I0632991

MISDIRECTION

BOREALIS: WITHOUT A COMPASS

BOOK 2

GREGORY ASHE

H&B

This is a work of fiction. Names, characters, places, and incidents either are the product of the author's imagination or are used fictitiously, and any resemblance to actual persons, living or dead, business establishments, events, or locales is entirely coincidental.

Misdirection
Copyright © 2021 Gregory Ashe

All rights reserved. No part of this book may be reproduced in any form, stored in any retrieval system, or transmitted in any form by any means—electronic, mechanical, photocopy, recording, or otherwise—without prior written permission of the publisher, except as provided by United States of America copyright law. For permission requests and all other inquiries, contact: contact@hodgkinandblount.com

Published by Hodgkin & Blount
https://www.hodgkinandblount.com/
contact@hodgkinandblount.com

Published 2021
Printed in the United States of America

This cover has been designed using resources from Freepik.com.

Trade Paperback ISBN: 978-1-63621-017-9
eBook ISBN: 978-1-63621-016-2

Misdirection, noun: the act of directing wrongly; the state of being led in the wrong direction; in theatrical magic, a form of deception in which the performer draws the audience's attention to one thing to distract it from another.

Shaw's note: For example, if you are at the State Fair for the first time in your life, and your friend has a substance abuse disorder, and he falls down a manhole while following the smell of fried cheese.

North's note: (the real story) I tripped. I am not a cartoon character. Misdirection is more like the time Shaw disappeared for two days to research lady boys.

Shaw's correction: That was my private time. I was doing research. For a term paper.

North's correction: Yeah? Well, you shot your research all the way up the wall, and I had to clean it up because I sure as fuck was not going to lose my security deposit.

Shaw's reaction: I hate you.

North's reaction: I'm the one who had to borrow a ladder.

Chapter 1

KINGSLEY SHAW WILDER ALDRICH was trying to finish his story, but he had to compete with the bass line of a Weezer song.

"—and that's when I knew I could do it because the power to achieve my dreams had been inside me all along."

North McKinney, his boyfriend, sighed, spun his beer, and said, "The power to buy pre-shelled pistachios had been inside you all along?"

"Don't say it like that. It was a very enabling revelation. Societal pressures have been holding me back for years. Understanding that the power had been—"

"Please don't keep saying 'inside me.'"

"—inside me all along was life-changing. I'm going to write a book. I'm going to free people from their chains." Shaw leaned back and stole a cheesy fry from North's plate. "And you didn't have any complaints about me using the phrase 'inside me' last night."

A pair of young gym-bunny gays was passing the table right then, and they shared a look and burst out laughing.

North's cheeks reddened, but his only answer was to drag his plate closer and curl an arm around it protectively, glaring at Shaw.

"Also, that cheese is mostly preservatives," Shaw said, "and it's hardening inside your small intestine, and you'll probably get a blockage and die."

North's eyes narrowed.

"A slightly smaller portion—"

"No."

"Or if you shared—"

"There it is. No. No. No. No fucking way, Shaw. Nibble on your lettuce."

"If you'd be nice to me, maybe I'd nibble on your lettuce."

North covered his face with one hand, but he didn't relax the protective curl of his arm around the cheesy fries.

The Unicorn Trough wasn't officially a gay bar, but with a name like that, it had a hard time being anything else. At least half the couples were men; of the remaining half, some were women, some were straights, and a few were clearly enby. A banner over the bar limply announced 90'S NIGHT, but that only seemed to refer to the choice of music—nobody else had gotten into the spirit of it. Colored lights spun and swiveled, illuminating patches of the haze that floated over the dance floor; a handful of couples were dancing, all of them young and clearly looking for an excuse to grind on each other.

"My parents would have killed me if they'd found out I came to a place like this," North said as he dragged a fry through the cheese sauce and glanced around. "Not that that ever stopped me."

"My parents would have cried with joy if I'd asked to go to The Unicorn Trough," Shaw said. "They made me do the whole gay-straight alliance thing in school after I came out. They were literally waiting for me to tell them; my mom had made t-shirts ahead of time."

"They made you join the GSA? That seems like a bit much."

Shaw shook his head. "They made me start it."

North rolled his eyes. "Parents have some fucked up ideas about knowing what's best. Exhibit A."

He didn't have to glance across the room for Shaw to know what he meant; Exhibit A was Nicci Lesperance, the woman they were following that night. Nicci had a chop of purple-gray hair and was probably too full figured to be wearing nothing but a leather vest (on the back, the name of her yet-to-be-discovered band, Bathtub Punchout) and leather leggings. She was a middle manager at Aldrich Acquisitions, which was the company owned by Shaw's father and which supplied most of the work for North and Shaw's private investigation agency.

Nicci's father, Ralph Lesperance, was an executive at the same company, and he had asked that North and Shaw look into a younger woman with whom Nicci was having an affair. Kelly Cann—fifteen years younger, with blond ringlets and cherry-red lipstick—was, from all North and Shaw had been able to discover, about what you'd expect from the lead-singer-slash-genius behind a band called Bathtub Punchout: no steady job, no education, heavy use of recreational drugs. The subtext when Ralph had given them the job had been to get rid of Kelly, and Shaw couldn't exactly blame the man—but that didn't make him blind to North's point either.

Fanning aside the sweat, artificial smoke, and skunky weed that cobwebbed the air, Shaw grimaced and said, "I'm going to have asthma from breathing all this glycol or glycerin or whatever it is. I'm going to need lemongrass and sage and—"

North took a long pull from his Schlafly—their pale ale, tonight. It was his turn to watch the women, and he was frowning.

"—ginger root and gingko biloba and—"

North lifted a finger from the Schlafly's brown glass, and Shaw went silent. Then, with a tiny shake of his head, North said, "Never mind. They're just getting more comfortable in the booth." He took another, quicker pull on the beer. "And you're not getting asthma."

"I might be getting asthma. I definitely feel like I'm getting asthma. My throat's all scratchy—"

"Because you've eaten four bowls of bar mix, and it's mostly pretzels."

"—and my tongue feels like corroded battery terminals—"

"Because you've had six Cokes."

"Four, North! I had four. You cut me off, remember?"

"I remember very fucking well, thank you. I also remember that you flirted with the piece of meat behind the bar and got two more while you thought I was in the bathroom."

"You can't—I didn't—" Shaw struggled to sit up straight. "First of all, trust is super important in a healthy relationship, and—"

North made a face as he retrieved his phone.

"Thank you, Vishnu," Shaw whispered.

When North saw the caller, his expression disassembled into a deadly blankness that Shaw had come to recognize over the last few months. He stared at the phone, unmoving. In Shaw's ears, the music became a background of pounding white noise—surf washing everything away.

Fighting the urge to close his eyes, Shaw said, "You can take it."

"No." But North kept looking at the phone. "No, he knows we're only supposed to communicate through our lawyers now."

"So don't take the call."

North sat there, staring at the illuminated screen that flashed with Tucker's name. "He's drunk. And he wants to scream at me. Or he wants me to think he's drunk, and he wants to scream at me. Or he doesn't think he's as drunk as he really is, but he wants me to think he—"

"I'm going to get some water," Shaw said, sliding down from the stool.

Behind him, North's voice was low and hard as he said, "What the fuck do you want, Tucker? What the fuck don't you understand about 'no contact'? Are you too fucking stupid to understand—" North broke off and resumed more fiercely, "I'll talk to you however I fucking want, you fucking imbecile. We're not—"

And then The Smashing Pumpkins were singing about tonight. Shaw kept his gaze on the bar, refusing to look back. He wormed his way through the press of bodies, flagged down the bartender, and ran a hand through his auburn hair—long enough now that he could hold it back with a scrunchie, which was a nice change from the crazy cloud of curls that North had described as Bob Ross-bred-with-a-poodle (the little yippy kind, he had clarified).

"Hey, beautiful," the bartender said, leaning on his elbows, a white towel crisp against his black shirt. He couldn't have been older than twenty, sandy haired, and he still managed to look boyish even though he must have spent a couple of hours at the gym every day. He had an inner bicep tattoo of a distorted clock and writing in what Shaw thought was Sanskrit. "You're making my night better and better. I'm glad you came back."

"Thanks," Shaw said, checking over his shoulder; North was bending over their two-top, one hand cupped around the phone, probably so he could eviscerate Tucker more thoroughly. "You're beautiful too. I bet you're a Pisces."

"Can I get some service?" a salt-and-pepper bro at the end of the bar shouted.

"What's Pisces?" the bartender said, smiling as he pulled the towel from his shoulder and flapped it at the bro. "What dates, I mean?"

"February 19th to March 20th."

"No way. March 1st."

"I knew it. It's because you're so pretty. And I bet you have a really beautiful soul. Have you ever had your chakras read?"

The bartender blinked. Then his smile got bigger. "No, but I'll try anything once. Do you want to—"

"Hey, buddy." Daddy-bro was shouting again. "Trawl dick on your own time."

The bartender shot him an angry look and turned back to Shaw. "I've got to, you know. Can I get you anything? Another Coke?"

For a moment, something nasty snapped its teeth inside Shaw, and he almost said yes. "Just a water. And another Schlafly, the pale ale."

When the bartender set the drinks next to Shaw, he took Shaw's wrist in one hand. His touch was warm and soft. His thumb traced the vein visible under Shaw's pale skin. "I'd really like to keep talking to you."

"I'd really like to keep talking to you," Shaw said with a smile. "And you know what? I'm really glad you said that I'm making your night better because now you're making my night better. North, that's my boyfriend, is being such a jerk. It's not like he tries to be a jerk. Well, sometimes he does. Like one time, he came home when I was using one of those as-seen-on-TV back shavers, and he told me if I really wanted to manscape, I could start, well, down there, because, quote, 'it's like getting lost in the pubic Amazon,' which was really rude, and I said—"

The bartender released Shaw's wrist and straightened. "You've got a boyfriend."

"Oh, yeah, he's the one over there who's trying really hard to look butch with the henley and—"

The bartender shot toward the other end of the bar, saying something like *wasting my fucking time* under his breath.

"I didn't give you the name of my psychic," Shaw called after the young man. "If you want your chakras read. It's Master Hermes!"

"Dude," one of the guys next to Shaw said, covering his ear.

At a more normal volume, Shaw repeated, "It's Master Hermes."

"Yeah, whatever, quit yelling in my fucking ear."

Shaw was carrying the drinks back to the table when Nicci got up and headed toward the bathroom. Kelly played with her glass, gaze fixed on the appletini in front of her, until Nicci had disappeared down a narrow hall. Then she grabbed Nicci's purse, slid out of the booth, and shot toward the door.

North was still whispering furiously into the phone.

"Something's happening," Shaw said, touching North's elbow.

With an inarticulate cry, North ripped the phone from his ear and hammered it against the table. When he pulled it back, he said, "No, you listen to me, you abusive piece of shit—"

"She's running," Shaw said.

"You want to talk about unfair? You want to talk about what's unfair, Tucker? What's unfair is every fucking minute I had to spend standing behind you, smiling and looking supportive—"

Shaw grimaced, set the drinks on the table, and went after Kelly. She was moving at a fast walk, sliding through the crowd without glancing back. Shaw copied her. She hit the door and disappeared into the night, fingers of artificial smoke curling after her. Shaw was five yards behind her. The April evening was cool, the air shockingly clean and sweet with spring after the weed-and-glycol haze in the Trough. A couple of guys were making out hard, pressed up against the brick façade. A woman in a matted fur coat smoked at the curb, the security light washing out her face so she looked like a picture from an old book.

Kelly was already halfway down the block, disappearing between the aprons of light from the streetlamps, and Shaw took off after her. She was wearing biker boots to go with the leather leggings and the leather vest, and they made her steps solid, heavy, the only sound in the universe. At the next alley, she jinked right, swallowed up by the yellow, fluttering light from deep between the brick buildings.

When Shaw came around the corner, she punched him, aiming for the face. He had good reactions, honed by sparring in the smattering of martial arts he'd picked up and then abandoned, and he managed to dodge so that the punch only clipped his ear. It still stung, and the rush of adrenaline narrowed his vision to a tunnel and sent his pulse racing. She kicked before he could recover, catching him in the hip, and Shaw went down. He landed on the cracked pavement, chips of cement slicing his palms.

Kelly came after him. A part of Shaw's brain told him things had gone wrong—she should have run again; now was the perfect opportunity for her to escape—but things were moving too quickly for him to figure out why. Her boot came down in a vicious stomp intended for Shaw's head. He rolled and came up against a dumpster.

The movement had reversed their positions: now Kelly stood at the mouth of the alley, and Shaw scrabbled backward, deeper into the cleft between the brick walls. Bringing back Nicci's purse as though intending to use it as a club, Kelly leapt forward. Shaw grabbed a broken section of pallet, driving splinters into his hands, and tossed it. It caught Kelly at the legs. She swore, stumbled, and almost lost her balance.

That delay gave Shaw time to regain his feet. When Kelly lunged again, Shaw was ready. He threw a jab that was meant to catch her in the solar plexus, but the uneven cement caused Kelly to lose her balance. Shaw's fist connected with her breast. Kelly's eyes got huge, and she screamed.

Shaw had already committed himself to the uppercut, launching up with as much force as his body could produce, focusing all of it behind his clenched hand. The blow caught her on the jaw, a perfect bell ringer. Silence. Lights out. Then the soft scuff of clothing as she slid to the ground.

Behind Shaw, in the alley, a man's voice said, "Jesus Christ, sorry I'm late. Toss me the wallet so you can get back in there before the bitch realizes—"

Shaw spun. Through red clouds of adrenaline, he was aware of his hand throbbing, his heart hammering in his throat. He locked eyes with a man who had at least six inches on Shaw and a hundred pounds. Bald, tiny eyes, and the evolutionary trade-off of a neck for shoulders that looked big enough to do some serious smashing.

His steps slowed. His tiny eyes were little black chips of confusion. "Kels, what…what did you do to her? I'm going to—"

"Hey." That was North, speaking out of the darkness near the bar's fire door and stepping into the middle of the alley. "Bozo."

Tiny-eyes lumbered around.

North grabbed a wooden slat and cracked it across the back of the big guy's head before he'd gotten farther than a quarter-turn. Again came the soft thump of flesh hitting cement. North tossed the broken length of wood aside, standing up straight, shoulders back, deep breaths making his chest rise and fall. The orange glow from the security light touched the mess of short blond hair, the pale eyes the color of ice. He was trying not to smile. He put his hands on his hips and glanced down at the big guy.

"Very het," Shaw called, shaking out his hand. Adrenaline was leaching out of him, and pain from his hand and a dozen scrapes and bruises was rushing in.

The half-hidden smile on North's face went out, and he scowled.

"No, seriously. It was super het. I'm really proud of you. I thought you'd still be busy on the phone, and then boom, 'Hey, bozo!'"

"Pretty big talk from a guy who just beat up a girl," North said, squatting next to the guy to roll him onto his back. He patted him down, stopped when he uncovered a knife, and tossed the weapon into a dumpster. Rising, North added, "You must be really proud of yourself too, knocking her around like a frat boy who can't get his dick up."

Shaw sat down crisscross applesauce on the broken cement. He emptied Nicci's purse onto the ground: Marc Jacobs mascara, a pack of face wipes, a baggie with several latex dental dams, crumpled tissues, and the wallet. As Shaw opened the wallet and began taking out credit cards, he said, "First of all it's the twenty-first century."

North's only answer was a grunt.

"Women have every right to get beaten up in a fair fight."

The clip-clop of those massive Redwings.

"And she started it."

A noise that might have been a laugh.

"And if I hadn't punched her, I would have been treating her differently because she's a woman, so basically it was a feminist imperative that I, you know, beat the shit out of her."

Kneeling next to Shaw, North made a rumble in his chest, but his touch was soft as he tilted Shaw's head.

"I'm trying to do something," Shaw whispered, but he'd forgotten about the wallet.

North took Shaw's hands next, turning them up, and he released a blistering string of swears when he saw the cuts and broken bits of glass and cement embedded in his palms.

"Where'd she get you?" North asked.

"I was stupid; I came around the corner, and she was waiting. She just clipped me on the ear, and the rest of it is mostly from the fall."

"This ear?" North asked. Then he kissed Shaw's ear lightly, his lips brushing the inflamed tissue. He kissed Shaw lightly on the lips and leaned back on his heels. "I fucked up."

"No, that was the right ear."

"I mean in there. I shouldn't have gotten distracted. I shouldn't have let you go after her alone."

"It's fine. I knew you'd have my back."

"But I—"

"I knew you'd have my back, North." Shaw shrugged. "I trust you. Besides, I can handle one skanky bitch on my own."

"That sounds like the feminist imperative talking."

"The feminist imperative is a real thing."

"Sure. And I'm sure that's what you were thinking about when you titty-punched her."

Shaw shrugged again. "At least I didn't pull her hair."

Kelly made a soft, groaning noise.

"Wake up, Sleeping Beauty," North said. To Shaw, he asked, "Anything?"

"Two Amex, three Visas, a hundred and sixty-three dollars in cash—"

"Jesus."

"—and the grand prize," Shaw flourished a card on a lanyard, "an Aldrich Acquisitions secure-access ID."

"What the fuck?" Kelly mumbled.

"Stay down," North said when she tried to sit up; either the words or the tone convinced her, or maybe she just didn't have the strength, because she fell back against the cement. "Police are on their way. What was this? Some sort of identity-theft scam? You toss bozo her wallet, and then you gaslight Nicci until he finishes copying everything? Nicci gets her purse back before the end of the night, none the wiser until she learns that somebody ordered eight thousand dollars' worth of Xboxes on her Mastercard?"

"Who are you?" Kelly said. "What the hell is going on?"

North made a disgusted noise. "You've got some fucked-up priorities, lady. Nicci seems nice. She seems like she genuinely cares about you. But her dad was right—you're garbage. You're going to throw away a chance with a decent woman for a few credit cards that will get canceled by the end of next week."

Kelly gurgled. It took Shaw a moment to realize that the sound was laughter. The words came more slowly, and Shaw was starting to realize he might have caused some damage with the uppercut. "Her dad?"

Shaw glanced at North.

More laughter. Kelly rolled onto her side, curling up slightly, but the muffled words kept coming. "Her dad's the one who hired me in the first place." She laughed again, raised herself up on one elbow, and spat blood across the cement. "Nicci was having a mid-life crisis. Nicci lezzed out, wanted to start a band. Daddy's little girl got wild, and that wouldn't look good to the board." The short, declarative sentences dissolved into huffing breaths.

"Her father hired you?" Shaw asked.

Kelly nodded. Her pupils were huge; the cone of orange light barely reached her face.

"To—what? Steal her identity?"

"To fuck her life every way from Sunday." This last sentence seemed to take the rest of her energy; she slumped against the cement, lines of tension relaxing in her body.

Shaw began returning everything to the wallet. North watched silently. Disapprovingly. When Shaw had finished with the wallet, he returned it to the purse along with the rest of the contents he'd dumped on the ground. Then he stood.

North caught his elbow. "He's the client. He paid."

"He's a monster. He's conducting this psych-ops warfare on his own daughter because he doesn't like her life choices and wants to scare her back into submission."

When Shaw tried to step away, North's grip tightened. "We're private investigators. We aren't going to like every job we're hired to do. We don't have to like the jobs we're hired to do."

"And we started our own agency so we didn't have to answer to anybody else. So we could help people. Is that what this feels like to you?"

"No, but he didn't ask us to—"

"He wants pictures of Nicci with Kelly so he can hold them over her head. For blackmail, maybe. Or just as a reminder of how stupid she's been. And he told us to run Kelly off because he figured we'd be more receptive to that. Do you think this is the right thing to do?"

North didn't answer. He held Shaw's gaze, his face coloring, and then he broke and looked away.

Shaw reached for the hand still clutching his elbow. He had half a mind to rip North's fingers away; instead, he was surprised to find himself taking North's hand into his own, squeezing.

"Compromise," North said, his voice rough. "She tells Nicci what her dad was up to, and then she leaves, and she never talks to Nicci again. We tell her dad we couldn't get any decent photographs, but we managed to put a scare into her, and she won't bother his daughter again."

"That doesn't solve the problem, North. He's going to try again."

"We can't solve all the world's problems. We're solving this one, right now. That's what we can do."

Shaw's eyes stung; he closed them for a moment. North's fingers tightened around his own, and after a moment, Shaw gripped him back.

When Shaw opened his eyes, he was looking at Kelly. She was still punch-drunk, her mouth loose, her breathing soft and shallow.

"Tell Nicci the truth," Shaw said. "And don't do anything like this again, or I'll punch you in the other, you know."

"Titty," North supplied.

Shaw sighed and headed back to The Unicorn Trough. North's hand, warm and solid, found the back of his neck.

"There are seventeen reasons," Shaw said, "why you shouldn't say tit or titties. Number one, it's sexist."

North squeezed the back of his neck and sounded suspiciously like he was laughing.

Chapter 2

NORTH DROVE THEM BACK to Shaw's house in Benton Park, on the south side of St. Louis. It was, for the most part, a quiet area, although with lower income and higher crime than the western neighborhoods. They passed Hodak's, windows dark beneath their green awnings (best fried chicken in the city). They passed the Dollar General, where a scrawny white man was trying to lift a motorized shopping cart onto a city bus. The April breeze chased a Big Gulp down the gutter. With the windows down, the smell of hops and malt and yeast from the Anheuser-Busch brewery floated into the car, and the 1968 GTO's engine rumbled pleasantly at the light.

Instead of dropping Shaw off, North took the alley and parked in the garage. The door rattled down behind them. Neither man moved. The automatic light flicked off. The air was cooler here, kept cold by the dark and the concrete slabs, and North shivered.

"I'm really sorry. About Tucker. About taking that stupid call. It's like— it's like he's in my head, and he knows exactly what to do to make me insane. I can't even think straight." North let his head fall back against the seat. "I swear to God, if he keeps trying to drag out the divorce, I'm going to drive over there one night and murder that son of a bitch."

The noise Shaw made was much, much sadder than a sigh.

North found his hand in the darkness, and Shaw hissed as their fingers slotted together.

"Christ, I forgot. I'm sorry." North thumped his head against the seat once. "Fuck me, I cannot believe I let you do that alone. I can't believe I let you get hurt."

"North, it's fine. It's—"

"It's not fine. It's very fucking not fine, Shaw." North turned in the seat, got into an awkward kneeling position, and lifted Shaw's hand to his mouth. He kissed the swollen knuckles. He kissed each fingertip. He turned the hand over and kissed each scrape and cut, gossamer kisses. Shaw shook himself once and let out a harsh breath. "I." He kissed the inside of Shaw's wrist. "Am." He kissed a few inches higher up Shaw's arm. "So." Another kiss, this one to the sleeve bunched at Shaw's elbow. "Sorry." He kissed Shaw's shoulder. Then, as gently as he could, he kissed Shaw on the lips, his tongue flicking until Shaw parted and let North in.

When North pulled back, Shaw's mouth hung open. Just a little, sure. But it did nice things to a guy's ego.

"Here's what we're going to do," North whispered. "We're going to go inside. I'm going to get a bath ready for you. I'm going to ice your hand while you soak in those healing salts. I'm going to tape up the worst of these cuts when you're nice and relaxed. And then I'm going to ride your dick like Paul fucking Revere."

As North leaned in for another kiss, Shaw said, "But you probably want to sleep in your own bed tonight."

North froze. Pulled back a quarter inch.

"You've been working so hard," Shaw said. "And I move around too much, and I elbow you, and I snore. So, you probably want to sleep in your own bed tonight." Shaw groped blindly for the door handle.

Gathering a handful of Shaw's jacket, North said, "I do not want to sleep in my own bed tonight. In fact, as I have suggested several times, I would very much like for us to have the same place and the same bed."

Shaw pulled the handle; the door popped open.

"Where do you think you're going?" North asked.

"You probably need to get home to the puppy. He needs you. He needs your full and undivided attention. He needs you to take him out to go the bathroom. He needs you to get his food and water. He needs you to play with him even when your boyfriend is trying to tell you about the psychosexual Mormon homoeroticism underpinning seasons one, three, and five of *Battlestar Galactica*."

North drew back another quarter inch, studying Shaw. "The puppy is with Pari and Truck. What the fuck is going on?"

"And you've probably got to take another phone call." Shaw would have slid out of the car, but North's grip was too firm. "And I'd hate to be a distraction when you've got to take an important phone call."

North's eyes narrowed. "You petty little bitch."

"North! You can't say bitch anymore either because—"

Shaking him by the jacket, North said, "Oh no. You're refusing to give me dick as a punishment? That is fucked up, Shaw. That is seriously fucked up."

In an easy, practiced movement, Shaw grabbed North's wrist and broke his hold. He slipped out of the car and slammed the door.

"Hold on one fucking minute," North said, throwing open his own door.

Shaw was already sprinting toward the door into the house, laughing.

North had to skirt Shaw's Mercedes SLC 300, which slowed him down, and he barely got to the door before Shaw could lock it. They played that game for a while, Shaw laughing uncontrollably as he tried to force the door shut and set the deadbolt, North growling and swearing and shoving just enough to keep Shaw from winning. Finally Shaw gave up, bolting down the hall. The main floor had been given over to the Borealis offices; North flew past them without even a glance, buttonhooking through the reception area at the front and following Shaw into the kitchen.

Shaw let North catch him at the top of the stairs.

North grabbed his ankle, dragged him down, and climbed on top of him. He trapped Shaw's wrists, pinning him; Shaw was still laughing. His auburn hair had come loose in the tussle, and now it formed a crazy cloud. For a moment, North just enjoyed the view: the refined features, the slender eyebrows, the sharp triangle of cheekbones and jaw that made Shaw more than handsome, more than beautiful. His hazel eyes were bright with amusement.

"Not fair," Shaw said. "I'm injured. You never would have caught me otherwise."

North made a noise low in his throat. He bent his head, nuzzling aside Shaw's collar and kissed the sensitive skin there. Then he bit. Shaw groaned, hips coming up, the beginning of his erection rubbing against North's belly. North ignored the silent request, sliding his mouth to Shaw's neck, kissing again.

"Not—" Shaw gasped. "Not fair. Not fair, North. I—" He made a high-pitched noise when North bit his collarbone, and this time, his boner was steel as he rutted up. North rocked back to meet him, coiling Shaw's hair around his fingers, turning his head to attack his neck again.

Unable to help himself, North bent down, his voice a low, hot whisper: "Still think I should take that phone call?"

Shaw shook his head wildly—or as wildly as he could, with North still clutching his hair. Then he froze, one hand on North's chest.

North froze too. "What happened? Shit, you got hurt worse than I realized, didn't you?"

Shaw's phone buzzed in his pocket; the faint notes of "Girls Just Wanna Have Fun" floated into the air.

Shaw's slender eyebrows drew up into innocent arches.

"Ignore it."

"It might be important."

North rubbed the bulge of Shaw's erection. "I'm going to be so nice to you. Ignore it."

Swallowing, Shaw blinked glassily. But he whispered, "It might be really, really important. Sometimes I get these important phone calls, and I have to drop everything else."

"You are a vengeful prick," North growled, yanking open the waistband of Shaw's pants. He hooked his fingers around the waistband and hiked the pants down to mid-thigh. As usual, Shaw was commando, and his dick sprang up and slapped the underside of North's chin wetly. Shaw groaned. He made another, more animalistic noise when North took the head in his mouth. Just the head. Suckling.

With what sounded like genuine pain, Shaw slid free and dragged himself up a few more steps. Pupils wide, he wrenched the phone from his pocket and met North's gaze.

"Don't do it," North said.

"It's my mom."

"At half-past eleven?"

"She'll be worried sick if I don't answer."

"This is the same mom who bought you a one-way ticket to London when you were sixteen?"

"She won't stop calling."

"She'll be just fucking fine for ten minutes."

"Ten minutes? That's all?"

"Fuck you, Shaw. Fuck—"

"I knew you'd understand. About taking important phone calls, I mean."

North dropped back on his heels, eyes narrowing, and Shaw accepted the call.

"Hi, Mom. No, no, you didn't wake me. Now's a good time. I have fourteen new kinds of wallpaper paste I need to tell you about."

Shaking his head, North rose, and he gave Shaw a hand up. Shaw did an awkward, hopping dance to try to tuck away his erection and keep his pants from sliding down. North took advantage of the opportunity to deliver a cracking, one-handed smack to Shaw's bare ass. The noise echoed in the stairwell, and Shaw yelped.

"No, Mom—holy shit—no, I just stubbed my toe. I don't know; that must have been on your end."

"Tell your mom hi," North whispered.

Shaw rolled his eyes.

"Hi, Mrs. Aldrich," North bellowed.

"You heard him? Ok, maybe now he'll leave me alone."

"Did she say hi back?"

Grimacing, Shaw gave North a fake push, and North pretended to topple down the stairs. Shaw just made an even more aggravated expression and turned away.

With a grin, North ruffled Shaw's hair and headed through the bedroom and into the bathroom. He brushed his teeth—real brushing, which involved using the tube of Crest he'd hidden under the sink instead of the coconut oil, for pulling, that Shaw had decided was going to cure his invisible goiter or Christ only knew what. He flossed. He washed his face, considered a shower, and decided he was too tired. When he got back to the bedroom, Shaw was stretched out on the bed, still on the phone with his mom. North lay next to him, head on Shaw's chest, and Shaw curled an arm around him and scratched his back lightly.

A text came from Haw Ryeo, their contact—and nominal boss—at Aldrich Acquisitions: *Attempted break-in at Nonavie. Be ready in case I need you.*

North texted back: *Any idea who it was? Security cameras get anything?*

But Haw didn't reply.

North checked their business banking accounts; he had nothing better to do. Johanna Griffin was a client who had hired them to find her missing father, who suffered from dementia. Her check had bounced the week before, and when North had called, she had told him it had been an error and the check would clear if the bank processed it again. When it bounced a second time and he'd called, she'd promised an electronic transfer and hung up on him. Surprise, surprise, the bank account showed that Griffin's payment hadn't arrived.

Shaw was still talking. He sounded different when he talked to his parents. Nothing easy to pinpoint. It wasn't like his vocabulary changed, or even the content—sophomore year, when Shaw had been living at home and recovering from being stabbed, North had walked in on Shaw and his mother debating dildo lengths, girths, and materials. With samples. But maybe a slight shift in manner, a hint of education and money that Shaw had dropped early in freshman year—one of the things, North remembered, that had made him hate Shaw at first sight.

Now, he burrowed deeper into Shaw, smelling the cigarette smoke from the bar and the slight musk of his hair product, Shaw's arm warm and comforting and possessive around him. Shaw's voice rumbled in his chest as he talked. North ran his hand over Shaw's ribs, tracing them, then pushing up the shirt to caress the wiry muscle and the dusting of auburn hair. He turned his head just enough to kiss Shaw's bare skin. In spite of his own best efforts, North was hard again. Really hard.

When Shaw ended the call, his hand came up to the short mess of North's hair, playing with it. North rolled onto his stomach, kissed Shaw's belly again, and pushed the shirt higher. He followed it with another kiss, leaning down to rub himself against Shaw's leg. Then he realized Shaw was soft.

He let out a slow breath, rested his chin on Shaw's abdomen, and looked up the length of that slim body. "You ok?"

"What? Oh. Yeah. Sorry."

North stroked bare skin in slow, calming movements. "What's up?"

"Oh, nothing."

"Great."

"Yeah," Shaw mumbled.

North crawled up the length of his body and then let himself drop, flattening Shaw against the mattress.

Shaw's breath whooshed, and he grunted under North's weight. Then he slapped North's hip. Then he tried to buck North off. Then he tried to shove him.

"North, come on."

"What?"

"Will you get off me?"

"I'm comfortable. I might fall asleep."

"This is so juvenile."

North took slow breaths that alternated with fake snores.

"You are a child. Do you realize that? You're a teenager at heart. A delinquent."

More fake snoring.

"A…a hooligan."

"Could you keep it down, please? I'm trying to get some shut-eye."

"I'm fine, ok? I'm totally, perfectly fine. It was just a bummer of a conversation. My mom is really stressed about these students in her studio, and I still haven't figured out what to get my mom and dad for their thirtieth anniversary, and they won't stop talking about—" Whatever he'd been about to say, he changed it at the last moment. "—the party, and then I had to hear about how my great-aunt's chemo port keeps coming out."

North turned his head, scruff dragging on Shaw's cheek, and kissed his jaw lightly. "What's the one you're worried about the most?"

"My aunt, I guess. She's eighty-three."

"Are you close?"

"Yeah. She's always been so nice to me. And now she's sick and miserable and nothing has gone right with the treatment."

Sliding onto his side next to Shaw, North said, "Maybe you should take a couple days off and spend them with her."

"I don't know." Shaw shook his head, staring up at the ceiling. The next part burst free, although he seemed to try to stop it. "And why can't they just drop it about the party? I don't—I don't know why I have to keep hearing about it. It's their party. It's for them. For their anniversary. Why am I involved at all?"

"I don't know. Why are you?"

"I don't know."

"How are you involved?"

"I don't know!"

"Ok, ok." North considered the stubborn-as-a-fucking-mule set of Shaw's jaw, prayed inwardly to whatever saint protected fools who got involved with complicated, beautiful men who owned an entire drawerful of assless chaps, and tried a different angle. "Should I be expecting an invitation? Delivered on a silver platter of course."

Shaw rolled off the bed. "I'm going to brush my teeth."

"Hey, I was just joking."

"I know." He delivered the words while walking, without looking back.

"Will you tell me what the fuck is going on?"

The answer was a slammed door.

Whatever the hell coconut oil-pulling involved, it apparently took a lot of time. North finally turned off the lights, crawled under the blankets, and closed his eyes.

Soft steps. The blankets being drawn back, the whisper of cool air, and then a warm body. One arm across North's waist. Shaw's head on his shoulder.

"I want you to go to the party with me."

"Great."

"It's a week from Saturday."

North didn't say anything about the preparations, about how long a family as rich as Shaw's might have spent planning and ordering and inviting and arranging. More than a couple of weeks, that was for sure. All he said was "I'll get my day planner."

"I'm sorry I'm being a pill."

North grunted. He had kept his eyes closed through this whole exchange, but now they opened. In the faint light from the window, the room was blue-black, bruised. He didn't mean to say it out loud. He definitely didn't want to say it out loud. But it slipped out anyway: "You know I'll be on my best behavior, right? I'm not going to get drunk and make a scene or pick a fight with your Uncle Al or look down your Aunt Suzy's dress. If you promise me treats, I bet I could even do some nifty tricks like use the right fork and drink out of a glass."

The silence had a heartbeat pulse to it.

"My Aunt Suzy got really good implants," Shaw finally said, his tone suggesting a joke to smooth everything over. "So, if you're into that thing, you actually probably should look down her dress."

North bit back the swear words. He bit back the reply. He couldn't help the rest of it, though: he rolled onto his side, his back to Shaw, and closed his eyes.

Chapter 3

IN MOVIES SOMETIMES—the kind North watched, the kind North made Shaw watch, even when there was a perfectly good four-hour QVC spot on empowerment gemstones—a guy stepped on a landmine, and then he froze because he knew if he moved at all, if he even scratched his nose, he'd get blown to Kingdom Come.

The next morning, Shaw knew how the poor bastard felt. Unfortunately, he couldn't seem to stay still.

The bed was empty when Shaw woke. It was a Monday, so Shaw found North downstairs, in their office, but North would only reply in grunts and monosyllables. He refused the coffee Shaw brought him. He ignored the slice of cherry danish. When Shaw tried to kiss him, he stood abruptly and left the room. When he came back, he moved his chair away from the desk, under the pretense of kicking up his heels and reading a sheaf of documents. When Shaw moved his own chair back as well, so that they were sitting side by side again, North made a noise and rolled his chair closer to the desk. When Shaw followed him, North looked over, wild-eyed, and dumped the cherry danish in the trash.

"Now you're making me mad," Shaw said.

"Good."

"I know I hurt your feelings last night, but you won't talk to me, and I want to apologize, and that was a perfectly good slice of danish!" Shaw lost it a little on the volume at the end.

North stood and pushed back from the desk so hard that the chair caught an uneven floorboard and tipped over. He stomped out of the room; when he came back fifteen minutes later, he smelled like cigarettes. Shaw caught his eye and opened his mouth, but the look on North's face made him reconsider.

It might have gone on like that all day, except Pari rapped on the door. She used what Shaw considered her professional voice (in contrast to her normal, I'm-going-to-harangue-you-into-an-undeserved-raise voice), which meant that a prospective client was in the reception area.

"There's a Mrs. Chittenden here to see you."

"We're not doing walk-ins today," North said without looking up. "And if it's your fault because you forgot to put her on the fucking calendar, you can apologize to her and find a better time for her to come back."

Stepping into the office, Pari shut the door behind her. She lowered her voice and said, "If the two of you could pull yourselves out of whatever high-school-relationship drama you're tangled up in for fifteen seconds and act like professionals, you might be interested to know that Mrs. Chittenden is a state senator from central Missouri—Maries County, Pulaski, Dore. That area. In other words, a fairly important person. And she wants to hire you. Although God only knows why; she'd be better off hiring the cheer squad."

North didn't exactly look at Shaw, but his voice was gruff when he said, "You'd probably better send her in, then."

Pari didn't reply; the look on her face said it all. A moment later, she was ushering a blond woman into the room. Shaw's first impression was of a waxwork Kim Novak—and not at the best point in her life. The short, tousled curls. The dark eyebrows. The high cheekbones. Her real age was most visible near her ears—and, of course, in her hands. She wore a navy suit under a scarlet jacket. A dark-haired young man pranced at her heels; Shaw had seen pieces of toast with more personality.

"Mrs. Chittenden," North said, coming around the desk to shake her hand. "And—"

"We'll have espressos," Mrs. Chittenden said, shrugging out of the jacket, which the young man caught like a relic. "Gavin, hold my calls."

"We actually don't have an espresso machine," Shaw said as he approached, "because North decided that only 'rich twats who have never done an honest day's work' own their own espresso machine, which was a jab at me because I had two in my dorm room." North's eyebrows were arching sharply now, so Shaw hurried to add, "We don't even have a Nespresso machine because the pods are so bad for the environment. But we do have coffee, if the coffeemaker isn't broken again, and we have a thistle tea that I brew, and—"

"Actually," North said, "we don't have thistle tea."

"No, we do. I picked all those weird, white twigs off the bush in the backyard, and if you pack it into a tea infuser, it tastes just like thistle tea."

"Oh my God," North whispered. In a stronger voice, he managed to say, "Coffee?"

Mrs. Chittenden gave each of them a long look. "Gavin, take their girl and get us some espressos. A double for me. For you?"

"Well, I like mine unicorn style—" Shaw began.

"A double is fine," North said, shooting Shaw a look.

Gavin, who Shaw now noticed wore a headset, was whispering furiously into the microphone as he pranced out of the room again. He pulled the door shut behind him, cutting off his words as he snapped at Pari, "Come on, I don't have all day."

North winced. Just barely.

"He's going to be lucky if she only rips out all his hair," Shaw whispered.

They got Mrs. Chittenden settled, and when they were seated behind their desks again, North said, "How can we help you?"

Mrs. Chittenden was examining the room. Success had made it possible for North and Shaw to update the office: comfortable chairs for clients, accent tables, a muted landscape painting they'd bought at the Francis Park art fair together. North's desk, as usual, was perfectly organized: the chrome in-out trays with their neat stacks of documents, the high-def monitor, the organizer with individual compartments for paperclips and binder clips and tacks and staples. North had shouted himself hoarse the one time Shaw had dumped it out to borrow it for his antique button collection. Shaw's desk, on the other hand, had a less traditional organizational system. Today, for example, was day seven of his exploration of metal racking and shelving systems, so he had a spread of trade magazines and sales catalogues spread across the desk. On top of those was the homemade kilt he was still working on, for which he had used a combination of black vinyl and rayon that was a color North described as "grandma's stirrup pants." The one bare spot on the desk was where Shaw had set a copy of the *Kama Sutra*, but when North had looked at it and then looked at Shaw for fifteen seconds, Shaw's whole face had caught fire, and he'd shoved the book in the bottom drawer.

Eyebrows drawing together, Mrs. Chittenden bent over the accent table next to her, picking up a figurine of dried pasta to examine it.

"That's elbow-macaroni Emery Hazard," Shaw said. "He's my best friend."

North pinched the bridge of his nose.

"Not the elbow-macaroni version. He's not a real person. I know that."

"Now," North muttered. "After fifteen conversations."

"I mean the real Emery Hazard. He's basically my best friend in the whole universe. He's got a boyfriend who's really sweet, and his name is John-Henry, and I was going to make an oatmeal-cream-pie John-Henry because, well, Emery is so stiff and prickly, and John-Henry is so sweet and gooey, but North told me I couldn't. North is always telling me what I can and can't do. But I just go along with it. I thought it'd be really nice to give elbow-macaroni Emery Hazard a boyfriend, but North said no, and I always do what North tells me to—"

"For fuck's sake, you said you were going to, quote, 'cream-pie John-Henry,' and when I said absolutely not, because God help me if I understood what you actually meant, you sulked for three days and then made the damn oatmeal cream pie anyway. And then you ate it."

"Oh," Shaw frowned. "Huh. I forgot about that."

"Are you the ones who caught the West End Slasher?" Mrs. Chittenden said, leaning forward, clutching the elbow-macaroni figurine without seeming to realize it.

"Yes," North said. "We had help, of course. And the police—"

"And that man who ran the youth shelter, the one who went missing?"

Shaw nodded.

"And there was something recently, an author who was murdered?"

Elbows on the desk, North leaned forward. "The official charge was manslaughter, I think. Mrs. Chittenden, are you in danger? Because—"

"The job is simple. My son, Philip, made a mistake. As a result, he is required to report for weekly drug testing. Since he has proven himself unreliable, you will pick him up at his school, accompany him to be tested, and take him home. I understand you typically require a retainer, so I've already written a check for five thousand dollars. Gavin will give it to you when he comes back."

Shaw glanced at North. "We appreciate the offer," Shaw said slowly, "and we recognize that you're placing a lot of trust in us."

"Unfortunately, we currently have a full case load." North tapped a key on the keyboard. "I'd be happy to refer you to—"

"No." The word was brittle. Color mottled her cheeks, red patches climbing her neck. Her knuckles were white around elbow-macaroni Emery Hazard. "I'm hiring you. I've researched your agency extensively. I'm impressed by the work you've done." A big, white smile broke out across her face; that was the politician, Shaw knew, poking her head out for the first time in this conversation. "My son means everything to me, and I'll be happy to pay your priority rates or whatever you believe is necessary."

"Mrs. Chittenden—"

"Celia."

North took a breath. "Celia, what you're asking us to do, it's not our specialty. If you want transportation, there are car services, luxury ones, who will do what you're asking and do it well. We've used a couple in the past, and I can recommend them."

"Unless it's more than that," Shaw said softly. "Unless you're worried about Philip for some reason. Do you believe he's in danger?"

"Don't be stup—" The smile slipped, and Celia plastered it back on. She was still white-knuckling the pasta figurine. "Don't be silly. Philip is perfectly fine. He attends The Gouverneur Morris School, which I'm sure you've heard of."

"It's very small, isn't it?" North asked. "Very exclusive?"

"Very rigorous," Shaw added. "All the students there still learn Latin and Greek."

"It's also very safe," Celia said. "I'm not worried about trouble finding Philip. I'm worried about Philip finding trouble. He's a good young man.

He's…he's almost perfect, in fact." The iron rigidity of her voice flexed. "I don't want to see him mess up his life. I don't need to hire a bodyguard, and I don't need to call him an Uber. I want you."

"Why?" Shaw asked.

The waxworks chill was back in her face as she turned her full attention on him. The silence dragged out a moment. And then another. Then the sound of the front door opening broke the stillness, and a pair of footsteps moved through the reception area.

"I'm sorry you've wasted your time," North said, "but you're asking us to babysit. That's not our specialization, and it's not the right fit for us as an agency. As I said, I'd be happy to put you in contact with—"

Her cry began wordless and low, but it climbed to an earsplitting pitch. Celia's hand tightened around elbow-macaroni Emery Hazard until the figurine cracked and broke. The bottom half fell and shattered against the floor, a starburst of macaroni spinning across the boards. Then Celia's shriek ended, and for a moment she sat there, shoulders hunched, chest rising and falling as she sucked in air.

The change, when it came, reminded Shaw of those stupid Transformers that North liked: twist a piece here, push this that way, fold that. Celia's back straightened. Her shoulders rolled back. Her chin came up. She opened her hand, shaking out the broken pieces of pasta that still clung to her flesh.

"I seem to have cut myself," she said. "Do you have a tissue?"

Both North and Shaw were frozen for a moment. Shaw moved first, grabbing a tissue from the box he kept in his desk. Celia accepted it, dabbing at the blood. She fixed her senator smile on them. Forget Transformers, Shaw thought. Forget landmines. This was Shark Week.

The door opened. Gavin minced into the room, holding a Shameless Grounds cup that he handed to Celia with what almost looked like a bow— there was certainly some kind of animal body language, some kind of groveling, that Shaw would have loved to analyze further. He didn't have a chance, though; Pari stormed into the room, a swirl of black hair and flashing eyes, the bindi a screaming red today.

"For my boss," she said, gritting her teeth in what was probably supposed to be a smile as she slammed a Shameless Grounds cup down in front of Shaw. "And for my other boss."

Then she stalked out of the room, her heels sounding like the promise of a nail gun to the forehead.

Gavin pranced away.

The door clicked shut.

Silence, and the perfume of good espresso.

"I think this would be a good point to end our conversation," Shaw said.

Celia sipped her espresso, made a face, and set the cup down.

"I'm sorry we couldn't help you," North said. "I hope you have better luck with another agency."

Smoothing the navy skirt across her legs, Celia watched them with glittering eyes. "Philip's first testing appointment is this afternoon. Gavin will provide your girl with the address for the school and a recent picture of Philip."

"She's technically not our girl because you can't own a human being and because Pari would probably bury me in fire ants if she ever heard someone describe her as—"

"There seems to be a misunderstanding," North said, "so I'm going to be frank. We're not taking this job, Mrs. Chittenden. It's time for you to leave."

"Celia," she said with that glad-handing smile. "Please." Then she stood. "And you absolutely will do this job, and you'll do it perfectly, because if you don't, the next time your private investigator licenses come up for renewal, I will make sure your applications are denied. You'll be out of a job. Now, isn't a little bit of carpool duty better than that?" She walked briskly toward the door. "Gavin will leave the check with your girl."

Chapter 4

"DOES SHE HAVE any idea how stupid something like this is?" North asked. He was wearing a hole in the office floor. One of the Redwings caught a piece of elbow-macaroni Emery Hazard and sent him spinning under Shaw's desk. "Threatening private investigators? And then trusting them with her son? We could rip her life apart, dig up every ugly thing she's ever done and put it on the front page. Hell, we could kidnap her kid, or kill him, or just let him do a hot shot and leave him in a gutter. I mean, what in Christ's name is she thinking?"

Shaw frowned, staring at his phone.

"Tell me you've already got something on her."

Expression blank, Shaw set the phone on the desk and reached up to fix his hair: undoing the scrunchie, smoothing the auburn mess, and then twisting the scrunchie into place again.

"Tell me you've already got a lead. Tell me you did one search on that crazy bitch and you've already got something. Corruption. Embezzlement. Christ, I'll take wire fraud."

Frowning, Shaw tapped the screen to wake it, his attention still riveted on the phone.

"Shaw, what the fuck?"

"Hm?"

"What do you have on her?"

"What?" Shaw looked up, a flush filling the sharp triangle of his face, and then he clicked the phone's screen off. "Sorry. I got a text."

"From who?"

"From whom, actually, because in that construction, whom is the object of a preposition, which takes the objective case."

"I know about the objective case. I wrote your fucking flash cards about the objective case junior year because you were too busy trying to knit your own bobby socks. I thought you were researching Celia Chittenden; what the fuck have you been doing?"

"Just—" He made a vague gesture. "A text."

"From?"

"Oh. My mom."

North grunted. He fought himself for thirty seconds and finally managed, "Is everything ok?"

"Yeah, yeah, sure."

In the reception area, Pari was playing "Walk Like an Egyptian" at full volume, accompanied by an ominous thumping. Probably nailing voodoo dolls of Shaw and North to the wall. Nails through the crotch, North guessed. Which Shaw would find either so endearing that he'd need a snack break or so horrifying that he'd need a four-hour meditation-nap to process it. Followed by a snack break.

"Fuck," North screamed.

When the echo died, the thumping had stopped, although the song continued. North ran a hand down his face.

"Feel better?" Shaw asked.

"No. She's insane. Did you see how she reacted when we told her no?"

"It was a little excessive."

"It was fucking nuts. She threw a tantrum. Like a child. She broke your preschool art project. She screamed."

"To be fair, you just screamed too. And sometimes you scream when we're really going at it, and you finally let yourself go, because normally I think you're too wrapped up in societal expectations chaining you to a performance of—"

"Shaw, we can't work for this woman."

"Ok."

"You can't say ok. We have to do this job or we're going to lose our licenses."

"Ok."

North drilled a finger into the desk. "It's not ok. Quit saying ok."

"Well, you're expressing your emotions. I'm just trying to be supportive."

"Quit being supportive and fix this fucking mess."

"Usually I make the messes. Fixing them is your job."

North dropped to sit on the desk, resting his head in one hand. Shaw rolled his chair back, stood, and came around. A moment later, he was slipping under North's arm, the spiky musk of his hair product filling North's nose, the warmth of his body pressed along North's side.

"It's just a dumb job. We'll handle the first testing appointment, just to make sure it's legit, and then we'll pass it off to Pari. We'll give her hazard pay. She'll scream her head off and then secretly be ecstatic."

North grunted.

"'That's a really good idea, Shaw.' That's your line."

"She's got our balls in a vise. Next time she wants something—"

"Next time, we record the conversation. In fact, maybe we should start doing that with all our clients, to prevent future situations like this."

North grunted again.

"Your line is, 'That's two really good—'"

North kissed him, which was an effective way of laying Shaw's bullshit to rest.

When North pulled back, Shaw said, "Are you still mad at me?"

"Probably. I usually am."

"I know I messed up. I want you to go to the party with me. I just—my parents are putting all this pressure on me, and I wasn't thinking clearly last night, and you're the most important person in my life so of course I want you to—"

"What are they pressuring you about?"

Shaw faltered. "Nothing. Dumb stuff. It doesn't matter."

"Right," North said.

Shaw reached for his hand, and North slid off the desk. Shaw leaned in for a kiss, and North headed for the door.

"If you're going to the kitchen," Shaw said, "would you make me some thistle tea?"

North indulged himself: he slammed the door so hard that it shook in its frame.

In the reception area, The Bangles were still singing about the cops in the donut shop. Pari, sitting behind her desk and currently devouring an entire bucket of Kentucky Fried Chicken, dark meat only, extra crispy, pressed something on her computer, and the music ended abruptly. The sound of North's heavy steps filled the void.

"This is mature," Pari said and then ripped a string of meat from a thigh.

"You're fired."

"You can't fire me," Pari said through a mouthful of extra crispiness. "Only Shaw can fire me."

In the kitchen, North yanked open the fridge door so hard that the bottles rattled, glass singing out against glass. He popped the lid off the container of nutritional yeast, dug around, and came up with the container of full-fat vanilla Noosa that he'd hidden there. That was the only way he could keep anything through Shaw's occasional purges. He knocked the container against the side of the sink a few times, loosening the last few granules of yeast, and then he rummaged through the drawers until he found a spoon.

Sitting on the counter, he ate the yogurt in slow, careful bites. He had a vision of himself twenty years from now, not understanding the fuck out of the man he loved and eventually eating himself to death with economy tubs of pistachio ice cream.

His phone buzzed. A message from Shaw.

I know you're mad at me. Again. But I've got to run over and help my parents with something.

North locked the screen.

The phone buzzed again. Another message from Shaw.

It's about the colors for the party.

Balancing the phone on his knee, North took another, slower bite of yogurt and waited.

My mom needs help picking colors.

With the spoon hanging from his mouth, North pressed the lid down on the Noosa container and returned it to its hiding spot in the yeast. His fingers would smell like feet for the rest of the day, thank you very much, Kingsley Shaw Wilder Aldrich. He kept the phone in one hand.

I really think she'd love this shade of blue.

A picture followed of one of the thirty-seven jocks Shaw had tried to convince North to buy "as an investment."

So I'm just going to run over and show her.

I'll just be an hour or two.

Do you want me to meet you at the school?

Just text me back and tell me what you want me to do.

I LOVE YOU I LOVE YOU I LOVE YOU I LOVE YOU I LOVE YOU and then approximately a million emoji with kisses and hearts.

North sent back a thumbs-up. Then he headed to the garage. Shaw's Mercedes was already gone, of course.

"Where are you going," North muttered as he climbed into the GTO, "you sneaky little fuck?"

Chapter 5

NORTH FOLLOWED SHAW USING his phone. Shaw had insisted that they both install a location-sharing app after the Slasher case; it was the kind that allowed the other person to check your location at any time—or, if you didn't turn off certain settings, it would send a stream of notifications about your movements, places visited, and time spent stationary. That had lasted until the day Shaw had claimed he was going to meditate with Master Hermes, and then North had gotten seventeen notifications about Shaw's visits to Popeye's, Ted Drewes, a head shop called Smoke Signals, two different adult stores (Pansy's Blue Box and Drill Bits), Jack in the Box, and Ted Drewes again. North had left his phone out, the notifications displayed, when Shaw came home. After that, the notifications had stopped.

But even without the notifications, the app still allowed North to track his lying boyfriend, and it had, after all, been Shaw's idea.

The April day was beautiful—at the end of the month, some of the trees were still budding—the redbuds, for example, in popcorn explosions of pink and crimson—while others had leafed out. The air was mild enough for North to drive with the windows down, and once he'd left Benton Park behind, and the stink of the brewery with it, the breeze smelled like spring. Somehow, it just made him angrier.

He was even angrier when he exited I-44 onto Kingshighway and made his first guess about where Shaw was going. He drove south, passed Tower Grove Park, where the new grass was an emerald carpet and the sun cut perfect shadows from the trees. He passed Uncle Bill's Pancakes, where the drag queens liked to go after their shows. He doglegged, Chippewa to Macklind, and passed the Conoco where, when he'd been eight years old, his Uncle Ronnie had bought him a Milky Way and a cherry slushie and asked him to sit on the curb while Uncle Ronnie took care of some business. It had been a day like today, perfect for being outdoors. What North had liked most—aside from the Milky Way, of course—had been watching the cars. And, of course, the independence. Being treated like an adult.

Shaw was parking on the west side of Macklind on the next block, in front of a pub called the Dublin Snug. The swears built like steam in North's chest. Then they became subvocalized. He looked for a place to stop the GTO, not caring if Shaw noticed him.

But an asshat stole the last parking spot on the block, and North had to park on the next one. He sprinted back, dodging the mommy gang treating themselves to boozy shakes outside an ice cream parlor, and caught Shaw halfway through the door to the Dublin Snug.

"North?"

"What the fuck are you—"

"Well, well, well. What do we have here?" That was Ronnie's voice. Uncle Ronnie. The Snug was dim inside, and North had to squint to make out Ronnie's shape near the bar: short, rotund, dressed as usual in a Hawaiian shirt, cargo shorts, and Birkenstocks. "North, my boy. And Shaw. In or out, boys."

"Out," North growled, yanking on Shaw's arm.

"In," Shaw said, his tone surprisingly cool as he met North's gaze.

"Are you off your fucking rocker?"

"I'm taking care of something."

"You have no idea what you're doing. No fucking clue. We're leaving, and after I finish telling you how very fucking stupid you've been, maybe I'll explain some of the things you don't understand."

The move was fast—Shaw was always fast—but it was also unexpected: a palm-strike to North's chest, not hard enough to knock the breath out of him, but enough to startle. And enough, it turned out, for Shaw to slip out of North's hold and head into the Snug.

Doing a hell of a lot more subvocalizing, North stepped into the pub and let the door swing shut behind him. The bar was exactly as he remembered, although it had been years since he'd set foot inside. Colored-glass pendants provided weak, moody lighting, and when patrons moved, their shadows danced in the tarnished mirror behind the bar. A burnt-sugar sweetness mixed with the yeasty, beery smells, underlaid by old tobacco and leather. The sound was tired bodies shifting, glasses settling on epoxied wood, the ponies on a swivel TV. The men, without exception, were men like North's father: hard faced, middle aged, white, tradesmen and union guys, wall after wall after wall mewing them in their tiny world.

Shaw was already halfway to Ronnie, and North massaged his chest and jogged to catch up.

"I'm sorry," Shaw whispered.

After a moment, tongue thick, North managed, "It's ok."

"I don't like being manhandled."

North surprised himself with a snort, and he was even more surprised to find a tiny, wry grin on his face. "Bullshit."

Shaw grinned—just a self-conscious gleam—and then they reached Ronnie.

"Now Shaw," Ronnie said in a mock-scolding tone. "You've been naughty. I thought we were going to have a private conversation."

"I followed him," North said.

"I'm a terrible liar," Shaw said with a shrug.

"Shaw is a devious, conniving, treacherous, weasely little shit, actually. But you have to give him time to prepare; he can't do it off the cuff."

"I wouldn't say I'm—"

"Yes. You are." North glanced around. "Are we doing this here?"

Ronnie's face was unreadable. Then he called over his shoulder, "Declan, three pints in the snug," and headed toward a door set off from the bar proper.

"Last chance," North whispered.

Shaw's mouth was set in a grim line; he shook his head.

When he started after Ronnie, North caught his shoulder, muttered, "For fuck's sake," under his breath, and went through the door first.

North's first impression was that the space was cramped, although after a moment he realized that wasn't quite right. It was technically a room, although it was barely large enough for the tables and chairs set next to a cold fireplace. The occasional whisper of air stirred flakes of ash on the hearth, which meant that it still saw some use—or that the Dublin Snug needed to hire better cleaners. Frosted windows bled milky light into the room. With the door shut, it was surprisingly pleasant.

"Sit down, sit down," Ronnie said, dropping into a chair by the window. He must have noticed North's considering look because he said, "Snugs used to be the fashion, especially in the old country. A nice little nook for the upstanding lady or gentleman who had a wee too much to drink. Sit down, I said."

North and Shaw sat. A man entered, carrying three pints, and set them on the table. He hesitated, and when Ronnie shook his head, he left, closing the door behind him. A thick door. And thick walls. Silence, except the intermittent whistle of air in the chimney.

"Well," Ronnie said, "tell your uncle how you've been."

"You're not my uncle. And I'm not interested in whatever game you're playing. The last time I saw you, you threatened us. You threatened Shaw. You threatened me. You threatened my dad. We're done, Ronnie. So whatever the fuck this is, say your piece, and then we're leaving."

"I thought he'd be like this," Ronnie confided to Shaw. "That's why I contacted you. He's always been stubborn. Digs in his heels."

"Like a mule," Shaw supplied.

"Yes, exactly. Like a mule. Although God knows I've never been within five miles of a mule, I don't think. But yes, exactly like that. That's why I contacted you, Shaw. I knew you'd be more reasonable."

"You said that someone needs help. You said you'd consider this going a long way toward squaring things with North. That's why I came."

"He lied," North said. "He always lies."

Ronnie tsked.

"This is another setup," North said. "Just like last time. You're going to point us the way you want us to run, and whatever you tell us, it's going to be half the truth, or a quarter, or just the skim floating on top. Whatever your angle, it's going to be about Aldrich Acquisitions, just like last time."

"He's dramatic," Ronnie said to Shaw. "He's always been a ham."

"Trust me, I know. You should see him sneeze. He does this whole thing where he winds up like he's throwing a pitch, and then—"

"What do you want, Ronnie?" North broke in. "We're not going to help you. We're not going to cave. Whatever you think you're going to get out of us, however you think you're going to manipulate us, you're wasting your time. The last time I saw you, you tried to extort me by threatening to put my dad in prison for jury tampering. As far as I'm concerned, we don't have anything else to discuss. Do whatever you're going to do."

"North, apple of my eye, you are a very bright young man, but you're a bit self-centered. Did it ever occur to you that I might not want anything from you except your help? That this might not be about you at all?"

"No. Because that's not you, Ronnie. And I know you."

With a sigh, Ronnie leaned back in his seat. He took a long drink of Guinness and glanced at their glasses.

"It's barely eleven," North said.

"It would be rude not to try," Shaw said. "I've never had—"

North took the glass before Shaw could pick it up and set it out of reach. "Clock's running, Ronnie."

"I admit that our last interaction was…unpleasant. That was on me; I'll take the blame. I've got a bit of a temper, as you know. But it's all flash-in-the-pan. It's over. And what you've got to understand, North, is that I deeply regret how certain events played out."

"Horseshit." North pushed his chair back. "Was that why you lured Shaw down here?"

"I didn't lure him anywhere. North McKinney, sit down!" Ronnie took a deep breath, hands cradling his bowling-ball gut. He dipped one finger in his beer and drew a circle on the epoxy-resin wood. Then he drew another circle, larger, encapsulating the first. Then another. And then another. Then he drew several circles that intersected the others. "This is the world, North, my lad. And you are a teensy-tiny part of it. I have other concerns. I have other interests. Frankly, although I hope it won't damage your ego, I have other priorities. I am part of a…group, if you will. A network of friends and acquaintances and business partners. We have a great deal going on, and if one of our interests turns out to be too much trouble, we simply shift to another interest. The world is a big place, and there's no point in hitting our heads against a brick wall. Such is the case with Aldrich Acquisitions."

A grin hooked the corner of North's mouth. "Oh, right. You and your business buddies, you just lost all interest in whatever you were after because it got a little too difficult."

"You're being snide, North. That's not an admirable quality."

"Fuck what you admire. Shaw, let's go."

Shaw shook his head. "You said someone needed help. Someone from our community."

"And they do," Ronnie said. "And they do. Give me just a moment." He eased himself out of the seat, stretched a stiff gam, and made his way to the door. After opening the door, he stuck his head out, said something, and then shuffled back to his seat. A moment later, a man slipped through the still-open door and shut it behind him.

He was tall, broad shouldered, still fit, but the way a guy is fit in his forties instead of in his twenties. Blond hair in a conservative part. Something about the mouth that suggested a winning smile. His blazer and wingtips had probably cost more than every piece of clothing North had bought in the last year put together. North's first reaction was to imagine kneecapping him with a tire iron, and then his conscious brain caught up with the lizard brain: this son of a bitch looked like Tucker.

"Gentlemen," Ronnie said, "meet Lee Wallace Searls. Mr. Searls, this is North McKinney and Shaw Aldrich. They'll the ones who'll be taking your case if they agree."

"Pleased to meet you," to North, then again to Shaw, and then, "Any connection to Aldrich Acquisitions?"

"Maybe," North said. "What's your connection to the company?"

Searls's gaze broke away to North only for a second before returning to Shaw. "None. I work in advertising, and I'd love to get face time with somebody over there."

"Are you working for any of Aldrich Acquisitions' subsidiaries?" North asked. "Or for a competitor? Or did you used to work for them in another capacity? Do you have family members, friends, sexual partners, or other connections at Aldrich?"

This time, Searls snapped a look at North for a moment longer. "What?"

"Answer the question."

"Questions," Shaw said. "You asked him more than one."

"No," Searls said more slowly. "I told you, I'm in advertising. We're based in Chicago, but we're setting up a satellite operation here, so I'm in St. Louis two weeks each month. I've got no connections or friends or whatever you said. I know the name because they're a big fish, and I'd love for our satellite office to land a big fish." To Ronnie, he said, "I thought these guys were professionals."

"In any of your advertising projects, have you had any interaction at any level with an Aldrich Acquisitions employee, or with—"

Shaw's hand closed around North's wrist under the table. He squeezed once, shook his head, and North cut off.

"How do you know Ronnie?" Shaw asked.

Ronnie chuckled, but when Searls glanced at him, he waved a hand and took a drink.

"I don't," Searls said. "Not really. A friend put us in contact. He told me Ronnie would be able to help me with a problem."

"Then here's a piece of free advice," North said. "Get out of here. Don't walk, run. And don't look back. Because you have no fucking idea what—"

"That's enough, North," Ronnie snapped. His features were tight and thin. "If you can't behave, Shaw and I will talk to Lee Wallace alone."

Shaw squeezed North's wrist again.

Somehow, North swallowed and ducked his chin.

"What's the problem, Mr. Searls?" Shaw said.

"My boyfriend." Searls slid into a seat at the table, with the air of a man who had just finished an interview. He unbuttoned his collar and ran two fingers under the cloth. "He disappeared. I'm worried he's hurt."

"Why would you think that?"

"He would have called me back. No matter how mad he is, he would have called me back. I think something bad happened. He gets reckless when he's upset; I think he might have been in an accident, or maybe he wandered into the wrong bar. That kind of thing still happens, you know."

"Why was he upset?" Shaw said.

"Why don't you call the police?" North said.

Shaw shot him a look, and North leaned back in his seat, caught up one of the untouched pints of Guinness, and drank deeply. The bitter, caramel-malt taste made him close to being sick, and he set the glass down too hard. Suds ran over his fingers.

Searls watched all of this.

"Why was he upset?" Shaw asked again.

"We had a fight. He's passionate. He's younger, quite a bit younger, actually, and he's still figuring things out."

"Not you, though," North said. "You've got things all figured out. You've got that window office. You've got that six-figure salary. You've got that loft apartment. Do you drive a Beamer? Let me guess: you play golf."

"Do you need to step outside for a minute?" Shaw whispered.

"No." North drew fingers, still soaped with beer, across his mouth. "No, I'm fine. Ask him about the police."

With a flinch, Searls glanced at Ronnie.

Ronnie nodded. "Best to be upfront about everything. They'll learn it all anyway; they really are good."

"I…hit him."

"Motherfucker," North said.

Shaw gripped his wrist so hard this time that it hurt. The pain was grounding, a red wire tethering North as he breathed the too-thin air of memories.

"I know," Searls said, one hand over his face. "I know. I know I'm a piece of shit. I know; you don't have any idea how many times I've told myself. And I don't expect Danny to take me back. I really don't. I just want to know he's ok. You don't have to tell me where he is. You don't have to tell me how to contact him. I just want to know he's ok."

"And we get paid?" North said. "Great. He's ok. That'll be five hundred dollars."

"His name's Danny Wilkintonis. He hates his last name." Searls took out his phone, unlocked it, and opened the photos app. "This is us."

The photograph showed two men in short swim trunks, framed by sapphire water and a blaze of white sand. Searls looked good, and from the way he stood, one arm hooked around the younger man, he knew it. The younger man, possibly Danny Wilkintonis, was attractive but not remarkable: a mess of long, sandy hair parted on the side; a great smile; a little jug-eared, maybe. Danny was scratching the back of one leg with his foot, his head turned slightly, as though Searls had just said something.

"I don't have any hard copies," Searls said, "but I can get them printed if you want. I've got a bunch of pictures of us together, and one or two of him by himself." Searls tugged on his collar again, his eyes sliding to the milky glass. "They're, um, adult pictures."

"Right," Shaw said, "I don't think we'd need any of him when he was younger, so that's probably for the best."

"He means they're sex pictures," North said. "Explicit."

"Oh," Shaw said, color rushing into his face. "Got it."

"I think he went home, maybe," Searls said. "He grew up near Cape Girardeau. I don't have his parents' address; there are a few Wilkintonis down there, and I was going to call all of them, but then I met Ronnie and he offered to put me in touch with you."

"Last chance." North walked two sticky fingers across the table. "Run away."

"North loves a touch of the dramatic," Ronnie said, squeezing Searls's shoulder in a way that made him rise. Walking Searls to the snug's door, Ronnie added, "He gets it from his mother. Have another beer. Sit down. Relax. I'll go over the specifics with you once we've got everything arranged."

As soon as the door shut, North said, "No."

Ronnie walked back to the table.

"No, Ronnie. We're not doing this."

With a wry smile at Shaw, Ronnie lifted his glass and sank the rest of his beer.

"You think this is funny?" North stabbed a finger at the door. "That guy is an abusive fuckwad. He beat the shit out of that kid, the kid was smart enough to run, and now we're going to help him track him down?"

"This is why I contacted you," Ronnie told Shaw. "This is why I asked you to come alone."

"Let's go," North said, catching Shaw's elbow to haul him up from the seat. "Final answer, Ronnie: no."

Ronnie slapped the table, and even though North was a twenty-six-year-old man, he jumped. "I didn't ask you to come here, North. And I didn't ask you to help him. I've reached the end of my patience with you; either be quiet or get out."

Heat filled every millimeter of North's face.

"He's one of your business friends?" Shaw asked in a subdued voice.

"No." Ronnie shook his head for emphasis. "He's not part of our little network. He's just a man who needs help."

"And who will owe you a favor."

"I'd like to think he'd help me if I ever asked."

Shaw was quiet for a long time. His fingers found North's, tracing the inside of his hand, but North couldn't bring himself to respond.

"Ok," Shaw said.

North stood. His chair scraped across the floor, and he headed for the door.

"North, wait—have him send us everything he has on Danny, including the pictures. Phone numbers. Apartments. Friends. Family. North, will you please—"

But North was already barreling out of the snug and headed for the street.

Chapter 6

SHAW TOOK HIS TIME driving back to the Benton Park house because he wasn't sure which was worse: finding North there, or not. The GTO was in the garage, and as the door rattled down behind Shaw, he found himself taking huge, gulping breaths, eyes stinging, as he tried to summon the personal mantra that Master Hermes had sold him for a hundred and seventy-nine dollars. The clock read 11:57 when he pushed the Mercedes' door open, the smell of cold cement meeting him, and walked into the house.

North was in the office, examining pages on the desk next to him and then typing carefully. Client reports. Or expense reports. Or invoices. Or something with taxes, which apparently you had to pay every year. Shaw shut the door and leaned against it. Through the wood, he could hear Pari moving around, accompanied by quiet voices and swells of dramatic music. Telenovelas had been a constant presence in the reception area lately. The smell of cigarettes was strong in the closed room.

"We've got to get over to the school by one-thirty at the latest," North said as he turned a page. "I'd rather be there by one, in case there's paperwork or the school administration wants to put us through our paces the first time. Do you want to work through lunch? Or we can run out and grab something."

"Actually," Shaw said, "I was hoping we could talk about what just happened."

North turned a page, flipped back, and made a tsking noise as he tapped the backspace key. "Ok."

"Maybe we should talk about our feelings first."

"Ok."

"I'm feeling really, really awful because I went over to meet Ronnie without telling you, and I lied, and then I took that case even though I know you didn't want to. But I did it because I'm scared that he's going to come after you, North, and because I'm really scared that you're going to get hurt or sent to prison or killed, and I don't know what I'd do without you. And I said yes because anything we can learn about what Ronnie wants and does, that gives us an advantage. Maybe just a tiny one, but we need all the help we can get. I don't know if that guy's telling the truth, I don't know if I did the right thing, but I'm scared all the time and I didn't know what else to do."

And then he burst into tears.

North bent over, and for a moment, through the storm of sobbing, Shaw had the idea that North might be climbing under the desk, having finally reached the end of his patience. Instead, though, North stood with the box of tissues he'd retrieved from Shaw's desk drawer, and he carried them around the desk. Plucking out two, he seemed to consider for a moment, and then he handed them to Shaw.

Shaw dabbed at his eyes. If anything, though, it only made him cry harder.

"Sit down," North said, hands on Shaw's arms, guiding him into the seats normally used by clients. "I'll get you some tea."

So, for a few minutes, Shaw did a magician's trick of never-ending tissues, and eventually North came back with a chipped mug that said PRIVATE DICKS DO IT IN THE CAR. Fragrant steam wafted up, and when North pressed it into Shaw's hands, the warmth soaked into him. North dragged another client chair closer, and they sat there, North's hand on Shaw's knee, until the worst of the crying was over.

After a bracing gulp of tea, Shaw managed to ask, "How are you feeling?"

"Grateful I didn't have to drink any tea. Chamomile tastes like grass."

Shaw closed his eyes.

"I'm fine, Shaw," North said. "I'm irritated you didn't tell me what you were doing, but I know you had your reasons. I understand why you took the job. We'll do it, and hopefully we'll figure out what Ronnie's after this time."

"So when you say you're feeling fine," Shaw said, opening his eyes, "could you talk more about that? I just need to know how you went from feeling, you know, upset, to feeling fine. Now."

North laughed. "I surely fucking can't. What about lunch?"

Shaw considered him: the voice was North's, but clipped; the hand on his leg was North's, but unfamiliar; the eyes were North's, but red-rimmed and leached of color, almost gray. The week before, Shaw had ordered their pizzas with a non-dairy cheese substitute, and North had delivered a forty-five-minute lecture that mostly consisted of readings from the National Dairy Council's website. Today, *I'm fine*.

"North, I'm really sorry about how that happened."

"I know."

"I think we need to take the case. I really think that's the smart thing to do."

"I know." North stood, hand falling away from Shaw's leg, and moved behind his desk. "We're taking it, right?"

"Right, but—"

"And I already texted Haw. She had messaged me last night about an attempted break-in; I'm starting to think this might be connected. It doesn't seem like Searls has any special access to Aldrich or its subsidiaries, but we don't know anything about this Danny guy. He might be what Ronnie's really after."

"That's a possibility." Shaw turned the mug in his hand. "Could we go back, though? If you could help me understand how you're feeling and what I can do—"

"For fuck's sake, Shaw." It was the first edge to his voice, and it was so mild that it sounded more like frustration than anything else. "I'm fine. We're fine. We talked about it. We processed it, or whatever you wanted us to do. What do you want?"

"I don't know. I don't know. I don't like this, and I just want things to be normal again."

"I don't know what you want," North said. "I talked about it. I told you how I felt. I'm sorry I don't have anything else to say."

Shaw's still-puffy eyes stung again, but he refused to cry a second time. He clutched the mug with both hands. His fingertips were white against the warm ceramic.

Shouldering into his Carhartt jacket, North said, "I just remembered I need to run an errand for my dad. Meet me at the school? One o'clock?"

"I could go with—"

"Better not," North said, boots thumping the boards as he passed Shaw. "You know how you get under his skin. If you want, you can call Haw. Or your dad. See if they've got any ideas about this Danny guy. Or about Searls."

And then he was gone, steps heavy as they faded down the hall.

Shaw waited until he was sure the GTO had left. Then he carried his tea into the kitchen. Pari said something; he couldn't make out the words. He dropped the mug in the sink without slowing, only distantly aware of the crack of ceramic, and took the stairs two at a time. He locked the door behind him, knelt on his bed, and screamed into a pillow.

Then Shaw dug through the joints in his nightstand until he found the fattest one.

Chapter 7

"GREAT," NORTH said when he met Shaw on the curb outside The Gouverneur Morris School. "You're high."

"I'm not high." Shaw tried for wounded dignity. He had changed clothes, and he appeared to be shirtless under a cream-colored jacket embroidered with dragons and cherry blossoms. Against the narrow vee of his chest that was exposed, he wore a necklace with a single, glossy black pendant, asymmetrical and probably abstractly representing something like eternity or his last incarnation. Buff-colored pedal pushers and lime-green Mary Janes completed today's choices. Shaw leaned closer. "Holy shit, do that again."

"Do what again? Are you serious with me right now? You got fucking blitzed, Shaw? We're working."

After another moment of staring, Shaw giggled. "Oh my God," he whispered. "Your eyelids are like," he mimed something moving up and down, "but for your eyes."

"I absolutely cannot fucking do this today. Go home, Shaw. I'll handle this."

Instead, though, Shaw trotted after him, and North found himself wondering if the last issue of *Marie Claire* had an article on spanking the hell out of boyfriends who did nothing but get your balls in a twist.

The Gouverneur Morris campus occupied twenty acres in the inner ring of St. Louis's suburbs. The grounds were perfectly landscaped: thick green grass, oaks leafing out, a fringe tree with its fluttering spring petals, flowerbeds with red and orange and purple tulips pushing up through the mulch. Dotting the rolling grounds here and there were buildings: a sprawling red barn with white trim, cottages with shake roofs and narrow windows, and then a quadrangle lined with brick colonials. The whole thing looked like you could have set it down next to Monticello, and nobody would have batted an eye.

The school's main building stood on the far side of the quadrangle. A pair of girls in blue-and-white uniforms were sitting on a bench, looking at North and Shaw and then putting their heads together and giggling. They clammed up as soon as North and Shaw were within range, switching over to looks of cool disgust, as though humans over twenty were something they had accidentally stepped in and needed to scrape off their shoes. North ignored them and caught Shaw's arm when the stoner veered off, obviously intending on talking to them.

The pediment over the doors said, *Patriotism. Liberty. Curiosity.*

Not a fucking word about spankings.

Inside, it was obvious that the building had once genuinely been a home: they stood in a foyer with sharply pitched stairs, white-washed paneling on the walls, and a softly glowing chandelier overhead. Signs indicated MAIN OFFICE to their left and GUIDANCE upstairs. North went left, heading through a pair of French doors.

It was a decent-sized room that felt cramped with all the office furniture, although they'd done a decent job of adding modern necessities to a room that still looked like Martha Washington would have been at home. The girl behind the desk was plumply pretty in a blue-and-white cardigan and a polo shirt proclaiming THE GOUVERNEUR MORRIS SCHOOL. The name plate on the desk said, *Leah.* West County white girl, North judged. Probably went to Parkway. She smiled, pushed back long hair, and said, "Good morning. May I help you?"

"We need to talk to the head of school for a few minutes. Could you let her know we're here?"

On the other side of the room, an open door offered a view of a private office. North could see a woman's shoes poking out from under a desk, and occasionally she clicked a mouse or tapped the keyboard.

"Could I get your names?" Leah asked.

"North McKinney and Shaw Aldrich. She should be expecting us."

"Kingsley Shaw Wilder Aldrich," Shaw said, and he tried to step forward to shake Leah's hand, stumbled on the uneven, hand-sawed boards, and crashed into North.

Doubt filtered into Leah's face.

"Would you let her know we're here?" North asked again, clutching Shaw's collar to hold him upright. "She'll know what it's about."

"North," Shaw said in what he probably hoped was a whisper and sounded, instead, like someone stoned trying to whisper. "I'm really dizzy. I think that peanut I ate gave me food poisoning."

More doubt. Leah was not pleased.

"Just tell her," North said, yanking on Shaw's collar again when his knees tried to fold.

After another moment and a glance at the desk—an inventory, North realized, in case they tried to steal anything—Leah took a few steps backward, turned and hurried into the private office. Low voices followed, and then Leah emerged again, pulling the door shut behind her. She sat at her desk and said, "I'm sorry, Dr. Latese isn't in the office right now. I'll be happy to—"

"She's not in the office?" North asked, hauling Shaw upright again.

"No, I'm very sorry. I'll be happy to take a message—"

"So, back there, you were just talking to yourself?"

"I wasn't talking to anyone," Leah said. Red stained her cheeks. "If you'd like to leave a message, I can do that. Or I can try to find her on campus. You're welcome to have a seat while I try to track her down."

North checked the clock; only half past one. He was willing to play this shit show out for a little bit longer.

"Do that," North said. "Quickly."

They sat in chairs that were surprisingly comfortable, and North got out his phone and sent a quick message to Celia's assistant—Gavin?—telling her that they were being stonewalled. Gavin responded with *On it*, then nothing. North pretended to read. In reality, he studied Leah, who was talking quietly into the phone, hanging up, placing another call, and performing an encore. It wasn't exactly surprising that Celia Chittenden hadn't alerted the head of school; people like her tended to assume the universe would fall into place once she made her wishes known. It was sure fucking annoying, though.

Shaw pawed through the magazines on the side table. "North, they've got everything. *Time, Midwest Living, Vogue,* the *Harvard Business Review, Scientific American.*" He froze and ran his hand down the cover of a National Geographic—lots of trees on this one; North preferred the ones with lions or deserts. Shaw grabbed North's hand and pulled it to the cover, drawing North's fingers along the glossy paper. "Do you feel that?"

"It's a magazine."

"But do you feel it? It feels like a magazine made out of light. How do they do that? Miss," he bellowed to Leah, who jumped in surprise, "how do they do that?"

"Ignore him," North said. In a low voice, he snapped, "Will you cut it out? I'm at the end of my fucking rope with you. Seriously, Shaw, what the fuck were you thinking?"

"I knew it," Shaw said with a triumphant smile, but his eyes were foggily sad. "I knew you were mad at me. You kept saying it was fine, but I knew you were mad."

"Great. You're the fucking Great Mouse Detective. I hope you're incredibly fucking proud of yourself."

"I said I was sorry—"

"I know. And I know you're sorry. It doesn't change the fact that—" North cut himself off.

Shaw put his face in his hands. His body was very still.

North stood, pocketed his phone, and grabbed a box of tissues from Leah's desk. He hesitated and said, "I know this won't mean anything to you, and you probably won't believe me, but I have to say it for my own sake: I swear to God we're professionals."

Leah gave him a brittle smile and went back to her bullshit phone calls.

As North dropped back into the seat, he decided it was time for the magic words. Pulling Shaw's hands away from puffy eyes, wet cheeks, and a snotty nose, he began to clean him up with the tissues. "I just need time to process what I'm feeling."

"Oh." Shaw perked up, took the tissues, and finished wiping his own face. "That's why you kept saying you were fine?"

"Yes. Because we are fine. We'll be fine. I just want some time to process all of this."

"Why didn't you tell me that?"

North shrugged.

"Thanks," Shaw whispered. "Thank you for sharing that with me."

North kissed his cheek, wrapped one of Shaw's hands in his own, and then settled back for fifteen seconds of blessed silence. He had no idea what Shaw thought processing meant, but it worked better than abracadabra.

"I'm going to find ninety-seven ways to make it up to you," Shaw said.

"Please don't."

"I'm going to write you an acrostic poem. North Magnanimous McKinney. 'N is for navel piercing, which I wish he would get. O is for orgasm, the best I've had yet. R is for—'"

"That's not my middle name."

"I'm going to learn a song like 'Greensleeves' and sing it to you while you take a bath."

"I don't take baths."

"I'm going to do that thing you like where I let my head hang off the bed and—"

"Shaw, for the love of God, you have to stop talking."

Leah was staring at them. In a kind of daze, she tugged on the sleeve of her cardigan.

"I'm really high," Shaw stoner-whispered.

North covered his eyes.

"Since we're being honest with each other."

"Yeah, I thought I might have noticed something when you started molesting *Popular Mechanics*."

"I'm so sorry," Leah said. "I just reached Dr. Latese, and she told me that she won't be back on campus today. She had to leave for personal reasons."

"Of course," North said, standing and stretching.

"If you have a card…"

"No, that won't be necessary." North walked around the desk.

"You can't come back here," Leah said.

"He's a complicated man," Shaw told her. "Sometimes he's really sweet and he's telling you he can't wait to listen to the forty-six-minute vocal fugue that you composed in your head based on 'Greensleeves'—"

"I never said that," North called back.

"I'm going to get security," Leah shouted.

"—and then sometimes—"

North drove one Redwing into the door. Both the door and the frame splintered—cheap wood, definitely not original, North thought—and the door flew open. The office on the other side was empty, but the computer was still running. More importantly, one of the wavy-glass windows was open. Someone had tried to force the sash down but had obviously not been able to get it all the way closed. Probably, North guessed, because she had been standing on the ground below after she climbed outside.

"—he's just a jackass in boots. That door wasn't locked, by the way."

North studied the door. "Oh. Huh."

"That's it," Leah said, although she still hadn't moved. "I'm calling the police."

"It's better if you just relax and let it happen. Oh. That's what North used to tell all the Chouteau boys he'd bring back to our apartment. I warned him that it sounded really rapey, but—"

"I said that one time, Shaw. Once. To a virgin who was so tight he could have cracked walnuts. Jesus Christ. You can't go around telling people I said that." North's phone buzzed. Gavin, sending them Philip's phone number. "Come on. We'll find Philip ourselves."

"What in the world is going on down here?" The voice was husky and sweet, and it came from a tiny black woman who stood in the foyer doorway with her hands on her hips. Her tight coils of hair were bleached reddish-orange, and her face was small and round. "Leah, I asked you a question. What's happening?"

"These guys broke into Dr. Latese's office!"

"That's an exaggeration," Shaw said. "I already explained the jackass-in-boots syndrome, and—"

"We're here to pick up Philip Chittenden," North cut in. "His parents sent us; you can verify that with them. We showed up to let the head of school know what was going on, only Leah gave us the runaround while her boss snuck out the window. So, consider yourself officially informed while I walk over and find Philip's scrawny ass and get this dumbfuck job over with."

The small woman's first word was, "Flip? Is this for his testing?"

"Philip," North said slowly. "Philip Chittenden."

"Yes. He goes by Flip. Leah, did you call security?"

"No, I'll do it—"

"No, no. It's fine. I'll handle this." She held out a small hand, and North pumped it once. "Countee Dove. I'm the guidance counselor. And you are?"

"North McKinney."

"Shaw Aldrich." Shaw squeezed past North in his determination to also have a chance to shake Countee's hand. "We're private investigators, and when

North told Leah that, Dr. Latese got really startled and climbed out the window."

"There's been some sort of misunderstanding," Countee said, glancing at Leah. North followed her look; Leah's expression conveyed very clearly that, a) there had been absolutely no misunderstanding of any kind, and b) she was seriously considering finding a new job. "Mrs. Chittenden told us that she'd hired someone to get Flip safely to and from the weekly testing, and I communicated that to Dr. Latese, although I didn't realize you were private investigators, which seems an odd choice for a transportation job. I'm sure we'll figure this out."

"Happens all the time," North says. "I show up at a private school. I introduce myself. Next thing I know, a woman with a doctorate is shooting down the drainpipe faster than you can say, 'Bob's your uncle.'"

Countee's mouth thinned into a line, and she said, "Let's go find Flip. I'm sure you need to get going."

When they emerged from the administrative building, the quad was alive with activity. A group of boys and girls who were so tiny they must have been ninth-graders was playing duck-duck-goose. Two boys with the sullen, combative expressions native to teen angst huddled at the end of a hedge, one of them quickly hiding something in his pocket when he saw Countee. A vape pen, North guessed, or a joint. A girl with a forelock of pink hair was playing the ukulele, while another girl tried to sing "What a Wonderful World" and kept jumping in early on the intro. All of them in blue-and-white uniforms— the options appeared to be jackets, shirt, and trouser, or sweater, blouse, and skirt. More than a few of the girls had opted for trousers, and North didn't blame them.

"I have that same skirt," Shaw said, halting abruptly as they passed a group of girls. "In pink plaid."

"Just keep walking," North told Countee. "You've got to maintain escape velocity with Shaw. I didn't, and look what happened."

"That's really rude," Shaw said as he trotted to catch up. "First of all..." He trailed off, head turning as he tried to track something invisible to North.

Sighing, North caught his arm and towed him along.

"So," he said to Countee, "you're the school counselor?"

"I am. It's really a jack-of-all-trades position here." North's face must have betrayed his skepticism because Countee added, "You'd be surprised how much these kids need."

"Oh yeah, I can tell. Two parents, food on the table, a private education at one of the most expensive schools in the state. Yeah, they've definitely got unmet needs. I bet some of them even have anxiety that they won't get straight A's."

The only sound was their steps on the sidewalk and the distant voices of the kids. Then Countee said, "I don't think you have any idea what you're talking about."

"Right," North said, "their lives are so hard. I get it. Makes perfect sense."

"Kids do a lot of crying in the laundry room," Shaw said. "Nobody can hear them when the dryer's running."

North stopped, caught Shaw's arm, and stared at him.

Yawning, Shaw covered his mouth with his arm. Then he managed to say, "North, I'm really sleepy now."

North considered him for a minute. "You went here?"

"Oh yeah. I wasn't even going to tell you because, you know, well, basically everything, but yeah. And not everybody here is happy. Lots of people are sad. Or messed up. Or messed up because they're trying so hard not to feel sad."

A minivan pulled to the curb a few yards away, and a girl in a Gouverneur Morris uniform emerged from the vehicle. A woman's voice chased after her.

"—not going to get any better if you don't practice. And make smart choices about what you eat, sweetheart. Two hours of practice a day. That's what we agreed on. And twenty pounds. And you're not keeping your part of the bargain, sweetheart, which means Daddy and I are going to have to take away your phone and the Amex if you don't—"

"Oh my God, Mom, I know," the girl shrieked. She slammed the door and stormed off toward a building on the opposite side of the quad.

North's gaze returned to Shaw as he tried to understand what he was hearing in Shaw's voice, laid bare by the weed.

"This is Flip's residence," Countee said.

"I had some really good friends here," Shaw said. "Oh. I should call them. I'm going to call them right now."

"Not just yet," North said, pushing Shaw's phone down. "Why don't you work on your vocal fugue until we drop Flip off? Then we can talk about going to school here and your friends and anything else you want to tell me."

"It's going to be three hours long now," Shaw said with a bleary smile. "I remembered one part I forgot."

"Is he all right?" Countee asked.

"This really isn't too far off normal, actually. Let's get Flip."

Countee gave Shaw several dubious looks as she led them up the walk. The residence was another of the brick colonials framing the quadrangle. Countee swiped an access card, and a lock disengaged. She led them inside, up the steep stairs, and down a hall. The decorations in the main areas all looked to be period reproductions, paintings and portraits that must have been meaningless to the students boarding there and, in North's opinion, gave the space a decidedly museum-like (and creepy) vibe. Countee led them up another flight of stairs, to a cramped third floor that had probably once been an attic, and then stopped. Her breath caught in her throat.

North saw it a moment later. The second door down the hall hung ajar, the frame splintered where repeated blows had forced the door open.

"Stay here," North said.

Countee listened to him; Shaw didn't.

In the doorway, North used his elbow to force the door open the rest of the way. The bed lay on its side. The dressers were overturned. The closet door hung open, and clothes were thrown across the floor. A crack in the wall's plaster, though, was what worried North the most.

"Call the police," he told Countee. "Someone was definitely trying to find something, and it looks like there was a struggle."

Chapter 8

THE POLICE CAME AND took their statements. Their phone call to Celia consisted of a battery of short, sharp questions, and then she had ordered them not to do anything until she contacted them. No one said the words, but *missing* and *kidnapped* floated just below the surface of every conversation. Then nothing; the next two days carried them into May, the passage marked by spring thunderstorms, the days dark with clouds that looked like they'd never move on.

North spent the days catching up on Aldrich Acquisitions jobs and one-off clients: he finished the report on Nicci Lesperance and sent it to her father; he spent six hours following the Armenian child-bride of a hedge fund manager, which consisted of two hours waiting for her to get her hair and nails done in a Clayton salon and four hours, on and off, of snapping photos of her affair with the owner of an Armenian grocery store in Bevo; North even tried following up on Johanna Griffin, their client who wouldn't pay. She'd stopped taking his calls, but that didn't mean he stopped calling. He offered her one last week before he sent it to collections.

Shaw had taken over coordinating with Haw, which consisted of a slush pile of carbon-copy memos on North's desk that said things like *No updates on the break-ins,* and *Haw says hi (she really didn't, but I'm being polite on her behalf), You have a cute butt, That was me making a pass at you, But seriously sexual harassment in the workplace is not a joke, Please buy me spaghetti,* and what looked like the beginning of a Shaw original, covering the front and back of the tiny rectangle of paper and which seemed to be a gay ballroom retelling of an Icelandic saga.

"Do you do any work around here?" North asked at the end of one day, scooping the haystack of messages into the trash. He was soaked from the rain, his back ached from all those hours in the car, and he had the sneaking suspicion that Shaw had done another fridge purge again.

Shaw pointed at the messages without looking up from the Legos he was playing with. It was supposed to be the Death Star, but judging by the completely inaccurate placement of the thermal exhaust port, North had a bad feeling about the final product.

"Any real work, I mean?"

"I've been working on finding Danny Wilkintonis."

North grunted.

"I ran down his parents," Shaw said, pausing to stick out his tongue as he studied where the next Lego should go. "And his best friend from college. And his one girlfriend before, as she told me, 'He started wearing those rhinestone jeans and slurping cocks.' And Searls sent over some of his bills, so I started going through those."

North made another of those acknowledging noises.

"Something really bad happened to Flip," Shaw said quietly.

"We don't know that," North said, because that was his line in this scene.

He watched Shaw for a minute. Watched how intently Shaw was focused on the Legos. Stretching his back, he let his shirt ride up, and he strummed his abs. Shaw threw a quick look before snapping his attention back to the blocks, and North smothered a grin.

"Come upstairs in five minutes," North said. "You need a real distraction, and my back is killing me. We're going to take a bath. If you want to be nice, you could bring me a couple of beers."

"I'm kind of busy. And you hog the tub. Your legs are too big. All of you is too big."

"All of me?"

"You've got the mind of a fifteen-year-old."

"Five minutes," North said, "or I come looking for you."

Shaw was there in four minutes and fifty-nine seconds, naked, hard, and carrying two beers by the necks.

On the news the next day, the story was everywhere: Philip Chittenden was missing, and police suspected kidnapping. The summons came at nine o'clock that morning—there wasn't any other word for it. Celia Chittenden demanded that they attend a meeting at her house in Maries County.

"Do you think we'll see Emery?" Shaw asked as they sped west on I-70.

"God, I hope not."

"Do you think we'll see John-Henry?"

"I doubt it. We're not going to Wahredua. We're not even going to Dore County. And please don't tell Hazard and Somerset we want to have lunch or check each other for lice or wash our hair and watch *Golden Girls* while we all wear towels or whatever you're about to do."

Shaw froze, phone in hand. "I wasn't going to—I wasn't going to suggest any of that."

"Then whatever it was, it would have been worse. Put your phone away."

The Chittendens lived in a farmhouse north of Vienna, although calling it a farmhouse was like calling the Sears Tower an office building. The place was an estate. Sure, it was white clapboard with a wraparound porch instead of brick and stone, and instead of a stable and horses and fox hunting or whatever the hell people did at estates, their preferences (to judge by what North could see through the open doors of the barn) seemed to be boats and four-wheelers. But this was rich people land, and the sprawling house and the perfect landscaping were just the beginning.

Gavin met them at the front door, gesturing them into the entry hall. It was open to the second floor, with wraparound stairs and a landing that looked down on the front door—presumably so the Chittendens could perform a downsized version of the Von Trapp family bullshit, or something like that. The walls were whitewashed, the floor a pale, scrubbed oak, with accent pieces that offered pops of dark wood and shades of blue and pink to complete the rustic-chic look. The sun had finally come out, and the house was full of light, the whitewash glowing with it. An opening connected the entry hall with a large space that was probably called the family room or the great room, where black cables snaked across the floor, and a pair of men in grubby tees were disassembling softboxes.

"Did they start the reality show today?" North asked.

Making a face, Gavin pointed at double doors that led off from the entry hall. "You can wait in there."

"I've got my lines all memorized," North said. "Keep your hands off my man!"

"He doesn't care about you or your fake tits," Shaw said.

"You can't say tits, remember?"

"No, it's not me. That's my character. Fiona Vandersaints. And anyway, it's in the script. Let's take it from: 'He doesn't care about you or your fake tits.'"

"He doesn't want you because your skanky ass got trashed at Ladonna's cat fashion show and you fell off your chair and gave everyone your own cat fashion show."

"All you want to do is spend his money. You never cared about him, and I have proof—"

"Just wait in there," Gavin screeched.

"Touchy," North said as he slid the double doors open.

"Rude," Shaw said.

"Respect the craft," North said. "And respect the scene."

"Even if North was stepping all over my lines."

"You little shit. You were taking forever to finish. It's not my fault—"

Gavin whirled and stalked away, heading toward the great room.

"You don't have to antagonize everyone," Shaw whispered.

North shrugged.

"It's not his fault he's a major drip. This place has some super creepy energy." Shaw looked around them at the farmhouse full of light and chafed his arms. "Creepy and dark and cold."

"I'll report it to the energy police," North said as he passed through the doors.

The room was an office, and it was immediately clear that this was Celia's private domain and not a space she shared with her husband. The furniture was in keeping with the rest of the house: blond wood with brush strokes of milk paint, a shiplap wall full of photos, lamps that were meant to look like they'd once served noble farm functions as moonshine jugs and blue-enameled percolators. Against all that, the computer was a black beetle crouched on the desk, all hard lines and glossy plastic. A red-felt display case held a small revolver: satiny stainless steel and black rubber grip. Stamped on the barrel was the Ruger phoenix.

The computer's monitor was dark, and when North jiggled the mouse, a lock screen appeared. He made his way around the room, examining the photographs. They all looked like they'd been taken relatively recently, perhaps within the last five years, because it was easy to spot Flip's entrance into adolescence, complete with acne and stooped shoulders, and his transformation into an attractive man-child on the cusp of adulthood. Celia Chittenden didn't change at all, and neither did the man, who must have been Flip's father. If Celia was Kim Novak, this guy was a puffy-faced, gin-soaked Jimmy Stewart, with his businessman's haircut and tassel loafers.

A drawer rattled. When North glanced over, Shaw was pawing through it.

"Don't take anything," North said.

Shaw made an indignant noise.

"Uh huh. Well, I have to tell you ever since you walked out of that dermatologist's house with an eight-thousand-dollar fountain pen."

"It had a unicorn on it! And I was going to give it back."

North let that one go. He moved to the center of the room, trying to take it all in at once. Energy and juju and all of that was bullshit, but he had to admit that something about the house gave him major creeps. The five-year span of the photos was one reason. And the stilted postures, the mannequin smiles, the way bodies didn't quite meet—a silhouette of some seriously fucked-up family dynamics.

"This is weird," Shaw said.

North joined him to look at the four-by-six in a plastic frame. Celia, her husband, and Flip were much younger. Flip couldn't have been older than eight, although North had a hard time being more specific than that because he had relatively little experience with children. The smiles looked real—or closer to real. Flip was pressed against Celia's legs, in overall shorts and a train conductor's cap, his face half-hidden against Celia's jeans with embarrassment. Or perhaps laughter. The husband was holding a little girl in a frilly pink dress. The child wasn't an infant, but she didn't look sturdy enough to release into the wild yet.

Voices moved toward them, and North said, "Put it back."

Shaw replaced the photograph next to the computer monitor. North slid the drawer shut. They moved away from the desk.

"Do I sound like I'm bullshitting you, officers?" A man.

"Detectives." That was a woman's voice, and it sounded familiar, although North couldn't place it.

"Whatever. Do you think I'm bullshitting you? I run a multimillion-dollar company. I don't bullshit. I expect people to do their jobs and do them well. If they don't, they're out on their asses. Not like you government types. Half you lot sit around scratching your butts all day, and there's no consequences. Nothing. Get a raise. Get a promotion. Move them up the ladder, and the whole time they're standing around picking lint out of their cracks. I was telling Celia the other day, just the other day I was saying, 'These are the people they want us to put in charge of our healthcare?' I mean, I expect results—"

"Francis," that was Celia's voice, cold and clipped, "shut up."

The silence had its own kind of echo.

A moment later, three women and two men entered the room. One of the men must have been Francis, and he matched the man in the photographs, right down to the tassel loafers. The other was a cop of some sort, although he was wearing a shabby green suit that was out at the elbows. One of the women was Celia Chittenden in a simple white blouse and a navy suit, the blue so dark that it suggested mourning. Another was a nervy blonde in what looked like the clearance-rack version of Celia's outfit. And the last was Diamond Kelso.

"Diamond?" Shaw said, a grin splitting his face. "What are you doing here?"

They had met her on the Slasher case; she'd been a uniformed officer who had helped them when she'd been able to, and they'd stayed in touch over the months when she'd occasionally passed along a tip or some helpful information. She had midnight skin, a sleek twist-up bun of hair that was now dyed a coppery color, and a fawn-colored suit that didn't look quite big enough. Her eyes, though, were her most remarkable feature: the irises a startling gold that demanded attention.

"I'm a detective with Juvenile now." She made a vague gesture at the blonde, as though that explained something.

"You got promoted?" North said.

"About time," Diamond said.

"Hey, that's great. Congratulations."

"You know these two?" the blonde asked.

"I know them," Diamond said. "What are you—"

"Mr. McKinney and Mr. Aldrich are helping with the investigation," Celia said. "Take a seat; I have an interview with the Kansas City Fox affiliate in forty-five minutes."

As soon as they were seated, the blonde spoke up: "Mrs. Chittenden, in my experience, private investigators are rarely worth the expense, and they're a classic case of over-promise and under-deliver. You could save yourself a lot of money and heartache by sending these two on their way."

"Thank you, Detective Raskowski, but it is my money, and I'll spend it however I please. Mr. McKinney, Mr. Aldrich, this is Detective Baker. Local police." She nodded to the man in the out-at-the-elbows suit. "And it seems you know Detectives Kelso and Raskowski. My husband, Francis. There, that's the introductions done."

Sure, North thought, looking around the room: Raskowski fidgeting in her seat, Diamond glaring at North and Shaw, Baker tapping nicotine-stained fingertips against his seat, Francis at the picture window, leaning against the glass and staring out into the world. Celia occupied the chair behind the desk. The way she and her husband had placed themselves, North thought you could have built the Great Wall of China between them and neither would have noticed. Sure, North thought again. All of us nice and introduced like feral cats in a drawstring bag.

"Detective Baker will continue to investigate any local leads, while Detectives Raskowski and Kelso take the lead in St. Louis. Mr. McKinney and Mr. Aldrich, you'll report directly to me." She flashed a smile, pearly and sharp. "Since it is my money, after all. Now that you've all met, I think you should exchange contact information, and then I'll need to speak to Mr. McKinney and Mr. Aldrich alone."

The three cops might have been too professional to share unhappy looks, but only barely. Raskowski snapped out a number before North had finished pulling out his phone, and she huffed loudly when he asked her to repeat it. Baker looked like a guy who just wanted to climb out of the lion's den, but his eyes were sharp, studying North and Shaw a little too closely for North's liking. Diamond just rolled her eyes; they already had her number, and she had theirs. By the time the cops had left, North's shirt was sticking to the small of his back. Shaw wasn't kidding about the bad juju.

"Alone," Celia repeated.

Francis glanced over from the window; his smile could have chopped wood. "Of course, dear." When he stepped into the entry hall, he rolled the doors shut with a kind of mocking bow, but the movements were stiff and stilted.

"You report directly to me," Celia repeated. "I'm paying the bills, so I'm the one who gets answers."

"That's how we always work," North said, "but you should be aware that we're professionally and ethically obligated to inform the police about illegal activity."

It took a moment, and then Celia barked a short laugh. "I'm not asking you to help me cover up any crimes, Mr. McKinney."

"What are you asking us to do?" Shaw said.

"Find my son. What in the world did you think I wanted you to do?"

"I'm not sure," Shaw said. "That's the whole problem."

"What Shaw means," North said, "is we seem to have been cut out of the loop for a couple of days. Why don't you bring us up to speed?"

"My son is missing. The police want to tell me he ran away, which is ridiculous. He was kidnapped. I fought tooth and nail to get an AMBER alert pushed out, but that didn't yield anything. Those first two days, I thought the police could handle this situation. Obviously, I was wrong, which is why you're here."

"Why do the police think he ran away?" Shaw said.

"Because they don't have to do anything if he ran away. That's the kind of entrenched governmental incompetence that I promised to uproot when I ran for office. The citizens of this great state elected me to—"

"Yes, I understand," Shaw said, "but do they have any other reasons?"

"He's seventeen."

"Lots of kids are seventeen. They don't all run away from home. Or from boarding school. Usually kids run away from home because there's trouble at home—trouble they don't know how to handle, or trouble they can't handle."

"He didn't run away," Celia asked. The flush was working its way into her face again. "What don't you understand about that?"

"Has there been something at home that might—"

With a short, shrill scream, Celia swept a hand across her desk. Object went flying: keyboard, mouse, a paperclip holder shaped like a galvanized milk jug, the four-by-six in its cheap frame. The paperclips hissed like metallic rain. The framed photograph cracked when it hit the floor.

North ran his thumb along the edge of the sofa, tracing the stitching, the leather stiff and resistant. After a moment, the hard lines in Celia's body softened, and she leaned back in her seat.

"I'm sorry," she said. "I've been under a great deal of pressure."

"You probably need acupuncture," Shaw told her.

That one slid right off her; her response was: "There hasn't been any trouble at home. Philip did not run away."

"We're just trying to get a feel for the situation," North said. "Why don't you tell us why you believe he was abducted?"

"The door had been forced. The room had been searched. There were signs of a struggle."

True, true, true, North wanted to say. He had seen them all himself. Instead, he only asked, "Was there anything else? A ransom demand? Contact of any kind?"

"No. Nothing."

"And his phone?"

"The police found his phone in his bedroom."

"Any unusual activity? Calls? Texts?"

"No, nothing. Texts to his friends. Texts to his girlfriend."

"And I assume the police spoke to all of them."

"Of course. They all claim they have no idea what happened."

"The head of school," Shaw said.

"Dr. Latese? What about her?"

"Her behavior was...odd," North said. "The day we went to the school. Extremely odd."

"Suspicious," Shaw said.

"Dr. Latese is an institution," Celia said after a moment. "She's the backbone of that school. I don't understand what you're suggesting."

"So the police didn't talk to her?"

"I'm sure they made contact, of course."

"All right," North said. "What about family and friends? Here or in St. Louis?"

"Of course we've talked to all of them. I don't have any siblings. Francis has two brothers and a sister, all of them in Kansas. We've called all our friends, all of Philip's friends from childhood. No one has heard anything." She shifted forward in the seat. "I don't understand why we're still talking about this. Philip didn't run away. He was kidnapped."

"But kidnappers are often already known to their victims," North said. "A stranger abducting Philip would be extremely rare."

"Why us?" Shaw said.

Celia didn't blink. "I hired you because a police investigation, no matter how good the officers, no matter how determined they are to help, are limited by their own policies, their own regulations, and the reality of the demands that full-time policing poses. For example, an excess of cases, which means they can't give my son their full attention. That's why I hired you. You can give me more hours, you can give me more maneuverability, and you can give me an independent account of what's happening."

North recognized the reasons. He ought to; he'd written them himself. Celia was cribbing from the Borealis website.

"I also hired you because you have a reputation for solving difficult cases. Impossible cases. And Philip's is impossible. His disappearance, I mean. It's impossible for him to have vanished like this, and yet he has."

"It might seem that way," North said, "but you'd be surprised how much we rely on the expectation of being safe rather than—"

"You don't understand. It's impossible. The Gouverneur Morris School is very prestigious. It has a healthy endowment. Top-of-the-line security because very important and very famous people send their children there. There are security guards on campus, and they're not just rent-a-uniform stiffs from a temp agency. These are former law enforcement professionals vetted by the school. The buildings all have secured doors that require an access card. The campus is lousy with cameras. And all of that seems to mean nothing, absolutely nothing, because all the police can tell me is that the cameras and the guards and keycards all tell the same story: Philip walked into his residence Sunday night around seven. The only other people who went into the building between seven that night and the next day, when you and Dr. Dove arrived, were students who lived in that residence. Nobody else went in. And Philip never came out."

Shaw's eyes narrowed, but he didn't speak.

"He never came out?" North said.

Celia shook her head.

"That is…strange."

"It's impossible."

"A laundry cart," Shaw said.

It took a moment, and then Celia shook her head. "Nothing like that, I'm afraid. There were no mysterious bundles being smuggled out of the building. No interruptions to the security feed. No blind spots." A dry smile dusted her lips. "No secret tunnels. My son went home the way he always went home, and the next day he was gone. Someone took him. I just don't know how."

In the distance, a gun fired, and North straightened in his seat.

"That'll be Francis blowing off some steam," Celia said, the smile inching open on her face again. "We're a hunting family. Competitive shooting as well. Philip is quite good. Francis, not so much, although he enjoys the sport tremendously. And it keeps him out from underfoot, so I let him indulge himself."

As though on cue, a series of shots followed in rapid succession.

"Is there anything else you can tell us about Philip? Recent changes in behavior? Anything, even if it seems small. Had he talked about anyone new in his life?"

"No. Nothing."

"You're sure?" When silence came back, North added, "Maybe you could give us an idea of what he's like, his habits, things like that."

"Philip is the perfect son." For the first time since North had met her, Celia Chittenden's mask slipped, and the woman underneath peeked out. Her eyes were distant, her face softly alight. "I'm sure every mother feels that way, but in this case, it's true. He's smart. He's handsome. He's athletic. He's a hard worker. He makes friends easily. He's done exceptionally well in school; in the fall, he'll be at Yale."

"Nobody's perfect," Shaw said. "I used to think North was perfect, and then I saw his toenails."

Celia blinked.

"I think that's why he wears those ugly boots."

"Enough," North muttered.

"I'm helping her understand—"

"Then stop helping." To Celia, North said, "You're sure there's nothing you might want to tell us? We'll do our own dig into Philip's life, but you could save us some trouble. What about the drugs?"

Frowning, Celia ran her hand through the spray of paperclips on the milk-paint desk. "I suppose you'll find out on your own, not that it's anything serious. Philip was arrested for possession of marijuana. You already knew that he'd made a mistake. A tiny mistake. It wasn't even his."

"He was holding it for a friend," North offered.

"Yes, exactly. How did you know?"

North carefully avoided looking at Shaw. "Lucky guess."

"That's why he had to be tested; his father and I insisted on it. He has a wonderful life in front of him, and there's no reason for him to throw it all away."

"What about his girlfriend?" Shaw asked.

"Abigail? She seems like a nice girl. She's come to dinner a few times with Philip. Her family lives in China; they're tremendously wealthy and very influential."

"Teenage relationships are often stormy—" Shaw began.

"Shaw would know," North said, "since he once broke up with the same guy sixteen times in one day."

"That's not really—"

"Over text."

"We're losing track of—"

"Of course, it didn't help that Shaw had never really been dating this guy in the first place. This guy just thought they were study buddies."

"All right," Shaw said.

"Straight as an arrow," North said. "The first fourteen times, he thought Shaw had the wrong number, and then—" North cut off, grinding his teeth to keep from yelping, and massaged his leg where Shaw had pinched him.

"What I'm trying to ask is if Philip and Abigail had hit a rough patch?"

"He didn't run away from home," Celia said, but she was suddenly busy scooping the spilled paperclips into neat mounds on her desk.

"But something did happen."

"They broke up," Celia said. "It's only temporary. She's going to Yale in the fall as well. Normally I'd encourage Philip to date around, but he and Abigail are a perfect fit. They'll work it out."

"We'll need access to his bank accounts," North began.

"Philip doesn't have any money of his own. After his…mistake, his father and I cut off his allowance. He'll earn it back, of course, because he has to be able to socialize with his friends. But right now, he's still being punished." She offered a cool smile. "Even if he had wanted to run away, he wouldn't have gotten far."

GREGORY ASHE

Not necessarily, North thought. Not while there were still people who picked up hitchhikers, guys who traded a blowjob for a lift across state, little old hippie ladies who sensed a kindred spirit, that kind of thing. But he just nodded.

"We'd still like access to his accounts, his phone records, social media, email, and some recent photos."

"Of course; Gavin will get it for you. And you'll need this, of course." She opened a drawer in the desk and withdrew a small plastic card. "I arranged for a copy from the school. You'll be able to access Philip's room; it's still a sealed scene, so you'll probably need to inform the police if you decide to examine it."

"Have they had someone watching it continuously?" North asked.

"I'm not sure. I can't imagine they did."

"Then it's not a sealed scene, no matter how much tape they put up." He took the card. "We'll give it a look anyway."

As North moved toward the doors, Shaw veered off and bent to recover the fallen photograph. He picked it up and handed it to Celia with a soft smile.

"You have a lovely family. Your daughter?"

Again, the mask slipped, and the woman looking out was sad and, North thought, quite lonely. Celia nodded.

"She's adorable," Shaw said.

"Sara Beth was such a happy child." Clutching the photograph to her chest, Celia stared at the floor, as though unable to meet their gazes. "Please find my son."

They saw themselves out.

When North and Shaw were halfway to the GTO, a voice called out, "Hold on a minute."

Francis Chittenden loped toward them across the manicured lawn. He'd traded the tassel loafers for shiny cowboy boots, and now he sported a revolver holstered at his hip. He'd even added a Stetson, white with silver stitching, and North wondered if it was everybody in the whole world who wanted to punch this guy in the face, or just people with good taste.

"Sorry about that," Francis said when he caught up. "What you had to see in there. She can be a royal cunt. Is, I guess."

North shifted his weight, face blank.

"She give you the good mommy routine in there? That's her specialty. Men don't like a woman who's smarter than they are, tougher than they are, and can shoot better than they can. You saw her little trophy winner on the desk, right? So she trots Philip out, Mother of the Year, and talks about gun rights and lowering taxes, and they all pat themselves on the back for putting a woman in office, convinced they aren't a bunch of sexist pigs."

"Is there something we can do for you, Mr. Chittenden?"

Francis gave them a smile. "You think I'm a bastard for talking about her that way. That's all right; I am a bastard. And a sexist pig, probably. But I know what I am, and at least I'm honest about it."

"If there's nothing—" Shaw began.

"If you find Philip, call me."

"Sure," North said. "That's what you hired us to do."

Shaking his head, Francis drew out a silver case, from which he drew a business card printed on linen cardstock. He handed it over. A little black tree, his name, a phone number, and the words DE WOLF FORESTRY – A FAMILY TRADITION.

"But not your family, I'm guessing," North said, as he passed the card to Shaw.

This time, Francis's smile was a little harder. "I'm telling you don't call Celia. If you find him—when you find him—if you care about what's best for Philip, you'll call me."

"Goodbye, Mr. Chittenden."

"You don't think it's strange, why she picked you two? She wasn't drawing names out of a hat, you know."

"What's that supposed to mean?" Shaw said.

Francis stood hipshot, one hand easy on the revolver like he thought he was the Man from Laramie. "Call me. When you find him, I mean. And I'll tell you all about it. Philip will tell you too."

He watched them go, and North didn't draw a deep breath until a windbreak of hawthorn and black haw hid the house and the man with the gun.

"What was that all about?" Shaw asked, craning to look behind them once more.

"I don't know, but I'm starting to have an idea why this case has felt messed up from the start."

Chapter 9

"CAMERA," SHAW said, "camera, camera, camera, camera."

"Oh," North said. "That's what those black camera-looking things are."

They finished their circuit of Flip's residence. It was mid-afternoon, and the May day was perfect: the sky clear, the sun bright, the air warm enough that North had ditched his Carhartt jacket in the car. Shaw was enjoying the admirable display of biceps provided by the red-and-black GameStop tee that was just a little too small for North. At the moment, the quad was quiet; if the schedule was anything like what it had been in Shaw's day, the students were all probably at phys-ed, participating in what Shaw had once tried to point out was ironically called a mandatory sport of their choosing.

He forced his attention back to the brick colonial. True to Celia's description, cameras covered every conceivable ingress and egress. Even if Flip had risked the fall from the third-story window, cameras would have caught him—Shaw had seen banks with fewer cameras.

"I still think he left in a laundry cart."

"My vote is for tunneling out with a spoon," North said.

"It's not a prison break."

"It might have felt like one to Flip; this place is not exactly cheery."

"Front or back?"

North smirked. "Are we talking your place or mine?"

"This setting is making you even more juvenile than usual. Let's try the front."

"Definitely. Back door action is third-date material."

"It's all that cheese," Shaw said as he waved the access card at the sensor. "Your myelin sheaths are probably like cement by now."

Inside, a familiar strain of odors met Shaw: body spray, furniture polish, teen boy funk that was a combination of too little deodorant and too many dirty socks. They made their way up the stairs, passing portraits of stern-faced old men and high-collared old ladies, landscapes of country fields and cottages, hounds and horses. The house was quiet; aside from the creak of the boards under them, the only noise came from outside, where someone was mowing the lawn.

"Must be a bitch to sneak out of this place," North said.

"Oh yeah," Shaw said. "There's a mom or dad in each residence, of course, and part of their job is to keep you from sneaking out."

"That sounds creepy as fuck."

"Oh, you don't have to call them that. Actually, it'd be kind of weird if you did. They're just teachers, so you just call them whatever you normally do. Ours was Mr. Huebner, and he was about a million years old and never trimmed his nose hairs. But when the kids talk to each other about that person, they'll say, 'he's my dad,' or 'she's our mom,' that kind of thing. There's a whole language here. Phys-ed instead of PE, for some reason. Bouching class instead of skipping class. I think a lot of private schools are like that, like these tiny, compressed worlds all on their own."

"High school is already like that," North said. "Add a lot of money, a lot of privilege, and a lot of entitlement, plus a maid and butler, and I bet every adult within five miles wants to put a drill through their eye."

Shaw laughed quietly. "Anyway, I lived in Jefferson, which is the next residence south, but it's basically the same as this one. We had to memorize which boards made the most noise—they all make some noise, so you just try to avoid the worst ones—and the best time to try to get out was when the house was settling. That was before all the electronic locks, so it's probably even harder now."

"Nobody goes out the windows?"

"Gracie Schwartz did. She had a girlfriend off campus who sold the best—" Shaw cut a look at North. "Um, candy. Anyway, Gracie slipped and fell because she was totally high, and she spent the rest of the semester in a cast, and the soccer team was furious because they probably would have won the championship if she'd been playing."

"What about the second-story windows? Or the ground floor? Why not ask a buddy to let you go in and out?"

"Alarms." Shaw winced at a particularly loud creak and then kept going. "They talked about sealing all the windows, but I guess that's too much of a fire hazard, so instead they alarmed the lower-level windows."

"Figuring nobody would be stupid enough to try to scale the building."

Shaw shrugged as he reached the third-floor landing. "Gracie liked to prove people wrong."

His memory of their first visit was buried under a pretty thick fug of weed, but Shaw remembered the splintered doorjamb and the open door. The door was closed now, although daylight showed where it didn't meet the frame. Police tape crisscrossed the opening.

"Sealed scene my ass," North said, but he still took out a pair of disposable gloves and passed them to Shaw. As he drew on his own, he continued,

"Anybody could have been in and out of that room by this point. If somebody did take Flip, and if they wanted to cover their tracks, there's not going to be anything for us to find. Hell, Flip's buddies could have gone in there and taken something important just for the hell of it. This is a fucking joke."

"Well, it's not like we could have searched it with Countee screaming about the police."

"Plus you were high as a kite."

"Plus I was—no! It was that peanut. I had indigestion."

Arching one blond eyebrow, North waved Shaw toward the door. Shaw parted the tape and gave an experimental shove; the door wobbled open. Inside, the room was still a disaster, with the finishing touches of a processed crime scene on top: a layer of fingerprint powder covered almost every surface; a section of the plaster had been cut away and removed, presumably to be tested for blood or tissue; the bed and dressers had been righted, but they stood at strange angles from the walls, as though whoever had put them upright hadn't cared enough to finish moving them into place. Clothes covered the floor, along with miscellaneous items: canisters of body spray (of course), loose change, a sandwich shop punch card, a leather bracelet.

"Jesus," North said behind him.

Shaw slid between the lines of tape and gave North a hand—those damn boots made him clumsy as hell. When North was standing inside the room, he gave Shaw a crooked smile and pecked him on the cheek.

"What was that for?"

"You're cute sometimes," he said as he picked a path past Shaw and toward the other side of the room.

"Sometimes?"

The room had a large window on the opposite wall, and the blinds were up; Flip's room looked down on acres of freshly cut grass, the clippings in windrows that some industrious maintenance worker would rake up—nothing but crisp, perfect lawns for The Gouverneur Morris School. Down a slight hill stood a greenhouse, a fenced garden, and a service road. Then the trees started up again, most of them still in bloom: big white blossoms on the hawthorns, yellow-and-orange flowers on the tulip trees. The real world reappeared in a line of three-bedroom homes with asphalt-shingle roofs and aluminum siding and Fords and Chevys that were twenty years old at a minimum.

North was moving carefully through the room, using one gloved hand to stir the clothes on the floor, checking each dresser drawer for false panels, items taped to the back or bottom, tilting the dresser itself to look underneath. Shaw moved in the opposite direction, starting with the bed. He lifted the mattress. He checked the seams. He ran his hand slowly over the surface, pressing down to search for anything that might be hidden inside. He checked the bed frame. Nothing. Then he started on the baseboards.

The search was agonizingly slow, like all good searches, but Shaw didn't mind. He and North were good at this kind of thing, and they could do the work without talking, without anything more than a glance and an unspoken question, a nodded answer. Once, a short, sharp bark of a board protesting made Shaw shoot a look at the doorway. North cocked his head. But after a minute, when they heard nothing else, they resumed their search.

And, of course, they found nothing.

"Nothing," North said, shoving the dresser. "Not a fucking thing. If there was anything, somebody else got it."

"Maybe Diamond will tell us what the techs found."

"Fat chance."

Something about the room nagged at Shaw—had nagged at him since they first stepped inside. Now it came to him. "Where's the rest of it?"

"Rest of what?"

"Teenage boy stuff. Where's all his normal teenage boy stuff?"

"Oh, right. Like his paisley kimono, his Farrah Fawcett-brand hair dryer, his cock ring that he leaves lying around on his dresser so that an innocent passerby accidentally touches it and then has to spend the rest of freshman year with cock cooties."

"Well, I hope you learned your lesson: in the future, don't put on rings that don't belong to you. You need to ask before you borrow my cock rings. And I was thinking more of, you know, his thug chains—"

North groaned. "I had one chain. One."

"—and his ironic bowling shirt—"

"That was a potential Halloween costume."

"—and, of course, posters."

"Don't you fucking dare. We agreed you were going to stop bringing this up."

"*Cats!*" Shaw traced a marquee with his hands. "America's favorite musical!"

"It did not say that. And, for the hundredth time, I did not buy that poster for myself. It was a gag gift for Percy."

"That you unrolled and looked at and then put under your bed, way at the back." North's face was painfully red, and he had that little tic of pulse showing in his temple, so Shaw hurried to say, "My point is: where's all Flip's personal stuff? I mean, being a teenager, especially being a teenage boy, is usually a cocktail of the same elements: sports, sex, rebellion, fantasy, hobbies. Where are the cool cars? Where are the baseball cards? Where are the hot babes?"

"I'm going to take a moment while my brain tries to digest you saying, 'hot babes.'"

"Flip doesn't even—"

North held up a hand. "Still digesting."

"You're an idiot."

North made a pained face.

"You look like you need to use the bathroom."

"Ok. Done. Phew." North wiped his forehead.

"You're the worst boyfriend sometimes. You like being mean to me."

With a shrug, North said, "Leaving aside the fact that I don't think anybody has touched a baseball card since Wally Cleaver, I think you're right. That's weird. I mean, 'hot babes'—"

"I'm going to kill you. In your sleep."

"—he can look at on the internet, and maybe he's not into sports, although Celia said he's athletic. But there ought to be something. A stack of sci-fi novels. Funko figurines. Manga. But you're right: aside from the clothing and a few basic toiletries, this room could have belonged to anyone. Good catch."

"I really doubted myself, but then I remembered that you and I are the best detectives in the entire world except maybe for Emery, my best friend, and then I realized that the power to be the best detective in the entire world was inside me all along."

"For the record, this is why I'm mean to you."

"You probably didn't notice all these important things were missing because you were still thinking about your *Cats* poster."

"It's amazing how your powers of observation are sharpened when you're not high as a kite."

Shaw grinned and said, "Maybe he took it all with him?"

"Maybe." But North's answer was slow and doubtful. "And I still have no idea how that kid got out of this building. Anything else you want to check in here?"

"One thing." Shaw opened the closet door and stepped inside. It was dark, and it smelled like fabric softener. He elbowed aside hanging clothes, the wire hangers chiming as they slid.

"Insert the obligatory back-in-the-closet joke here."

Ducking under the hang rod and shelf, Shaw pressed along the back panel of the closet.

"What are you doing? North asked.

"Checking for—damn, no, not this one." Shaw backed out, the clothes brushing over him until he was free, and then turned. North smirked. "What?"

North beckoned him closer. When Shaw was within reach, he undid the scrunchie and smoothed Shaw's hair into place before securing it again. "So you don't look like a cumulus cloud." Then he raised an eyebrow. "A little gratitude?"

Rolling his eyes, Shaw leaned in and kissed him.

"Why was my boyfriend going back in the closet?" North asked.

"These used to be single-family homes. When they turned them into residences, they had to close off some of the connecting doorways. They turned them into closets, actually. But, as you can imagine, over the course of a hundred and twenty years, teenagers found a way around that."

"No shit. These rooms have secret passages?"

"Well, they're not very secret. And they just lead you into another dorm room, so it's not like they're that useful. Unless the guy next door is a super closeted baseball player and sometimes he's down for a fiver. In this case, it doesn't matter because Flip's closet doesn't connect to anything—it's a solid wall."

"Back up: the baseball player thing. Is that a real scenario or wishful thinking?"

"Wouldn't you like to know? Come on, let's take a look at the rest of the building."

They went door to door, testing handles. Flip's room was the only one in use on the third floor, which explained why no one had noticed the broken frame and lock until North and Shaw had come to pick him up. On the second floor, most of the rooms were unlocked, which Shaw had expected but which seemed to surprise North. The rooms varied—one was clearly possessed by a juggalo, while another seemed to belong to what Shaw suspected might be The Gouverneur Morris's only male cheerleader, and several were empty—but they all exhibited that degree of personality that had been missing from Flip's. They saw no one, although the old house's creaks and cracks made North glance around more than once.

By the time they'd gotten to the ground floor, North said, "This seems like a really inefficient way to house students. How many of these old houses do they have? And how many students? Why don't they just build a dorm?"

"Eight houses," Shaw said, "four for girls, and four for boys. And around a hundred students, although some years it's fewer. I think it must be a low enrollment phase because so many of these rooms are empty."

"You went to school with a hundred students? And you boarded? And it was this fucking nutso place? How the fuck did I not know any of that?"

"Because you hated me at the beginning of freshman year, and by the time we were friends, we had other things to talk about."

North frowned. "But you know all about my school stuff. You know stuff about my elementary school, which is a little freaky sometimes."

"I love you," Shaw said as he jiggled the handle of a door marked CUSTODIAL. Locked. "I like knowing things about you."

North opened his mouth, but he didn't say anything, and then Shaw started walking again.

They passed through a small kitchen, with an efficiency stove, two microwaves, two toaster ovens, and an enormous fridge.

"I could live inside this fucker," North said, swinging the double doors open. "Oh my God. Shaw, I made up my mind. I'm enrolling at this fuckhole. I'm going to stay here forever."

"How many pizza rolls do they need?" Shaw screwed up his nose. "And that is definitely too many ice cream sandwiches. I don't see a single hemp-milk popsicle. I should probably write a letter to the board of trustees."

"Why do you break my heart over and over again? What did I ever do to you?"

"One time you used all those clothespins on me."

"Oh my God," North whispered, slamming the doors and hurrying away.

"I know I asked you to, but you really seemed to enjoy it, and you teased me way too much when you were taking them off."

Shaw caught up to North downstairs, in the laundry room. Four white economy washers and four stainless-steel jumbo dryers stood in opposite rows. The walls were cinderblock, and exposed lightbulbs overhead left deep pockets of shadow.

"This is where people come to cry," Shaw said. "And do their laundry, I guess, although a lot of people just had the cleaners pick it up."

"I wish you could hear yourself sometimes." North looked around. "You said that before, about the crying. What's that all about? Did you like it here?"

"I guess. I mean, yeah, I did. But high school is hard. I was trying to figure out a lot of stuff about myself. Not just the gay stuff. I mean, I pretty much knew I was gay as soon as someone explained the word to me. But figuring out who I wanted to be, not who my parents wanted me to be, that was hard."

"I thought they were happy you were gay."

"They were. They are. I'm talking about other stuff." Shaw shifted his weight. "I'm not explaining it right. There's a lot of pressure at a place like this. I know you think the kids who come here are all spoiled and indulged and have never had to struggle, and you're right. They never had to worry about missing a meal or not having clean clothes or living out of a car. But that doesn't mean they have it easy. A lot of them come from really ugly home lives. And even if things are ok at home, they're all under tremendous pressure. Their parents are investing all this money in them, and they're all expected to be the best at something, so they can go to the best schools, so they can get the best jobs, so they can make more money than their parents did. It's…a lot."

North was quiet for a long time. Then he reached out and took Shaw's hand, lifted it, kissed his fingertips.

Shaw rolled one shoulder. "It's fine; I'm over it. I've disappointed my parents enough times that they're used to it by now, and the past is the past. That's one thing Dr. Farr has helped me bring into focus."

"Shaw, if your parents are disappointed in you, they are out of their fucking minds. You're incredible. Whatever you think they wanted out of you, you became something better. I don't even have the words for it. Brighter. Purer. God, I can't even imagine someone being disappointed in you."

"Yeah, well, my mom has an expressive way of folding up grad school applications. She communicates the message pretty effectively." He looked around. "There are some old rooms down here; we can check them and see if any are in use, but I don't think they house people in the basement anymore. It's too gloomy."

"I bet the ley lines in this place are twisted up like catguts."

A surprised laugh escaped Shaw, and he squeezed North's hand. Hard. All he said was "Because of all that crying."

"Obvs," North said and kissed Shaw's fingertips again.

They moved back into the hall and began testing doors. Unlike the rooms above, these were locked. Shaw produced a key ring, sorted through them, and tried a key. No joy.

"Did you seriously keep your keys from when you were a student here?"

"Yes, duh, but they're in my shadowbox at home."

"And you do realize that not every door uses the same key."

"I know you're trying to be mean to me as a way of compensating for how sweet and gentle you are, but this is a teachable moment, so I'm going to ignore the toxic masculinity bubbling up. Yes, in theory, every lock has a unique key. In reality, locks and keys are mass produced." Shaw beamed at North. "Even though I knew the power to be the best detective in the world was—"

"Please stop saying 'inside me' so loud."

"—inside me all along, I also realized I needed to keep growing as a detective. So, I've been learning about locks."

"You can pick a lock. You're shit at it, but you can do it."

"I'm very good at picking locks. But this is a good tool too." He jangled the keys in North's directions. "If you have seven or eight of these really common keys, you can unlock most standard locks in the United States. Obviously it won't work for security doors, but inside—ha!" The key turned, and the door swung open.

A wave of cold, damp air met them with the faint smell of mildew. The room on the other side was dark and silent; he found a light switch blindly, flipped it, and got nothing. Then, somewhere else in the basement, the furnace kicked on, a chugging, struggling noise that broke the stillness. At first, the only thing Shaw could make out was a rectangle of cement-colored light—a dirty window behind a rusting security mesh. Then, as his eyes adjusted, he could make out the rest of the room: the shape of a bed frame, two dressers stacked on top of each other, stacked chairs filling in the empty spaces.

"Storage," Shaw said.

North cocked his ear at a faint scuffing noise. "And rats."

"Gross. There's not any rats. Are there?"

They checked the other rooms and found them all repurposed for storage and full of dusty furniture. The only difference was that the furnace actually seemed to work, and the rooms warmed up as they went. When they'd finished, they headed back to the stairs.

The residence's back door was located in the kitchen. North and Shaw opened it, inspected the frame, the lock, and the strike plate. Like the front door, this lock was electronic and opened with the same access card. When they'd finished, they shared an irritated look; no signs of forced entry. That made sense because the cameras hadn't showed anyone suspicious entering the residence, but the cameras also hadn't shown Flip leaving.

"Why does this place have two staircases?" North asked, pointing to the steps leading up from the kitchen.

"Servants' staircase," Shaw said. "Plus it's easier to sneak down for a midnight snack."

"Rich people are a real fucking treat."

"To be fair—" But Shaw cut off because a floorboard creaked violently above them.

"Somebody came home from PE early?" North whispered.

Shaw shook his head.

North pointed to himself and then to the front of the house. He pointed to Shaw and to the servants' stairs. Then he headed out of the kitchen, making surprisingly little noise for a man wearing the equivalent of leather buckets on his feet.

Shaw had visited this residence as a student, but he'd never had to learn its ins and outs the way he'd known the Jefferson building. Still, he remembered a few tricks, like keeping to the edge of the stair treads and testing his weight before moving up. It was slow going, but it allowed him to move quietly.

Then another board groaned above Shaw, and a man said, "Shit."

Shaw grabbed the canister of pepper gel from his pocket and got a good grip on it. He kept climbing.

More creaking boards overhead. More muffled words. Something that sounded like "—fucking ridiculous."

Whoever this guy was, he wasn't exactly a B-and-E genius.

"Stop right there," North shouted.

The answer was footsteps hammering the boards above Shaw, moving toward the servants' stairs. Shaw braced himself against the wall of the stairway. The footsteps turned into a staccato on the steps, and then a man came into view: dark brown skin, young, fit. He was looking over his shoulder, and as his head swiveled, his eyes widened as he took in Shaw.

His eyes got really wide when Shaw landed a palm strike to his solar plexus.

The guy's legs came up. His butt hit the stairs, hard, and then his head bounced back from a step. He was carrying clothes, and they flew into the air. As he slid a few steps before coming to rest, sweatshirts and joggers and underwear and socks rained down around him.

Chapter 10

WHEEZING, THE MAN who had collapsed on the staircase tried to sit up.

"Stop that," Shaw said. "Or I'll have to do something I won't like."

The man considered this. Then, bleary-eyed and still gasping for breath, he sank back down.

When North appeared above them on the stairs, Shaw said, "He might have a concussion. He hit his head really hard."

North squatted and held up a pair of gray compression shorts.

"You know I like those on you," Shaw said, "but I'd really rather have you wear those bikini briefs I bought you."

"No, thanks. I don't wear panties."

"Really? A lot of men find it sexually stimulating and freeing. It's an opportunity to explore being beautiful and desired in a way that they're traditionally excluded from."

Shaw was rather proud of this delivery of psychological insight, but all North did was hold up a Cardinals sweatshirt.

The man on the stairs was on his side, sliding down another step.

"Kick him in the head if he moves again," North said.

"What the hell?" the guy croaked. He tried to sit up, and then he sagged back again, rubbing his head. "Oh my God, who are you? What's going on?"

"North McKinney. Shaw Aldrich. Private investigators. Shaw's going to handle that second one."

"Well, that's an interesting question," Shaw said. "The way I see it, life is a cycle of existence. We are born as an opportunity to learn to grow and live in harmony with the universe—"

"Fast forward to the part of this particular existence where he's stealing Flip's clothes."

"Oh, right. You were stealing Flip's clothes and being really noisy about it, and when you saw North, you tried to run, and then you and I met, and I think you're probably a really great guy, but I had to put you on your ass because you were trying to get away."

The man's only answer was to cover his eyes.

"Sit the fuck up," North said, "and start with your name and what the fuck you're doing here. Shaw, call the police."

"No!" After another struggle to sit upright, the man let out a groan. "No, come on. This is—this is a huge misunderstanding."

He was handsome, Shaw decided. Probably around their age, in his mid-twenties, with skin a beautiful dark brown and glossy black hair in an undercut and part that managed to look both hip and professional.

"My name's Kishor. Kishor Virani." He tried an uncertain smile and held out a hand. Shaw pumped it. When he tried to repeat the gesture with North, North snorted. Kishor's smile got a bit steadier. A bit brighter. He rubbed the back of his head, rueful now, like he'd done something dumb and knew it. "Jeez, you really got me good. I guess I deserved it. This is so stupid."

"You'd better talk a lot faster," North said, "or we'll skip straight to the police."

"No, no. You don't need to do that. I'm a teacher here. I live here."

"Here here?" Shaw said. "In this residence?"

Kishor nodded. "I'm head-of-residence for Washington. That's this residence."

"Keep going," North said.

"Oh, um, right. The clothes. Look, it was dumb. I made a really dumb mistake. I'll put them back, and it won't happen again. I swear to God."

"What were you doing?"

Kishor swallowed; he looked sallow now, and his gaze swung from North to Shaw.

"Don't look at him," North said. "He can't help you. Answer my fucking question."

"I could give him a motivational speech," Shaw said.

"No, you can't."

"I could help him understand that the power to answer our questions has been—"

North was making a guttural noise.

"—inside him all along!"

"What the fuck were you doing?" North snapped, taking one heavy, booming step down.

Kishor flinched and threw up his hands. "I was going to sell them!"

"What?"

"I was going to sell them, man. That's all. I know it's messed up, but there are a lot of weirdos out there, and they'll pay good money to own clothes of a boy who's been—" He cut off, eyes darting to the steps.

"Kidnapped?" Shaw said. "Murdered?"

"I said I know it's messed up." Kishor's gaze came up fractionally. "Look, they pay us shit. I love the job, but they pay us shit. There's this whole song and dance about how free room and board makes up for the low salary, but the truth is, they're just cheap. I'm young. I like to go out. If there's a guy I like, I want to show him a good time. They're just clothes, right? I mean, it's not like it's hurting anyone." He hesitated. "You probably want to talk to Abigail. I could help you."

"Why would we want to talk to Abigail?"

"Isn't that what they always do? The girlfriend, I mean. When something bad happens."

"Did something bad happen to Flip?"

"I don't know—I thought—I don't know!" Gulping air, Kishor said, "I just went in his room! I didn't do anything wrong!"

"Except it's a sealed crime scene," North said. "Except you're contaminating possible evidence. How many times have you been in there?"

"Just this once, I swear to God. And I heard one of the police officers telling Dr. Latese that they were pretty much done with Flip's room. I never would have gone in there if I thought it would have hurt him." He turned big, dark, puppy-dog eyes on Shaw. His hand, warm and surprisingly large, came to rest on the inside of Shaw's thigh. "Please. It was a dumb mistake. Please don't ruin my life because I made a dumb mistake." His tongue teased his lips. "I could make it up to you guys. Show you how sorry I am. You could make sure I learned my lesson."

"Well," Shaw said.

"No, you fucking degenerate—I'm talking to you, Shaw. The answer is no. And you, get your hand off my boyfriend. You've got five seconds before I start breaking fingers."

"He's very possessive," Shaw confided.

Kishor was cradling his hand against his chest, eyes wary.

"He thinks it's attractive. I've really been trying to work with him on non-ownership ways of expressing his feelings for me—we've really been trying to work on that, haven't we, North?"

"No."

"I think a three-way—"

"Go ahead and finish that sentence, Shaw, and see what happens."

Discretion being the better part of valor, Shaw tried a redirect. "Lots of couples find that adding a sexual partner…" The words dried up under North's gaze. Shaw sighed. To Kishor, he said, "I guess not this time."

"Not ever," North said. "Get the fuck out of here. And if I even get a hint, even a whiff, that you're trying this stunt again, I will come back here and destroy your ass."

"That's the spirit," Shaw said. "Now you're getting into it. We'll come back and we'll destroy your ass. North's actually really good at that, and—"

"For the love of Christ," North whispered in a strangled voice. Then he roared at Kishor, "Go!"

Kishor scrambled downstairs, and a moment later, the back door slammed shut.

"We ought to call the police anyway," North said, crouching again as he collected the fallen clothing. "Creepy little fucker. For all we know he was taking these for his next jerk-off session."

"I don't think so," Shaw said, passing North a pair of socks. "He was freaked out, but I didn't get that kind of vibe."

"He literally made a move on you."

"He made a move on us, actually, and he did it because he was trying to get himself out of trouble."

"He's young," North said as he lifted the bundle of clothes and started up the stairs again. "He's gay. And he's alone with horny adolescents around the clock. A lot could go wrong there, Shaw."

"Maybe," Shaw said as he followed North. "But I really don't think so."

They returned the clothes, which meant dumping them inside the room, and North pulled the door shut. With the lock broken, it only rested in the frame, but it was better than leaving it completely open. North stared at the shut door for a moment.

"We should have asked him if he'd noticed anything strange. People hanging around campus. Changes in Flip's behavior. Anything unusual Sunday night."

"If he did notice anything, he would have told the police. And he's not going anywhere. We'll track him down and talk to him again. Besides, now we've got leverage on him; it'll make it easier to get him talking."

North grimaced, glanced at Shaw, and looked away.

"What?" Shaw said.

"I'm just thinking. The cameras didn't show anyone entering the building who didn't belong here. But that includes Kishor. And now we know there's something really sketch about him, and he's gay—"

"Being gay doesn't make him more likely to abuse children, North."

"I know that, for fuck's sake. But it's a boys' residence. And he was stealing those clothes. And he made a pass at two strangers and pitched a three-way."

"Your puritanical side is showing."

"I'm just saying he's weird, and if we're supposed to trust that camera footage, then it sounds like it could have been an inside job."

"And what happened to Flip? He chopped him up and is taking him out in neat little bundles?"

North's expression only grew grimmer.

"You're joking," Shaw said.

"I'm just saying, we've got to consider the possibility that the people who live here were involved."

"And I think there's another way someone got inside. Something that's going to be really obvious once we figure it out."

"But we agree that it doesn't seem likely Flip ran away?"

Shaw let out a breath and shook his head. "It doesn't seem likely."

"Well, this was a bust. Want to see if we can track down some of Flip's friends?"

Nodding, Shaw headed for the stairs.

They were stepping out into the May sunlight, a breeze tugging at Shaw's tee, when a woman shouted, "Excuse me!"

She was tall and dressed to the nines—Louboutin heels, a gray silk suit that flowed like running water, a pashmina draped across her shoulders. Her hair was cropped close to the scalp, and the only sign of age was a touch of gray at her temples. She moved like brick walls would be smart to get out of her way.

"You gentlemen need to leave right now."

"My name's North McKinney—"

"I know who you are, and I want you off this campus right now."

"And who are you?"

"I'm Shaw."

"Not you," North muttered.

"Dr. Trinity Latese, head of school. I've already called security; I understand you assaulted a staff member. You can be sure I'll report that to the police."

"Not cool," North said. "If you know who we are, then you know that the Chittenden family hired us to look into Flip's disappearance. We're just looking around, trying to figure out what happened."

"I know why you're here. What I don't know is why you laid hands on my best teacher. What I don't know is how you got inside a student residence without a school representative accompanying you."

"Your best teacher—"

North cut off when Shaw touched his arm.

Since Trinity seemed not to know about the access card that Celia had given them, Shaw decided to lie: "The latch didn't set. We just wanted to look around."

"Regardless, you're not allowed to be on campus, especially not after your behavior today. Please see yourselves to your car." A golf cart's motor whined as it came around a building farther up the quad. "Security will escort you off campus."

"The Chittenden family has a right—" North began.

"And the other students here have rights too. Our staff have rights. We have to consider them too. If you need to look around campus, if you need to do anything on campus, you can contact my office for preapproval. We'll arrange a time and someone from the administrative staff to accompany you."

"This is bullshit." North waved at the brick colonials and the freshly trimmed grass. "It's not Fort Knox."

The golf cart's whine grew louder; the two men in the front seat wore navy windbreakers and slacks.

Shaw pointed. "They look like the FBI. Or like they think the FBI looks."

"If you refuse to leave, I'll have the police here in five minutes." Trinity's gaze didn't waver.

"Want to tell us why you crawled out the window when we stopped by your office?" North set himself, hands on hips. "Want to explain what that was all about?"

"All right," Trinity said, producing a phone. "We'll let the police handle this."

"We're going," Shaw said, tugging on his arm. "We're leaving right now."

They'd made it ten feet before Trinity called after them.

"Mr. Aldrich, I understand you're an alumnus."

Shaw glanced back.

"You can be sure I'll be contacting your father about this."

North made a quiet, huffing noise that might have been a laugh.

"Very not cool," Shaw finally managed before stalking toward the GTO.

Chapter 11

ANGIOLETTO'S WAS AN ANCHOR store in a strip mall less than a mile from The Gouverneur Morris School. It consisted primarily of a large, open dining room with floor-to-ceiling windows on three sides, a deli counter, and retractable-belt stanchions that kept the line to order clear and neat. Those were a recent addition; the last time North had been there, he'd witnessed two nonnas slapping each other with phonebook-sized purses in a fight for the last cannoli.

"Why are you smiling?" Shaw asked; behind the counter, a woman drew out a pan of breadsticks from a warmer, and Shaw's expression changed to horror. "North, no. Please. No. We've been so good."

North got in line behind a middle-aged woman with an acre of blow-dried black hair.

"We've been avoiding nightshades."

"You've been avoiding nightshades."

"We've been cutting out processed foods."

"Actually, I eat more of them when you're not around to keep my intake steady."

"We've almost completely eliminated dairy."

"That's an adorable fantasy."

After glancing around, Shaw let out a breath. "Ok, ok, no reason to freak out. We can do this. Nothing fried, please. No cured meats. I think we'll be ok with a nice salad. No dressing, obviously. No cheese. And no sugar, of course."

North nodded, smiled, and stepped up to the register. "The salsiccia sandwich, garlic-cheese-bread style. Sub toasted ravs for the salad. And two of those Missouri Baking cookies. No, better make it four. And a fountain drink."

"Four?" Shaw protested. "No, only give him one. I'm basically his doctor, and he's not allowed to have more than one."

But by then, North was paying. He moved to claim a table; in the background, Shaw's queries about a seitan alternative to the veal blurred into a pleasant white noise. North filled the waxed-paper cup with Sprite, found a clean table, and watched. Shaw was using his hands to demonstrate the size of the cages where veal calves were kept. The guy behind the counter was getting splotchy. Shaw was getting splotchy. The air smelled like garlic, onion, tomatoes, and Italian sausage. North briefly considered opening a little shop like this; it had to be better than the shit job he currently had.

"He threatened to put me in a cage," Shaw said, face still hot with color when he came over and slammed a waxed-paper cup onto the table. "He said if I liked talking about cages so much, maybe I'd like to see one from the inside."

"Huh."

"And when I said he was creating a hostile environment, he said it was going to feel a lot more hostile after he shoved his foot up my ass."

North took a swig of Sprite.

"North!"

"What?"

"Go beat him up."

"Pass."

"Fine. I'll do it."

Laughing, North caught his wrist and pulled Shaw into the empty seat next to him. They sat there for a while, Shaw glowering at the man behind the counter, North drinking his Sprite.

"Why are you so grumpy? Usually I'm the grumpy one."

"I'm not grumpy."

"Is this about your dad?"

"No." But the note was pure, adolescent petulance.

"You need to eat something. Something real. Not just grass."

"I don't eat grass."

North rubbed the spot between his eyebrows. "Will a Coke make you feel better?"

"I'm not a child." After a struggle with silence, Shaw burst out, "And he's a willing participant in an act of torture. He's the one who ought to be put into a cage."

"He works a register at an Italian sandwich shop, Shaw. He's not exactly masterminding the veal industry."

"It's the principle of the thing!"

Sighing, North collected both their cups. "I'll get you a Coke."

When he came back, Shaw still had his gaze set to death-ray. North slid the Coke in front of him and kissed his cheek.

Shaw's gaze darted to him. It was a very dirty look. A very suspicious look.

North chuckled. "I'll beat him up after we eat if you still want me to."

"I will."

"Ok."

"Fine."

"Ok."

"I'm going to hold you to that."

But after that he was mostly focused on the Coke, and North was focused on limiting Shaw to three refills. Their food came. North sighed again when he saw that Shaw had ordered a salad with no dressing and no cheese and no meat, which meant he had ordered a paper tray full of iceberg lettuce. He cut his salsiccia sandwich, put half in front of Shaw, and set the toasted ravioli between them.

"I think I'm going to go off meat entirely," Shaw said before biting into a ravioli. He took an enormous bite of the sandwich next. "No. No. I'm going to infiltrate Big Meat, and I'm going to bring them down from the inside."

Putting a hand over Shaw's cup, North moved it out of reach. "Let's slow down on the Coke."

They ate, which meant that Shaw devoured all of the food in front of him, almost all of the toasted raviolis, and three of the sugar cookies.

When he figured the sugar had hit Shaw's bloodstream, North asked, "Do I still have to murder an innocent restaurateur?"

"I guess not. Although he's not really innocent. Ignorance is no excuse for—"

"If I let you have another Coke, will you please stop talking?"

"You can't let me have anything, North. I'm a grown man. I make my own decisions."

"You can fill it all the way to the top. You don't even have to put ice in it."

Shaw was out of his seat before North had finished talking. After filling the Coke, he stopped by the service counter again, where he and the man behind the register began talking. North kept an eye on them while he called Diamond Kelso and told her about the teacher, Kishor, and the stolen clothes. Diamond's answer was mostly swear words before she disconnected.

When Shaw sat down again, he was smiling.

"You look pleased with yourself. Did you convince him to become a vegan?"

"What?"

"Is he going to join a commune and wear a sarong and play the sitar all day?"

"You're so dumb sometimes."

North waited.

"I apologized," Shaw said, chin held high. "And then we started talking. He's a really nice guy."

"Please don't tell me he asked you to meet his gay cousin."

"No." Shaw bit his lip. "He does have a step-brother who's a caterer, and he said he thought we'd really hit it off, and I said I probably needed to talk to him to convince him to stop catering with meat, and he invited me to his daughter's First Communion next Sunday because his step-brother is catering, and—"

"Fantastic. Have fun on your first date."

"North, it's not a date." But Shaw chewed his lip for almost a full minute and then said, "North, it might be a date."

"Uh huh."

"I think Big Meat might have corrupted me."

North let a beat pass, pretending to look at his phone. "I'll give you some big meat."

Trying not to laugh, Shaw said, "You're really dumb sometimes. Like really, really dumb."

They sat in silence for a while; it was mid-afternoon, still too early even for the early-bird dinner rush, and they had the dining room to themselves. North placed a couple of calls—trying again to collect on Johanna Griffin's account, and then checking in with Haw on the lab where there had been an attempted break-in. He let a call from his dad go to voicemail, listened to the first two blistering minutes about the family name and responsibility and everything Ronnie had done for them, and deleted it. Then he did some research on De Wolf forestry—as he'd guessed, it was a business owned by Celia's side of the family, which meant Francis's position was probably due to nepotism rather than competence. Shaw was busy on his phone too, a combination of web searches and phone calls; when North cocked a questioning look in his direction, he mouthed, "Danny Wilkintonis."

"Any luck?" North asked when Shaw had finished another call.

"I think I've got a lead; his ex-boyfriend thinks he still has one of Danny's credit card passwords saved on his computer. He's going to call me back if there's any unusual activity. What about you?"

"I told Haw that I think we've got an idea of who's behind the attempted break-in. She's doubling security, including more cameras." North blew out a breath. "So there's something really fucked up at that school, right?"

Shaw hesitated. He gave his phone a one-fingered spin, and it wobbled on the laminate tabletop. "My, um, dad has left a few messages. I didn't call him back, but I'm getting the sense he's not happy that Trinity called him."

"Like you said, you're a grown man."

"Yeah, but my parents are really into that school. They've both been on the board at different times. Trinity wasn't head of school when I was a student there, but it still feels a lot like I'm fifteen again and I'm in trouble because I was supposed to write a two-page paper on love in literature, and my parents keep asking why I didn't just write a two-page paper, and I can't give a good enough explanation for why cutting all of the naughty parts out of *Lady Chatterley's Lover* and then stitching them together to make a blanket seemed like a better way of expressing the theme of love in literature."

North stared.

"That was a hypothetical example," Shaw said.

"Sweet Jesus."

"Purely hypothetical."

"What did I get myself into?"

"Hypothetical!" Shaw hurried to add, "But to answer your first question, yeah, something felt really...off. Trinity's behavior on Monday. The way she acted today, kicking us off campus and threatening to call the police. Kishor. The fact that the whole thing might have been an inside job."

"So you agree it's worth spending some more time figuring out what's been going on there?"

Shaw nodded.

"Even though it might mean you get another phone call home?"

With a sigh, Shaw nodded again.

"We'll be more careful," North said. "Where would we find kids right now?"

Shaw checked the time on his phone. "Now might not be a good time. They're probably wrapping up phys-ed, and then they'll shower, change, and eat in the refectory. After that, it'll be easier. On a nice day like today, some of them will be outside, some of them will be in the library, and some of them will be in the dorms."

"With the dorms, we run the risk of the head of residence catching us, right?"

Nodding, Shaw said, "Not to mention the kids might be freaked out if we just showed up in their bedrooms."

"And I'd bet Trinity's going to have security zipping all over the place in that fucking golf cart."

"So," Shaw said with a smile, "the library."

"The library," North said, gathering their trash. "And if it's empty and you're very, very good, maybe I'll give you some inspiration for your novel."

Shaw tripped over the chair when he tried to get up.

Chapter 12

"HOLD ON." North tightened his grip on Shaw's arm. On the other side of the quad, the golf cart whirred around. "Ok, go."

They were old hands at this, at being where they weren't supposed to be and looking like they might belong. A brisk pace, but not too fast. Head up, shoulders back. Guys with a destination in mind and a job to do. Ahead of them, the library's glass atrium caught the last daylight in ribbons of fire.

After leaving Angioletto's, they had killed a couple of hours catching up on other jobs before returning to campus. Instead of using the main drive, though, they had followed a service road that Shaw had directed him to. They had parked the GTO by the greenhouse, and they had kept behind the brick colonials as they looped to the other side of campus, where the Eichacker Memorial Library looked like a Lucite cube. North had had one on his desk as a child, a rare gift from his father, with a baseball signed by Stan Musial. After the Red Week, North had taken it into the alley with an aluminum bat, beat it to shit, and swept the pieces into the dumpster.

Perhaps because it was clearly a later addition to the campus, or perhaps because The Gouverneur Morris School one day planned on housing an irreplaceable collection of books that needed precision control of temperature, humidity, etc., the library's main entrance consisted of two sets of doors, with a vestibule between them. As North and Shaw stepped into the vestibule, North caught Shaw's arm. Shaw stopped and threw him a look.

On the other side of the second set of doors, a high-traffic runner marked the path to what was clearly a librarian's version of a security desk: slightly elevated from the floor, teak paneling, lots of chrome, and then the RF security gates. Behind the desk sat a blunt-faced, square-jawed woman with glasses on a beaded chain and an enormous brooch dragging down one side of her cardigan. She was reading something, although North was too far away to read the title.

"*Fatal Shadows,*" Shaw whispered.

"There's no way you can—" North cut off.

"By Josh Lanyon."

"You recognized the cover."

"No."

"Fine. You can read the title, and you already knew the author's name."

"I knew your eyes were bad, North, but I didn't know they were this bad."

"My eyes are just fucking fine, thank you. She's holding it at a weird angle."

Shaw nodded in a way that made North understand why some spouses preferred face-to-face killings. "You're right. Perfectly vertical, with the front cover facing us, is a hard angle to read at."

"Will you let it go? We need to—"

"I mean, after you tried to use that flaphead screwdriver on the wrong screw, I knew we needed to talk about glasses again—"

"It's a flathead screwdriver, moron, and I was only using it because you said you had recognized the soul of my Phillips head the last time you did peyote and you made it a Viking funeral boat out of newspaper and sent it down the Meramec."

"And after you groped that waitress because you mistook her breasts for our takeout bags, I really knew we needed to talk about glasses. Oh, and about groping."

"I tripped. You tripped me. You tied my shoelaces together because you'd spent the morning watching *Loony Tunes* reruns."

"But this is really a new low."

North felt a little bit like he was being strangled. In a thin voice he managed to say, "Get your ass in there and distract her long enough for me to check out the place. Then you leave. I'll text you when I find a door where I can let you in."

"Why me? You should be the distraction this time. Last time I ended up with custard all over me."

"That's because you insisted on impersonating a custard delivery driver, which is a thing that has never existed since the beginning of time."

"But it should."

"Just get in there." North managed not to scream, but only barely.

With what might have been a tiny, wicked smile, Shaw slipped through the doors. North watched him approach the desk. Then he started talking, pointing at the book, yammering away. The librarian's fixed expression shifted first into wariness, then into a smile, and then into that inexplicable affection most people seemed to have for Shaw. Probably because they didn't have to spend more than five minutes at a time with him. Or because he'd never cut up all their high school football shirts to make matching rag wreaths for their doors. Or because he was the adult male equivalent of a lost puppy.

In less than five minutes, Shaw had finagled his way around the desk and was showing the woman something on his phone—a tropical parasite, a homemade astrology chart, Shaw's sixteen-hundred-tier taxonomy of fictional wizards. Who the fuck knew? North opened the door and strode across the lobby, heading for the RF gates and the library proper.

"—tied up to one of those rolling ladders, you know," Shaw was saying, "but the date due cards really add—"

"I'm not saying they don't add a nice touch," the librarian interrupted, "but in the first place, I'm worried the ink wouldn't be enough lubricant, and in the second place, it might be illegal to use withdrawn stamps that way."

North walked faster and tried not to hear any more.

The library consisted of one vast, open space, with two walls given over entirely to windows and metal accents that lent the space a futuristic feel. On the other side of the glass, the sunset streaked red and purple across the sky, ruddling the campus and the white walls inside the library. One portion of the library had been given over for the bookstacks, while the rest—the majority of the space, actually—was some sort of reading and study area: private carrels, clusters of soft seating, white laminate tables that continued the futuristic theme. North counted a dozen students: two were together, hunched over massive textbooks; four sat silently at the same table, each of them scribbling something without any apparent need for notes or references; and the other six sat individually, some reading, some listening to music, some tapping away at laptops.

North followed one wall, and it led him into the stacks. The first door he came to was unlocked and led into a service corridor, which he figured he'd come back to. On the next wall, he found a fire door, which wouldn't be any help for getting Shaw inside. On the third leg, he was heading back toward the reading area, and the wall consisted entirely of windows. He'd need to check the service corridor for an employee entrance. As he was about to cut through the stacks, though, he stopped and tried to keep the glare from his face.

Shaw was standing on this side of the RF gates, staring around the space with what might have been nostalgia. North stared until Shaw met his gaze, and a grin broke out across Shaw's face. He hurried around the room to join North. If the kids had noticed either of them, they gave no sign of it—thank God for high expectations, endless homework, and this generation's preference for escaping into screens.

"Oh my God," Shaw whispered, "this place brings back so many memories! That was where I read *Catcher in the Rye* for the first time. And that was where I wrote my sonnet cycle about Jonathan and David from the Hebrew Bible. And that was where Ian Daugherty kissed me on the cheek and asked me to go to prom with him. And I can show you the spot in the stacks where I had to go after I'd been reading Lord Byron all day and knew that my balls were going to explode if I didn't—"

Red infused his cheeks. His gaze drifted to North's, checking, and then cut away again.

"—write a poem," he finished lamely.

"It's like one of those mystery boxes," North said. "You shake it. You listen to it. You think about the shape and the size. All the possibilities. And every goddamn time, it's not what you thought."

"Oh," Shaw said, cocking his head. "Thanks."

"It wasn't a compliment. More importantly, give me five minutes with you in these stacks, and you won't remember Ian Daugherty. Or Lord Byron."

Shaw grinned. "So, where do you want to start?"

"How about with Flip's girlfriend?" North pointed to an Asian girl. She was wearing a pink fleece jacket, pink fleece joggers, and pink slides with wild pink tufts coming off the straps. Next to her was a backpack: silver with purple-sequin monogramming.

"Are you sure that's her?"

"Well, Celia told us she was Chinese, and none of the other kids in here are Asian. Her name's Abigail, and the monogramming is AMQ. And this school is tiny. I think it's a good bet."

Shaw shrugged.

When they reached the table, North said, "Abigail?"

Nothing. Her head bobbed in time with silent music; earbuds, North realized.

He waved a hand in front of her face, and she started. After tapping one of the earbuds, she glanced up at them. Pretty, with her dark eyes and her ponytail of dark hair. But North had seen plenty of pictures of Flip Chittenden, and under normal circumstances, Flip would have been in a different league than this girl. And that made North want to know what the special circumstances were here.

"Abigail?"

She nodded. She looked like she was trying to move as little as possible. Petrified, the word came to North.

"We need to talk to you about Flip."

That sealed the deal. She was so still North wasn't sure she was still breathing. Her eyes glimmered.

"Are you all right?" Shaw asked. "We just have a few questions."

"Not—not here." The words were unaccented, and they sounded stilted from emotion more than anything else.

"Ok," Shaw said slowly, his eyes rising to North's. "How about outside? Grab a breath of fresh air."

Abigail gave a jerky nod and began shoving her belongings in her backpack. When she was ready, she rose, and they walked through the gates and toward the doors.

"Have a nice—" the librarian began. When she saw North, though, she said, "Who are you? How did you—"

"My consultant," Shaw said without slowing. "He's a crucial research component for my book I'm writing."

"You really can't—"

But apparently they could, because they had, and a moment later, the spring air met North, with a hint of chill and the dew that would settle overnight. North's next breath brought the perfume from a line of black cherries planted on the verge; in the thickening darkness, their white blossoms were luminescent. Like bone, North thought, and he didn't know where the thought had come from, and he didn't like it.

"I'm not eighteen," Abigail said, arms wrapped around herself as she stared at the ground. "You can't talk to me without—"

"The police can't talk to you without an adult," North said. "We're not police, and we're not trying to cause you any trouble. Flip's parents hired us to find him. We've just got a few questions."

Abigail shook her head. "Maybe I shouldn't—"

"The only reason you wouldn't want to talk to us is if you didn't want to help Flip. Is that what's going on?"

"What? No, but—"

"No? Because you broke up with him, right? Why would you still care what happened to him?"

Head coming up, Abigail shot each of them a look of compressed teenage disgust. "I didn't break up with him. It was mutual. We weren't working out. Nothing was working out. I love Flip; I don't want anything bad to happen to him."

North waited; in the distance, at the edge of hearing, boys were screaming with excitement. Something about a frisbee.

"Oh my God," she whispered, "did something bad happen to him?"

"That's what we're trying to find out," Shaw said. "That's why we need your help. Do you have any idea what might have happened?"

Abigail shook her head.

"Flip never talked about running away?"

She shook her head again, but this time, with a slight hesitation.

"What does that mean?" North said.

"He never talked about running away."

"But?" Shaw prompted.

"He...he wanted to be away from here. He talked about it a lot. Graduating. In the fall, he talked about graduating early, but his parents told him absolutely not."

"He didn't like it here?"

"No, that wasn't it. I think he was happy. As happy as Flip ever is, I mean."

"What does that mean?"

"I don't know. He's just—he's got a lot going on. I guess we all do. He's sweet, and he's funny, and he's kind."

Shaw's question came out of nowhere, but North understood it at once, and he kicked himself for not thinking of it when the topic of running away first came up: "What was Flip's home life like?"

"Have you met his parents?"

Both men nodded.

"They're nice to me. I went out there a few times for dinner. They were all right."

"How did they treat Flip?"

"Fine, I guess."

"He's asking you," North said, "if you think Flip was being abused?"

"What? Oh my God. No."

"You're sure?"

"Absolutely. I mean, they were fine. And Flip never said anything like that."

"Sometimes kids hide things like that," North said, "but the signs are there. There are behaviors, avoidance mechanisms, things they can't explain—"

"I'm telling you no. They're fine. He just wanted to be done with school and start his own life. I mean, I know something bad happened with his sister, but he wouldn't ever talk about it."

"You don't have any idea what happened to her?"

Abigail shook her head.

North shared a frustrated look with Shaw, and Shaw asked, "Do you think he ran away?"

Another hesitation, longer this time, and then Abigail shook her head again.

"What do you think happened?" North asked.

"I don't know!" The outburst was half despair, half protest.

"But you've got an idea," Shaw said. He was watching her closely, hazel eyes intense.

"I think—" Abigail drew a deep breath. "Headers, I mean, Dr. Latese, she told us in assembly a couple of weeks ago that those guys weren't going to come around anymore, and we weren't supposed to worry. But they did come around. And we all saw them. And I think maybe they had something to do with Flip." She started to cry, turning her face away, her thin shoulders shaking.

"What guys?" North said. "Tell us about these guys."

"They were just here. A first-year saw them, and nobody believed her, and then Liam, he's a third-year, he saw them with Katie and Pranav, and then Dr. Latese made that announcement, and then Ward and Rich saw them the next weekend."

"What did they look like?"

Another dose of withering teen contempt as she dashed tears away. "I don't know."

"Somebody had to say something."

"They just said they were sketch. Shady. Katie said they were gangsters, but she loves to exaggerate."

"Except now you think she might have been right," Shaw said. "You think they had something to do with Flip."

Again that hesitation, the wall between the pack loyalty of adolescents and the foreign tribe of adults. "Flip used. Sometimes."

"He got arrested for possession," North said, "but his mother swears it wasn't his."

Abigail snorted, the sound surprisingly mature. "It wasn't just weed, and it wasn't just that time. He really liked to party. And when the police came and talked to me the first time, I didn't put it together, but then I thought about all the times Flip didn't have money, and how that never stopped him from partying, and I wondered if maybe he owed them money, you know?"

"Did you call the police?"

"No. He might come back, right? He might just be getting away for a few days. I don't want him to get in trouble."

"You need to call the police and tell them," Shaw said. "If you're right, the worst that will happen is that he gets in trouble. If you're wrong, though, the police need to follow up on that information as soon as possible."

Abigail was crying again, silently now, wiping under her eyes in quick, repetitive movements.

"Who did he party with?" North said. "Where did he get the drugs?"

"I don't know."

"Abigail."

"I don't! I mean, Hiwet is…she's like this international party girl. She's been to all these different schools and keeps getting kicked out. And Flip liked to hang out with her. So maybe Hiwet."

"Last name?"

"Zerai."

"And where is she?"

"She's in Ross—no, wait, let me check." Abigail pulled out a phone in a furry pink case and tapped the screen. "Hiwet's always posting on Instagram." Turning her phone to display it, she added, "See?"

The photograph was of the sunset over what looked like tennis courts. The caption was just a series of hashtags about teenagers and photography. The timestamp said it had been posted four minutes ago.

"Where are the tennis courts?"

"The jungle."

"The phys-ed buildings," Shaw clarified.

"Call the police," North told Abigail. Then he nodded to Shaw, and they set off across campus.

Chapter 13

ONCE, WHEN NORTH had been eighteen, he had watched the sunset from scaffolding on the job site. Shaw liked to tease him about having worked construction; that was fine. But it had been part of North's life once, and he remembered that evening in particular, the darkness of Illinois, the purple bleeding across the river. He had learned in school that purple was the color of kings, and he had empty air beneath his legs and the wind in his hair and the whole world had belonged to him. So he could understand why a girl named Hiwet had chosen this spot to watch the sun go down.

They found her on a swell of ground that overlooked the tennis courts. Darkness was rolling in. The evening air carried a hint of fresh mulch. Below them, lights were popping on, illuminating the blue-and-white acrylic of the courts and outlining a steel-and-glass monstrosity of a building. The words ABELMAN HEALTH CENTER glinted on the windows.

She was thin, almost to the point of malnutrition. Sticks-and-bones arms and legs. A neck that barely looked capable of holding up her head. A heart-shaped face; she had dark brown skin, and it looked flawless. Her hair hung in tight, oiled coils. She was not alone. The boy next to her was on the verge of manhood, his body filling out, the rangy leanness of adolescence almost gone. His blond hair was shaggy, and his eyes were hard. Neither had noticed North and Shaw yet.

"Hiwet?" North said.

The girl turned her head. Her hand went instinctively to a backpack, but she didn't run. Not yet.

"Who are you?" the boy demanded.

"Who are you?" North asked back.

"Let's go," the boy said in a low voice.

Hiwet was still watching them.

"My name's Shaw, and this is North. We're private investigators." Shaw smiled and tilted his head toward her bag; a can of tennis balls was stowed in the mesh pouch designed to carry a water bottle. "Do you play?"

"No," Hiwet said, her voice musical and with a faux-English accent that reeked of boarding schools. "What are you wearing?"

North blinked. Sometimes he got so used to it. Today, Shaw's ensemble consisted of a raglan tee, one sleeve pink, the other sleeve camo; skinny jeans cuffed to mid-calf; and a pair of silver chukkas—sockless, of course.

"Do you like it?" Shaw said, plucking at the pink sleeve. "I had to make it myself because I saw it in a trance and then I couldn't find it online anywhere, not even Amazon."

"Oh no," Hiwet said.

The boy flashed a mocking smile.

"I know. So then I had to buy a sewing machine, only North wouldn't let me—"

"I didn't say I wouldn't let you. I said you didn't have space for an industrial sewing machine and it seemed like a lot of money to make one shirt you'd seen in a fug of weed."

"—so instead, I asked Pari's mom to help me, her name's Bud, well, that's probably not really her name, but that's what she goes by, and Pari is our secretary, only sometimes she wants us to call her an administrative assistant, but then she brought in a coffee mug one time that said 'world's best secretary' on it and she screamed for forty-five minutes because she said we should have bought it for her ourselves and she always has to buy herself things and then she threw it in the fireplace to break it—on purpose—"

"She didn't," Hiwet said.

"She did! And I said if you're going to act like a spoiled child, you ought to be treated like a spoiled child, and she said—wait, what was I telling you?"

"The clothes," North muttered.

"Oh, right. And the jeans I got at the Gap, only North calls it Lady Gap—"

"Because you were shopping in the women's section."

"—and I had to spray-paint the chukkas myself because, um, weed vision. I mean trance."

"Oh my God," Hiwet breathed, a nasty little giggle lurking in her eyes. The boy next to her was smirking. "It's so cute." She dragged out the word so.

"Thank you."

"Very homo-forward," the boy said.

"Oh, that's an interesting term. I've never heard it before."

"He's making fun of you," North said.

"I don't think so. I am a homo, and forward is always good, so homo-forward sounds really good. Oh, except forward isn't always good, like that one time you tried to joyride in one of those motorized shopping carts but you got stuck in that tampon display and I told you to back up but you just kept going forward and you got buried in tampons and all those tampon ladies had to help you because I was laughing so hard."

"There's no such thing as a tampon lady," North snapped. "They were just ladies who were shopping there. And you told me the wrong way to back up and—" He forced himself to take a breath and looked at the boy. "Name."

"Who the fuck are you two?" the boy asked.

"They're ancient is what they are," Hiwet said.

"I'm the club tennis pro," Shaw said.

"I'm a caddy," North said.

"Oh, like on *Caddyshack*."

"They don't know *Caddyshack*."

"Or on *Happy Gilmore*."

"They don't know *Happy Gilmore*."

Shaw directed a worried look at the teenagers. "Really? Because they're great movies, and they're at a very good school, so I'm sure their education is comprehensive."

"What the fuck are you two talking about?" the boy asked, rising. "Who the fuck are you, and what do you want?"

"*Happy Gilmore* is a movie about why it's ok to abuse the elderly—"

"We told you our names," North said. "And we told you we're private investigators. We're looking into what happened to Flip, and we want to talk to Hiwet."

"No. Go away."

"Kid, either shut up or get your ass lost."

"You going to make me? A couple of fags like you?"

"Oh," Shaw said, "you really shouldn't use that word."

"You going to—"

"Ugh, Jos, cut it out." Hiwet stood; barefoot, she was as tall as the boy she had called Jos, and he wasn't much shorter than North. "Why do you want to talk to me?"

"Someone said you like to party. Someone said Flip liked to party with you."

She shrugged one birdlike shoulder.

"Is that true?" Shaw asked.

"Americans are so uptight. I miss Amsterdam."

"Is that where you're from?"

Jos laughed. It was a mean sound.

Shaking her head, Hiwet said, "Eritrea. But I've lived all over."

"Because you get kicked out of school for drugs?" North asked.

"Sometimes. For lots of reasons. My parents are overprotective." She frowned. "Who told you those things about me?"

"You still haven't answered his question," North said. "Is that true about Flip and the partying?"

"It doesn't matter if you tell me. I'll find out eventually; I find out everything. All these little secrets. This one makes herself throw up in the toilet after lunch. This one's parents have lost all their money. This one had to pay someone else to take the SAT for them. This one likes to suck cock." The crudeness of the words sounded even worse coming from that smooth, innocent face, delivered in that faux-English accent.

"I haven't spent a lot of time at this place yet," North said, "but I'm a pretty fast learner. I had to be, because my parents didn't have shit when I was growing up, so I had to be smart, and I had to work hard. And do you know what I've figured out about this place?"

Jos rolled his eyes. Hiwet's smirk was almost invisible, just a slash to her mouth.

"Half the problems in this place would go away if somebody would just beat your asses with a belt once in a while."

Color flooding his face, Jos took a step forward before Hiwet caught his arm.

"Does Flip go to your parties?"

"Everyone comes to my parties," Hiwet said. "Everyone I invite, that is."

"Does he do drugs?"

Hiwet shrugged. "He likes cocaine. It is very expensive. He was angry when his parents took away his allowance."

North looked at Jos. For some reason, the boy seemed to take it as a challenge, and he tried to step forward again. When Hiwet held him back, he sneered and said, "I saw him do a rail off a girl's ass. That's Flip: the golden boy snorting coke off some dumb gutter bitch's ass."

"So Flip isn't the golden boy? Because we've heard from a couple people that he's pretty much perfect."

Jos's scowl was starting to look like a permanent fixture, but it was Hiwet who answered. "Nobody's perfect. Flip is close. He works hard in school. He's friendly. He's good at soccer. He treats Abigail right. So he likes to come to my parties and let loose. Is that bad? Is he a bad person, when the rest of the time he tries so hard to be good?"

When North glanced at Jos, the boy looked away and mumbled, "He's all right."

"Do you think Flip might have gotten in over his head?" Shaw asked. "We heard about men on campus, and we thought maybe—"

Hiwet's laugh was bright and sudden and genuinely amused. "No, that's not—that has nothing to do with Flip."

"Really? How do you know that?"

Hiwet's smile just got bigger.

"Why were they here?"

"That's not your secret."

"Whose secret is it?"

Still smiling, lips sealed, she shook her head.

"Do you have any idea where Flip might be?"

Jos shook his head first. Hiwet hesitated and then signaled no as well.

"Did he talk about running away?"

"Jesus, this is so stupid," Jos said.

"No," Hiwet said. "He wanted to graduate, but he didn't want to run away."

"Do you think someone took him?"

Jos nodded. Hiwet shook her head.

"Why do you say yes?" Shaw asked.

"The door. I saw the door; somebody kicked it in." He set his jaw, his expression challenging. "I live in Washington too. When the police left, I went up and looked at his room. I didn't touch anything."

"Why do you say no?" North asked.

"It's too much." Hiwet gathered coils of hair and looked off past North's shoulder. "It's like an American movie."

"Then what do you think happened?"

"I think Flip is on vacation. Maybe he's tired of being perfect and for a few days, he only wants to be Flip."

"Great," North said. "Does he have a timeshare?"

Hiwet laughed. Jos's scowl deepened, and he asked, "What's a timeshare?"

"What were things like for Flip at home?" Shaw asked.

After a shared look, Jos shrugged. "Fine, I guess. He didn't really talk about it much. He went home when we had days off from school. His parents came a few times and they seemed all right. His mom's some kind of big deal. They've got a ton of money."

When North looked at Hiwet, she shrugged and nodded.

"Did it ever occur to you, even briefly, that Flip might have been abused?"

"No," Jos said immediately.

"What about his sister?"

A frown line appeared between Hiwet's eyes. "She had leukemia?"

The door to the Abelman Health Center opened, and a pack of teenage boys burst out into the night. One of them was repeating the word, "Bonker!" over and over again, while another laughed so hard that he staggered and couldn't keep a straight line. The third boy kept his distance, shoulders high and tight, stalking away from his friends.

"Flip got in an argument."

The statement was delivered in a low, flat voice; Jos was studying the boys down the hill, his arms crossed now, his body in profile to North and Shaw.

"This," Hiwet said in a tone of disgust. "This again."

"All right." North fought to keep his tone level. "A fight. With?"

"It was nothing. They fought. The end."

"His name's Louis." Jos shot them a look; his eyes were quicksilver with the halide glow of the lamps. "You'll love him; he's a fag too."

"What were they fighting about?" Shaw asked.

Hiwet had become a statue. Jos shrugged. "I don't know, but Louis said, 'I'll kill you.' It all happened in the refectory. Everybody heard him."

"Where can we find him?" North asked.

"The nat."

When North looked at Shaw, Shaw said, "The pool. It's in the health center."

"So just say pool."

Shaw shrugged.

"You're sure he'll be there?"

"He's always there," Hiwet said. "When he's not in class or sleeping, he's there."

"Ok." North handed each of them a card. "If you think of anything else, let us know."

"What are Flip's secrets?" Shaw asked suddenly.

Hiwet gathered coils of hair again. She barely looked like she was breathing. A second passed, and then another, the May air cool now against North's skin, the basketball boys' laughter swallowed up by the night.

Shaw's gaze shifted to Jos. "You'd better be careful. Secrets have a way of hurting people, and even if you think she's your friend, that doesn't mean you're safe."

Jos gave them what North was beginning to consider his default mode: a furious look, brows drawn together.

"Jos doesn't have anything to worry about," Hiwet said, the words lilting with amusement. "Jos's only secret is that he's poor."

Chapter 14

NORTH AND SHAW MADE their way down the hill toward the Abelman Health Center. Twilight threw a pall over everything: the last embers of the day behind them, and ahead, the world long brushstrokes of blue that smoked away like dry ice. Another group emerged from the gym, girls this time, all in their early teens, all in shorts and tees, all tall. The way they moved suggested that The Gouverneur Morris School's girls' basketball team wasn't half bad.

The access card that Celia had provided unlocked the front doors. Inside, they found a two-story atrium, the skylights dark and opaque overhead. To judge by the smell, the linoleum was new, and the building contained a lot of sweating teens. Shaw made a face and pulled the collar of his tee up over his nose.

"Baby," North said. "This is nothing compared to the boys' locker room."

"I've been in boys' locker rooms," Shaw said. "That doesn't mean I have to like this."

As they headed deeper into the gym, North had to admit that either his memory might have faded a bit, or teens were much more pungent these days.

A quick tour of the building took them past three multipurpose gyms, their wood floors marked with basketball courts, a room with rolled-up yoga mats, a room with a full-size indoor soccer field, a weight room, a second, smaller weight room, and then a wall of windows that looked down on the pool.

"We could have come around that way," North said. "Why'd you bring me on the scenic route?"

"I haven't been here before. This is where the old gym was, but they tore it down and built this one after I left." Shaw frowned and pointed to a flight of stairs. "I think we go down there."

"Down the stairs that say POOL and SWIMMING LOCKER ROOMS?"

"That's right."

North managed not to say anything else. Somehow.

After passing through a pair of fire doors at the bottom of the steps, they found themselves in the pool area proper. Chlorine made North's eyes sting.

Their footsteps echoed back from the tiled walls, syncopated with the slosh and splash of the water in the Olympic-sized pool. If Louis was here, he wasn't swimming; North and Shaw were the only ones in the vast room.

"We should go swimming," Shaw said.

"We're a little busy right now."

"I meant later. Next time we have a break. We should go; I like going swimming. And I like seeing you in those shorty-shorts that you wear. And I like when you ask me to put sunscreen on you."

"I never ask you to put sunscreen on me."

"Well, you should. You always burn."

"I got one sunburn. Once."

"You're very fair."

"Oh my God."

"It's a good thing. Mostly. Once I put on my ski goggles."

"You're possibly the whitest person I know."

"But I'm not fair. There's a difference."

North slapped the wall next to a door marked BOYS' LOCKER ROOM. "How about this? How about no more talking? We'll make a game out of it. I'll time you and see if you can break your own record."

"That doesn't sound very fun."

"You can think of a prize. Something you want me to do."

Shaw hemmed. "I do find you very sexually attractive."

"Fantastic."

"And I want you to do all sorts of dirty things to me."

"Make a list. Happy to oblige."

"And I did get a little, you know, semi, when you threatened to beat up those children earlier."

North threw open the door to the locker room and strode inside.

"North, wait, I didn't finish telling you about my Woodrow Wilson!"

North couldn't help it; he stopped, glanced back, and whispered furiously, "It's called a woody, you fucking mental defective."

The smile on Shaw's face was just a flicker, there and then gone.

North was practically jogging as he tried to get away.

Ahead, a wall of lockers met them. The smell of boy funk and chlorine was tempered now by the slightly harsh perfume of soap. Somewhere, a shower hissed, and a steamy haze hung in the air. The locker room branched left and right.

"We should probably stick—"

"Like fuck," North said. "You go that way. I'll go this way."

"What if we—"

"Stop talking," North ordered in a tight whisper.

North went right, following the perimeter of the room. He passed an office door, the varnish peeling, the pebbled glass lettered in gold with the word

COACH. He tested it. Locked. If they didn't find Louis, maybe he'd come back and take a look inside. Lockers continued ahead of him, with narrow benches placed at regular intervals. The drum of falling water from the shower sounded louder now. Ahead, a locker stood open, a towel hanging from the door.

North threw a look over his shoulder; the room was clear. He approached the locker, nudging the door open with the back of his hand, and glanced inside. The long vertical space was divided by a shelf about three-quarters of the way down. A rugby shirt banded in yellow and black hung from a hook on one side of the locker. Mesh shorts were puddled on top of the shelf, with a partially balled-up sock next to them. North patted the shorts, felt a hard, rectangular shape, and worked a leather wallet out of the pocket. The driver's license showed Louis Yates Albee, seventeen, blond, green eyes. He was a decent-looking kid—cute now, although he wasn't a beauty. The license gave his height as six-two, weight one-sixty. Even from the picture, North knew that was a lie; the kid was stacked.

Aside from an Amex Gold and a Visa that was so heavy it felt like it was made of gold, the wallet contained a Gouverneur Morris access card, two hundred and forty-one dollars in cash, and what North thought at first glance might be a cheat sheet. It was a small piece of paper, obviously cut and laminated by hand, that was tucked behind the cash. It took North a moment to understand what he was seeing: macros. Protein, carbohydrates, and fats. After another moment's consideration, North returned the card and the wallet. He was about to step away from the locker when he noticed the gym bag under the locker's bottom shelf.

Working it loose, North was surprised by both the weight and the sound of crinkling plastic. He let it hang half out of the locker, tugged on the zipper, and studied the contents: protein powders; blender bottles; Twix, Snickers, Milky Way, all of them king size; Ding Dongs, Twinkies, Zingers, Ho Hos; individual packets of creatine supplements and something called Monster Bulk-Up, which might or might not have something to do with bowel movements. Swimmers, especially teenage swimmers, could burn up to twenty thousand calories a day, and that number probably went up with all the supplements this kid was taking.

Voices echoing on the tile made North shove the bag back under the shelf. He gave the locker door a tap to send it wobbling back toward its original position, and then he began working his way around the locker room again. When he turned again, he realized that the room was roughly the shape of a square—four connected aisles of lockers, with something at the center. The showers, he guessed.

The wall to his left opened. The voices were stronger, as was the hiss of the showers. The steam was thicker here, dampening North's shirt, and the tile had a sheen of condensation that caught the glow from the fluorescent lights.

"A little higher." The voice was young, male, confident, and surprisingly firm.

Shaw said something North couldn't make out.

"Higher," the younger voice repeated.

Showers on the left. Through an opening in painted cinderblock, North could see the ring formation of the showerheads. Two of them were still running. Water puddled where the floor was uneven.

"I said higher. Jesus, do I have to do—like that. Thank you." He didn't sound particularly thankful, though. North moved slowly across the slick tile toward an open door on his right where the voices were coming from. The young man spoke again. "A little higher now."

"Are you sure?" Shaw said. "Because you said it was a hamstring, but now I'm starting to think you pulled your groin."

"Which one of us would know where I got hurt?"

"Well, you, I guess—"

"Then do what I tell you: higher."

North leaned in the doorway. The room obviously belonged to the school's trainer. An exam table and a massage table occupied the center of the room. Cabinets took up one wall, and on top of a stainless-steel counter rested ACE bandages, splints, and various tapes and wraps. An ice machine rumbled in one corner.

On the massage table, a naked young man lay prone, his head turned away from North. He was blond. His hair was wet and dark. Water beaded across his back. He was jacked, muscles visibly defined in a way only teenagers could accomplish, and even then, only with tremendous discipline. He had enough real estate shoulder to shoulder for a tract development. This, North figured, was Louis Albee, who had threatened to kill Flip the week before. Shaw stood at his side, one hand rubbing the inside of Louis's leg.

"Any higher," North said in what he hoped was a conversational tone, "and you're going to be committing a felony."

Shaw whipped around. The kid shot upright and slid off the massage table, keeping it between himself and the doorway.

"North," Shaw said with a note of relief. "Hi! This is Louis. I met him when he was coming out of the shower, and we started talking, and he told me he pulled a hamstring at practice, and I told him about reiki healing and said I could generate an 8.7 reiki healing factor but we probably needed a massage table, and he said, 'What a coincidence, there's a massage table right over here,' and then it turned out not to be a hamstring at all because I think he really pulled his groin."

"Did he say he wanted reiki healing with a happy ending?"

"Actually, he did!" Worry crept into Shaw's voice. "How did you know?"

"Because you were about five seconds from giving him a tugaroo."

"Oh no, I wouldn't—I mean, he didn't—I mean, I would never—"

North put a finger to his lips. Shaw cut off, swallowed, and nodded.

"If it really matters," Louis said, clasping his hands behind his head in a pose that made muscles pop along his torso and arms, dick still bobbing in front of him, "I'm seventeen, so it's totally legal."

"It matters."

"I've never done it with two guys before, but you're hot. Riley's got lube in that cabinet over there."

"Pass."

"Then fuck on out of here and let your friend get me off." He cast a look at Shaw. "He's gorgeous."

"No."

"North!" Shaw protested. He shut his mouth again when North looked at him, but then he managed to add, "That's really rude."

"I'm not saying you're not gorgeous, dumbass. I'm saying you're not going to give a teenager a fast-five in a trainer's room. Jesus Christ." To Louis, he added, "Do you see what I have to put up with?"

"Are you guys, like—"

"Yes, although God only knows why."

"North!"

But when North directed a furious glare his way, Shaw cut off again, color flooding his face.

"You're kind of intense," Louis said. He dropped the pose and reached down to stroke himself once. "Normally I like to be the one in charge, but, fuck, I think I want you to yell at me."

"Oh, he's really good at that," Shaw said.

"Go put some fucking clothes on," North said. "Do your fucking algebra homework. Pick up your fucking room. How's that for a start?"

"Yeah, we can play it like that. What if I don't pick up my room, Daddy? What if I'm bad?"

"You don't even want to know," Shaw said. "One time he told me I had to pick up my room even after I'd been really nice to him after he destroyed this model I was working on, and then I was about to beat the world record on *Duck Hunt*, the old NES one, and he ripped the cord out of the Nintendo and turned off the TV. Because I hadn't picked up my room."

"I didn't ruin a model you were working on," North said. "I reached under the bed for my socks and accidentally put my hand into that fucking nightmare banana-cream-pie skyscraper—" To Louis, he interjected, "it's exactly what it sounds like—that you'd left under there for two weeks. And I turned off the fucking game because you started sobbing every time you shot one of those damn ducks."

"But the dog was so cute! I had to!"

North closed his eyes and counted to ten. When he opened them, Louis was watching him with a small, unreadable smile.

"So we're not going to spit-roast your boyfriend?"

"No," North said. "Go get dressed. We're here to talk to you about Flip."

"Damn. Ok, I'm going to rub one out in the shower."

Thirty seconds after Louis left, the sound of fapping echoed back from the tile. Shaw, who was inspecting the cabinets, paused, and his face turned scarlet. It looked like he was trying not to meet North's eyes.

"This is why I hate children," North said. "This is why I hate teenagers in particular. This is why I thank God every morning that I'm never going to have kids."

Shaw, busy now trying to wrap his wrist with blue athletic tape, frowned. "I think you'd be a great dad. You already like to sit around in your underwear and drink beer and watch TV. And you strutted around for almost a week after you bought yourself that Weber grill. And you even sound like a dad sometimes like when you say, 'When you're in your own house, you can do whatever you want, but when you're under my roof, you live by my rules.' Which is kind of ironic because you have the ground-floor flat; technically, Mr. Winns has the roof because he lives above you."

"I'm sorry that I didn't want you to install what you kept calling a 'sex spiderweb' in my living room. Forgive me for being worried the landlord might not like it."

"It wasn't a sex spiderweb," Shaw said, tearing the easy tape and then pressing the loose end into place. "It was a sex web. A sex spiderweb just sounds silly. Also, I think he's done."

The shower's hiss had gone silent. The five-finger percussion was over. North headed out of the trainer's room, passed the showers, and followed the corridor back to Louis's locker. Louis was sitting on the narrow bench, wearing electric yellow bikini briefs, the curve of his spine on display as he rummaged around in the locker. Zero percent body fat might not actually be possible, but North figured this kid had come pretty close.

"You wanted to talk about Flip?"

"That's right," North said. "We heard you got in an argument with him."

"I've got a temper."

"What were you arguing about?"

"Stupid stuff. It doesn't matter."

"You threatened to kill him; I think it matters."

Louis sat back, emerging from the locker, and looked up at them. "Did I really say that?"

"You don't remember?"

Louis shrugged. His posture was changing, one arm coming up across his chest now, hand on his shoulder, then his neck, then his throat. A defensive movement. Because he was lying? Or because he was suddenly realizing he was alone with two strangers who might be accusing him of murder?

"I don't know," Louis said. "When I get really mad like that, it's all a blur."

"Why don't you tell us what happened?" Shaw suggested.

"He cut in line at the refectory. When I told him to move his ass back, he mouthed off. I grabbed his arm. He knocked my tray out of my hand. My food went everywhere." Louis shrugged. "I lost my shit. I kind of remember screaming at him, and then I went back to my room and calmed down. The end."

"That's all?"

"That's it."

"Seems like an extreme reaction," North said. "Do you always lose your shit when somebody ticks you off?"

"Pretty much."

"When was the last time you saw Flip?"

"Sunday. That thing at the refectory, that was Thursday. Friday, we weren't talking. It sucks at a place like this; it's so small, everybody knows everything. Fridays and Saturdays we're allowed to go off campus, although curfew is at nine on Friday and ten on Saturday, which is total bullshit. Normally, the fourth-years go out together—well, not Abigail because she never does anything fun—but I was still pissed at Flip, so I did my own thing Friday. Saturday, things were cooling off. We went out together, the fourth-years. Sunday, I saw Flip at lunch. And in the house, of course."

"You live in Washington too?"

Louis nodded as he pulled on the rugby shirt. When his head popped through the collar, he added, "Yeah."

"Do you have a best guess what time you last saw him on Sunday?"

"Early afternoon? I don't really know. The house was pretty empty. I think I left around two or three. I'd finished my homework and I wanted to get in some pool time, and I think the house was totally empty."

"You think?"

"It's not like I went door to door." He cocked his head. "You guys really don't seem like cops."

"I never said we were cops," North said. "I said we wanted to ask you about Flip. Do you have any idea where he might be?"

"Maui? Tahiti? A friend's house, laughing at all the dumbasses who are looking for him?"

"You think this could be a practical joke?"

Rising, Louis pulled the mesh shorts from his locker. He stepped into them; the fabric barely hit the middle of his thigh. "Flip wasn't really a joker, but what else could this be? I mean, nothing happened to him. So he's doing this because he wants to."

"Why would he want to do this?"

"Maybe he just needed to. Haven't you ever needed a fresh start?"

"He's about to graduate. He's about to have a fresh start."

Louis considered his socks, dropped them on the floor, and shoved his feet into a pair of slides. "Nah. Not with his parents riding him."

"Are there problems at home?"

He made the classic teenage noise that expressed the ineffable stupidity of adults.

North refused to acknowledge that he understood, so he said, "What does that mean?"

"You know what kind of kids go here?"

"Rich, bratty ones."

"Sure, all right. You know what kind of parents they have?"

"Rich, bratty ones."

"There you go."

"What about his sister?"

"Oh, yeah." Louis sobered for a moment. "That was really sad."

"What happened?"

"Um, she drowned or something?"

"Or something?" North asked.

"I don't know, man. Flip wouldn't talk about it at all. I heard she drowned, but I don't know where I heard that."

"We're trying to figure out if Flip's home life might have been worse than usual," Shaw said.

"He doesn't have a home life." Louis closed the locker. "None of us do. That's the whole point. He never seemed to mind going home, if that's what you mean. Nobody was beating the shit out of him; I had a couple of friends with parents like that. He wasn't cutting himself, he wasn't anorexic or overeating, he wasn't depressed. I know what you're asking, and I know what it looks like, and that wasn't Flip."

"But you think he ran away to escape his parents?"

With a practiced roll of his eyes, Louis shook his head. "I told you: I don't know. I'm just saying what he might have done. He might want a fresh start. He might be playing a joke."

"Would Flip have done something like that?"

"Jeez, I don't know."

"Sure you do," Shaw said. "You know him well enough. Is he cruel? This is a cruel prank, if that's what it is. When he knocked the tray out of your hand, did he do it on purpose? Is he a bully? Does he like to cause trouble?"

Louis's face screwed up, first in irritation, and then in something else. "Is it weird if I say, no, but…"

"But what?"

"He's always trying so hard to be perfect. It's fucking annoying. Perfect student, perfect athlete, perfect guy. The teachers are obsessed with him. Everyone is, really." A surprisingly mature laugh escaped him, droll and dry and pained. "Even me, although I guess I did threaten to kill him. But it's like something is off. Or missing. Or not quite real. Ever been in his room?"

"Yes."

"Like that. Flip would be perfect all day, all week, maybe even a month. And then one of his little gears would slip, and robot boy would blow a gasket and do something really stupid. Like that stuff with Lauren."

"Who's Lauren?" North asked.

"She thinks she's one tough bitch." Louis grabbed the gym bag from his locker and cracked his back. "She's a student here. She calls herself a drug dealer, but I've never seen her sell anything. I think smoking cheap weed behind the greenhouse is about as close as she's ever gotten. Flip and Lauren got in a huge fight in Kish's classroom; I didn't see it, but I guess Flip went ape. Broke a desk in half or something. And there's been guys on campus, sketchy as hell. Put it together yourself."

"Someone told us those guys had nothing to do with Flip."

"Hiwet?" He said her name like he wanted to scrape his tongue clean after. "Little *Gossip Girl* bitch baby Beyonce?"

"Try saying that three times fast."

"And I bet she had Jos with her, right?"

Shaw nodded. "He was there."

For some reason, Louis found that funny, although the sound was mean this time. "She likes to pretend she knows everybody's shit because we all know her shit. It gets old after a while, and after a while, you realize she doesn't know anything the rest of us don't already know."

"What's her shit?" North said.

"I'm not a gossipy old queen," Louis said. Then, with a smirk, he added, "Yet. Look, it's been fun, but if neither of you is going to stick a cock in me, I've really got to—"

"What's your relationship with Flip?" Shaw asked.

Louis adjusted his grip on the gym bag. After a moment, he said, "What does that mean?"

"It means, you said you're interested in him, and the argument you described looked minor but escalated quickly. That's a classic symptom of fights between people who have very strong emotions for each other."

"My very strong emotion was that Flip was being a prick cutting in line. That's all."

"There wasn't anything else? Even something unofficial? Maybe you—"

"Maybe I jerked him off under the covers at night, is that what you mean? Grow the fuck up. I've got a phone. I've got Grindr and Scruff. If I want to get laid, I hang dick and let some loser thirty-year-olds beg for it." His voice softened, but the edge only grew sharper. "I'm the only fag boy at this school. The rest of them can pat themselves on the back for how open and accepting they are, but I know how they look at me. Fuck them. In two years, I'm going to be swimming in Tokyo. At the Olympics. These pieces of shit can suck vag."

The intensity of his rage left North speechless for a moment, and before he recovered, a door opened and footsteps echoed off the tile. "Louis? What the hell is taking so long? We've got to break down tonight's practice before I go home, so move your ass."

Louis's whole body tightened at the sound of the man's voice. With an angry look at North and Shaw, as though this were somehow their fault, he hurried away and disappeared around the corner.

"You were swimming for shit tonight," the man said, voice fading now as he and Louis headed for the exit. "You picked up those two-tenths of a second you dropped last week. That's bullshit; you're better than that."

Louis answered, but the words were muffled.

Whatever he'd said made the man laugh. "I don't think so. If you think I didn't notice the extra three pounds when you weighed in today, you're out of your mind. Power versus resistance, that's the trade-off. You're dropping those three pounds. And maybe an extra, just to see if it helps you lose those two-tenths again. Last night, your mother was saying that she thinks—"

But whatever she thought, the words were cut off when the door slammed shut.

"Wait," Shaw said. "That was his dad?"

"Or coach is doing double duty," North said. "Come on. This place smells like bleached assholes."

"It probably brings back fond memories," Shaw said as he kept pace.

"What happened to the quiet game?"

"All those swimmer boys you'd bring back and bang so loud I could hear them screaming at the other end of the hall."

"Enough, Shaw."

"And it does explain why you were reading that article on DIY asshole whitening."

That was too far, which meant they had to spend the next five minutes with North trying to shove Shaw inside a locker, and Shaw fighting to escape and giggling so loudly that North barely managed to keep a smile off his face.

When they finally stumbled outside, the May air was sweet and clean after the chemical tang inside the pool area, the breeze cool enough to raise goosebumps on North's bare arms. The world had gone black except for the security lights, which shed hazy spheres like dandelion puffs. A night bird called softly, and then something a little too large for North's liking—a possum, he guessed—shot away from the dumpsters next to the health center and into the brush. Branches shivered and rustled. Then silence.

"What do you say we try to track down Kishor? He's got to be home by now, and it sounds like he might know something about Flip's fight with

Lauren. If nothing else, we can sweat him a little more and see if he gives up anything else."

"Ok," Shaw said, "but—"

His phone buzzed. He answered, caught North's gaze, and mouthed, *Jadon*. "Uh huh. Uh huh. Well, I don't see why—I'm not saying you did, I'm just—ok. Yes, ok. Thank you."

"What crawled up his butt?" North asked when Shaw disconnected.

"He's probably just tired."

"Jadon never cuts you off. Once I watched him listen for an hour and a half while you explained how you were going to recreate Susan B. Anthony's brassiere, which you claimed had been revealed to you in a dream."

"You were listening too!"

"No, I was trying to watch the Super Bowl. I was just too lazy to move the TV. Or kick your ass out."

"You were taking notes. I saw you!"

"I was trying to figure out if women at that time even wore bras, and it fucked up my search results for a month, Shaw. And don't try to get me off topic. Jadon is irritatingly patient with you; why did he keep talking over you right now?"

"Oh. Well, why don't I tell you while we walk very quickly back to the car?"

Shaw didn't wait for an answer; he caught North's hand and tugged, leading him in a brisk walk up the hill and past the tennis courts.

"Shaw."

"He's going through a really rough patch. He tried to work things out with, um, that guy. And it didn't work out. And I said maybe they should try—"

"Nope. The real bit."

"Jadon might have been the tiniest bit worried about me. About us, really, because I know you're basically his best friend."

"I fucking better not be. Why is he worried about us?"

As though in answer, blue-and-red lights whirled to life, and a siren blatted once as a cruiser pulled onto the access road.

"Maybe because of that," Shaw said with a sigh.

Chapter 15

AFTER TWO HOURS, Diamond let them go. Most of that time, North and Shaw spent sitting at her desk in the Juvenile bullpen. The smell of sour sweat and old cigarettes competed with an artificial air freshener labeled Jumpin' Juniper, which stank worse than the rotgut gin Shaw remembered North loving during senior year of college.

"This should have been a trespassing charge," Diamond said when she walked them out. "Do you understand that? The school is private property, and you don't have any right to be there unless you've cleared it with them. Especially not after the head of school told you that to your face."

"We were hired—" North began.

"Don't raise your voice to me," Diamond said.

North managed to swallow whatever he thought about that. In a tight voice, he asked for an update about Kishor, the teacher who had been trying to steal Flip's clothes.

"I'm going to talk to him when I get around to it."

"Talking to him won't—"

"I'm sticking my neck out for you two because Jadon asked me to," Diamond finally said. "Don't piss me off. And don't make me regret it."

When they got in the GTO, Shaw squeezed North's arm. Neither man talked as they left the parking lot. North drove hard: sharp bursts of acceleration, sudden braking, turns too fast. He must have been lost in thought because they were halfway back to his Southampton duplex when he swore, signaled, and cut toward an exit.

"It's fine," Shaw said. "Let's just head back to your place. I don't need to go home, and we're both exhausted."

North didn't answer; he just accelerated again, the GTO tearing up asphalt as they slingshotted along the curve of I-44.

The puppy greeted them, tail wild, when North let him out of his crate. A note on the whiteboard from Pari said, *In crate at 9*, which meant the puppy had only been alone for an hour. At first the puppy just pranced around, nails clicking on the floorboards, whining at North and then occasionally pausing to yap at Shaw. He was probably getting too big to be called a puppy, Shaw thought, but he didn't have a name yet. Then North scooped him up, grimacing as the puppy licked his face, and carried the puppy outside. After the puppy had done his business, North let him back inside and locked the door, which required an extra push because the door no longer hung plumb in the frame.

They undressed, took their turns in the bathroom, and crawled into bed. The puppy spent a good half an hour walking on top of North, sniffing, and turning every once in a while to growl at Shaw—all of this while North read on his phone. Shaw tried to coax the puppy onto his lap, but the puppy would have none of it. Then Shaw tried to commune psychically with the puppy, which turned into meditating, which turned into snoring himself awake a couple of times. He jerked awake again sometime later. The room was dark, and the mattress shifted as North stood.

"Go back to sleep," he whispered. "I'm just putting him in his crate."

But Shaw was awake with that strange clarity of interrupted sleep, and he lay, warm and comfortable and staring up into the darkness, until North came back. North lay down, and Shaw rolled onto his side and kissed North's arm.

North made a quiet noise. "I thought you were going back to sleep."

"Don't want to sleep." He slid closer. North had chosen cut-off sweats and a loose tee for pajamas that night. Shaw rucked the tee up a couple of inches and kissed the bare skin of North's abdomen. Warm, salty, dense with muscle.

"Baby, I'm tired." North's hand ruffled his hair. "And if I'm honest, kind of not in the mood."

"You're mad."

North made another quiet noise. When Shaw kissed his belly again, he carded Shaw's hair and said, "Bullshit way to end the day. Come on, let's go to sleep."

"You've got all those feelings pent up." Shaw curled his fingers under both waistbands—cut-offs and boxers—and slid them down a few inches, exposing the thick mat of dark blond pubes. North's dick was halfway to erect, but it was pinned down now by the elastic. North wiggled his hips in silent frustration, but Shaw tightened his hold on the waistbands, keeping North trapped. "Maybe you should do something with them."

"I don't want to do anything with my feelings. I want to go to sleep." But his voice was hoarse, his cock hardening, the discomfort of the elastic barrier making him reach down.

Shaw nuzzled his hand away and then planted a kiss on the patch of hair, breathing in North's scent.

"You're such a fucking tease," North said, his breathing shallower now, faster.

"What are you going to do if I stop teasing you?"

"Lie here and make you do all the work for once."

"That doesn't sound very nice."

"Fuck nice. I want you to fuck my brains out. Is that too much to—oh Jesus."

In one quick move, Shaw yanked the cut-offs and boxers down and took North in his mouth. He went slowly at first, teasing, suckling, even nipping—and being rewarded, in turn, by muffled swearing that grew more and more frantic. Then he took North to the root. He'd gotten better at this over their months together, and if Shaw were honest with himself, he'd been surprised by how much he liked it. Especially when North took over, grabbing him by the hair or ears and setting the pace.

Tonight, though, North only clutched the bedding. His breath hitching and then releasing slowly, a steam whistle, the defined muscles of his abdomen rippling as he struggled to keep himself still.

Finally Shaw pulled off and sat up. Drool and spit covered his chin; he left it there because he knew North liked it. North's eyes were heavy-lidded, but his chest rose and fell rapidly, unevenly.

"What do you want now?" Shaw whispered, stroking North's thigh, the thick blond fur there bristling under his touch.

"I already told you." North had to stop to clear his throat. "I want to go to sleep. If that's no longer an option, I want you to fuck me."

"You're grumpy."

"Why the fuck would that be, I wonder?"

Shaw stretched over North to retrieve the bottle of lube from the nightstand, and he let out a shriek that he barely managed to muffle when North reached up and tweaked his nipple. Hard.

"Oops," North said, his gaze still hooded, a smirk ghosting at the corner of his mouth.

After a few moments preparing himself, Shaw straddled North and lowered himself slowly. North hissed. His hands came up, as though of their own accord, and clutched Shaw's hips, dragging him down to seat him fully.

"Slow," Shaw whispered, a throaty noise breaking out of him when North rolled his hips. "Slow, slow, I need a minute."

A minute. A minute suspended like that, his body adjusting, the sense of fullness making Shaw's whole body tremble. And then he nodded, raising up to—

Whatever he'd planned, it went out his head when North slid free and rolled them over. Shaw landed on his back. North hooked one of his legs over his shoulder and slid in again. The shock was less this time, but Shaw's back still arched.

"This is what you wanted?" North asked, his voice a rough attempt at casual as he began to thrust.

"Oh fuck," Shaw moaned, trying to rock back to meet him. "Oh fuck."

"That's not an answer. Is this what you wanted?"

"Yes, yes, God, yes." Shaw reached down to grab himself; his own cock felt like steel, aching, neglected during all that time he'd been focused on North.

North intercepted him, catching his wrist. With surprising agility, North bent forward, pinning Shaw's arms over his head, hips bucking as he slammed into Shaw over and over again.

"North, oh shit, hold on, North, please, just—I just need to—"

"I could have gotten eight hours of sleep," North growled. "I could have gotten a nice, leisurely fuck."

"Please, I'm serious, I just need five seconds. North, I'm so close, North, North, North!"

"Instead, I've got a boyfriend who gets one thing in his head and won't. Fucking. Stop." He punctuated the words with long-dick thrusts.

The combination of aggression and stimulation sent Shaw over the edge. His vision waterfalled white. He was vaguely aware of North's name on his lips, a grunting call that barely sounded human. North's hips jittered, and Shaw heard his muffled cry as he pulled out and wet warmth sprayed across Shaw's hip, balls, and leg.

North collapsed on the bed next to him. For a while they lay there, breathing syncopated. Then North raised himself on one elbow, kissed Shaw, and rolled off the bed. He came back with a washcloth and two towels, cleaned them up, and spread the towels over the wet sheets.

"Now can I go to sleep?" North grumbled as Shaw slipped under his arm and laid his head on his chest.

Shaw barely heard him; he was already halfway there himself.

Chapter 16

THE NEXT MORNING, Haw Ryeo, their Aldrich Acquisitions contact, called them to come in for a consultation about the attempted break-in at the Nonavie lab. North finished up the client report that he was typing, while Shaw ran upstairs to change clothes.

"This I can't wait to see," North said without looking away from the monitor.

North finished the report, printed it, and added it to the file. He grabbed his Carhartt jacket, passed Pari in the reception area, where she was trying to teach the puppy to bark on command, and stopped in the kitchen at the bottom of the stairs.

"You coming?"

Shaw stepped out onto the landing, pulling the door shut behind him. When Shaw had gone upstairs, he'd been wearing a purple-and-ivory serape, a straw boater, and what he had described to North as Suzanne Somers-spring-collection leopard-print leggings. Now he was in a white polo, jeans, and penny loafers.

"What?" Shaw asked.

North had to take another second before he managed to say, "Nothing."

But Shaw still eyed him suspiciously as he came downstairs.

They took the Mercedes, at Shaw's insistence, and headed toward University City, a St. Louis suburb that bordered Washington University, as the name suggested, and where the Aldrich subsidiary lab was located. Halfway to the lab, a call came in on Shaw's phone, and the car's display lit up with an unfamiliar name.

"Who's Jerome Kramer?"

"That's one of Danny Wilkintonis's exes. The one who said he might still have his credit card information. Hold on." Shaw tapped the accept button on the steering wheel. "Hi, Jerome. Tell me you've got something."

"Hi," the voice camped. "Yes, oh my God, I think I found him."

"You did?"

"A pending charge showed up for the Stay-Rite Motel. I looked it up, and that's outside Sikeston."

"How much was the charge?"

"Thirty-nine dollars. That sounds like a cheap motel, doesn't it?"

"It does. You did good, Jerome."

"Now, you mentioned a reward, and I looked you up online and you're absolutely dreamy, so I was thinking you should—"

"We'll talk later," Shaw said, punching buttons on the steering wheel, his face red. "Thanks, Jerome!"

North found the Stay-Rite on his phone. A blurry photograph showed a board-and-batten building with peeling white paint; an ell extended from one end. Flowerbeds full of weeds lined the perimeter, and decades of rain and neglect had packed the gravel lot until it looked more like cobblestone. The motel didn't have a website, but the search included a phone number. North called.

On the eighth ring, a gravelly voice answered, "Stay-Rite."

"My friend checked in last night. Can you put me through to his room?"

"Name?"

"Daniel Wilkintonis."

"Just a second."

Silence, then a click, and then nervous breathing. North opened his mouth to introduce himself, but the other man spoke first: "Stop calling me! Just stop! I'm not going back, and you can't make me, and if you try, I will kill you, Lee. I will."

"Whoa," North said. "This isn't Lee. Don't kill me. Don't kill anybody if you can help it. Is this Danny?"

For a moment, the rapid breathing was the only answer, and then the voice said, "Who are you?"

North took that for confirmation and placed the call on speaker. "Danny, my name is North McKinney. You disappeared, and a lot of people are worried about you. A lot of people want to know you're ok."

"He hired you, didn't he? Lee did. It's not enough that he ruined my life. Jesus Christ, I knew he wasn't going to let me go." Danny sounded on the brink of tears. "Just fuck off. It's no use coming down here; I'll be gone by the time you do. And if you've got a conscience at all, you'll give him his money back and tell him I'm gone. I'm hanging up now."

"Wait, wait, wait." North shot a glance at Shaw. "Searls—I mean Lee—you're trying to get away from him?"

"He put me in the hospital on Christmas."

"He hits you?"

"Sometimes. Not usually. He's just got this way of getting inside my head. If I don't do what he wants, he rips me to pieces. If I talk back, it gets worse. If I—if I try to leave, he won't let me. I took most of a bottle of Tylenol on

Christmas because that was the only thing I could find. I'm going to hang up. I need to hang up."

"Just a second. We're talking. That's all. Sometimes it helps to talk."

Movement came from the other end of the line. Then a metallic crinkle. Danny parting the blinds, North guessed. "I've seen that car three times," Danny mumbled. "That's not his car, but I've seen it three times."

"How about this?" North said. "How about I give you some advice, and you think about it, and if you want some help, you call us back? I'm not going to lie to you: Searls did hire us. But if you're trying to get away from him, we're not going to bring you back—not if you're telling us the truth."

"I am telling you the truth. Ask anyone. Ask all those people who said they were my friends."

"All right. Here's the free advice. Go into Sikeston—or, better yet, Cape Girardeau—and find somewhere to pull out some cash. Then, ideally, you should drive as far as you can today. Is that an option?"

It took another of those long moments, the cheap motel microphone crackling with static, before Danny said, "I don't—I don't think so. My car's old, and Lee kept promising to get it fixed, but I think he liked that I'd have to call him for help or beg for rides. There was a lot of black smoke the last ten miles."

"I'd say don't risk it. Get the cash, pick another motel in the area, somewhere like the one you're in now: small, cheap, and off the main road. Pay cash. Don't use your legal name. If they ask for ID, offer to pay more. If they still want ID, go somewhere else. How are we doing so far?"

"Yeah," Danny said. The blinds rustled again on his end of the call. "That's stuff they do in the movies. I can do that." With a note of embarrassment, he added, "I haven't been thinking too clearly lately."

"Once you're settled, if you want us to help, call me." And then North gave Danny his number. "Does the name Aldrich Acquisitions mean anything to you? Or Nonavie?"

"I don't think so."

"You're sure?"

"Why are you helping me," Danny asked, "if you're working for Lee?"

"I don't work for clients who lie to me. And I definitely don't help abusive assholes track down their victims. Think about those names, if you can figure out any connection to them."

When North disconnected, Shaw was throwing sidelong glances at him.

"Don't do that," North said. "I do not need to be psychoanalyzed right now."

"I'm not psychoanalyzing you."

"Can you stop looking at me, then?"

"I like looking at you."

North grabbed the tiny bun of hair that Shaw had tied back with a scrunchie. He used it to turn Shaw's head forward. "Eyes on the road, Speed Racer."

They drove like that until Shaw turned on Forest Park Parkway, and then North's hand relaxed, sliding down to rest on Shaw's nape, his thumb massaging his neck lightly. The May morning was bright; it glittered where friction kept the Metrolink tracks shiny. Opposite the tracks, brick and timber walk-ups offered student housing. You couldn't tell from this stretch of road, but one of the best green spaces in the city was only a few hundred yards away. One summer, while they were still in college, North and Shaw had gone to Forest Park almost every day. They'd gone for pick-up games of frisbee golf. They'd gone on walks, and once, North had been ripping the seed-heavy heads off stalks of prairie grass, not even thinking about it, and Shaw had caught his hand and said something about how the grass probably didn't like that. They'd gone to see Shakespeare in the Park, and North had watched *Othello*, and it had been before Tucker had opened doors in North's life that North didn't even know existed—hadn't wanted to know existed. He had watched *Othello*, and he had wondered how a man could do those things to someone he loved.

"Not to complain," Shaw said, "because you know I love your shiatsu massages, but I think you might be pinching a nerve."

"Jesus." North relaxed his grip, stroking the skin where he had been clutching Shaw. "I'm sorry."

"It's ok."

"Kind of got in my own head."

"I think maybe that's the point."

"I know you think I need to see a therapist. I don't. I'm fine."

Shaw's breath sounded distinctly unhappy, but all he said was "I meant, I think distracting you is the point of this job. With Danny, I mean."

North grunted; he scratched lightly at Shaw's neck. The Metrolink tracks burned like fire, leaving blue-green tracers when he closed his eyes. He opened them again to brick and concrete and glass blocks. "We knew the job wasn't legit. Ronnie doesn't give two fucks about helping a guy track down his lost boyfriend. Under ordinary circumstances, I might believe that he's doing this so that Searls will owe him a favor down the road, but it's too close to the attempted break-in. He's working another angle. I bet if we dig a little deeper, we'll find out either Searls or Danny has something that Ronnie thinks will help him get closer to whatever he wants from Nonavie."

"I don't think so." Shaw shifted under his touch. "I mean, not completely. The job is bogus. But I think—I think Ronnie wants you to lose your head. I think he knew you'd find out that Searls was abusing Danny, and he wants you to do something stupid because you—"

"Because I what?"

The hum of tires answered. North dropped his hand and turned to look out the window. His eyes followed the powerlines, tracing their parabolas, something hypnotic about the swoop and fall and rise. Then he looked forward again, settling into the seat.

"Do you want to finish that thought?" he asked.

Shaw shook his head.

"Because if you think I can't do this job, if you think I'm so damaged that I can't handle this case—"

"That's not what I said."

"—then maybe I should take the stuff with Flip, and you can handle this shit with Danny. Since I'm a liability."

They went under an overpass. The shadows winged over Shaw's face. His eyes were tight. His jaw was tight.

"You're being a real jerk about this," he finally said.

"I'll talk about it with my therapist."

Shaw shook his head, and they finished the drive in silence.

The Nonavie lab looked like a repurposed warehouse, which is probably what it was, although North guessed that security hadn't been nearly so stringent when the low, concrete-block building had housed toaster ovens or children's shoes or industrial chemicals. A chain-link fence topped with razor-wire formed the first line of defense, and they had to stop at the gate to show their IDs and have their visit confirmed before they were waved through. The next checkpoint was at the building's main entrance, where their IDs were checked again. While they waited, North examined the doors and windows. Everything was reinforced—heavy metal doors, security glass—in a way that suggested nothing less than a tank was getting through there.

"Mr. Aldrich?" a heavyset woman in a lab coat called from where she stood, propping open a door that led deeper into the building. "Mr. McKinney? I'll walk you back."

She didn't give her name, and North didn't ask. His mind was full of other questions that seemed so much more important right then: why couldn't Shaw just keep his mouth shut sometimes? Why did he have to go around saying things that everybody already knew? Why couldn't he let the bad stuff stay buried? And this one kept popping up, the whack-a-mole question that North couldn't get rid of, why in the seven fucking hells was Shaw wearing a polo? Because there were no good answers, he made himself count cameras and motion sensors instead.

The inside of the building didn't match the outside. Inside, the building could have belonged to any other 21st-century corporation: lots of white, lots of chrome, better-quality fluorescent lights, carpet squares with dirt-masking geometric patterns. And the room where North and Shaw were led could have been any office anywhere, with catalogue furniture and neutral art prints and leather club chairs. The only difference was that in this room were two people who had recently become very important in North's life. One was his nominal boss, Haw Ryeo, who handled all their work for Aldrich Acquisitions. And the other was Shaw's father, Wilson Aldrich.

Wilson was a little shorter than Shaw, although that was probably due to age more than anything—he had to be past sixty. He had Shaw's build, too, wire thin, and with the same whipcord energy. His features were broad and strong, masculine without exactly being handsome. What most people noticed when they saw him, North decided, was the fashionable haircut, the Brooks Brothers suit, the Patek watch, and a man who knew how to wear them all well. Most people, North figured, probably didn't remember getting called on the carpet by this man when they were nineteen for drinking an entire bottle of fifty-year-old scotch and then puking it up in his best friend's bedroom.

"Wild," Wilson said, standing and setting aside a file so that he could wrap Shaw in a hug. He peppered kisses on the side of Shaw's face. "God, you're thin. Are you eating? North, is he eating?"

"He made me stop for two breakfast croissants on the way here," North said, but Wilson was already turning his attention back to Shaw.

"You know you don't have to do a speech, right? Your mother won't let it go about that speech, but you don't have to do one."

"I'll do a speech," Shaw said. "I've already got most of it."

Which North took to mean the paper lunch bag with mayonnaise stains that he had seen on Shaw's desk that morning. The paper bag on which Shaw had written, *My mother and father got married thirty years ago. Let's all congratulate them. Please do not drink all the Schlaflys at the open bar because those are North's favorite.*

"We can talk about it later," Wilson said. Then, turning, he stuck out his hand, his tone neutral as he said, "North."

"Hello, Mr. Aldrich. How are you?"

"We don't really have time for chitchat, North. This is a serious situation."

"But one which is completely under control," Haw said. She was petite, her hair buzzed to jarhead-approved length, and she passed a dry, callused hand to North first and then to Shaw. "As I told Mr. Aldrich earlier, this doesn't require his valuable time. I have complete confidence in my team and, of course, in the two of you."

"You may not require my time," Wilson said, "but you've got it anyway. Let's go over this and see what our experts suggest."

"We're really not security experts, Dad." Shaw stuffed his hands in his pockets. "We're investigators."

"A second set of eyes never hurt," was all Wilson said. "Haw?"

Haw didn't frown; the only expression, if it was one, was the tightness around her eyes. "I'll give you an overview, and then I can explain more if you have questions. Last week, someone tried to gain access to proprietary information. He almost succeeded. We'd like your help tracking down the person behind this and helping us figure out how he got as far as he did." With a glance at Wilson, she added, "And, of course, your feedback on improving security protocols would be most welcome."

Sure, North thought. About as welcome as a knee to the balls.

"What happened?" Shaw asked.

"A delivery driver made it all the way to Lab 14. That's our most secure lab. It should have been impossible."

"But he didn't get inside?" North asked.

"No. The biometric lock stopped him. The driver only made one attempt; after three failed attempts, an alarm sounds, and the building goes into lockdown. Apparently after realizing he wouldn't be able to get into the lab, the driver decided to leave. The only reason anyone knew anything was wrong was a lab tech saw him in an access-controlled hallway. He wasn't wearing a lab coat, so he definitely stood out. The tech waited too long to report it; by the time the guards were looking for him, he was gone. It's all on camera. While the truck is being unloaded, he walks through the rest of our security as though it wasn't even there."

Shaw threw a look at his father, but he directed his question to Haw. "What's in Lab 14?"

"That's proprietary information."

Wilson waved a hand. "Do you know what Humira is? The drug is actually called adalimumab, but people tend to know the brand name better."

"I've seen the commercials. It's a drug for psoriasis or something, right?"

"It's an immunosuppressive, a monoclonal antibody approved by the FDA. It treats an amazing range of conditions. It's also one of the highest-selling drugs in the world; in 2016, it generated sixteen billion dollars' worth of revenue."

"And you've got the next Humira in Lab 14," North said.

"Something like that. Maybe. If it's actually as effective in clinical trials as we hope. But that's a way off, and so for now, we've relied on a low profile and secrecy as the first line of defense."

"It doesn't seem like it's a secret anymore, though."

"Hence the security. And hence our concern. As Haw said, it should have been impossible for the delivery driver to penetrate our security as far as he did. But 'should have' isn't worth beans, as my grandfather used to say. He did penetrate our security. That's what matters."

"We've already begun an internal investigation," Haw said, picking up a folder from the desk. "And the guards who were monitoring our internal video feed have been fired. The human element is usually the most susceptible part of any security system. Typically, industrial espionage happens one of two ways: either someone is greedy enough to sell out, or they're stupid enough to get caught up in it without meaning to. So we're vetting—again—everyone who has biometric access to Lab 14. We want your help finding this man."

It was a high-definition color photograph of a squat, round man in a brown delivery uniform. The camera had caught him looking up, as though he were looking for the security system. There was no mistaking the goblinish face with its fringe of white hair.

"That's Ronnie."

"Who?" Haw said.

"You know him?" Wilson said.

"Yes," North said. "He's—"

"He's someone we've had to deal with in the past." Shaw caught North's eyes and gave a tiny shake of his head. "He's very dangerous."

"What's his full name?" Haw asked.

"I don't know." North shook his head. "I've tried to find out, and I haven't had any luck. For all I know, Ronnie isn't even his real name. That's just how I know him. I'll do some digging. I know some places he hangs around, although my guess is that he'll have gone underground until this blows over."

"Something is better than nothing," Haw said. "Make a list, and I'll see what I can do."

"I don't understand; aren't the computers password protected? What was he going to do once he got inside the lab?"

"The computers are secure, of course, but he doesn't necessarily need to access the computers. What he needs is a sample from the cold storage room; with that, it would be relatively straightforward for a competitor to sequence the gene already inserted into a high-yield production strain. All he has to do is secure it in a cryoflask with dry ice and walk out of here. Well, roll it out of here on a cart, but you get the idea. Stealing the production protocols that pertain to the strain would be an added bonus, but it's the genetic material that is the real prize."

Wilson drew an access card from his pocket. It was stamped with NONAVIE on one side and, on the other, the Aldrich Acquisitions logo. "In the meanwhile, I'd like you to do what you do best: figure out what's going on here and how this man almost managed to get into Lab 14. This card has the same permissions as mine and as Haw's; you'll have full access to this facility, even overriding the biometric locks. The staff have also been instructed to answer all your questions."

"I don't need to tell you," Haw said, "that what your father just gave you needs to be protected at all times."

"I understand," Shaw said.

"Do you have somewhere secure to store it? A safe would be my recommendation."

"We have a safe for the business; I can keep it in there."

"There's a clock running on this, Wild." Wilson squeezed his son's shoulder. "If there's a rat inside the lab, this man is going to try again before we can ferret him out. I need you to work fast."

"We will."

"I know you will."

North figured that *you* didn't include him.

"I can introduce you to a few people," Haw offered.

"You have a full day," Wilson said. "Go ahead. I'll introduce them to Campbell—he's head of security for this facility."

"Be in touch," Haw said with a warning look at North as she left.

"I'll let you boys get to work," Wilson said, "although I'd like a quick word with my son, North, if you don't mind."

"Not at all." No one moved or spoke, and a prickling flush worked its way up North's chest and throat. "Oh, right. Sorry."

He stepped out into the hall and pulled the door shut behind him. He considered moving down the hall, decided not to, and then heard Wilson's voice clearly even through the closed door. His last rational thought was that he should walk away.

"Have you given your mother's offer any consideration?"

Shaw's answer was muffled.

"I know that, Wild, but Imani's chapbook line is highly regarded. Your found poetry is excellent, and it deserves a home. You don't need to see this as a favor; your mother simply mentioned your poems to Imani and gave her a couple, and Imani was crazy about them."

Shaw spoke again, the words too quiet for North to make out.

"I don't know why you won't at least send her something," Wilson replied. "Let her make that decision. The only thing you have to do is show her your work."

The next moment was silent, and North recognized its texture: Shaw digging in his heels, the maddening obstinacy that lurked under the crystals and the hemp bracelets and the tie-dye jock straps.

"Consider it," Wilson finally said in what he probably hoped was an easygoing tone. "Now, Dean Noguchi will be at the anniversary party, and I want you to at least say hello. Good Lord, don't make faces, please; you're almost thirty years old. I think you'll hit it off, and then we're having the dean and her wife for dinner the week after next, and I want you to come." With a speed that suggested he was cutting off a familiar response, Wilson added, "As my son, of course. That's all. And because I think you'll like them."

This time when Shaw spoke, the words were distinct, a combination of the sharp edge that anger gave the words and an increase in volume. "I'm not going to grad school, Dad. And I'm not going to law school. I'm a private investigator. Borealis is my career; what don't you understand about that?"

"I understand perfectly well. You manage to throw that in your mother's face every time you see her, and do you have any idea who has to deal with the fallout after you're gone?" The silence was a knife's edge. In a softer voice, Wilson continued, "You're very good at your job, son. I'm proud of what you've done. So is your mother. And I know you love the work you're doing. But is this a job you'll still want to be doing in ten years? In twenty? I'm not just talking about getting bored, although we both know that's your Achilles' heel. You've chosen a job that's physically demanding. You've been hurt, seriously hurt, several times already. I know this is what you want right now, but you need to start thinking about your future."

Shaw's reply was too low for North to make out.

"I'm glad to hear it. But while North is a nice young man, I'm sure, he's not exactly functioning at your level."

North made himself walk away, but he heard both men laughing behind the door. He made it to the end of the hall. He cut around the corner. A mousy woman in a lab coat gaped at him, but North barely saw her. He leaned against the wall. Once, when he'd been nine or ten, Michael McCann had found a hornet's nest in the linden tree in his backyard, and Derek Cleary had gone at it with a branch, and after that, North remembered a series of still images, like his brain had lost the filmstrip version of his memories: the nest on the ground, split open, the quasi-honeycomb structure, the squirming white larvae; then, the first hornet stinging North; and then all of them running, chased by a cloud of wasps. He blew out a breath and wanted the American Spirits stashed in the GTO.

"There you are." Shaw and his dad stood at the intersection. "Are you all right? What happened?"

"Fine." North pushed away from the wall.

"You look—"

"I said I'm fine. We don't have a lot of time, so if we're going to talk to people today, we'd better get started."

Chapter 17

THEY WORKED AT THE Nonavie lab until classes ended at The Gouverneur Morris School, and then they drove south and west to the campus. Their interviews at the lab had been fruitful, although Shaw was pretty sure anyone could have put the pieces together—one of the security guards hadn't reported for his shift, and when they inspected his account activity, they found that he'd made an access card two weeks before. The card was unassigned to a specific staff member, which was against protocol, and it was given the highest level of access the guard was authorized to create. North had called Haw, who canceled the access card and promised to follow up and see if the guard had skipped town.

All of that was fine, as far as Shaw was concerned. What bothered him was North. North had been pale and quiet; when he did speak, he alternated between a flat, dead tone and biting mockery. It hadn't interfered with their work; it had just made the work absolutely no fun at all.

When they got to the school, they used an access road again and parked the Mercedes behind the health center. They hiked up the grassy slope, following a line parallel to the quad. True to Louis's description of her, they found Lauren behind the greenhouse smoking cheap, stinky weed inside the fenced nursery. At least, Shaw assumed this girl was Lauren. She was short and on the heavier side, and she was growing out a bad dye job—half her hair was still bottle blond, while the roots were dark brown. At the corner of one eye, she'd drawn a teardrop in black marker. She was sitting on the edge of a raised bed, where bare wire tomato cages waited for this year's planting. Trash littered the soil: cigarette butts, scraps of rolling paper, even a dusting of weed that must have fallen from the innumerable joints that had been rolled down here.

"Lauren?" North barked.

She jolted, but when she looked at them, her eyes were glassy and undisturbed.

"Are you Lauren?"

Blowing smoke out of the side of her mouth, she considered them. She stubbed out the joint. She stood. She slung a courier bag over one shoulder and only then seemed to realize they were blocking her way.

"I asked you a question," North said.

"Easy," Shaw whispered.

"Are you Lauren?"

"Who's asking?"

"I'm asking, and I'm going to take that as a yes. We're looking into Flip's disappearance. We heard you might know something about what happened to him."

After a moment, she shook her head slowly.

"How high are you?" North asked.

"Not high enough. Can you move? I've got to get to lacrosse."

"Bullshit. We're going to talk. Then you can go get stoned somewhere else while mommy and daddy put together your future in a nice little package. You can smoke your ass off, and in five years, you'll probably be running a Fortune 500. School can be a joke, and you'll waltz into Harvard or Yale, and hell, you won't have to worry about scholarships because mommy and daddy have got that all lined up too."

"North," Shaw whispered, touching North's arm, "ease up."

North jerked away. "But that's in the future. Right now, we're going to talk. Tell us about the fight with Flip."

The wind shifted, carrying the smell of cold soil and last year's leaves, the vegetable decay of a garden that needed cleaning out before new life could come in. Lauren dropped her bag, resumed her perch on the wooden frame, and lit her joint again. Exhaling, she held out the joint in a stream of smoke.

"I don't think—" Shaw began.

North grabbed the joint and took a serious toke. He held his breath; his eyes were watering, and now Shaw noticed that the hand holding the joint was shaking slightly. When he finally blew out the smoke, a patchy flush covered his cheeks, and he held out the joint to Shaw.

"No, thanks," Shaw managed to say, but he took the joint anyway and said, "Let's hold off on that until we're done talking."

"You guys blow," Lauren said. "This is lame. Can I go?"

"We just want to hear about the fight with Flip," Shaw said. "And anything else you can tell us that might help."

"He was being a dick. I called him out. He lost his shit and broke that desk."

"Really?" Shaw said. "You called him out, and he got so angry that he broke a piece of furniture in the middle of class?"

"You ever hear of anger management issues? His whole family is like that. Can I get a hit, please?"

"When we're done. How was he being a dick?"

"Don't remember."

"Everyone else has told us that Flip is basically the perfect guy. Now you're telling us he was being a dick that day. What did he do?"

Her eyes came alight, and her smile was nasty. "I want my joint back."

"That weed is shit," North said, a faint rasp to his voice now. "You should buy better."

"Fuck you."

"You're tough, huh? That's why you have a teardrop? You're the toughest shit this school has ever seen, is that about right?"

"Maybe you should let me handle this," Shaw said.

"Fuck you." Lauren stood again. "Fuck both of you."

"Cheap-ass weed, and a poser girl who thinks she's tough." North's smirk was hard enough to match Lauren's. "I knew you never sold to Flip. What a fucking waste of time."

Lauren shot out of her seat again, grabbed her backpack, and made a lunge for the joint. Shaw let her snatch it out of his hand. He waited for her to storm off, but instead, she stood there and took a long, defiant hit. When she'd cleared her lungs, she said, "I sold to Flip? Fuck, you'd better believe it. I sold that boy more shit than everybody else combined."

"Yeah," North said. "I bet all those ten bags really add up."

"It isn't just weed. He uses all sorts of shit when he wants to let loose. Oxy. Coke. Just last week he wanted—" She seemed to realize what she was saying because her jaw snapped shut.

"How does he pay? His parents cut him off, and before that, he had a credit card. Cheap-ass potheads who deal behind the school greenhouse don't take credit cards, do they?"

"I'm done."

"What kind of deal did you have going with Flip?"

"I said I'm done. Get out of my way."

"Who were those guys on campus? Who sells to you? What did Flip get himself into?"

"I don't know anything about that stuff. Get out of my way, or I'm going to scream!"

North opened his mouth, but Shaw gripped his arm, hard, and dragged him sideways. Lauren edged along the back of the greenhouse, not taking her gaze from them until she reached the end of the nursery. Then she turned and hurried down the hill, throwing backward glances as she went.

"What the hell?" North snapped. He tried to yank his arm free, but Shaw tightened his grip. "She was about to tell us—"

"She's a teenager, and you were terrifying her. It doesn't matter how tough she acts; she's a kid, North. We could have gotten a lot more out of her if you'd been patient."

"Oh boy. Sorry. I forgot; these are your people. Fuck me for not handling them with kid fucking gloves."

"Excuse me?"

"Get off me, Shaw."

"What does that mean, my people?"

With a surprisingly ferocious shove, North broke free and stalked toward the nursery's exit.

"North, God damn it." Shaw hurried after him. "What's going on with you?"

"She didn't head toward campus."

"She's not going to talk to us, North. She's scared, and she's pissed, and she's got a right to—"

"She's about to do something stupid. Either she's going to take us to whoever she buys from, and maybe that way we get a lead on the thugs who were roaming campus, maybe we figure out if they actually had anything to do with Flip disappearing. Or maybe it's something else." North's laugh was all jagged edges. "Maybe we'll get lucky and she'll take us straight to Flip."

They followed the hill in the same direction Lauren had gone. It took them back toward the health center. Lauren ducked inside the building; she had stopped looking back. North and Shaw separated, moving around the building in opposite directions so they could cover all four sides between the two of them. Shaw found an old oak to stand behind. When a troupe of teenage boys, shirtless and sweating in spite of the relative coolness of the day, jogged past, he held his breath. The last thing he needed was to get hauled in on a trespassing charge again. But the boys all looked exhausted, and none of them even glanced in Shaw's direction.

Seven minutes had passed according to the clock on Shaw's phone when Lauren emerged from a pair of red fire doors on the back of the health center. Shaw took out his phone and texted North: *I see her, but she's not going anywhere.*

Lauren paced for a few minutes, hands stuffed into her pockets. Then she dragged an overturned plastic bucket to the edge of the cement pad and sat. She sparked a joint and smoked it down, but her movements were restless and abrupt. Like someone angry, which Lauren had a right to be. Or someone afraid.

On the other side of the building, music blared—classic Kylie, pop that hadn't been pop for twenty years, and to judge by the girls' laughter that followed, something now enjoyed ironically. Keeping one eye on Lauren, Shaw drew out his phone and texted North: *She's still here.*

Five minutes later, North ambled into view. He came around the front of the health center, cutting a wide arc to approach Shaw without entering Lauren's field of vision. The volume of the music swelled and then Kylie cut off, replaced by Britney. "...Baby One More Time."

"They're playing our song," Shaw said, leaning into North.

North grunted and shifted a few inches away, until they were no longer touching.

"What is going on with you?"

"No talking; she'll hear us."

"She can't hear us. I could scream pi to the hundredth digit and she wouldn't hear us."

North's eyes narrowed. "No. Talking."

"Three point one—"

That was as far as he got before North clapped a hand over his mouth, his weight bearing Shaw against the tree, the heat of his body and the musk of the weed an explosion that detonated inside Shaw's chest. North gave him a surprisingly gentle shake, but his voice was hard as he whispered, "Why are you determined to drive me fucking crazy?"

Shaw raised one finger. After a moment, North peeled his hand away.

"Because," Shaw said, "you seem really unhappy, and I hate when you're unhappy, and you really enjoy yelling at me, and I like to provide a useful service."

Nothing.

Then North said, "That makes no sense. I don't like yelling at you."

"Sometimes you start smiling right in the middle of it. Like that time I was trying to sew a puppy-sized snuggie and you got mad because I cut up all your sweaters and then the puppy crawled out of the pile of sweater scraps and you made a little noise like it was the most adorable thing in the world."

"I didn't make a noise." North looked like he was struggling with himself before he burst out with "And it was fucking adorable, Shaw, so sue me."

They were silent for a moment, and then North kissed him on the cheek and stepped back. Shaw straightened and moved away from the tree, and then he slipped an arm around North's waist.

"What's wrong?" Shaw asked.

"Nothing. Just stuff. My stuff." Before Shaw could open his mouth, North added, "That I don't want to share or talk about or communicate or process."

"Oh."

"Yeah."

"But you know if you did want to…"

"Yes, I know. God, Shaw. How could I not know?"

On her plastic bucket, Lauren was rolling another joint, but she was having trouble. Twice she had to start over, and when she'd finished, it was lumpy and misshapen, and she made a sound of disgust that carried even over the volume and the excited screams from the other side of the building.

"What's going on over there?" Shaw asked.

"Cheer practice."

"This school doesn't have a cheer squad."

"I think it's a joke. Or an art installation. Or alien invaders who just want to ruin a national treasure."

"I don't think anyone has ever described Britney as a national treasure before." When North turned a flat stare on Shaw, Shaw added, "But of course, you're totally right."

Lauren stood, shoved the misshapen joint in a pocket and resumed pacing.

"Something doesn't feel right," Shaw said.

"I said I'm sorry. I told you, it's just my own stuff, and I'm dealing with it."

"No, I meant earlier. At the lab. Why would Ronnie be the one who tried to break in? Why not use someone else? Hire a professional thief? And the camera getting a perfect shot of his face—that seems impossible, right? I mean, it looked like he wasn't even trying to hide."

North made a considering noise.

"It just all seems so obvious," Shaw said. "I had an idea about security, and I was thinking about how banks strategize for robberies. Ink packs. Things like that. My dad thinks his IT people—"

Words erupted from North: "Your dad thinks. Your dad thinks. Who fucking cares what he thinks?"

Startled, Shaw glanced over; red stained North's cheeks.

"What's going on with you?" North demanded, rounding on Shaw. "You've never changed your clothes for your parents before. Never. One time you let your mom into the apartment with nothing but a sock hanging off your wiener."

It took Shaw a moment to catch up with the conversation's jink sideways. "What are you talking—"

Before he could finish, Lauren was on the move, and Shaw grabbed North's wrist and jerked his chin in her direction. Her stride was quick and determined as she set off down the hill again, heading straight into an overgrown wooded section of campus. North and Shaw waited until she'd passed the tree line, and then they set off after her.

"Called it," North said, his voice a facsimile of normalcy. "She's about to do something stupid."

Shaw debated pressing the issue and settled for "No one likes a told-you-so."

The swatch of trees and brush thinned in proportion to the growing sound of traffic, and less than five minutes later, Shaw pushed through a blossoming tangle of honeysuckle, the smell sickly sweet and the branches cool against his hands, and stumbled onto the littered verge of a two-lane road. North emerged a moment later, one of his Redwings catching a Monster can and sending it skittering onto the asphalt.

Traffic was steady but not exactly busy, and the cars that whipped past looked like standard-issue suburban gear: minivans and crossover SUVs and sedans, a lot of Fords and Toyotas. On the other side of the street, Lauren was crossing the parking lot of a shopping plaza. If she still thought she might be followed, she gave no sign of it; her attention was fixed on the line of urban farmhouse-style buildings ahead of her, with their corrugated metal roofing flashing in the May sun and their exposed timbers and verdigris weathervanes. The offerings were suburban-plus. A nut-milk only ice cream and smoothie shop. A pharmacy. A health food market. A yoga studio. Take-and-bake pizza.

But Lauren was cutting across the lot at an angle, not heading for any of the stores.

When the next break in the traffic came, Shaw sprinted across the street, North at his side. They reached the plaza just as Lauren disappeared around the side. The faint smell of fresh asphalt still hung in the air; it reminded Shaw of the constant repairs in the parking lots at Chouteau College, all the late summer days he'd jogged past freshly patched asphalt. Freshman year, before he'd decided alcohol didn't always agree with him, he'd had half a can of Natty Light, and he'd tripped over one of those patches and lain on the still-warm lot, laughing, while North tried to get him upright. He hadn't realized it until he'd sobered up, but he'd twisted his ankle badly, and North had spent the rest of the weekend taking care of him, disguised as bullying and yelling.

The clang of metal interrupted his thoughts. The sound came from the alley at the back of the shopping plaza, and Shaw thought he recognized it as a dumpster lid falling closed. He quickened his pace, North mirroring him, and they took the corner into the alley.

Lauren was walking toward them. She froze. Then she spun and took off running.

Shaw was about to launch after her, but North said, "Let her go."

With a sigh, Shaw nodded. "Whatever she came down here to get rid of, she already did it."

"So let's see what required a special trip to the Nuts About Milk dumpster."

As they moved to the closest dumpster, Shaw said, "I'm nuts about your milk."

"That sounds way too much like the first line in a squirrel-fetish porno."

"Squirrels don't drink milk. What about this one? Your nuts have the milk I need."

Grunting, North threw open the dumpster's lid. Then he laced his fingers together. Shaw stepped into the stirrup, balancing himself with one hand on the dumpster's rim, and North boosted him into the container. "You're getting fat."

"North!"

"You weigh seven ounces now. I could feel the strain when I lifted you."

"You're just losing muscle from all the time sitting in front of a computer."

"Fuck that."

"When was the last time you went to the gym?" Shaw asked, heaving aside a black garbage bag. A sour almond smell wafted up, and then a stronger wave of odor, years' worth of garbage runoff and bacterial growth. He rolled the first bag back into place and tried another. Wherever Lauren had been trying to get rid of, it would be near the top—she hadn't had time to bury it deep.

North was being suspiciously silent. When Shaw risked a look, a worry line had appeared between North's eyebrows.

"I have weights in my garage," North finally said.

"You told me it was too cold to work out in there during the winter. I'd try to remind you of the exact date by telling you it was the same night you had a second bowl of ice cream, but that's basically every night, so it wouldn't really help."

"Wow, Shaw."

"I know. I've begged you to cut back. I'm glad you're having this moment of realization, although I'm sure it's painful."

"What I'm realizing is that my boyfriend has been taking fucking master classes in stabbing me in the back."

"The truth hurts," Shaw said as he rolled aside another bag.

"They're small bowls!"

Shaw bit his lip and tried to keep his face serious.

"I've got a schedule," North was saying. "Back and biceps. Biceps and triceps. Legs and back. Legs and chest. Chest and back. I just got off my schedule."

With a small crow of triumph, Shaw spotted the wallet. He scooped it up—top-grain leather, hand stitched, and inside, a Missouri driver's license for Philip Chambers. There was more, but Shaw wanted to examine it with North, so he sat on the dumpster's rim, swung his legs over, and gave North a look.

Rolling his eyes, North caught him around the waist and helped him down.

"See?" Shaw said. "You're still very strong."

"Two bowls of ice cream my ass."

"That's exactly where they're going. North, what happened a few minutes ago between us? Back on campus, I mean."

North had the good grace to blush and look away. "Nothing. I just—your dad puts me on edge. I know he doesn't like me, and somehow that gets in my head. You're close with your parents, and I think that's awesome, but I can guess how they feel about us dating. Then you changed clothes, and your dad—" He cut off. When he spoke again, he was trying to smile. "I'm surprised your mom hasn't hauled me in for an interrogation."

Shaw's face felt stiff, his expression unnatural. He managed to say, "Good thing my parents don't get to decide who I date. And anyway, they like you."

North laughed, but it was too short and pitched too low for any real amusement. "No, Shaw, they don't. But it's ok. I just don't want it to mess up your relationship with them."

The only answer Shaw could think of was "Flip has a fake ID."

North's gaze focused on the wallet, and Shaw opened it again, extracting the driver's license and several reloadable debit cards.

"No cash," Shaw said.

"I'm guessing Lauren helped herself to that. If she were smart, she would have kept the reloadable cards too; it's not like those can be traced back to Flip. Why did Flip have a fake ID?"

"Drinking."

"Possibly, although it doesn't sound like they had any trouble getting what they needed for parties on campus. And what about the money?"

Shaw frowned and shook his head. "Celia said they'd cut Flip off, but obviously he was still getting money somehow. Maybe there's a relative? Or maybe his dad has been slipping him some cash on the side without Celia knowing?"

"We'll have to ask." North leaned closer. "What's the address on the license?"

"You know what my great-aunt does? She holds it out really far like this, and then she brings it in closer and moves it out farther until she can see it. That's only when she forgets her cheaters, which is almost always. Here, you try it."

North had murder in his eyes.

"Or we can run into the pharmacy. I bet they have cheaters."

"Give me the fucking license," North said.

"You're going to give yourself a headache with all this eye strain."

"My eyes are fine!" The shout echoed back from the alley walls, and North snatched the license from Shaw's hand. He peered at it. And then, with a challenging look sideways at Shaw, slowly moved it away from him. After a moment he passed it back and took out his phone.

"I bet we could get you contacts. Or a monocle!"

"That address is less than a mile from here."

"It's a fake ID. Wouldn't he just put a fake address on there?"

"Maybe. Maybe not. It depends on why he needed the fake ID. It's only a mile, and since you're wearing those ultra-comfortable penny loafers that your mom gave you last Christmas, you'll be fine."

"Well, they're actually not that comfortable because I've never worn them before. I only put them on because—"

North raised an eyebrow.

"Not because of my dad, if that's what you're thinking."

"That's an interesting thing to say."

"I only put them on because I had a vision from a former life this morning. While I was meditating. Something that has to do with penny loafers. So I took it as an omen and decided to wear them."

The explanation had been too long, and the silence after it, with North looking at him, was too vast.

"Maybe in your last incarnation," North finally said, "you were a penny loafer."

"Oh my God, I'll have to ask Master Hermes. That's probably exactly right. That's definitely what it was."

"Sometimes I wonder what guys with normal boyfriends talk about all day."

"Don't feel bad. I've always thought of you as a normal boyfriend, and I didn't fall in love with you because of your conversational verve."

North was still for a moment. Then he released an explosive breath, turned, and walked away.

"North, I'm sure there are lots of guys who talk about cheese as much as you do."

"Shut up!" he shouted over his shoulder.

The address was for a gray stucco walk-up, and although the street-facing side had received cosmetic upgrades sometime in the last ten years, the rest of the building looked like it hadn't been touched in decades. Most of the paint had flaked away from the railings, leaving rust trails that snaked down the metal and stained the concrete. The outdoor carpeting was spongy, although it hadn't rained for a couple of days, and the smell of mildew competed with an exhaust draft of bleach fumes from what Shaw guessed was the laundry. The doors looked like particleboard, and the windows had thin glass that shivered every time North took a step.

When they reached apartment 2F, North knocked, and the door swung open an inch. The air that wafted out was foul: piss and shit and a hint of decay. Shaw's brain immediately began its spider web of associations. Flip was dead. And Shaw pictured himself telling Celia Chittenden that her son was dead. And then he could imagine being Celia, hearing that her only son had been taken from her. He made the list he imagined she would make: she'd never see him walk across the stage at graduation; she'd never adjust his tie before his wedding; she'd never watch him hold his own child, and hope that he'd do better than she had, even while her heart was bursting with pride.

A warm hand cupping his face made Shaw take a wet breath. Ice-blue eyes held his.

"With me?" North asked.

Shaw nodded.

"Stay here. I don't want you to see this."

"I can do it."

A look of something—not pity, although that was Shaw's first guess, but something more complex and much more tender—flitted across North's face. All he said was "I know you can, but I don't want you to. Once you pick this shit up, you have a hard time putting it down. Just stay here."

"North, I can do this."

With a sigh, North elbowed open the door and called out, "Hello? Is anyone here?"

The gust of death and corruption made Shaw gag, and he pulled his polo up to cover his nose as he followed North into the apartment.

Part of Shaw's brain ramped up. The part that never turned off, the part that Dr. Farr told him had to do with unregulated empathy, that part was incandescent, filaments of imagination branching off: Celia's pain, Francis's grief, Flip's last moments alone before death.

He was so caught up in those thoughts that it took him a moment to realize that the body lying in the center of the apartment wasn't Flip. It was a girl. The heart-shaped face, the tight coils of hair, the too-thin arms and legs. It was Hiwet, the girl they had spoken to the night before, on the hill that looked down on the tennis courts.

"She's been shot," North said from where he crouched near the body. "Twice."

Chapter 18

THEY LOST THE REST of the day to the police: giving statements at the apartment, and then being carted off to the station to give their statements again. The hours dragged on. Shaw found himself wandering in a labyrinth of thoughts about Hiwet, trying to understand why she had been in an apartment that Flip had rented under a fake name, and then getting dragged down by the undercurrents of his own brain, lost in the pain and fear she must have felt at the end of her life. A moth was trapped behind the pebbled plastic cover of the light panel overhead. The fluorescent tubes fluttered in time with the trapped moth's wings, and the stretches of darkness got longer and longer.

"Shaw."

Shaw started. North was kneeling next to his chair, one hand on Shaw's arm, one hand on Shaw's knee. With a shaky grin, North smoothed Shaw's hair. Then he gave the bun a tug. "Hey."

"Hey."

"So, you're kind of freaking me out."

"Sorry."

"You don't need to be sorry. I just need to know if you're ok."

"I'm ok."

North was silent a moment. Then he held out a wad of tissues, and Shaw took them and touched his face, surprised to find that he'd been crying.

"Let's go home," North said.

"We're done?"

Nodding, North stood and helped Shaw to his feet. They made their way to the Mercedes, and North took the keys without asking and drove them back to the house in Benton Park. The south side of St. Louis was a post-industrial warscape of rusted rails and Quonset huts, shipping containers and abandoned pallets. All of it lay under the ashy haze of ancient discharge lamps.

When they pulled into the garage, Shaw said, "Do you mind if we don't do a sleepover tonight?"

"No, but I will point out that this is another reason why I wished we lived together. I don't want you to be by yourself tonight."

Shaw said nothing.

After a moment, North rubbed his eyes. "Are you sure you want to be alone?"

Shaw nodded.

"Let me rephrase that: I don't want you to be alone."

"I'm just tired, North. And I'm not going to be good company."

"You're always good company. I love you." North took a breath and braced himself with both hands on the steering wheel. "I don't know what to do. This world fucking sucks, and it hurts you, and it goes on hurting you, and I don't know how to stop it or make it better or keep you safe."

The smile felt wan on Shaw's face. "You can't keep me safe from life, North. I just need to figure out how to handle things better." He leaned across the car and kissed North. North caught the back of his head and kissed him again, deeper.

"I'm not going home, dumbass. Let's get inside and—"

He cut off; the sound of his phone vibrating filled the car. After a moment, he retrieved the phone, and Shaw watched as hatred stripped North's face down to the bones.

"He's just messing with you," Shaw said. "He's trying to get a reaction out of you. The best thing to do is just dismiss the call."

"Right," North said. The screen's glow washed out his face, highlighting sharp angles and leaving deep shadows.

"North, just dismiss the call. Or ignore him."

The phone made the decision for them and sent the call to voicemail.

Shaw let out a breath.

The phone began to buzz again.

"That little shit," North said.

"Hey, you know what, I think it would be a good idea if you came in and took care of me—"

"What?" North pressed the phone to his ear. "What the fuck do you want, you fucking asshole? Do you have any fucking idea what time it is? I'll talk to you however I want, you great big bleeding hemorrhoid. Hurry up and tell me what's so fucking important that you have to call me over and over again, when you know perfectly fucking well that we're not supposed to be talking."

When Shaw opened the car door, North glanced up, his face a furious mask, and held up a finger.

"Are you out of your fucking mind? What kind of fucking claim do you think you have on my half of Borealis?" Cutting laughter burst out of North, and he raised his voice. "No, you listen to me you bag of syphilitic dicks. You are not getting one fucking cent of Borealis—"

Shaw had heard this one before. He got out of the car, shut the door, and headed inside. As he was setting the deadbolt, he heard a savage scream from North, and he closed his eyes and let his head rest against the jamb. A few minutes later, he heard the GTO rumble to life, and then North was leaving, the engine growing fainter, and the garage door rattling down.

Upstairs, Shaw stripped and thought he could still smell Hiwet's loose bowels and the toner-and-burnt-coffee fetor of the police station. He showered, tied his hair back again, and crawled into bed naked.

He woke to the smell of Pari burning something in the toaster. Shaw flopped onto his back, took a deep breath, and began to cough. Sitting up, he blinked, trying to clear his stinging, watering eyes. For a disorienting moment, he thought he was crying again, and his first, clearest thought was that North would be upset, so he needed to stop crying. Then he realized that the room was full of smoke.

Adrenaline rushed through him, high-octane fuel for his brain, and he threw back the bedding. The floor was warm underfoot, bordering on hot, and his next breath brought another round of vicious coughing. Shaw dropped onto the superheated boards, crawled to a dresser, and pulled out the first things he could grab: a khaki short-sleeve button-up and unicorn-embroidered hot pants. Socks and fleece Chucks completed the outfit. Then he grabbed his phone and wallet, made sure the Aldrich Acquisitions access card was still tucked behind his credit cards, and crawled to the door that led to the back stairs. He touched the handle, which was hot, and fanned away the smoke boiling up at the bottom of the door.

Shaw reversed course and headed toward the front of the building. The house had originally been a duplex, with a top unit and a bottom unit, which meant it still had two front doors. Shaw rarely used the front door that led upstairs, preferring instead to come up through kitchen, but the door was perfectly functional. As he moved away from the bedroom, the haze of smoke thinned, and Shaw got to his feet and jogged down the hall. His lungs burned as he inhaled the hot, suspended particles of soot and tar, but he managed to avoid another coughing fit. He threw open the door, ran down the stairs, and turned the handle on the door that led out to the street.

The handle turned, but the door wouldn't open.

Shock paralyzed Shaw for a moment. He tried again, yanking on the handle, part of his brain telling him that maybe the door was just stuck. The handle turned easily, but when Shaw pulled, the door refused to budge. Wood groaned on the other side of the frame, and then Shaw understood: the door had been boarded shut.

Heat radiated through the drywall, and smoke wisped across the ceiling. Shaw gave the door one last tug and headed back upstairs. He wasn't sure if it was his imagination, but the stair treads felt like they gave slightly underfoot, as though the fire were already eating away at them. In a half-crouch, he jogged across the living room, cut into the bathroom, and shoved the window open. Cold, wet air—clean, with the tang of rust—rushed in off the fire escape. It smelled better than anything in Shaw's entire life. An animal hope reared its head. Escape. Away from the fire, away from the smoke, out into the dew and the night breeze. For a wild moment, Shaw wanted to laugh; it was a two-story building. Why the fuck did it have a fire escape? Then he was pulling himself up onto the sill.

A gun cracked, the sound audible even over the roar of the burning building. Splinters sprayed the side of Shaw's face. Blood ran down his temple, hot, stinking. He stumbled back from the window, tripped, and landed half in and half out of the tub. He lay there, back aching where the cast iron had caught him, and stared at the chunk of the window frame that a bullet had ripped out.

Someone was out there, his brain told him, as though enjoying stating the obvious. Someone was out there waiting to kill him if he tried to escape the fire.

After another stunned moment, Shaw dragged himself out of the tub and lay on the floor, eye to eye with a rubber ducky and a bottle of Mane 'n Tail. The tile might as well have been a griddle. No more gunshots. Nothing but the sound of the flames. How had no one noticed that his house was on fire? All the neighbors, all the traffic on Gravois. How had nobody noticed? Why wasn't anybody helping?

Hearing that note of helpless panic in his own thoughts made Shaw stop and draw in a sooty breath. He drew in two more, summoning the mantra that Master Hermes had revealed to him, counting his breaths like Dr. Farr had made him practice. And then he was back. He pulled the phone from his pocket and called 911. He gave his address, reported the fire, and warned of a gunman, and then he disconnected. He called North next. It rang until it went to voicemail. He called again, and he got voicemail again.

"Someone's set the house on fire," Shaw said. "They've got a gun, and I'm pinned down. Be careful."

As he was disconnecting, he had the brief but all-consuming thought that maybe North wasn't answering his phone because he had problems of his own. Fear locked Shaw in place for a heartbeat before he made himself start moving again; he couldn't do anything for North until he got himself out of this situation.

Army-crawling back into the hall, Shaw grimaced at the thicker pall of smoke that blanketed everything. Even on the floor, he had trouble getting enough air, and what he did get was too hot and too thin. His brain raced ahead, trying out possibilities. He couldn't go down the back stairs; the fire would only have gotten worse in the last few minutes, and he'd never make it out that way. He couldn't go down the fire escape without risking being shot. If worse came to worst, that's what Shaw would have to do—at least he'd have a chance if he moved fast. If he stayed here, he would die.

His brain kept running down the same dead-ends: the burning building, the boarded-up door, the shooter watching the fire escape. And then Shaw drew in another shallow, ashy breath, and dragged himself toward the bedroom.

The shooter. One shooter? Or two? Or three? Or a dozen? How many men did you send to murder a private investigator? Shaw's gut told him one. Maybe two, but one would be better because the more people involved, the messier it got. And of course the shooter would have chosen to watch the fire escape, to wait until Shaw tried to go through the window. It was the most reasonable exit.

But if there was only one shooter, then Shaw might be able to make it out another window. The only issue was getting down without breaking a leg.

Shaw got onto his knees and opened the window that looked out over the alley. This time, the air had a hint of garbage and the yeasty sourness of the brewery. No movement. Shaw stood. No gunshot. He sucked in a breath of the relatively clean air, sprinted across the room, and stripped the sheet from the bed. Back at the window, he tied one end of the sheet around a leg of the dresser. Then he flung the rest of the sheet out into the night. It wasn't nearly long enough—the sheet was probably ninety inches long, and some of that length had been used up in tying a knot. Shaw considered the remaining distance to the ground. He shoved the dresser closer to the window. Then he flipped the dresser so that the legs were up in the air. He gauged the distance again and figured he'd earned himself an extra foot of improvised rope.

He pulled himself up onto the sill, rolled onto his belly, and a frisson ran up his spine; if someone were going to shoot, now was the time. But no shot came. Shaw clutched the sheet and began to lower himself. His chin scraped against the sill. He scrabbled for purchase between the bricks with his Chucks, and the rubber soles offered a decent grip. Then he reached the end of the sheet.

The night air seemed much colder now, brushing bare skin where his shirt rode up. His feet swung in the emptiness. Shaw cast a final glance down. Shadows made it difficult to tell, but he guessed that there were still eight feet between the Chucks and the alley's brick pavement. He counted to three and let go.

When he hit the ground, the landing drove spiking pain through his feet and up into his knees. But a moment later, in the surge of adrenaline, he barely noticed. He could stand. He took a few steps. He could walk. He started down the alley; the heat of his burning home slapped him in the back.

Faintly, in the distance, sirens.

Headlights swung into view at the mouth of the alley, and then a car sped toward Shaw, bouncing on the uneven bricks. Shaw stumbled back, started to turn, and caught a hint of green. Springmist Green. Original color of the 1968 GTO.

Brakes squealing, the GTO skidded to a halt, and North stumbled out barefoot, in boxers and a Chouteau College tank top. He had the CZ in his hand, and he brought the pistol up as he sprinted around the car toward Shaw.

"I'm ok," Shaw said.

North caught his arm, yanked him toward the car, and shoved him into the passenger seat. A moment later, they were flying down the alley, and then out into the south side's warren of shadows and orange-gray vapor light.

Chapter 19

THEY SPENT THE NIGHT in a motel south of the city, on an abandoned frontage road outside of Arnold. The lamp shades were shaggy with dust, and the room smelled like cigarettes and microwaved lasagna, and the curtains were printed with Underdog, sun-faded until they looked like watercolors. On the all-purpose dresser and TV stand, someone had burned a meticulous pattern of circles from the tip of a cigarette to form the word C*NT; someone else had scratched out the U with a knife.

The hyper-alertness of the adrenaline gave out as soon as Shaw made it through the door, and he could barely keep his eyes open. He was vaguely aware of North undressing him, aware of the small sounds of discomfort he made when North popped off his Chucks, aware of North settling him in the bed and then pulling Shaw's legs across his lap so he could massage Shaw's aching feet and ankles. And then exhaustion hit, dragging Shaw down into something that was sleep, but restless and stalked by dreams.

He woke once in the night, the heat of the flames very real on his skin, smoke choking him, and then understood that the flames had been a dream. But this, too, this felt like a dream: a chink in the curtain; light from the highway dusting everything; North upright in a chair, the CZ on the table next to him. The smell of cigarette smoke in the small room seemed stronger. North's eyes had an icy glitter. It was all unreal, all of it, the slow swivel of North's head to take in Shaw, and the utter motionless of the rest of the universe, and the silence a hissing white noise like an ash cloud.

"Go back to sleep," North said in a stranger's voice.

And to Shaw's surprise, he did.

When he woke again, late morning light made its way through the gap in the curtains. On the other side of the thin door, North was talking on the phone.

"And I told you, we'll be in to make a fucking statement when we can get there. Someone tried to murder him last night. I'm not going to—don't fucking interrupt me!"

Shaw stumbled out of bed, wincing at the ache in his heels, and opened the door.

Phone to his ear, North scowled at him. "You're naked." Into the phone, he added, "For fuck's sake, of course I'm not talking to you."

"That explains why I'm chilly. Although maybe it's a good thing. Benjamin Franklin believed that air baths—"

"Shower. Now. I ran to the Dollar General this morning and picked up something for us to wear that doesn't smell like burned rayon."

Shaw tapped his lips.

Growling, North leaned in and pecked him once. Shaw turned for the tiny bathroom, and he was surprised by a slap to his ass. When he grinned over his shoulder, North just tried to make an even scarier face and shouted into the phone, "I don't know what you want me to say. We'll be there when we'll be there. If you don't have anything useful to tell me, quit wasting my fucking time."

Shaw shut himself in the bathroom, wondering if North had been trading conversational tips with Emery again. He ran the water and sat on the toilet while he waited for it to get hot. It only made it to lukewarm, so he unwrapped the silver-dollar-sized soap and stepped under the spray. He was working the bar across his shoulders when the door opened.

North stripped off the Chouteau tank with one hand and tossed it behind him. He hooked his thumbs in the boxers' waistband and hopped out of them. Then he stepped into the tub, his bigger body framing Shaw against the fiberglass panel. Water flecked his face, and North blinked into it. He ran his hands down Shaw's arms and settled them at his waist. Then he pulled Shaw against him in a crushing embrace. He was shaking, Shaw realized, and when Shaw rubbed his back, he pressed his face into Shaw's neck and shook harder.

The water was warm. North was warmer. And Shaw felt like with all this wet, slippery contact, he couldn't exactly be blamed for his reaction.

North chuckled against his neck and clutched him tighter.

"I like you," Shaw protested. "It's not my fault you came in here and got all slick and nakedy, and this shower definitely wasn't designed for two people, and sometimes I think you forget that you're kind of this giant, clodhopping oaf, and—oh sweet Jesus."

North, wordless, had slid down to his knees and taken Shaw in his mouth. He moved Shaw's hands to his hair. The straw-colored mess was dark with water, and when he looked up at Shaw, lips distended obscenely, his pupils were wide, shading his ice-blue eyes to the color of a storm.

In part, it was the reaction to near-death. In part, it was the unfamiliar setting. In part, it was simply because this arrangement was new for them. Shaw was slow at first, and then faster, and then rougher, until North gagged and coughed. When Shaw eased back, North pulled off, returned Shaw's hands to his hair, and said in a rough voice, "Did I tell you to stop?"

"Oh fuck," Shaw groaned.

He didn't last much longer. When the orgasm ripped through him, North cupped his ass and helped him stay upright. Then Shaw slid free, and North rocked forward, his head pressed against Shaw's belly. Shaw stroked his hair, the side of his face, tracing his ear and the bristle of golden stubble. North's face was an ember against the sensitive skin there. After what felt like a long time, he turned and kissed Shaw just below the navel and got to his feet.

"Can I—"

North gave a brusque shake of his head, elbowed Shaw aside, and said, "Give me the soap. And quit hogging the hot water."

They showered and dressed in the clothes that North had purchased from the Dollar General. The jeans were very, very blue. And the t-shirts were very, very white.

"I feel like I'm in a 1950s gang of ne'er-do-wells."

"Great. That's a step up from your usual look of 'I raided my hippie grandmother's lingerie drawer.'"

"My grandmother was a hippie," Shaw said.

North shook his head as he stepped into a pair of plasticky slides. "Why do people wear this shit? What's going to happen if something falls on my foot?"

"And I did raid her lingerie drawer. After she died, I mean."

"Stop talking before I have to break up with you."

They got breakfast and drove back into the city; at the station, people gave them plenty of looks, and more than a few amused grins, but it didn't take long before they were in separate interview rooms. They spent most of the rest of the day there. Shaw told his story to a fish-eyed detective who was mostly interested in the arson angle, and who seemed to think Shaw was hard up for money. Then Shaw told his story again. And again. And again. He told it once to Diamond and her partner, who shared a look but refused to answer any of his questions. And then Shaw had to tell it again.

At sunset, he found North sitting on the steps outside the station. "I've been trying to get in touch with Ronnie," he said when he saw Shaw. "But no dice. I wanted to give that murderous little troll warning before I tracked him down and killed him."

"Remember when we were at Rufus's party and I was telling everyone how you and I had looked at sex swings together, and you got really red and later you said sometimes certain conversations are better in some places than others?"

"It wasn't a party. It was his mother's wake."

"Maybe you shouldn't be talking about murdering Ronnie outside the police station."

North grunted. "I want that little fucker to know how much shit he's in for going after you. It's weird that he's been quiet this long; I thought we'd have heard from him by now, if only so the ghoul could double down on his threats."

"Forget about Ronnie," Shaw said, giving North a hand up. "We should probably call Pari. And Truck. And Zion. They're going to want to know they can't show up for work for the next little while."

"They already know." North looked wrecked; dark circles marred the fair skin under his eyes, and his gaze had a hollowed-out quality. He smelled like cigarettes. "Diamond sent a couple of uniformed officers to check out my place; we can go back there." His hesitation was so awkward that it was almost physically uncomfortable. "Unless you'd rather stay at your parents' place."

"What? No. I want to be with you."

A tired smile raised the corners of his mouth.

"So you can sit up all night with your gun."

"Jesus."

"And be all butch and protect me."

North turned and headed down the block.

"It was very inspiring."

"Stop talking."

"I composed eighteen erotic haikus about it."

"Please stop talking."

Instead, Shaw recited the first four erotic haikus on the drive home; he'd forgotten the others.

While Shaw tossed a rubber bone for the puppy and listened to voicemails from the insurance adjuster, North changed clothes. He was stepping into a pair of sweat shorts, the muscles in his back flexing, when his phone buzzed. He gave it a dirty look.

"If you ignore it, I'll let you order pizza."

"I'll order pizza if I want to order pizza, Shaw."

"I'll let you get the one with all the murdered animals."

"You know what it's called. You know perfectly fucking well. Meat-lover's. And you ate five slices last time."

"I'll let you—"

"It's Celia," North said, eyeing the flashing screen. He picked it up; his side of the conversation consisted of fewer than six words. When he lowered the phone, he looked even more tired than before. "We've been summoned again."

Chapter 20

AT NIGHT, THE Chittenden farmhouse reminded Shaw of turn-of-the-century phantasmagoria: the white clapboard was ghostly, pearlescent in the moonlight, shifting behind the windbreak of black haw. Moisture in the air refused to settle into either mist or dew, and it gave everything a warped, kaleidoscopic look. They parked, and when Shaw opened his door, the smell of spring onions and raw Midwestern humidity rolled over him. An owl hooted in the distance, and then cut off abruptly before branches crackled against each other in an explosion of movement.

"Fuck this," North said. "If I want the fucking haunted house experience, I'll go to Disney World."

"We could go right now," Shaw said. "I've got six different Disney World maximizer apps on my phone already, and my Donald Duck romper was at the cleaner, so it didn't get destroyed in the fire, which is kind of a miracle, North, right?"

"Why do I say anything?" North asked as they approached the door. "Why do I open my mouth at all?"

"Well, earlier, you opened your mouth because—my tit!" Shaw stumbled sideways, trying to rub out the sting of the titty-twister.

"Don't say tit."

"You can't—but you—"

"It's sexist."

"What's going on? What's happening? Who are you, and where is the real North?"

"I don't know," North said. "I haven't had any cheese today; maybe my body is shutting down."

Then he knocked, and Shaw decided the rest of this conversation might be one of those things North kept saying was better to save for private time.

Gavin the assistant opened the door. Behind him, darkness flooded the entry hall. The only light came from somewhere on the second floor, an oblong panel that illuminated one end of the landing with harsh, electric clarity. Where North and Shaw stood at the front door, the sanded pine boards had darkened to the color of honey, and the walls that last time had seemed the white of a tungsten filament were dingy now. Pigeon colored. The rest of the house dissolved into a void. Gavin's eyes drooped, and his coffee breath mixed with an overpowering blast of vanilla air freshener.

From beyond the second-floor kliegs came screaming: two voices, a man's and woman's.

"Mrs. Chittenden will be with you in a moment," Gavin said as he ushered them into the office.

"Tell her no rush," North said. "Make sure she rips his balls clean off; don't hurry on our account."

Gavin's face rippled with anger, and he rushed out of the room.

The office lay in shadow too. A single lamp on the desk provided light, and the objects that on their last visit had seemed middle-class banal—the milk pails, the shine jugs, the blue-enamel percolator—had been rendered down to blobs of shadow. Inside its red-felt display case, the revolver looked dull and leaden. Even the shiplap wall with its photographs had changed. The lamp threw a glare, turning the glass into mirrors that winked when Shaw moved. North took a seat; overhead, the screaming continued. The woman's voice, almost exclusively now. North stood again, hands in his jacket, and paced to the window.

Shaw tried counting his breaths. He hummed the first four bars of "Screaming Infidelities." He applied a transposition cipher to fragments of "I heard a Fly buzz—when I died" that he remembered. When the front door opened, he started, and he was weirdly relieved to see that he wasn't the only one who was jumpy: North's hand had gone to the CZ holstered under his arm.

Gavin's voice was a murmur, and then footsteps moved toward the office.

"—and I'm telling you, we can't just—" Detective Diamond Kelso cut off as she passed through the office's double doors and saw them.

"Yes, we absolutely can," her partner was saying. Raskowski was tucking her blond hair under a Cardinals cap and hadn't noticed them yet. "Pick them up, hold them for twenty-four hours, and let them go before we have to arraign them."

"Gee willikers, North," Shaw said. "That sounds like false imprisonment."

Raskowski stopped moving. Then, shoving the last of her hair under the cap, she raised her gaze to look at them.

Diamond let out a sigh. "Should have known you'd be here."

"Long time no see, Detective," North said. "I thought you and your partner had just about worn yourselves out trying to prove that Shaw burned down his own house. I figured you were due for some shut-eye."

"You need to take it down a level." Like her partner, she was dressed in jeans and a t-shirt, which made her larger build more obvious than in her tailored suits. She took a seat on the tan leather sofa, and after a moment, Raskowski joined her. "You know we have to ask those questions. You might be the first person who's lucky to have a killer trying to silence him, just because it gives you some sort of alibi. The arson squad got hard-ons just smelling all the accelerants around your place."

"Right," North drawled. "Shaw boarded up his own doors, crawled up the fire escape, fired a rifle at his window, and set the place on fire. Oh, and escaped out the back." Then he frowned. "You think whoever killed that girl came after Shaw?"

"Now they're going to try to twist everything around," Raskowski said.

"It seems pretty straightforward." Diamond's luminous golden eyes narrowed as she studied North. "You found that girl, and the same night, your partner almost gets murdered. Someone wants you to stop looking into this case. Did you think it was just a coincidence?"

North's face was painfully blank, and Shaw could practically hear him thinking about Ronnie, but all he said was "I didn't think it through, I guess."

In the silence that followed, something crashed upstairs. Raskowski flinched.

"Don't you want to check that they're ok?" Shaw asked.

Settling back onto the sofa, Diamond ran her hand along the cushion.

"She's a state senator," Raskowski said. "I'd like to get to my twenty."

The screaming picked up again, rising in intensity before another crash punctuated the harangue.

"What do you have on Hiwet?" North asked.

Raskowski shook her head, but Diamond glanced up at the escalating voices and said, "She was killed with a nine-millimeter. Two shots from close range. It looks like she was killed there; the blood spatter seems consistent, although that'll have to be checked."

"Any idea why she was in that apartment?"

"Or how she got there?" Shaw added.

"We can talk about this—" Raskowski began.

"It's either talk about it now or sit here and go crazy listening to that." Diamond flinched as a thud sounded above them, and the whole house seemed to shiver. "She had travel papers. Train tickets to Chicago, and then connecting on a bus to Bemidji."

"Minnesota?" North glanced at Shaw. "Why was she going to Minnesota?"

"No, they were for Philip Chambers, which matches the fake ID you found in that wallet."

"Shit. How the hell did she get her hands on those?"

"It's pretty obvious, isn't it?" Raskowski snapped. "She showed up. The kid was still there. She threatened to tell everyone he was running away. Grabbed his papers or something, said she wouldn't let him leave. He shot her and took off."

North didn't exactly roll his eyes, but it was close.

"Do you have any idea how she found out about that apartment?" Shaw asked again. "Or when she went there?"

"Her head of residence says Hiwet was in bed by curfew the night before; our best guess is that she snuck out and went to the apartment. She didn't show up for classes on Friday, and the school notified her parents, but apparently this was a semi-regular occurrence. From what we can tell, the girl's been on the move her whole life—her dad was some sort of bigwig in Eritrea twenty years ago, but he's been on the run since that girl was a baby. God only knows why." Diamond blew out a breath. "That's a long way of telling you that no one was particularly worried when she didn't show. We're not sure how she learned about the apartment. It doesn't seem to be common knowledge; you might think we just sat around waiting to talk to you about your house burning down, but we spent most of today talking to students and staff. If anybody knew about that place besides Hiwet, they're a grade-A liar—everyone we talked to swears they didn't know Philip had a fake ID, let alone an apartment, and I'm inclined to believe them."

"What about Lauren?" North dropped into one of the farmhouse chairs. "Have you hauled her in and pressed her? How did she get that wallet? She had to know about the apartment, right?"

Diamond pressed her lips together and looked away.

"Lauren," Raskowski said in a mocking tone, "is back with her parents in Vermont. Behind an army of lawyers."

"Jesus," North muttered.

"The most we could get out of her was a story about Flip dropping his wallet; she claims she picked it up and meant to return it to him, but then he disappeared."

"Convenient. But as soon as someone shows up to ask her about Flip, she runs and buries it in a dumpster."

Diamond gave an aggressive nod. "She swears she didn't know about the apartment; she assumed the address was a fake just like the name."

"She says," Raskowski said with that same mocking sneer, "you guys scared her, and that's why she threw it away. She says if the police had asked her about it, she would have turned it over immediately, but she thought she was in danger from you two."

"Bullshit." North slapped the arm of the chair. "That is fucking bullshit. She knew something was wrong, and she's tied up in it somehow."

"You think she had something to do with Hiwet?" Diamond asked.

"I think every time she opened her mouth, she was lying. Why would this bullshit be any different? She knows something about Hiwet; I'd bet on it. And I bet she knows a hell of a lot more about Flip than she's telling us."

"You can fly out to Vermont, then. Good luck."

"Fuck," North growled, pounding his fist on the chair again. "What about that fake ID? Did you get anything?"

"We're waiting on warrants to see if he has accounts in those names. As far as we can tell, he hasn't booked any flights, but—"

"That kid is dead," Raskowski said.

Diamond turned to look at her. North did too. Shaw couldn't turn away.

Raskowski shifted, playing with her ball cap and looking away. "He is. And you all know he is."

A door opened and slammed shut, a gunshot sound that made all four of them bolt upright. Heavy steps moved along the upper hallway, and then stairs creaked.

Celia's screams suddenly became audible. "—at least I'd have a husband with a functioning dick." The words grew clearer as she came closer to the entry hall. "I should have listened to my father when he told me not to marry the cockless wonder."

From where he stood, Shaw could see through the double doors into the entry hall's gloom. Francis raced across the floor, threw open the door, and plunged out into the night. The door hung open behind him; tendrils of damp chill and spring-onion smell worked their way into the house.

The next scream, when it came, sounded like Celia was standing just outside the office. The noise was guttural, animal, and it rose in pitch into a kind of insane rage. A moment later, something crashed—shattering ceramic and splintering wood. Then the only sound was ragged breathing.

"Jesus Christ," North whispered.

Footsteps. Celia, in another navy suit and sensible heels, clicked her way to the front door and shut it. Then she turned, staring into the office, her eyes skating over Shaw before fixing on an empty space in the middle distance. The only sign of her distress were two ruddy spots in her cheeks, barely noticeable in the shadows. She walked into the office, her stride smooth and unhurried, and Shaw fought the urge to step back, to grab North's hand, to dive out the window.

From her seat behind the desk, Celia leveled a look at each of them and then said, "You're fired."

The house creaked as it settled.

"Excuse me?" North said.

"You're fired. You're done. Send a final invoice; you can keep the balance of the retainer."

"Mrs. Chittenden, with all due respect—"

"Get out of my house."

"—we're the only ones who have made any progress in this investigation. We found an apartment that Flip has been renting, and we found a girl who has been murdered, and we—"

"I didn't hire you to find a dead girl," Celia said, her voice swelling again. "I hired you to find my son!" With what seemed like a masterful effort at self-control, she took several breaths. "I appreciate what you've done. I'll be sure to praise your efforts, and if you want to send a press kit to my assistant, I'll do what I can to publicize your—"

"For fuck's sake," North said, shooting to his feet. "We're the ones that blew this case open. We're the best in the area; you need us."

"As you pointed out, you found a girl who has been murdered. This is no longer trying to track down my runaway son. This is a police investigation; if Flip is in danger, which seems like a real possibility, I want the police to handle it."

"We—"

"North," Shaw said.

North's jaw clicked shut, and he headed for the sliding doors. Shaw followed him outside. He was pulling the front door shut when a hand caught it, and then Gavin slipped out of the house. He was crowding Shaw, the reek of coffee breath and now whiskey fumes making Shaw's eyes water.

"What?" North snapped.

"Don't even think about going to the press with this. Don't even think about it." He blinked, his eyes red and watering. "Don't even think about it. Don't even—don't even think—"

"For fuck's sake," North growled, planting a hand on Gavin's chest and shoving him into the door. He turned and headed down the porch steps.

Shaw cast a backward glance; Gavin was struggling to stay upright, the combination of North's shove and drink making him clutch the jamb for support.

"I will—" He tried the phrase a couple of times. "I will—I will—"

He was still trying to finish as North and Shaw made their way down the drive, and the half-formed threat unraveled behind them.

"This is the biggest fucking crock of horseshit I have ever seen," North said. "This is a fucking joke. That's what this is. A fucking travesty." He kicked a rock, and it whirred toward the house and thunked against the white clapboard. "This is—"

An ember flared ahead of them; Shaw caught North's wrist, and North went silent, his head snapping up.

"It's just me," came Francis's weary voice.

After a moment, Shaw and North moved forward again, but Shaw remembered their last visit, and Francis venting his rage with target practice. He remembered the revolver at Francis's hip.

Tonight, though, there was no revolver, no Stetson, no furious swagger— just a stooped man with the puffy, fleshy face of an alcoholic, his executive's haircut spilling over his forehead. Francis took a long drag off the joint he pinched between two fingers, and then he tilted his head back, holding his breath before a long exhalation. The wind slashed the smoke into ribbons, and then it was gone.

"Sorry about that. What you had to hear in there. Don't know why I'm the one apologizing, but I guess it takes two to argue."

"That sounded like more than an argument," North said.

Francis was still looking up; the night sky was black, the stars hazy through the blanket of wet Midwestern air. "My parents argued like that. In public. I'd be eight, nine, and we'd be in the middle of Sears, and they'd take out the knives and go to work on each other over the price of blue jeans or a power drill. I'd go down the fucking bike aisle and look at the bikes and pretend I was a normal kid with normal parents, just looking at bikes. I smell rubber these days and it gives me anxiety."

"Lavender is good for that," Shaw said. "You could carry around a little roller bottle of lavender and it would help a lot, I think."

The next toke was longer, and Francis coughed when he blew the smoke up at the stars and then wheezed as he tried to clear his lungs. After another long moment, he brought his head down and stared off at the wall of oak and pike, just a line of bristling shadows that marked a deeper edge of darkness. Wordlessly, he held out the joint.

"Maybe just to be polite," Shaw said.

North caught his fingers, squeezed gently, and asked, "Should you really be smoking that?"

"What are they going to do? Arrest me?" He laughed, which turned into another long drag, and then more coughing.

"Mr. Chittenden—"

"I'm going to ask you again. You never said yes, so I'm going to ask you again. If you find him, will you call me? Not her. Me." His eyes were bloodshot, but they were surprisingly intense as they fixed Shaw.

"We're no longer working this investigation," Shaw said.

"Your wife fired us."

"That fucking cunt. Pardon my language." He considered the joint, and then he squatted and butted it out against the glistening asphalt with a stoner's exaggerated movements. When he stood again, he looked at them. "She fired you?"

"That's right. She said this is a police investigation now because there's a murdered girl and Flip might be in danger."

"Flip." Something like an echo of a smile crossed his face. "I haven't called him that in years."

"We're sorry we couldn't find him," Shaw said. "But I think we should leave. And I think you should probably go back inside and see what the police need from you."

But Francis stood there, weaving slightly, the night breeze stirring his Jimmy Stewart hair. "She fired you because—" He stopped, seeming to catch himself. "A dead girl in the city, and we're paying two fag detectives to look for our son because the police can't do their job. Those are her words, by the way.

That's what she said to me. How's that going to look? How am I supposed to win this election if people think I don't support the police?"

"I don't think your wife would place the election above Flip's safety."

Francis's bloodshot stare didn't waver. In the distance, an engine rumbled, and lights swept past the Chittenden home, picking out the gravel shoulder of the road, flecks of quartz and mica, and then the car was gone, and they were standing alone under the bleary stars.

"Out here," Francis said slowly, "who do you think they're going to vote for? The high-powered woman whose husband works for the family business, the woman who boards her son at an expensive private school so she doesn't have to raise him herself, the woman who bails her son out of drug charges and has private investigators drive him to his weekly drug tests? Or the woman whose son disappeared tragically, the grieving mother who wants to go to Jeff City to fight for the rights of other mothers, help them keep their kids safe?"

"What are you saying, Mr. Chittenden?" North asked slowly.

"I'm saying dead kids get votes." He put one hand over his eyes, and his shoulders shook like he might be crying, but when he spoke again his voice was clear and even. "Spoiled brats don't."

"We need to go," North said. "Goodnight, Mr. Chittenden."

He shuffled away from the GTO. "You're not working the case. Fine. But if you think of something—anything—call me, would you? Don't—don't call her."

They backed down the drive. When they pulled out, just before the windbreak closed the house off again, he was still standing there, a charcoal smear against the perfect white house, watching them.

Chapter 21

THE BENTON PARK HOUSE was a burned-out shell: two of the brick walls still standing, the fire escape blackened and drooping like a burnt chicken wing, soot-stained rafters collapsing to drag the remaining asphalt shingles down and in. A ribbon of caution tape fluttered in the occasional eddy. The air smelled like fire, obliterating the normal aroma of hops and malt, but this wasn't a good, clean woodsmoke. This was the smell of a fire that had eaten through textiles, electronics, wiring, plaster, fiberglass insulation—a greasy, chemical residue to every breath that made North want to take a shower, even though it was barely eight, and the Sunday morning promised a perfect day.

Pari was crying softly; the bindi was a 90s shade of purple today. Truck was crying loudly. Hir huge shoulders went up and down with sobs, and Pari was holding hir as though ze were a child. Zion's dark eyes were dry, but he kept taking off his headband and retying it, and his gaze never settled anywhere long. Shaw, balanced on one tumbled-down wall, was picking through ash and debris. He held up a piece of wood that had been chewed by fire and considered it. Then he tossed it over his shoulder. The clatter of wood against brick startled Pari; the only other sound came from old Mrs. Romero, who was trying to clean ash from the gutter with a rake, the tines scraping against the concrete in shrill, rattling strokes.

"North!" Shaw stood up quickly, almost lost his balance, and windmilled to steady himself.

North picked a path across the rubble to join him.

"Emery survived!" Shaw held up the elbow-macaroni figurine. "Well, the part of him Celia didn't break. I think it's a sign."

"Is it a sign that he's such an unstoppable asshole that I'll never get him out of my life?"

But Shaw was staring at the pasta figurine. His eyes were dry. His face was clear. He was swimming in a gray Chouteau College hoodie that North had given him, sleeves cuffed to the elbow, and the too blue, too stiff jeans from the Dollar General. The pair of old Adidas were North's too. And North thought about all the caftans and tunics and peasant blouses and clogs, and he had to look down the street for a few breaths. He settled for fixing a glare on Mrs. Romero, that nosy bitch, who had given up all pretense with the rake and was now staring at them openly.

"Why don't we go visit them for a few days?" North said when he trusted his voice again. "Get away from this shit. You can hang out with your best friend Emery, and I'll get a motel room and practice drowning myself in a stranger's toilet, which would be moderately more fun than having to listen to him talk about the history of treacle or whatever the fuck he was going on about last time."

"The history of treacle-related tooth problems," Shaw said absently. Then, looking up, he said, "North, I don't think this was Ronnie."

The rake started up again, that high, metallic rasp. North balled up his hands and then worked the fingers open one at a time.

"I know you think he was behind this," Shaw said. "I know you think he tried to kill me to punish you for not doing what he said. But I think we have been doing what he said. We found Danny, right? And it's only been a couple of days. I think he meant for us to see him on the Nonavie cameras, but even if I'm wrong, why would he make a move against us so quickly? It doesn't add up."

"What are you saying? You think some stranger boarded up your door and tried to murder you for kicks?"

"No. I think Diamond was right: whoever killed Hiwet did this."

The words were a bucketful of cold water. "Why?"

"I think he's panicking."

"Or she."

Shaw's smile was tired. "Or she. They're panicking, whoever they are. I don't think Hiwet was supposed to die. She was collateral damage; maybe she figured out too much. But this is about Flip, and I don't think it's a coincidence that the night after we found Hiwet's body, someone tried to kill us."

"Tried to kill you."

"But I don't think they realized you weren't here. We're partners in just about every way that matters."

"Not bridge partners."

"Because you refuse to learn. I begged you to learn bridge. My mom's entire bridge club would simultaneously orgasm and die if we showed up to play."

"That's going to be in my nightmares," North muttered.

"My point is that whoever did this, I think they assumed we were both here. We were both supposed to die, and that would be the end of the investigation into Flip's disappearance."

"You're guessing."

"I'm intuiting."

North drew a breath and considered. "They'd have to be someone who didn't know us very well. They're operating on an assumption that we live together. They couldn't know your craptastic list of one million reasons it's better if we live separately for now."

"You're very set in your ways. You keep all those dairy toxins mingling with the non-poisonous food."

"Reason number six: Shaw needs a separate washer for when he needs to dye his pubic wigs."

"It just says wigs! Reason six didn't say anything pubic—" He cut off, jaw snapping shut.

"Let's say you're right." North glanced up and down the street—aside from Mrs. Romero and the Borealis employees, they were alone. "Let's say someone wanted us to stop looking into this. Is it a coincidence that, when we survived, the next thing the Chittendens did was fire us?"

Shaw wore a pained expression.

"They're shady as fuck, Shaw," North said. "I don't trust either of them, but at least Francis is upfront about his own agenda."

"Maybe."

"You didn't feel that weird vibe? That house, those people, it's like what the Donner party must have been like around dinner time?"

"I like when you talk about vibes. Did you feel when we drove over that ascendant ley line—North, come back, you're very spiritually sensitive when you're not polluting yourself with carnal pleasures."

"You were polluting yourself with carnal pleasures for fifteen minutes in the shower this morning," North shot back as he headed toward Pari, Truck, and Zion. "You left me zero fucking hot water."

"Are they always like this?" Zion said, riffling his tight curls.

"Sometimes they're worse," Pari said, still stroking Truck's back. "Sometimes they kiss."

"For the next few days, while we figure things out, we're going to have to ask you to be on leave," North said. "But we promise we're going to find a new place to work, and we're going to keep Borealis going."

"Paid leave," Shaw said.

"Well, I'm not sure—"

"Thank God," Pari said. "I told Truck you were going to try some neo-capitalist white privilege to get out of paying us."

"We're not," Shaw said.

"We're not," North said, "because you're not getting paid for a perfectly valid reason."

"Do you think it's a coincidence that both of the bosses are white?" Pari said. "And your employees are all people of color?"

"That's not—hold on—" North took a breath. "Shaw and I founded—"

Zion was smiling, just a tiny one, and ducking his head to hide it.

"Fuck all of you," North said as he stalked toward the car.

"Great speech, North," Truck called after him—the words only made worse by the one-hundred-percent sincerity behind them.

Zion was laughing.

When North looked back, Pari was smiling.

He turned forward and walked faster.

When Shaw slid into the passenger seat, North started the car, but he didn't shift. He looked over. "Are you ok?"

Shaw's eyes were still dry, but he sagged against the headrest. "Oh yeah. We're not letting this go, North. Someone murdered an innocent girl. Flip might be hurt. He might be dead too. We're going to get to the bottom of this."

North wove their fingers together, kissed the back of Shaw's hand, and pulled away from the curb.

Chapter 22

HIWET ZERAI HAD A room in Adams, which was yet another of the brick colonials that marched around the campus's quad. It had been an easy piece of information to find; she mentioned the residence frequently on her Instagram feed, which was public. With the GTO parked on the edge of campus, North rummaged through the trunk. He settled on a black windbreaker with the initials CST on the sleeves and back.

As he shrugged into it, Shaw said, "Sexy piano tuner?"

"What?"

"Last time you wore that, you were a sexy piano tuner. Conestoga and Sons Tuning. It was that lady who dressed up all her cats like Victorian princesses and you made me stay for the princess parade."

Closing the trunk lid, North said, "I have no idea what you're talking about."

"Yes, you do. She thought her neighbor had stolen one of her cats, and you were mad because I said you were prickly with clients sometimes, so you decided to bond with her, and you started talking about how one time your dad was sick and you had to take care of his cats and one fell asleep in your lap and you started thinking about your mom, and then you started crying and—"

"Ok, ok, ok. Yes. I have a vague recollection of that. Although I definitely didn't cry."

"You did. And it was very sweet. I would have given you an amazing handy, but we weren't dating then, and you probably wouldn't have wanted one. Well, you might have wanted one, because back then you actually had a sex drive unlike now. Actually, come to think of it, you used to be randy as a goat, so you definitely would have wanted one, like that time we shared a twin and you humped me all night, but Tucker might have objected."

North thought about running away. Alaska, maybe. He could work nine months of the year on a shrimping boat. There was no way Shaw could find him on a shrimping boat. Then, smoothing out the sleeve, he touched each letter in turn. "Crime Scene Technician."

"Cool. Sexy crime scene tech. That's a new one."

"It's not sexy. Not every costume is sexy."

"Of course they are; play to your strengths."

"I'm not some himbo who—what the fuck are you doing?"

Shaw was undoing the buttons of North's henley. Then he fluffed the blond hair visible where the collar parted. "Voila: sexy crime scene tech."

"Can we please do our jobs? Can we please be grown-ass men who just do our jobs?"

"Sure," Shaw said with a shrug. He gestured at North's shirt. "Do you want me to de-sex you—"

"No. We're not wasting any more time."

"It won't take any time. If you're uncomfortable being objectified, I want to make things right."

"It's fine. It looks fine, right?"

"You look fantastic. But I could have already done it with all the time we've spent—"

"Just leave it," North growled as he set off across campus. When he caught a glimpse of himself in the half-light of the Adams front door, though, he had to admit that the buttons had been a nice touch.

The access card that Celia had given them still worked, and in less than a minute they were inside. Red, white, and green streamers hung across the entry hall; a pudgy girl on a ladder was stringing red, white, and green letters onto a length of fishing line. HAPPY DRINKO DE MAYO. The air smelled like overheated hair dryers, wet fabric, and teeny bopper perfume.

"Could you point us to Hiwet's room?" North tapped his sleeve again. "Couple of follow-ups."

The girl pointed to the righthand hallway off the second-floor landing.

After a moment, when it seemed nothing more was forthcoming, North took the steps two at a time.

"Maybe I should have a windbreaker too," Shaw whispered.

"Be quiet."

"I'd go shirtless though. I think people like my nips."

"Dear baby Jesus, in your infinite manger, please deliver me to a shrimping boat."

"Wait, what?"

The hallway that the girl had directed them to held four doors: two on the left, and two on the right. It was obvious which belonged to Hiwet. Police caution tape formed an X across the door, which was closed. When North tested the handle, it was locked.

"Do your trick," he told Shaw.

"Oh, no, it actually takes some time to get all the beads up in there and I haven't prepped—"

In a strangled whisper, North managed to say, "Open this goddamn door."

"Oh. That's what you should have said then."

North couldn't be sure, but he thought the little shit was smiling as he flipped through the universal keys on his ring. The first one he tried worked, and to North's questioning look, Shaw said, "That's the same one that worked on that basement door in Washington."

"Good to know."

North nudged the door open and took in Hiwet's room. It was a disaster zone, but he guessed that was only because of the police search. Fingerprint powder covered almost every surface. Drawers hung open, clothes hanging out or dumped onto the floor. The mattress had been propped against one wall, and slivers of broken glass suggested that at some point, the people processing the scene hadn't been nearly as careful as they ought to have been.

Passing over a pair of disposable gloves, he asked, "Ready?"

Shaw nodded, and they began to search. The search was hampered by the fact that other people had already gone through the room, which meant that nothing was where Hiwet would have originally put it, which meant that details that might have been important had been erased. They worked in silence until someone cleared her throat at the door.

He didn't recognize the woman, but he put her age in the easy forties or the hard thirties, and that combined with the robe and slippers made him guess that this woman was the head of residence for Adams. She was white, carrying extra weight, with hair color that had come out of a box some industrious clerk had probably clearanced out.

"No one told me that you'd be working here again today," was her opening salvo.

"I'm sorry, Miss…"

"Oglevie. Layla Oglevie. I was very clear when I spoke to the detectives: the girls are already dealing with a lot, and I don't need strangers tramping through the residence. You scared poor Marnie to death."

North stood from where he'd been removing drawers from a built-in dresser and crossed to the doorway. He stood close but not too close, and he added a smile. "I'm sorry about that. Miscommunication. The liaison was supposed to call and let you know we were coming, but you know how bureaucracies are."

Layla Oglevie actually sniffed like the matron in a Dickensian boarding school. "I really wish you'd cleared this with me. The girls have planned a cultural celebration—"

Drinko de Mayo, North wanted to say.

"—and they're trying their hardest to put this horrible situation behind them."

"I want to apologize again. I'm really sorry." He leaned closer, inspecting an enamel pendant. "Is that a Dalmatian necklace?"

"Well, yes, but I don't see—"

"Tell me you've got one of those big lugs around here, please? Those were my favorite dogs growing up; I'm saving up for a house so I can get one of my own."

"Well, no. We're not allowed to have pets, which is something of a relief because I'm still in counseling about Pongo's death."

"Pongo like, *101 Dalmatians*?" North set his smile to endearingly sad. "God, break my heart, why don't you?"

"Hey," Shaw barked. "We've got work to do."

"Sorry," North said quietly. "My boss is a real hard-ass."

Layla offered a sniff in Shaw's direction. "Please have one of those detectives contact me about any future disturbances. We really have to think about the girls, you know."

"I know. And I'm really sorry."

But Layla hesitated in the doorway. "If you'd like," she drew the words out, "I could tell you a bit more about what to look for in a Dalmatian. I have some books in my apartment I could—"

"Nordyke," Shaw snapped. "Get your ass back to work."

"Well, really."

"Sorry," North mouthed, and then, before he got abducted into a Dalmatian date, he smiled and closed the door.

Shaw had the good grace to wait until the woman's footsteps had faded before repeating North's words: "God, break my heart, why don't you?"

"Shut up."

"You should have twirled your hair."

"Someone had to handle her, and you were too busy picking lint out of your crack."

"You should have giggled."

North decided ignoring him was the best policy and returned to the built-in dresser.

Undeterred, Shaw came across the room. "You should have—" He humped the air. "—you know, really given her the business."

"You're going to be lucky if you ever get the business again if you don't cut the shit," North said, and when Shaw tried to hump him, he laughed and shoved him away.

Shaw had to ham it up, of course, which meant he ended up crashing into the mattress, which immediately fell on top of him.

"Serves you right," North said. "Stay there."

But when Shaw crawled out from under the mattress, he said, "We're missing something."

"You're missing some critical brain cells. That's what you're missing."

Shaw didn't rise to the bait, though. He was looking around the room. "She found out about the apartment Flip was renting. She had his travel plans. She went there. And she was enough of a threat that someone had to kill her."

"She said she was good at digging up people's secrets," North said. "Maybe that makes sense. She spent her life with her parents on the run, hopping from school to school. She must have known from a young age that secrets could be very powerful. I don't understand, though; why kill her?"

"Because she was a threat or an obstacle. Or both."

"She showed up at that apartment. She had his travel info. But if Flip was just running away, why add a murder charge to it? Why not change your travel plans? Why not do anything except shoot someone twice?"

"That's assuming Flip ran away."

"You think he's dead?"

Righting the mattress, Shaw said, "I think he could be. Or he could have been abducted, and the kidnappers didn't expect this much public attention. In either case, someone would have a reason for getting rid of Hiwet, and the travel papers might have been a misdirect."

After several moments, North finally said, "Maybe. So we've got a girl who's always on the move and who likes secrets. So where does she keep those secrets? On her phone? If so, we're screwed; the police must have it by now."

"She'd definitely have them on her phone. But I think she'd have them somewhere else too. Backup. This is a girl who's had her life change drastically with little warning—getting uprooted every time her parents have to run again. She's probably had to ditch her phone before. More than once, I'd guess. That means she's got something else."

"I don't see a computer."

"Police probably took her laptop too."

"She liked secrets," North said, glancing at the closet. "Maybe she hid stuff in the secret passage."

"Secret passage is a tad dramatic."

"This from the guy who put on an eight-minute pom-pom routine to celebrate the first time I bought him hot chocolate."

"The anniversary of the first time you bought me hot chocolate," Shaw corrected, opening the closet door. "It was a very important date."

The clothes had been pulled from the hangers, and the top shelf was empty, but Shaw didn't see any sign that the search had extended to the removable panel. When Shaw got his fingers under the edges and pulled, the false back came loose easily, which suggested regular use. He passed the panel to North, turned on the flashlight on his phone, and played it back and forth. The cavity between the rooms was about ten inches—deeper than the thickness of a modern wall, but too small for most teenagers or adults. Shaw pressed lightly on the panel on the other side of the cavity, but it seemed stuck; Hiwet must not have used the passage to sneak between rooms. Or perhaps her neighbor had decided to block the false back of her own closet.

Running the light up and down, Shaw inspected the rest of the cavity. Mouse droppings and dust formed the major elements of the scene.

"Well?" North said.

"Oh, she's got a whole evil genius's lair set up back here. Computers, ICBMs, sharks with lasers on their heads—ow!"

The kick caught Shaw right in the ass, and he rocked forward, knocking his head against the opposite panel.

"Sorry," North said in a syrupy voice. "Tripped."

Shaw ran his hand along the studs, searching by feel, and on his way back, he slid his fingers along the header. Dust furred up under his touch, but he got nothing.

Until plastic crinkled under his fingers.

He pulled out the bag, extricated himself from the closet, and held his discovery up to the light.

"Molly," North said.

"She liked to party. That's what everyone told us. I guess this is proof."

"Fuck. Another dead end."

"Asking for a friend," Shaw said, "but do you have to tell the police if you find—"

"Give me that." North shoved the bag into his back pocket. "That is the last fucking thing I need. Jesus Christ. All right. We'll have to try another angle. We talk to the students again. We check out her social media feed. We still haven't caught up with that sketch-as-shit teacher, and we probably need to run down the head of school and figure out what game she's playing."

While North continued to ramble through their options, Shaw studied the room again. He was trying to figure out what he'd missed. Hiwet was a girl who'd been on the move. Hiwet was a girl who hadn't trusted easily. She must have learned early on not to feel too comfortable anywhere. Never get too settled. She needed to be ready to go at a moment's notice. Shaw's pulse quickened. Yes, that seemed right. She needed to be ready to run whenever trouble—whatever the trouble was—caught up with her family again. So she'd be ready. She'd have a plan. She'd have—

"What do they call those bags? The survival guys have them. Like a 72-hour kit, only extreme?"

"Bug-out bags. I'm surprised you have to ask; your best friend," the scorn in the words was audible, "Emery Hazard sent you a fourteen-page list of what you need to pack in yours."

"Like my *HMS Pinafore* still-in-the-original-packaging action figures."

"They're called dolls when they're designed for little Victorian girls. Also, no, not like that at all."

Shaw sensed a fun argument, the kind that he could spend all day using to push North's buttons, but he decided to let it slip because his brain was caught on something else. A bug-out bag. Hiwet would have had something like that, although not the way most people imagined it. Something she could grab if trouble came and she had to flee in the night. Something with everything that was most important to her.

But the only bag in the room was the backpack Shaw had seen her carrying the night they'd met above the tennis courts. He studied it again. It was simple, although clearly high quality, and designed not to draw too much attention. He dropped into a squat. On the outside, the only thing of note was the three-pack of tennis balls, still secured in the elastic pouch intended for a water bottle. Shaw worked the zipper open. Notebooks. He flipped through them, saw nothing of interest, and shut them again before North decided Shaw's life really wouldn't be complete until he understood the joys of logarithms. Loose scraps of paper, something with scribbles that might have passed as class notes. Crumpled foil wrappers that still smelled like Big Red gum. A hairbrush. The laptop compartment was empty, and Shaw's heart fell; if there had been anything valuable in this bag, it was gone. Someone had beaten him to it.

"—start with that teacher," North was saying. "Come on; I bet we can catch him at home."

"She didn't play tennis."

"What?"

Shaw hadn't understood why his gaze was fixed on the tennis balls until he said the words again, more slowly. "She told us she didn't play tennis. I asked her because of the tennis balls and because they were sitting on the hill overlooking the courts, but she told us no, she didn't play."

"So why does she have tennis balls?" North asked.

Working the tube free from the pouch, Shaw popped the lid off. Then he dumped the balls out. He heard something rattle, and he picked the balls up one by one. He heard the same noise again and squeezed the tennis ball in his hand. A slit appeared in the green felt. When Shaw turned the ball over his cupped hand, a flash drive tumbled out.

"Shit," North whispered. In a slightly stronger voice, he said, "I knew I liked you for some reason."

Grinning, Shaw wagged the flash drive at him. "Want to see what Hiwet was hiding?"

Their own computers had been back at the office, and the office was now a pile of charred timbers, so they stopped at the head of residence's apartment. Layla Oglevie answered the door, clutching the neck of her robe. A smile started on her face and then stopped when she noticed Shaw.

"May I help you?"

"We need to borrow your computer," North said with an apologetic look. "I'm afraid we don't have time to go back to the station."

"I suppose—"

But North was already pressing his way into the room, and Shaw tagged after him. In only took a matter of minutes to get settled in Layla's kitchen, which was crammed with Dalmatian-themed paraphernalia: a Dalmatian clock ticking softly on the wall; Dalmatian salt and pepper shakers (a little on the nose, Shaw thought); a Dalmatian table runner; a drooping silk floral arrangement in a massive ceramic dish patterned with Dalmatians, and which looked like it might originally have been intended as a water bowl for dogs. Layla made a few matronly noises at being ejected from her own home, but by then North had booted up the computer.

As soon as they had privacy, North inserted the flash drive. He whistled as he scanned the contents. "There are hundreds of files here."

Some were images, and from the thumbnail previews, Shaw could tell that they were scanned documents. Others were clearly compromising photographs. Each file was named with a string of letters and numbers that made no sense to Shaw.

"She's got them encoded. Damn it, I have no idea how long this is going to take."

"She's got the names encoded," North said, "but the files aren't encrypted. All we have to do is sort by date and, boom. Let's see what Hiwet has been working on recently."

The file was from the Saturday before Flip had disappeared. It was a video file, and when North clicked it, Shaw couldn't help himself: he let out a gasp.

On screen, two young men were having a hard, furious fuck. They were in a bland room: a bed, a window with the blinds down, nothing distinctive that might help someone identify where the video had been filmed. Shaw recognized it as Flip's secret apartment, where Hiwet had been killed. One of the young men was Flip Chittenden. He lay on his back, his ankles hooked over the other young man's shoulders. His face was red. His eyes were glazed. Baked, Shaw guessed, and that guess was confirmed a moment later when the other young man took a long toke, bent, and shotgunned the smoke into Flip's mouth, all without altering the breakneck pace of his thrusts.

The first problem was that the second young man, the top, wore a Spider-Man mask. Shaw looked for identifying marks, but he came up empty. The man must have been close to Flip's age, although it was hard to tell exactly without seeing his face. He was muscular, with skin that was either a light brown or a dark tan. Dark pubes. Pits shaved. And, although Shaw couldn't have explained exactly why, something about the way he fucked suggested an immense fury—a rage whose only outlet existed in punishing Flip through sex. Stoned out of his gourd, Flip just moaned and bounced and sucked in more of the shotgunned weed.

The second problem was the watermark at the bottom of the screen: MyFans.

North's voice sounded raw as he said, "It's a private porn site. Indie porn, if you want to call it that. Whoever was selling this must have been making a shitload. Jesus Christ, it's like he wants to hurt him."

Shaw stopped the video. They tried the rest of the most recent files; they had all been downloaded over the space of several hours on the same day, and the conclusion was obvious: the Saturday before Flip disappeared, Hiwet had discovered these videos and downloaded them one by one. In all of the videos, Flip appeared with the same partner, although the masks changed: sometimes he was Batman; sometimes he was a dinosaur; once he was a unicorn. In every video, Flip's face was exposed, and in most of them he was on something— probably several somethings, weed being the least worrisome.

North's face was troubled.

"What?" Shaw asked.

But North just shook his head.

Collecting the flash drive, Shaw shut down the laptop. "Let's go talk to Louis."

"Maybe he wants to reconsider his fucking sob story," North said as they passed a three-quarters-sized Dalmatian statue that was staring at them, "about being the only gay boy at this school."

Chapter 23

WHEN THEY LEFT ADAMS, it was late morning, and kids covered the quad. Many of them seemed to be doing nothing in particular; it was a Sunday, and the day was warm without being hot, with puffy clouds hanging low overhead. The perfect day to relax outside after months of being cooped up. Shaw turned his face to the sun as they walked, taking deep breaths of air that smelled like new clover and the mixture of perfume and vegetable decay—the last of the redbud blossoms, most of them already papering the sidewalk, nature's version of the hangover morning after a parade.

"Kishor," North said in a warning voice.

Shaw checked the direction North was looking. Kishor stood on the opposite corner of the quad, his handsome face alive with a smile as he talked to a group of boys—judging by their size, they had to have been first-years, which made them fourteen and fifteen at the oldest. Kishor wore a Manchester United jersey and white mesh shorts that barely passed his crotch; the jersey showed off his developed shoulders and arms, and the shorts left bare a couple of miles of thickly muscled brown legs. One of the boys was juggling a soccer ball, and when Kishor said something, the whole group dissolved into laughs. Kishor smirked at their response, tugging on his crotch, his gaze sweeping the area before coming back to fix the boys with another killer smile.

"Are you seeing what I'm seeing?" North asked.

"I don't know what I'm seeing. I don't have enough information."

"Bullshit."

Shaw didn't have a good reply to that because if he were honest, he was pretty sure he knew exactly what he was seeing.

"That's the same piece of shit who was stealing Flip's clothes to sell. Or to jerk off into. Who the fuck knows?"

"Let's walk faster; he's looked over this way twice, and I don't want him to notice us."

They looped around Washington, and their access card opened the back door for them. Inside, the house smelled like overcooked eggs and, of course, teen feet. Someone was playing music—The Smiths, God bless that retro emo boy's heart—but the music was muffled and distant, and otherwise, the house was silent. A chore chart, held on the fridge by a magnet shaped like a pickle, was organized by floors. Louis was listed on the second-floor roster.

Shaw took the lead on the servants' stairs, and they climbed to the second floor. The music was even quieter up here, almost inaudible, and no other sound reached Shaw. Most of the doors were unlocked; those that weren't opened to the same key he'd used in the basement. They worked their way down the hall, checking each room briefly until they found Louis's.

"He didn't exactly hide it, did he?" North said with a meaningful glance at the massive Tom Daley poster. The diver was naked except for a pair of glasses in chunky black frames and a towel that was approximately the size of a Kleenex held in front of his crotch. Similar posters of male swimmers and divers, their incredibly defined musculature fully on display, covered the other walls.

"Keep calm and jerk off," Shaw suggested as they began to toss the room.

North was the one to score this time: behind the removable panel in the closet, North found two massive black garbage bags. One was full of trash, although as North pawed through it, Shaw could see that it consisted exclusively of candy bar wrappers, the little paper trays that snack cakes came on, and crumpled bags that had once held potato chips. Lay's Cheddar and Sour Cream seemed to be a particular favorite. The other bag, less full, contained junk food still in its packaging. The relationship between the two was obvious. What wasn't obvious to Shaw was why a teenage boy with a high metabolism and a demanding sport was caching food and trash. No answer came, and they resumed their search.

"What the hell is going on here?"

Shaw, currently rooting around under the bed, sat up so fast his head hit the frame. By the time he had wormed his way free and turned around, Louis was standing inside the room.

"I asked you a question," Louis said. "What the fuck is going on?"

"Good, you're here," North said. "We wanted to talk to you."

"No, you didn't. You wanted to go through my stuff. I'm calling the police."

"Call them. And call your dad. And we'll all sit down, and you can tell us about the first time you stuck a finger down your throat to make yourself puke."

The transformation in Louis's face was instantaneous: his expression screwed up into fury, and he launched himself at North. Shaw scrambled to his feet, but he was too slow. Louis closed the distance, swung, and missed. His momentum carried him too far. North grabbed his arm, turned into Louis's movement, and slammed him into the closet door. The thud echoed through the room, and Louis's breath exploded from his lungs. North pulled the teen's arm up behind his back until his fingers were almost between his shoulder blades. Louis let out another sharp breath and twisted, and North grabbed Louis's collar with his free hand and slammed the kid into the closet door again.

"Calm down," North barked.

Louis bucked and thrashed. "I'm going to kill you, I'm going to kill—"

This time, North's hand moved up to his hair, and he cracked Louis's head against the door. "Calm the fuck down before you hurt yourself."

It might have been the words, but Shaw guessed it was the blow to the head that quieted Louis. He sagged in North's grip, his breathing frantic and ragged.

"If I let you go, are you gonna be smart?"

"He will," Shaw said. "He'll be smart." Elbowing North out of the way—and, in the process, forcing, North to release his hold on Louis's wrist—Shaw said, "That's right, isn't it, Louis?"

Louis brought his arm down, flexing it once as though testing it, and then turned slowly. A red mark on his cheek showed where he had made contact with the door. His eyes were wet, but the expression in his face was still a trembling fury.

"Let's sit down," Shaw said, not really thinking about what he was saying, just slipping into the kind of patter that worked most of the time in these situations. "Come on, let's sit down on your bed. Good job. Yep, I'm just going to hold your elbow because you hit your head pretty hard. You're doing so great. Ok. Hey, look at that. Perfect."

Perched on the edge of the bed, Louis stared at North, every muscle in his body drawn wire tight. North stared back from where he slouched against the wall.

"Don't worry about him," Shaw said. "Forget about what he said. He doesn't know what he's talking about. He's just taking out his own body issues on you. He's got a thing with his feet."

"I do not."

"It's why he wears those big boots."

"Thin ice for a guy who spent two weeks clip-clopping around in unicorn fetish hooves."

Louis's gaze still transfixed North; he was quivering, and Shaw guessed he was about five seconds away from standing and starting the whole thing again.

"Tell me everything you know about planetary harmonics," Shaw announced.

That was enough to make Louis throw a quick look at Shaw.

Shaw caught his eye, nodded, and said, "Planetary harmonics?"

After a moment, Louis shrugged.

"Planetary harmonics," Shaw said, "basically refers to this amazing fact that planets are like strings in a cosmic guitar. Or something like that."

"I'm getting a real Eric Clapton vibe right now," North muttered. "Stairway to Heaven."

"Only so much gayer," Shaw said. "Like if God were an enormous gay Eric Claptop. That's exactly right."

"Clapton," Louis corrected in a murmur, a tiny smile touching his lips. Up close, his breath was minty, but with a hint of halitosis underneath. "Planets aren't strings, though. And the universe isn't a guitar."

"No, I just say that because one time North tried to learn guitar, and he painted his nails black, and he spent an entire weekend writing these incredibly bleak thrasher love songs."

"Louis, you're free to go," North said, straightening out of his slouch. "I'm going to murder my boyfriend now."

"But music, at least at a physical level, really just means the vibrations of mechanical systems, so anything that vibrates at the right frequency is also emitting a musical note. And planets vibrate. And they're in harmony. So basically whenever you feel bad, you can remember that the universe is singing you a love song, even if you can't hear it."

"Maybe it's a hate song," Louis said, and then he wiped his eyes. In a thick voice, with a smile skimming across his expression, he managed to add, "Maybe it's a thrasher hate song."

North groaned.

"It's not," Shaw said. "God is love. And the universe is love. And the whole reason I told you is because you seem really upset, and I thought maybe it would help you to hum an A. Or maybe an A-sharp."

Louis wiped his eyes again, but the tears were coming faster. "Why an A-sharp?"

"Because that's Jupiter's note, and Jupiter is the most calming of the planets."

Even on the brink of weeping, Louis managed to deliver the perfect teen look of scorn.

"You might as well do it," North said. "He'll just keep bothering you until you do. Like the time he wanted to paint my fingernails black."

"Don't listen to him," Shaw said. "He's an artist. They're all temperamental. This is an A-sharp." He hummed a note. "Now you."

After another furious glance at North, Louis turned his attention back to Shaw. He hummed the note.

"That's good. Again."

While Louis hummed the note again, Shaw took Louis's hand and inspected it, noting the nicks and cuts and calluses along the knuckles. Louis faltered and tried to pull away.

"You're doing so good," Shaw said. "Keep going." Lowering Louis's hand, he said, "I'd like to see your teeth."

Louis was still humming, but he opened his mouth. Again, the combination of mint and underlying bad breath wafted over Shaw, but the teeth still looked relatively healthy, and after a moment, Shaw nodded. Louis closed his mouth, and the note cut off.

Shaw waited.

Pulling up the collar of his tee to wipe his eyes, Louis began to cry in earnest.

It didn't last long, but it was intense, and Shaw held the kid against him until it passed. When it was over, North handed Louis a bottle of water from the dresser, and Louis took it, expression dull, and swallowed a few mouthfuls. When he spoke, his voice was low, the words practically uninflected.

"I don't even know how it started. One day I was just so sick of it all. Sick of Dad. Sick of the pool and sick of times and sick of trying to beat the next record. Sick of having to eat a million eggs every day. Sick of the stupid protein shakes and the supplements. I just went out and bought whatever I wanted to eat. And then I felt like shit, which makes sense because I was eating shit, but I looked at myself and saw how gross I am, and I figured that's why I can't get a boyfriend, and I don't know, it just clicked. I wanted to get to two-percent body fat. It was like magic, like I finally had an answer. I was already in really good shape, but two percent, that was a number. I could control that. We'd had to see the videos in health class, so I mean, I knew the general idea, and it seemed like this one-time thing. I went into the bathroom." His shrug was the ellipsis at the end.

"Have you talked to anyone?" Shaw asked.

Louis shook his head, but after a moment, he said, "Flip figured it out. It was a total accident. I slipped up, and he walked in on me in the bathroom. That's why we had that huge fight in the refectory. He said he was going to tell someone because I needed help. I said I was going to kill him. Honestly, for a minute, I would have. I really would have. I'd worked so hard. I read all the blogs and websites. I knew not to brush my teeth right after, I knew to use fluoride mouthwash. Nobody was going to figure it out, and once school was done and I could tell Dad to fuck off, I'd be fine. But Flip, he just kept talking about it. Insisting on it." Louis wiped red eyes again. "I didn't do anything to him, though. I swear to God."

"What was your relationship with Flip?" North asked.

"I told you," Louis said, a challenge in his voice. "We were friends, I guess, until he found out what I was—what was going on."

"That's all?"

"That's all."

"Louis," Shaw said, "we need to tell you something. We found videos of Flip having sex with someone. We think it might have been you."

The shock on Louis's face was comic. "He was gay?"

"Or bi."

"But Flip wasn't—I mean, I never, we never—" Louis gave an odd, fragile laugh. "Are you fucking serious?"

"The other man, he would have been close to your age. He had well-defined muscles, an adult build. Like you, and not like most teens. He was dark haired—"

"You could see his face?"

"No. He wore a mask."

"Then how do you know it was the same guy? And how do you know he had dark hair?"

"His dick." Shaw shrugged. "Well, and his balls."

"Umm."

"Dicks are actually pretty distinctive. Think of it as a penis fingerprint."

"Shaw once sent a forty-two-page manifesto to the Supreme Court supporting this theory. He also tried to patent his DickPrint system, which almost got him hauled in on felony charges."

"It was an amicus brief, not a manifesto. And anyway, this was definitely the same guy. And we know he's got dark hair because his pubes are really dark. And he had brown skin or a heavy tan."

"Shaw Aldrich, everyone. The modern Dick Tracy with his patented DickPrint system."

"I don't understand," Louis said.

"He's saying that because Dick Tracy was an old detective, but he didn't have anything to do with dicks. Well, not that I know of, anyway. I'll have to consult the history of dick-printing literature."

"No, I mean—" Louis shook his head. "I mean, it's not me. Look, I don't even have pubes; I shave."

"No, no, no, no," Shaw shouted as Louis got his thumb under the waistband of his shorts.

"Oh my God, I'm naked or in a Speedo all day. Who the hell cares?"

"We care," North said. "We'd really, really like not to go to jail."

Another of those nonverbal teen deliveries of mixed contempt and pity. "Whatever. And I have freckles on the inside of my thigh, right by my taint. So you can prove it's not me. I'll show—"

"No!" North shouted. When Louis grinned, North added, "You little shit."

Louis's grin got bigger. "I'm serious about the freckles, though."

"Yeah, well, I'm not sure we're going to be able to see that on the video."

"We'll check," Shaw said. When North fixed him with a look, Shaw felt his face heat, but he raised his chin. "In the name of forensic diligence."

"You're a gross old man."

"I'm only six months older than you!"

With a shrug, North turned his attention back on Louis. "If not you, then who was Flip hooking up with?"

"I don't know. We're in a city, right? I mean, he could have hooked up with a guy on a ton of different apps."

Shaw shook his head. "We're pretty sure it was someone from school, and we're pretty sure the same person was involved in Flip's disappearance. I don't want to go into it, but the circumstances make it really hard to believe it was anyone else."

"Have you talked to Kish?"

"Is that Mr. Kishor?"

"Well, it's technically Mr. Virani. His first name is Kishor, but the soccer guys started calling him Kish, and pretty much everybody does now. Dr. Latese doesn't like it because she says it's not respectful, but Kish is really cool about it."

Shaw thought about Kishor holding court on the quad, the fresh-faced boys lapping up attention from an older, confident man. He thought about that absent-minded—or maybe not-so-absent-minded—tug on his dick that Kishor had performed in front of those kids.

"Why do you bring him up?"

"Well, I walked in on Kish and Flip one time."

"You walked in on them?" North said.

"No, no." Louis laughed nervously. "No way. Not like that. Kish is super cool. He gets ass all the time, I mean, of course he does, he's gorgeous, and he'd never, you know, do that with a kid."

"So why'd you bring him up?"

"They were arguing. When I walked in on them, I mean."

"About what?"

"I don't know. It was right after class; he teaches history. I forgot I needed to ask him for an extension because I was going to be out of town for a meet, but when I walked in, Flip was there. And—" He drew in a deep breath. "Man, Kish was pissed. I mean, scary, and he's normally so chill about everything. Flip was pissed too, and that was weird because he's usually cool too. They both stopped talking right when I walked in, and the whole thing freaked me out, so I made up something and left. But now I think—what if Kish found out about those videos? He would have hauled Flip's ass over the coals. Or maybe he found out who Flip was fucking."

Or, Shaw thought, he found out their playtime videos were being sold on MyFans to Flip's dedicated audience of teen-porn afficionados. The same kind of guys, Shaw guessed, who would pay top dollar for their favorite porn star's underwear—especially if he had died tragically. Which added a sinister layer to the already creepy encounter when they'd caught Kishor trying to steal Flip's clothes.

"We'll run him down," North said, and the tone of his voice suggested he'd reached the same conclusions as Shaw. "What about Hiwet? How do you think she got tangled in all this?"

Louis had a thoughtful expression on his face.

"What?" North asked.

"I don't know how Hiwet got involved in this, but I think you might be on the wrong trail. I've been texting with Lauren and Abigail. There have been these weird guys around campus. Scary guys, actually, although Jos called me a pussy faggot for admitting I was scared. We all think they had something to do with Flip and Hiwet. I mean, Hiwet really liked to party, and when Flip slipped a gear, he really liked to party too. Hiwet bought a lot of shit, and I don't know if she could always pay for it. Flip used a lot of the shit she bought. I think they got caught up with some really bad people."

"Lauren's people?"

Louis rolled his eyes. "Lauren buys weed from this Somali kid she dates on and off. Brandon is fifteen, and he's pretty much the sweetest person you'll ever meet. He got a perfect score on the ACT last year. He didn't do this. Trust me, if I could get him to turn, I wouldn't let him go. He's perfect."

"Most people usually have some degree of homosexual—"

"Nope," North said.

"The Kinsey scale—"

"Do not encourage him to trawl for straight boys." Before Shaw could answer, North turned back to Louis. "Do you know something about these guys? So far, all people have been able to tell us is that they're scary or shady or sketchy."

"Not exactly. But—" Frowning, Louis worked his phone out of his pocket and tapped the screen a few times. A video began to play; North moved to loom over Shaw's shoulder so he could watch it as well. In a small voice, Flip explained, "I wanted to prove to Jos that I wasn't a pussy faggot, so I followed them."

On screen, at the back door to The Gouverneur Morris School's administration building, Dr. Trinity Latese was talking to two men—one shorter and balding, one taller and balding, both of them shady as fuck in Easter-egg-colored track suits. And then, with what looked like resignation on her face, she stepped aside and waved them inside.

Chapter 24

WHEN NORTH AND SHAW stepped out of Washington, the sun dazzled North momentarily, and he took a long, deep breath of air that smelled like wet grass and teeny-bopper body sprays and something cool and dank, like freshly turned earth. Then his eyes cleared, and the day, blue and bright, came into focus. On the far side of the quad, Kishor was talking to a young man. Kishor, in his pretty boy shorts and his pretty boy jersey. Kishor, with his pretty boy hair. And North remembered the hate fucks he'd seen in those videos, Flip bent in half while this dickwad piledrove him.

Shaw must have sensed some of it because he caught North's arm.

"I'm just going to murder him," North said, trying to shake off Shaw. "Really quickly."

Shaw grabbed him tighter.

"Fine. I'll settle for sodomizing him with that fire hydrant."

Laughing softly, Shaw squeezed his arm. "What do you think that's all about?"

The question made North pull back, and now he saw what he'd missed: the sharp, cutting gestures of hands; the stiffly held bodies; the faces tight with attempts to moderate strong emotions in public. This wasn't the pretty young teacher soaking up adolescent praise; this was Kishor furious, and the young man—Jos, North recognized him now, his blond hair and fair skin in stark contrast to Kishor—was equally angry.

"I don't know," North said, "but let's find out."

They headed across the quad. Jos stood with his back to them, and Kishor was so caught up in their argument that he hadn't noticed them yet. Their voices were still too low for North to make out the individual words, so he picked up his pace; he wanted to hear at least a little of what they were saying before they realized he was there. Once they spotted him, they'd either split or try to snow him, and North wanted to have something for leverage first.

Before he had a chance, though, a frisbee flew in front of him. It hit the grass, skipped once, and landed on one of the sidewalks crisscrossing the quad. As it skated across the cement, the plastic disc rattled, and Kishor glanced over.

The change in his expression was immediate. He said something that sliced through whatever Jos was saying, and Jos glanced over his shoulder. The sudden rush of color, the wide eyes, the shoulders climbing almost to his ears—North had seen a lot of people look guilty, and Jos could give a master class. With a meep that North could hear halfway across the quad, Jos took off at a power walk.

Kishor, on the other hand, dug out his phone and stared at North and Shaw as he spoke into it.

"Damn it," Shaw said.

"We'll give him a chance to double down on this shit," North said with a grin. "Come on."

The teacher was pocketing his phone when they reached him.

"Trouble in paradise?" North asked.

"I called security. It's time for you to leave—if you want to avoid the police, you'll go now."

"That must have been very empowering," Shaw said. "People look for empowerment and validation from all sorts of external sources, but the only thing that will be truly empowering is when you realize that the power to achieve your dreams was inside you all along. For example, I never thought I could cook, but then just the other day, I told myself, 'Shaw, the power to cook has been inside you all along,' and then I made North tuna surprise casserole, and I totally nailed it."

Kishor turned to North. "Is he being serious right now?"

"You'd be surprised too," North said, "if you took a bite of the driest, nastiest, burnt-and-raw-at-the-same-time tuna surprise casserole forced on you and bit down on a toy soldier."

"That was the surprise," Shaw shouted with excitement. "Like king cake!"

"What in the—"

"What just happened?" North asked. "Your boy toy didn't look too happy with you."

"You ought to watch what you say; people take those kinds of allegations very seriously."

"I know what I said."

Across the quad, the frisbee kids were laughing uproariously about something; North glanced over to see that two of the boys had co-opted the game and were now flinging frisbees at each other.

"He used a homophobic slur." Kishor shifted his weight. "I let kids slide on a lot of things, but I won't stand for that. Jos knows I'm gay; I'm very open about it. He wanted to provoke me because that's what a lot of teenagers do when they feel threatened: attack, attack, attack."

"Yeah, you're the patron saint of gays," North said. "Young guy like you. Good looking. You're funny and athletic, not some campy old queen. And I bet there are a lot of boys still trying to figure themselves out. Trying to understand what they're feeling. Is that right?"

Kishor's look hardened even further. "Of course. All teenagers are trying to figure themselves out."

"And I bet you're willing to help those boys. I bet you're willing to give them some private coaching so they can figure themselves out with a helping hand."

North couldn't decide if the look was shock or guilt or both. The emotion, whatever it was, wiped Kishor's expression clean. After a moment, he started up, his voice pitchy: "I never touched—"

Before he could finish, a golf cart sped into view, motor whining. The same security guards sat in the front, with Trinity Latese in the back. The golf cart cut straight for the middle of their group; Kishor stepped back in one direction, and North and Shaw retreated in the other. The motor whined. The laughter on the quad had stopped, and when North risked a look, he saw that the frisbee duel had ended and that the kids were watching to see what happened next.

"Mr. McKinney," Trinity said. "Mr. Aldrich. You're being placed under citizens' arrest for trespassing on private property after repeated warnings. Please come with us; the police have already been called."

North smiled, rocking back on his heels and studied the security guys: thin, soft-faced men with windbreakers and tasers and Berettas in shiny leather holsters. Somebody had unboxed their Super Accountant action figures and mixed them up with the tough guy set.

"It's eighty degrees," he said. "Drop the jackets."

"North," Shaw whispered.

"No, it's ridiculous. These guys are playing their Nerf-gun version of cops and robbers. I'm guessing that if you unwrap those badges, and you'll find chocolate under the foil."

One of the men stepped forward, hand going to the Beretta.

"Are you out of your mind?" Trinity snapped. "Stop this. Mr. McKinney, let's go."

"I didn't know they made orthopedic shoes with soles that thick. These guys are walking on clouds."

"You didn't miss the lumbar support pillow, did you?" Shaw asked.

"Fuck, of course I didn't miss it. I had it worked into this whole piece about how they take naps."

"Mr. McKinney," Trinity said again.

"Now it's ruined," North said. "I was doing the setup, Shaw. Why can't you just hold your fucking horses?"

"You take too long on the setup! How was I supposed to know that you were lining them up for a pillow joke?"

"I've got great setups, Shaw. I like to build up to a joke. I don't step all over myself like somebody I could name."

"I know you've been working on landing your jokes, but I really think you need to pay more attention to the setups. People don't have the attention spans they used to. Smartphones—"

"Mr. Aldrich!" Trinity's voice was a teacher's lash. "Mr. McKinney!"

"Jesus Christ, lady," North said. "What?"

"You guys think you're real funny," one of the Super Accountants said.

"Yes," North said.

"Obviously," Shaw said.

"Come with me right now," Trinity said, "or—"

"No," Shaw said. "You come with me."

North looked at him. Trinity looked at him. The Super Accountants looked at him. Kishor looked at him.

"Um," Shaw said, "but could we use your office?"

"What my partner is trying to say in his ass-over-tit fashion is that it's time for us to have a nice, long chat, Dr. Latese. We've got a very interesting video— a few of them, actually. And we need your expert opinion."

Trinity's lips parted slightly as though she'd been slapped.

"And you should probably tell the police that you don't need them anymore," Shaw said with a sunny smile. "You've got bigger problems now."

To the security guards' outrage, Trinity agreed and called the police. Worse, she left the Super Accountants behind with Kishor, driving the cart herself to the administration building, with North and Shaw along for the ride.

"These pillows really are comfortable," Shaw said, plumping the lumbar support and then falling back against it again. "We should get you one for your car."

"Don't talk about the pillows. I'm still pissed at you about the pillows."

Trinity's secretary, Leah, stared at them as they followed Trinity into her private office.

"Hi, Leah," Shaw said with another of those gratingly happy smiles.

"Don't talk to her," North said.

His last glimpse of Leah was her surprise transforming into wounded indignation.

Trinity's office was pretty much how North remembered it from the last visit: the desk, the computer, the awards and degrees framed and hung on the walls, a bookcase with what was obviously intended to be a decorative set of the *Encyclopædia Britannica* and the Harvard Great Books collection—both sets in sober leather, with gilt-stamped letters. The windows were open, a concession to the perfect spring day, and the air smelled like the dogwoods in bloom. In the distance, someone was talking in tones that sounded like exaggerated enthusiasm, although too distant for North to make out what they were saying.

Collapsing into her chair behind the desk, Trinity said, "If you think you can blackmail me, you're wrong. I don't even know why I agreed to this. The police should be arresting you."

"You agreed because you know what's on these videos and because you don't want the police to see them. That's why you agreed."

Trinity's controlled posture dissolved; slumped in her executive's armchair, she shot rapid glances at North and then away, at Shaw and then away. Her hand played with the bail pull on a desk drawer, and every time she let the pull fall, it gave off a tinny tinking.

"Let's see them," she finally said, leaning across the desk.

North played the video Louis had given them, which showed Trinity speaking to the two track-suited thugs and then letting them into the administration building.

"God damn it," Trinity said, although she sounded tired more than angry.

Without any setup—fuck Shaw and fuck his complaints about long setups—North played one of the MyFans videos.

The effect was electric: Trinity shot upright in her seat as though galvanized, one hand jerking sideways to knock a WE LOVE OUR HEAD OF SCHOOL mug. The mug made a chinking noise against the carpet, and coffee sloshed out, filling the air with its smell.

"Turn it off," Trinity whispered. Then, more loudly, "That's enough."

North paused the video. "Start talking."

Pointing one perfect nail at the phone, Trinity said, "I did not know about that. I don't know what that is, and I don't want to know."

"Bullshit."

"I don't!"

"Don't give me that. You've got two students at this school, one dead, and one missing who might be dead. Hiwet was murdered for something she knew, and Flip disappeared in a way that should have been impossible—and in a way that suggests someone inside had to be involved. The first time we showed up, you ran. Crawled out that fucking window right there. You've done everything you could to keep us off campus since. You're neck deep in this. Why did you help those men kidnap Flip? What did they do with him?"

"No!" The word was shrill. Trinity cut off, took a deep breath, and managed to even out her voice when she said, "The loss of our students is a terrible tragedy—one that I had nothing to do with."

"But you know something." Shaw inched forward in his seat. "Dr. Latese, whatever you know about this, it's time to come clean. A girl is dead. Flip might be dead. If you really didn't have anything to do with those things, then tell us what you know, and help us find the people who did."

Trinity's expression was vacant, her eyes dead. The stink of cold coffee was giving North a headache. Voices moved closer, carrying clearly through the windows now. "And this is the administration building, which was built in

1898. It's the first building of the original campus of The Gouverneur Morris School, and from 1898 to 1927, this served as the home for the original head of school and our founder, Dr. Jabez Buffum. The dogwoods were planted by Mrs. Buffum the first year they lived here, and—"

"Our Ainsley is very allergic," a woman's briskly self-assured voice interrupted. "She would have gotten first place in the state 5k, but her allergies got her. I asked the organizers to move the event to a day with a lower ragweed count, and this horrible woman laughed at me."

"An old place like that must cost a fortune to keep up," a gruff, blustery man's voice said. "Is that why I'm paying thirty-seven-thousand dollars a year for my daughter to go here? I went to public school, and I turned out all right."

A tiny silence, like a record skipping, and then: "And over here, you'll see our library which is one of the newest buildings on campus. The original library was torn down in…"

The voices trailed off.

Trinity wore a grim smile. She gave the bail pull a final flip and sat up. "I don't suppose there's any way to come to an agreement about this."

"I thought you refused to be blackmailed," North said.

"I had a student like you my first year teaching," Trinity said. "I let him ride me pretty hard because I was new and didn't know better. He had a smart mouth, and he always played it safe: little sniping comments, ironic distance, wall after wall between him and the world. I'll tell you what I wish I'd told him, Mr. McKinney: shut the fuck up."

Heat rushed into North's cheeks, and he opened his mouth. Shaw's hand on his knee stopped him.

"I meant an arrangement where you didn't take this to the police." Trinity waved a hand. "I'm sure you'll tell me that you have to hear what I have to say first, and I think in the end you'll take it to them. But God, I love this job." She blew out a breath, tracing her mouth with those perfect nails, pinching her lips into a bow. Then she dropped her hand and said, "I was all right until 2007. My game is craps. I'd never touched a pair of dice before 2007; my grandmother taught me games of chance were of the devil, and that stuck with me until I was a grown woman. Then, one night, one of my friends wanted to have her bachelorette party at this new casino right downtown. Lumiere Place. I was feeling sorry for myself. I was single, and although I'd done well in my career, I kept telling myself I'd missed the boat to have a family. I can't even really tell you how it happened that first night, but I liked how it felt when I rolled the dice, and I liked even better how it felt when I won. But I didn't win as much as I lost. It got bad last year. I took out loans. My car. Then my house. Check-cashing stores. And then I couldn't get loans, so I took money from people who…you should not take money from. And I missed a payment." One hand hovered above her ribs. "They made me thank them for not leaving marks where anyone could see them."

The wind soughed in the dogwoods; old branches creaked, and a spindrift of white petals whirled in through the open window and patterned the carpet.

"Are you fucking kidding me?" North asked. "You went to a loan shark, and now he's sending Beavis and Butthead in track suits to collect?"

Trinity shrugged. "They came around a few times to talk. To threaten me, I guess I should say. And then, the last time, they hurt me. When Leah announced two men to see me, I assumed they were here for a more serious punishment." Her gaze cut to the window. "So I ran. If I'd known it was you, I would have smiled and walked you over to Flip's residence, and we wouldn't be here right now."

"What about throwing us off campus?"

"Whether you like to believe it or not, Mr. McKinney, I am a good head of school. I care about my students, and I meant what I said about their own rights being infringed by having private investigators on campus."

"No." Shaw shook his head. "You're lying again."

Trinity's eyes narrowed. "I've told you everything, and I've told you the truth. Those men had nothing to do with Flip's disappearance. I'm ashamed of what I've gotten myself into, but I'd never let a child—"

"You're telling the truth, but you're walking around the thing you don't want to tell us."

"Well," North said, leaning back in the chair, "that's very fucking interesting."

"You're mistaken," Trinity said huffily. "There's nothing else to say. And I don't appreciate being treated in this way, especially not after I've answered your questions."

"Come on," North said to Shaw. "I think the police will be interested to hear about the gambling angle. People will do a lot of stupid things when they've got their back to a wall. I think I'll float the idea that maybe you and your buddies decided to kidnap Flip; the Chittendens could pay a ransom that would more than cover whatever you owed the loan shark."

Shaw unfolded himself slowly from the chair; they were halfway to the door when Trinity let out a strangled, "Please don't." Her chest rose and fell; her voice was still thick when she said again, "Please. I didn't do that, what you said."

"But you did do something," Shaw said, and the hard edge to his voice took North by surprise. "What did you do, Trinity?"

Spilled coffee now soaked the dogwood blossoms studding the floor; instead of freshly fallen, now they looked like they were in the late stages of decay.

"I made a mistake," Trinity said.

"What kind of mistake?"

"It was the first week of school."

"When? This year?"

"This year. This school year. We start the week after Labor Day. It was the first week of school, and I got a call from Mr. Gutierrez. He's a retired teacher, one of our substitutes now, and he was covering for Mr. Virani as head of residence over the weekend."

"Does that mean what I think it means?" North asked.

"Mr. Virani was out of town to attend the wedding of a family friend. Because he's head of residence, we have to find someone to assume his responsibilities—otherwise, the boys would be unattended. It was Friday night of the first week of school, and Mr. Gutierrez called and told me there was a disturbance. He's in his seventies, and like many retired teachers, he seems to have used up whatever patience he might have once had for teenagers. I anticipated that he'd call me if there was any trouble; we pay him fourteen dollars an hour, and I know that's not enough to make him exert himself." She took a breath and seemed to run through what she'd just said. "Because I was expecting something like this, and because the first week there are always discipline issues—boys, especially new boys, go through a transition period, and there are always pranks and fights and hurt feelings. When he called, I didn't think anything of it; I live on campus, so I simply walked over to Washington. I could hear the screaming as soon as I stepped through the front door."

"Flip?"

"And his father."

"What?" Shaw asked.

"When I got to the third floor, Mr. Chittenden was dragging Flip out of his room. In his other hand, he had a roller bag. Flip was screaming that he didn't want to go, that he wouldn't go."

"What the fuck?" North breathed.

"Both of them froze when they saw me. The look on Mr. Chittenden's face..."

"Angry?"

"Murderous. I honestly believe he might have killed me if he thought he could get away with it."

"That's a serious accusation," Shaw said.

"I grew up in a nice, quiet home, Mr. Aldrich, in a nice, quiet subdivision. I can count the number of times I've been that afraid on one hand, and keep in mind, nobody had even done anything yet. They were just standing there, both of them, looking at me."

"What happened?"

"Mr. Chittenden told me that they were leaving; he was taking Flip out of school because of a family emergency, and they'd settle the outstanding tuition as soon as things settled down. Flip looked me straight in the eye and said, 'Please don't let him take me.' After that, it was a lot of back and forth: I told Mr. Chittenden the situation was highly unusual and making me uncomfortable; he said it was none of my business; I said I insisted on talking to Mrs. Chittenden before he and Flip left; he said he was Flip's father, and it was his right to take his son out of school whenever he wanted. Finally, I threatened him. I said I would call the police and report him for parental kidnapping. That's when one parent—"

"We know what it is," North said. "What was Flip doing during all of this?"

"Nothing. Just standing there."

"He didn't fight? He didn't run?"

"No. He stared at me. At me." Trinity spread her fingers on the desk, studying her nails. "That boy was terrified. When I mentioned the police, Francis changed his tune. He shouted and threw a fit, and it went on for another fifteen minutes, but he wasn't going to risk a criminal charge. After he left, I got Flip settled. I required him to talk to Countee, our counselor, and after a long conversation, Countee told me that he had refused to tell her anything."

"Was that the end of it?"

Her gaze came up and slid away. She rocked her weight from side to side in the chair. "I don't know what else I could have done. I helped Flip; I made sure his father understood that the school would be keeping a close eye on Flip. But I couldn't go to the police and say that Flip's father wanted to remove him from school and acted strangely about it."

"Yes," Shaw said quietly, "you could have. At the very least you could have filed a report. What did Mrs. Chittenden say when you told her?"

As the silence dragged on, North understood. "You never told her. You decided to do a little blackmailing of your own."

"No." The word was sharp and peremptory. "I wouldn't—he called me. Do you understand? He called me. The next day. He said he'd been upset about a situation in their family, and would I be understanding enough to forget that anything ever happened, and was there any way the Chittenden family could show their support for the school. I needed the money. And nothing bad had happened; Flip was fine."

"He was scared to death. He was alone. He needed an adult he could trust, and you sold him out."

Trinity flinched at the end of each declarative.

"No wonder this whole thing felt like a setup," North growled. He swatted a pencil holder off her desk. "No wonder it felt like an inside job. No wonder the family has been so fucking weird about this from day one. Come on; we've got to tell Diamond about this."

"What about Hiwet?" Shaw said. "Where does she fit into this?"

"I don't know." Trinity wiped her face. "I really don't. She liked to snoop. Once, she used a pair of those wireless earbuds to record a private conversation, and I had to talk some angry parents out of turning the whole thing into a lawsuit. But I have no idea how she got involved with this or—or why such a horrible thing happened to her."

"What's the part you're really upset about?" Shaw moved to stand opposite Trinity, bending down to catch her eye. "What aren't you telling us?"

"I was curious." Trinity raised her head, a trace of defiance reminding North that this woman headed one of the most prestigious and selective schools in the nation, that she was smart and competent and savvy. "I wanted to figure out why Francis tried to take him."

"So you could blackmail him some more," North said.

"I found a will. Flip's grandfather's. It was probated years ago; it's public record. He left a great deal of money to Flip, to be held in trust until Flip is twenty-five."

"Fuck me," North breathed.

"I'm no lawyer, but I think if something happens to Flip, everything goes to his parents."

Chapter 25

AFTER CALLING DIAMOND AND relaying the information they had gathered, Shaw got only a bitten-off response: "Stay out of this."

North raised blond eyebrows.

"The phone cut out," Shaw said. "I didn't catch that last part."

"Want to go for a drive?"

"Yep. I want to see his face when we tell him."

The drive to the Chittendens' took them through some of the most beautiful country in the world: the Midwest in full spring. The late redbuds were still in bloom. Catalpa trees with their big, trumpeting blossoms. Oak trees budding. One maple had jumped the gun, the silver-backed leaves foiling sunlight back at them. North rolled down the windows, and the air smelled like loam and diesel and the winter-wet leaf litter drying in the sun.

When they got to the Chittenden farm, it had changed again. The same white clapboard. The same wraparound porch. The same windbreak, white flowers perking on the haw. Now, though, black satin bows marched along the split-rail fence. On the porch, someone had set up a piece of poster board, the kind Shaw remembered from grade-school science fairs. Hair-sprayed rose petals, so dark red that their edges looked black, were glued to the poster board to spell out words: NO ONE IS LOST TO JESUS. PRAY FOR FLIP.

"Damn," North muttered as they took the steps. "That's morbid."

Shaw knocked; no one answered. He strained to hear, but the only sounds were branches creaking and then a car whipping past on the road. He knocked again, and when he got nothing, he went down the porch and around to the garage. A silver Lincoln Aviator was parked next to a big black Ford F-150. He went back to the porch and shrugged. "They're here."

Grimacing, North checked the handle. It turned, and the door opened. Inside, the house was full of spring sunlight, the whitewashed walls glowing. A food smell hung in the air—no one particular note, but meats and starches mingling in a way that reminded Shaw of the Chouteau College dining hall.

North was making a face. At Shaw's glance, he whispered, "Casseroles. I hate casseroles."

They took a few steps inside; North shut the door behind them. Every movement echoed inside the entry hall, bouncing back from the high ceiling.

"Hello?" Shaw called. "Mr. Chittenden? Mrs. Chittenden?" Silence; then something clicked, and an appliance hummed to life deeper in the house. "This is Shaw Aldrich and North McKinney. We need to talk to you."

"Jesus," North said under his breath. "If this is a fucking murder-suicide, we're going to Cancun. For a month."

The rumbling discharge of an ice maker made Shaw jump. When he settled, North's hand came to rest on his shoulder and squeezed once. Then North glided forward, making surprisingly little noise in those ridiculous boots.

They crossed the entry hall, which led them into what was probably called a great room or a family room or a hearth room: a massive leather sectional, an even bigger—if that were possible—television, and a few blandly anodyne paintings of horses and rural landscapes. A dried-flower arrangement of rust-colored grasses needed to be updated for spring. The food smell was stronger.

"I bet it's chicken and celery." North's mouth twisted like he wanted to spit. "Might as well eat a mouthful of dirt. Mrs. Saill brought it to every fucking church potluck. Every fucking one."

"You shouldn't say fuck and church in the same sentence," Shaw whispered back. "Unless it's one of those sex-positive churches."

North laid a finger over his lips, which seemed unfair since he was the one who had started talking. When Shaw opened his mouth to point that out, though, North's glare doubled, so Shaw settled for rolling his eyes and nodding.

An opening from the great room connected with the kitchen. Miles of granite and stainless steel and distressed oak cabinets. The oven door stood ajar, and under the warming light lay two casserole dishes covered with foil.

North sniffed. "Definitely chicken and celery." More sniffing. "I don't know what the other one is. Yet."

"That's amazing. You're like a dog. Or a rat. Or—what's another trash-eating animal?"

"What don't you understand about no talking?" And North put his finger over his lips again.

"But you—"

"Shaw!" North repeated the gesture more emphatically.

Shaw began composing a North McKinney shushing invective in his head. He figured he'd keep it short; no more than four thousand lines of iambic trimeter.

Before he could get very far, though, a door on the far wall of the kitchen opened, and Francis Chittenden stumbled out of what looked like a pantry. He was carrying a bottle of amber liquid, and judging by the cloud of fumes wafting ahead of him, Shaw reached two conclusions: Francis liked scotch, and he was well on his way to being drunk. It took Francis two staggering steps before he paused, clutched the breakfast bar to steady himself, and seemed to notice them.

"What are you—" His voice was soft and slightly fuzzy. "You shouldn't be here."

"Mr. Chittenden, we need to talk to you." North cast a quick, assessing look at Shaw, and Shaw nodded. "It's time to start telling the truth."

"The truth." After a wobbly moment, Francis sat at the breakfast bar, drooping on the stool. He set the bottle down too hard, and the glass chimed against the granite and then slid sideways, threatening to slip out of his hand. Francis fumbled it upright at the last moment. "You want to know the truth? The truth is, my little girl is gone. The truth is, my wife is a sexless iron cunt. The truth is, I've got nothing, absolutely nothing. She takes everything away. She gets off on it."

"We were at Flip's school—"

"I work for her daddy's company. Did you know that?"

His waiting had a drunken belligerence that demanded an answer, and after a moment, Shaw said, "We figured it out."

"A man shouldn't have to ask his wife for permission to spend money. He shouldn't have to ask for an allowance. Am I right?"

"Mr. Chittenden—"

"Do you—" Francis weaved slightly on the stool and had to release the bottle to steady himself with both hands. He addressed himself to North. "You two fuck. You know how it is. Do you have to ask him for an allowance?"

North snorted. "No, although Shaw would fucking love that."

"I just think you spend a lot of money on those Japanese snack boxes."

"Says the guy who spent four hundred dollars on snail oils."

"For my face! You love my face! I'm doing it for both of us."

Francis's gaze had followed the conversation, sluggishly pingponging to each speaker. Now he started to laugh. "You guys are all right. She fired you, but I think you're all right. But you get it, right? You get it? She makes a couple of calls, and no matter what I say, my paycheck gets put into our joint account. But it's not joint. I've got to ask. And it's my money. I earned it, even if it is her daddy's company."

"Is that right?" North said softly, although the words were razor sharp. "Is that why you wanted Flip dead? So that his trust would dissolve, and you'd finally have some money for yourself?"

Francis stilled himself with drunken solemnity. He slid the bottle away, the glass chittering across the breakfast bar. He didn't sound sober, but his voice had taken on a distinct clarity when he spoke again: "You don't know what you're talking about."

"I'm talking about Flip's grandfather. I'm talking about the money he left in trust for Flip until he reaches twenty-five. I'm talking about you messing up the first time you tried to get rid of Flip. Flip made too much of a fuss, and you got busted by the head of school. What did you do this time? Who helped you get rid of him?"

For the second time in their conversation, Francis began to laugh, but it was hard and unpleasant. It turned into nothing more than a choking noise, and when Francis was finally quiet, he wiped his face with both hands.

"Fuck you," the words were easygoing. "Fuck both of you. You've got no clue what you're saying."

"We know about the will. We know about the trust."

"Yeah? Well, apparently your faggot superpowers don't include knowing how to read. Did you look at the will?"

North's color was high, red spots burning in his cheeks.

Francis gave another of those choking laughs and cut off only to drink from the bottle of scotch. "Somebody told you what was in it," he asked, wiping his mouth with one arm. "Is that it?"

"Are you telling us there isn't a trust?" Shaw asked.

"Oh, there's a trust. If something happens to Philip before he comes of age, though, the money doesn't come to me. It doesn't even come to Celia, at least, not directly; it's supposed to be divided up the way the rest of the estate was. Celia has a brother and a sister, so they'll each get a cut. And my cunt wife wouldn't let me anywhere near that money, in case you're wondering." He'd never looked more like the puffy-faced Jimmy Stewart than he did right then, grinning at them. "You can verify that with any lawyer who knows how to read a will, by the way. Next time, boys, check your facts."

"Then what were you doing the night—" North began.

"I was kidnapping my son," Francis said and took another belt of scotch. "Obviously."

"Excuse me?"

"You're looking for someone who would want him dead. I wanted the exact opposite; I needed him alive. The trust specifies that whoever is Flip's legal guardian when he turns eighteen will remain in control of the trust until he's twenty-five. I'm tired of the iron cunt. I'm tired of being shat on at work. If I divorce her, I get nothing—her daddy made sure of that when we got married. But if I divorce her and I'm Flip's legal guardian, even if it's only for another six months, then I have the trust for seven years. I wasn't trying to rob my son; I just needed a cushion while I started a new life." Another *It's a Wonderful Life* grin. "Kidnapping him seemed like the obvious solution. I set up house, get Flip settled somewhere new, let him finish high school. The divorce would be ugly, but possession is nine-tenths of the law, and having Flip under my roof and showing that he was happy and safe would go a long way to ensuring I got custody."

North shook his head and muttered, "This fucking family."

"I know," Francis said with another of those clipped laughs. "You really want a suspect? Then maybe you ought to think about this: there's an election coming up, and this is a very conservative part of an already conservative state. What do you think is going to get my dearly beloved wife back in the senate? A faggot whore son who sucks cock on camera? Or the perfect son who is mysteriously abducted and tragically dies just before an election?" Something must have showed on Shaw's face because Francis grinned and rolled his eyes. "God, you boys really aren't any good at this. I felt bad when the iron cunt fired you, but maybe she was right." He managed to work his phone free from a pocket, unlock it, and slide it across the breakfast bar.

Shaw caught it before it could fall.

Francis stood and walked around them to the oven, where he retrieved the casserole dishes. He peeled back the foil; the smell of cheese and onions rolled through the kitchen.

On the phone's screen, a video waited to be played.

"Gotta love funeral potatoes," Francis said as he scrambled the cheese-and-potato casserole with a fork.

The face was Flip's; Shaw recognized him from the photographs and videos. The background was cement-block walls. Something thin and dark, barely more than a shadow, ran behind his head. When he spoke, his voice was husky, still slightly boyish but thick with emotion.

"My name is Philip Chittenden, and today is Saturday, May fourth." A sad smile curved his lips. "May the fourth be with you. I thought things would get better if I left, but you can't run away from your problems, and you definitely can't run away from yourself. I'm sorry to everyone I hurt. Goodbye, Jos, Hiwet, Lauren, Louis. Bye, Abby. I'm sorry."

Then the camera fell sideways, and Flip's body jerked. The shadow behind his head became a rope. Then only his feet were in the frame, and he kicked for a long time before he went still.

Chapter 26

NORTH GOT THE PHONE out of Shaw's hands, although Shaw's fingers were stiff, his joints locked. Francis watched them over the pan of funeral potatoes, his glassy, drunken gaze expressionless. After forwarding the video to himself, North tossed the phone on the counter. Then he took hold of Shaw's arm.

"Think about what I said." Francis gave a smile that was so wild that North couldn't decipher the strong emotion behind it: grief or madness or amusement. "Can I make you up a plate before you go?"

"He killed himself."

"Somebody sure wants it to look that way."

Shaw swallowed then, the noise dry and painfully audible, and his eyes closed.

"Come on," North whispered. "Let's get you out of here."

Somehow, he walked Shaw out to the GTO. Somehow, he belted Shaw into the passenger seat. Somehow, because ninety percent of North's brain was dealing with a combination of murderous fury and crippling fear. Fury for Francis, for making Shaw see that. Fear for Shaw, who never grew calluses, who never stopped getting hurt, who couldn't stop feeling no matter how bad things got.

Crouched next to the car, North turned Shaw's head by the chin. "Hey."

Shaw licked his lips. "Hi."

"I'm going to call Dr. Farr."

Shaw shook his head. "I'm fine."

Only he wasn't fine. His jaw was slack. His shoulders loose. He had a thousand-yard stare. Their freshman year, before North and Shaw transitioned to friends, North remembered Shaw crying for two days straight after someone told him the ending of *Old Yeller*. He remembered holding court in the dorm common room, expounding on the rich twinkie queen who was just being self-indulgent and trying to get attention. He remembered, later, realizing the truth, and the nights he had lain awake, staring at the acoustic-tile ceiling, calling himself every awful name he could imagine.

After that, North had understood. He'd understood when Shaw started bawling on the quad after seeing a candlelight vigil for Jo Kopel, who had died in a car accident. He'd understood when Shaw had taken all of North's Progresso soup and hauled the cans to a food bank in a wire shopping cart because he'd read an article about shortages. He'd understood after Shaw's grandmother had died and Shaw had worn a black armband for six months, and he'd meant it—North had been the one who had listened to his sobs at night, who had gone into that dark room smelling like eucalyptus and weed and finger-combed Shaw's hair until he fell asleep. That had been one of the rare fights he and Tucker had before their wedding: Tucker wanted Shaw out of the wedding party if Shaw insisted on wearing the armband, and North had refused to give up his best man.

And it wasn't that Shaw wallowed. It wasn't that he sulked, or that he was a crybaby, or that he was seeking attention. It was simple: every grief was the first one; Shaw had no scar tissue to desensitize him. What North feared was that one of these times would send Shaw back into the same place he had gone after the Slasher attack, because North didn't know if he could bring Shaw back from that again. Finding Hiwet dead had been bad enough. For Shaw to have seen that video, to have seen what Flip had done to himself, was much worse.

"Let's get you home. I bet Dr. Farr will FaceTime you."

"North, I'm fine. Really."

North opened his mouth, but his phone vibrated. An unknown number. He answered.

"He's here. He's definitely here. He's sitting in the parking lot; I can see him."

It took a moment to place the voice. "Danny?"

In a hysterical whisper, Danny repeated, "He's here." After a few hyperventilated breaths, he managed to say, "I pushed the bed up against the door, but there's a big window. He can get in through the window."

"Where are you?"

"A motel. I went to a motel like you told me. You told me I'd be safe, and Lee is out there. I can see him in his car. He's watching my room." Danny released a low, despairing moan. "I think he just saw me. I pulled back the curtain to check, and he was looking right at me."

"Did you use a credit card?"

More of those rapid, shallow breaths. And then, in a protesting whine, "They won't let you use the internet unless—"

"For fuck's sake, Danny." North managed to bite off the rest of it. "Give me the name of the motel. If he gets out of his car, call the police and lock yourself in the bathroom. Until then, don't move. Not one fucking inch."

"It's called Bertrand Rooms-4-Rent. It's a four like the number. I'm in room twenty-nine."

"Fine. Let me figure some things out, and I'll call you back."

"He's right out there. He's going to do something really, really bad this time. I can tell by his face."

"Keep an eye on him. If he gets out of the car, you call the police and then lock yourself in the bathroom. Say it back to me."

Danny sounded on the break of tears. "If he—if he gets out of the car, I call the police."

"And then?"

"Lock myself in the bathroom."

"Good job. I'll call you back."

He disconnected, cutting off another terrified moan from Danny. Straightening from his crouch, he put a hand on the top of the door to shut it, but Shaw prevented him by holding out a hand.

"What are we going to do about Danny?"

"Nothing. We're going to make sure you're ok. I'll send Truck and Pari; Pari is desperate for a chance to use that new taser."

"I'm fine, North."

"I like hearing that. Keep telling me that."

When North tried to close the door, Shaw pushed it open again. "This is serious. This isn't an ordinary case. Ronnie wanted us involved in it for a reason. I don't think it's safe to send Pari and Truck; I think we should be the ones to handle it."

"That's the exact opposite of what you told me last time. Last time, you said Ronnie was manipulating me into getting over-involved. Now you're telling me I'm under-involved. This is a simple job: they drive down there, pick up Danny, and either bring him back or get him on a bus."

"What if Lee is going to hurt Danny really bad? What if he's going to kill him?"

"He's not going to kill him. What if this is all just a decoy to get us out of town so Ronnie can try again at the Nonavie lab?"

"He's going to kill him," Shaw said. His eyes were huge; the pupils obliterated the hazel irises. Voice rising, Shaw began to repeat with breathless intensity, "He's going to kill him, he's going to kill him, he's going to kill him, he's going to—"

"Fine, fine, fine, fine, fine!" The last one was a shout, loud enough to cut Shaw off. Shaw drew a shaky breath and wiped his face. The old oaks creaked and groaned. The air shifted and carried a tang; someone had fertilized their fields recently. "You're freaking me out."

"If you don't want to go, I'll go by myself."

"Yeah? With what car?"

"I'll rent one."

"Jesus Christ."

"Maybe it would be better. You stay here in case Ronnie tries something. I'll go get Danny."

"Move your goddamn arm so I can close the goddamn door."

"I'll call Hertz right now."

"Move your fucking arm!"

The ammonia smell of the fertilizer hammered between North's eyes, the tattoo of a migraine just getting started. He shut Shaw's door, moved around to the car, and stood there. He stared at the trees for a ten count. Wind slapped the oaks hard, and fragile buds fell in a shower that sounded like rain on an old roof. Then he opened the driver door and got behind the wheel.

"I'm scared shitless," North said as he put the key in the ignition.

Wan and colorless, Shaw nodded and looked out the window.

"About you, I mean."

"I knew what you meant."

Before they left, North called Haw and explained as much of the situation as he could.

"I don't understand," she said when he'd finished. "What is this guy's connection to Nonavie? How would anybody even know you were going out of town?"

"It's a long story; just trust me. If someone's going to try something, it might be now."

"I'll head over there myself. I want to hear this long story when you get back."

North figured telling her would be a quick way to get them fired, so he made a noncommittal noise and disconnected. Then he called Danny and told him they were on their way.

"North," Shaw said. "If Ronnie is using Danny to lure us somewhere, maybe I shouldn't take the Nonavie access card with me."

"Shit," North said. "We're really racking up the miles today."

From the Chittenden's farm, they drove back to St. Louis, and North waited in the car while Shaw ran into the Southampton duplex to stash the access card. When he came back, he offered a lusterless smile. "Pari is teaching the puppy to roll over, and she's lying on the floor demonstrating."

"Sounds like the puppy is teaching her to roll over. Maybe next he'll teach her 'down' and 'stay' and 'quiet.'"

Shaw smiled again, like winter sunlight, and rested his head against the passenger window.

The Bertrand Rooms-4-Rent was east of Sikeston, on US-60, next to a lot with corrugated-metal fencing and a sign advertising RENICH DUMPING – 24/7 – WE TAKE YOUR DUMPS FOR YOU. In contrast to this spiffy advertising scheme, the Bertrand Rooms-4-Rent had settled for the more traditional accoutrements of a sign with its name and, below it, a flashing neon sign announcing VACANCIES. The lot was paved, the asphalt buckling along the edges, the yellow lines faded into ghostly suggestions. Four other cars occupied stalls in front of the motel: a panel van with TREVOR

ELECTRICIANS stenciled on the sides; a pinkish Toyota All-Trac that had probably once been red; a Cavalier with a crumpled rear fender; and a Missouri staple, the white Ford F-150 with steel balls hanging from its trailer hitch.

They parked in front of room twenty-nine.

"I don't see Lee," North said.

Shaw shook his head.

Squeezing Shaw's fingers, North gave him a considering look.

"Do you want me to go in and get him?" Shaw asked.

"No. I'm trying to decide if leaving you here is the equivalent of forgetting a baby in a hot car."

Shaw rolled his eyes; it looked like it took effort.

North tapped his lips. More eye-rolling. But then Shaw leaned over the seat and kissed him.

"I get so worried about you," North whispered, smoothing Shaw's tied-back hair. "Tell me what I can do."

"I swear to God, I'm fine. Really."

Clearing his throat, North nodded. "If Lee does show up, feel free to blast him with that pepper gel."

"Duh. And I'll chop him in the nuts a few times."

"God help him."

North's phone buzzed as he approached the motel. He checked the phone, saw Joanna Griffin's name, and dismissed the call with an irritated swipe. He did not want to hear another excuse about why he shouldn't take her to small claims for her unpaid account, not with the day he was already having. He hammered on the door to twenty-nine and said, "Danny? It's North. Open up."

A picture window with thin, wavy glass opened the wall next to the door. The curtain twitched. Then furniture groaned inside, a bolt was thrown back, and the door opened on a chain. It was the same jug-eared kid with the same mess of long, sandy-brown hair.

"How do I know you are who you say you are?"

"Danny, it's the wrong fucking day to test my patience."

The boy swallowed, undid the chain, and poked his head out. "I swear to God he was here. He left twenty minutes ago. I was going to try to hitch, but then I thought he might come back and catch me on the road."

"You were going to try to hitch? Jesus Christ, I told you not to fucking move."

"You can't yell at me," the kid said, shrinking back. "You're not supposed to yell at me."

North let out a brief, inarticulate scream and then managed to say, "Get in the fucking car."

After a few minutes of packing, the kid staggered out to the GTO, his roller bag slapping against his leg. North threw the bag in the trunk, and the kid stared doubtfully at the GTO's back seat.

"Do I have to climb over your seat?"

"Mary, Mother of God," North growled and adjusted the seat so Danny could get in the back.

They drove to the parking lot of an Arby's, where Danny devoured two roast beef and cheddars and started crying halfway through his chocolate shake. That seemed to knock Shaw out of his torpor. He read Danny's palm and opened his third eye—or tried to, anyway, which mostly seemed to consist of flicking Danny on the forehead while Danny squirmed and flinched and said he didn't think it was working. Then he gave a long, meandering speech that dealt with such topics as the time Shaw had met an erotic ghost in the Palace of Versailles, the American steel industry, and recreational use of peyote as a civil rights issue. Peppered through the speech was the phrase "the power was inside me all along," which Shaw made Danny repeat back to him at key moments.

North murdered some curly fries and enjoyed his front row seat to this new shit-show. If this kid was a plant by Ronnie, Danny was wasting his talent on a con like this; he should have been doing theater on Broadway or infiltrating a terrorist cell. North dodged a phone call from his dad, caught the drift from the first words of the voicemail: no hello, only "You have a goddamn responsibility to pay your uncle back. I didn't raise you to welch—" And then North hit delete. He considered, briefly, the strangeness of Ronnie's silence after he had contacted them with this job. There had been no follow-ups, and Ronnie had avoided North's attempts to contact him. He thought, again, about how eager Ronnie had been to be seen on the security camera footage. And he thought about Shaw's oblique comment about bank robberies. After a while, though, North gave it up and turned his attention back to the dynamic dufuses.

After many, many, many conversations about their best options, they got Danny loaded onto a Greyhound headed for Los Angeles. He had an aunt there who would give him a place to stay—or so he told them. North wasn't entirely convinced that he wasn't just heading for the gay-boy fantasy of southern California. North repeated his warning about credit cards, and Danny nodded dutifully and, when he must have thought North wasn't looking, rolled his eyes at Shaw. Shaw, the little shit, rolled his eyes back. And then Danny was on the bus, and the bus was pulling away, and they headed back to St. Louis.

It was after nine, dark, and where light pollution reached the low hanging clouds, the sky had the faintly uneven blankness of cleaved slate.

"Shit," North said, steadying the hand with one wheel as he dug his phone out of his pocket. "I've got to call that Griffin woman back."

"Oh, I talked to her."

"What?"

"Yeah, when you were getting Danny packed. She called me because she said you weren't answering."

"What'd she say? Is she going to pay her bill?"

Shaw shook his head. "I told her not to worry about it."

The GTO's stereo was playing the Pussycat Dolls.

North put both hands on the wheel. "You what?"

"I told her not to worry about it." Shaw must have heard something in the silence because he shifted in his seat. "She was crying, North. You should have heard her. She was so upset because she couldn't pay, and she knows she owes the money, but things are tight, and she thinks the financial strain will give her a heart attack."

"And you told her that she didn't have to pay the bill." It didn't sound like a question when it came out of his mouth.

"Well, yeah. I mean, it's not like we need the money—"

"We do need the money, Shaw. God damn it. We invoiced her for almost five thousand dollars. Zion worked that case; I've got to pay him."

"You said we were way ahead of where we were last year."

"We were. Now, because you're a soft touch, who fucking knows?"

"I don't know why you're talking to me like this. We've got plenty to pay the bills, and—"

"Because we did the work, Shaw. We earned that money. It's ours; she owes it to us."

"She's in a really bad place. And there are more important things than money."

"Easy for you to say."

The GTO passed over a patch, bouncing North in his seat.

"What was that?"

"If we talk about this anymore, I'm going to lose my shit."

"Fine."

North stifled the urge to have the last word, and they drove the next forty miles in silence. The Pussycat Dolls explained that they didn't need a man. North was right fucking there with them.

When they hit the city limits, Shaw said, "I didn't like that video. With Flip."

"I know." The brusqueness of the response made North wince internally, and he softened his voice as he added, "I'm sorry you had to see it."

"No, I mean, something felt off about it. Wrong."

"Ok."

"You think I'm making it up."

"I think," North said carefully, "that it would be nice to think that Flip didn't kill himself, but that video was very convincing."

"He said goodbye to Hiwet."

"What?"

"He said goodbye to Hiwet, but she's dead."

North waited.

"He didn't know she had died," Shaw said. "He thought she was still alive. He didn't have anything to do with her killing."

"But that doesn't mean anything in terms of the video itself. He could have killed himself whether or not he knew what had happened to Hiwet."

"Isn't it strange, though? I mean, why didn't he know? I'm telling you, something feels really hinky."

"Shaw, he said his name, he said today's date, and he said goodbye. You saw the video, and you saw what it did to his dad. It seems pretty straightforward."

"But—"

"If he faked it, why? He'd already gotten away. Why would he need to fake his own death?"

"I don't know, but I'm telling you, I don't like it."

They followed I-55 into the city, cut up I-44, and exited on Kingshighway toward North's Southampton duplex. The streets had the amber glow of late night; the garage door rattled down behind them, and they sat in darkness with the smell of cold metal and motor oil.

"Are you going to call Dr. Farr?"

"It's late. It's not an emergency; I don't want to bother her at home."

"First thing tomorrow, then."

"I guess."

The engine ticked as it cooled. North pulled on the door handle, but not all the way. Then, after another moment, he let out a breath and gave the handle a jerk. The door popped open, and he pushed his way out of the car.

"I'm going to do some laundry so you'll have something to wear besides those ugly-ass jeans."

"I like these jeans," Shaw said, sliding out of the passenger door. "You bought me these jeans."

"I bought them from the Dollar General because I had literally no other option, and they practically swallow your skinny ass whole—"

"Oh my God."

"Come on, you know I like your ass. I'm talking about the jeans."

"Oh my God."

North threw a look over his shoulder. Shaw was halfway around the GTO, but he had frozen with one hand on the hood. The weak light filtering in through the street painted a mask of shadows across half his face; the other half, though, was rigid with shock. No, North corrected himself. Realization.

"I know why we couldn't figure out how Flip disappeared," Shaw said. "He never left the residence. He's still there." A grin broke out across his face.

Groaning, North shook "Don't say it."

"Flip has been inside me the whole time."

North raised an eyebrow.
"It sounded better in my head."
"Please shut up."

Chapter 27

THEY TOOK THE STEPS down into Washington's basement slowly, trying to make as little noise as possible. The access card had allowed them into the kitchen, and the house was dark and silent. Or mostly silent. It was an old house, and it creaked as it settled, the occasional pop of a joist as wood shrank and expanded. But there was no sign that anyone else inside the residence was awake, and North wanted to keep things that way. Especially if this batshit idea of Shaw's was right.

The perfume of detergent floated up from the laundry room, and North remembered what Shaw had told him the first time they had walked the campus, that kids did their crying in the laundry rooms, where the noise from the machines would cover up other sounds.

Shaw stopped, and North brushed up against his back before catching himself. A fumbling sound came from the right. Then fluorescent panels flicked on overhead, illuminating the length of the hallway. Ballast buzzed and hummed. One of the panels flickered—rapidly at first, and then more slowly, a strobing effect that made North blink. The only open door in the hallway led into the laundry room, where the ghostly white and stainless steel of the appliances glimmered. Shaw reached through the doorway and hit that light switch too. More fluorescent tubes hummed to life.

"I knew the background in that suicide video looked familiar," Shaw whispered as he pointed to the cement-block walls. "And look." He pointed to the gap between the machines. "If you plan it right, you can have the camera fall so it looks like you're hanging, but really, he was just supporting himself with a hand on each machine and kicking his feet."

"It's a public room. Why take that kind of risk? Someone could have walked in on him."

"Well, like I said, lots of kids don't do their own laundry, so it actually wasn't that big of a risk, and it's common courtesy—at least, it was back in my day—not to come inside if the door was closed. In case, you know, you were sobbing your heart out because your parents sat you down for an incredibly passive-aggressive conversation about 'your potential' and 'thinking long-term' and 'law school.'" He drew air quotes around each the phrases. "The polite thing was to go back upstairs and give whoever was bawling a chance to finish crying and leave so everybody could pretend nothing had happened."

"Jesus. And you think I'm bad about not expressing myself? You rich twats have it down to an art."

"Don't say twats. And don't be classist. Anyway, he also could have recorded that video in the middle of the night, and that would have lowered the risk of being caught even more."

"Especially if he had somebody in this house helping him. Why this room, though? Why not one of the bedrooms that aren't in use?"

Shaw pointed to the exposed joists. "The ceilings in the other rooms are finished, and he needed somewhere to tie the rope, even if it was just for show."

They moved back into the hall, and Shaw produced his set of common keys, opening each bedroom door as they went. Again, they were assaulted by the chill, mildewed air of rooms that had been closed up for a long time. They left each door open, the lights burning in each room, as they moved down the hall. A diligent security guard might wonder why the basement lights were on at almost midnight, but this was a fat-cat school in a cushy suburb. The guards had proven their own general lack of prowess up to this point; North guessed that the lights would be attributed, if they were noticed at all, to rich kids doing dumb shit.

And then they came to a room that was different from the ones before it. The air was warm, and it smelled of an unwashed body and greasy take-out— a kind of desperate, holed-up rancidity that North had smelled on previous jobs with hoarders and shut-ins. It was packed with all kinds of junk: metal bed frames on adjustable lifts, stackable plastic chairs, a plaid loveseat standing upright, cardboard boxes marked PTO 1972. Like the other basement rooms, it was clearly doubling as storage space, but the longer North studied it, the easier it was to spot the differences. Several of the metal bed frames had been pushed together, and they were all lofted to create the maximum space underneath; a folding table, legs collapsed, lay on top of the frames; the loveseat's cushions and the cardboard boxes were stacked to form a wall. Together, the arrangement created a kiddie fort. When North took a step toward the door, Shaw caught him, one hand on North's chest.

"Flip?" Shaw called into the room. His voice was soft, but it wasn't quiet, and it held no doubt. "Flip, you can come out now."

Nothing. After a moment, Shaw pointed down the hall to the door to the next room, and North moved to stand in front of it.

"Flip?" North opened the door and turned on the lights, inspecting another collection of boxes and dusty furniture. "We know about the false panels in the closets. We're watching both rooms. If you make us, we'll drag you out. This'll be easier for everyone if you play along."

Shaw shot North a hard look and jerked his head. "We got off on the wrong foot. Let's start over. Hi, Flip. My name is Shaw Aldrich. My friend's name is North McKinney. Your parents asked us to help them find you because they're very worried about you. I'm guessing the last few days have been really hard. Really scary. You've been down here hiding, hoping things will just get back to normal because you're ready to move on with your life. I bet you feel like nobody can help you. But we want to help you; we just need you to tell us how." Shaw waited; when no response came, he added, "Maybe you can start by opening the closet door so we can talk to each other a little more easily.

Another long silence. And then the closet door must have opened because the sound of hinges protesting came from the room that Shaw was watching. North rejoined Shaw.

"Please just go away." Flip's voice; North recognized it from the videos. He sounded close to tears. "Please. Everything was going to be ok, and now it's all ruined. Please go away. Please, please, please go away."

"We can't do that," North said.

Shaw threw another look his direction. "Why don't we start with just talking? Can you come out of there so we can talk? We'll stay in the hallway if it makes you feel better, but I'd like to see your face and know that you're all right."

A fine-boned hand emerged first, nudging the door open further, and then Flip stepped into view. It was the same kid from the photographs at the Chittenden house, the same kid from the MyFans videos: a boy growing into manhood, his brown hair oily and lank from days without washing, his eyes hollowed with shadows. He wore a sweatshirt and joggers and sneakers. He hugged himself and looked away.

"Hi. I'm Shaw."

"Please don't make me go back. Please. You're ruining everything."

"Look, kid," North said, "whatever you think you're fixing, running away isn't the answer. Your parents are going crazy worrying about you."

"They're not worried about me."

"Maybe. I don't know. They sure seem like they are. Either way, though, you've got to go back. That's the law. And, in case it makes you feel any better, it's what's best for you. Right now, as far as most of the world is concerned, you're dead. You can't have a life if you're dead. You can't go to college. You can't get a job."

"I don't care." The words burst out with a teenage petulance so classic that it almost sounded rehearsed, but the look on Flip's face, the look he flashed at North before turning away again, was genuine. "I just want it all to be over."

"It doesn't matter—"

"North," Shaw whispered. "Back off."

North raised his eyebrows, but he whispered back, "He's going home. He shouldn't get any false impressions about that."

"Ok, but he's also a kid and he's freaking out. Can we just talk to him for a few minutes?"

North made a be-my-guest gesture.

"I bet these last few days have been awful," Shaw said.

After a moment, Flip gave a sullen shrug. "It's not too bad. I've got one of the school tablets and a space heater, and I could get food delivered sometimes."

"But no bathroom? No shower?"

"There's a bathroom down the hall. I bought one of those chemical toilets just in case. I put it down here with a lot of water. And some of those protein bars."

"That's really impressive. It sounds like you thought things through."

He let out a short, unhappy laugh. "Yeah, I did great, didn't I?"

"Do you want to tell me about it?"

"What do you care? You're, like, a hundred years old and you wouldn't understand."

North couldn't help it: the look of outrage on Shaw's face was so strong that he smiled. Then he grunted when Shaw elbowed him without looking over.

"Sometimes it helps to talk about things. I tell North everything. Well, pretty much everything."

"He tells me too much," North said. "He told me about a dream he had where he was playing parcheesi with Rasputin, and then they both had to go vote in the municipal election, and there was something about Dracula eating cereal."

"Count Chocula," Shaw said. "And that part was a sex dream."

A wet laugh burbled up from Flip; this one sounded much closer to genuine amusement. He wiped his eyes and cast a long look at them before his gaze cut away again. "You guys are, like, boyfriends?"

"Yes," North said. "Unfortunately."

"No," Shaw said at the same time.

"Excuse me?"

"Well, you never asked me. You just showed up with the champagne and fucked me one day. Actually, first you shot a load all over my floor. And I had to clean it up, North."

Face hot, North said, "What the actual fuck, Shaw? We'd known each other for eight years. I didn't just show up on a stranger's door, buttfuck him, and then start pretending he was my boyfriend."

"No," Shaw said patiently, "you shot a load on my floor first. And you didn't wipe it up. That's really bad manners. Especially without asking."

Flip giggled and wiped his face. He looked feverish, with his cheeks flushed and his eyes dilated. "You can just go away, right? You didn't tell anyone, so you can just leave and pretend you never found me, and in a couple of days I'll be gone. As soon as people stopped looking, I was going to leave. And I'll never bother anyone again. I can take care of myself, I promise."

"What's going on?" Shaw said. "We can't help you if you don't tell us what's going on."

"Nothing!" With what looked like a great deal of effort, Flip brought his volume down again. "Nothing. I just—I just want to be done with all of this. I hate them, and I hate who I am, and I want to be done and be someone else."

"You're almost legally an adult," North said. "It's going to be over soon enough, and you won't have to destroy your life to get away from it."

"You don't understand," Flip moaned, near tears again. "It'll never be over. If I stay now, I'll never get away."

"Flip, please." Shaw took a step inside the room. Flip flinched, and Shaw held up his hands and made a coaxing noise. When he took the next step, Flip didn't move, so he kept advancing. "Is someone hurting you? Whoever they are, if they're hurting you, we can make it stop. We can help you."

"No," Flip said, shaking his head as he began to cry.

Shaw reached him then, wrapping Flip in a hug, and Flip dissolved into wracking sobs. It went on and on, and all North could do was watch, his heart breaking as Shaw rocked the boy and stroked his hair and whispered to him.

Finally Flip calmed down enough to sit on the floor; Shaw kept an arm around him, and Flip rested his head on Shaw's shoulder. For the first time that night, North could see how thin the boy had been stretched, the layers of comfort and security and shelter stripped back, and all that remained was an exhausted, terrified man-child who had been pushed to his limits.

"We can't take him back," Shaw said quietly.

"Are you kidding me?"

"North—"

"He's not a stray kitten, Shaw. He's the son of a state senator. He's an unemancipated minor. He's legally a runaway, and that means harboring him is against the law. We'd lose our licenses."

"No one would ever find out."

"It's not ethical. He belongs with his parents. On top of that, we made a commitment. We gave our word to find him. Those people trust us."

"They fired us. We don't work for them anymore. And when we found Danny, you didn't care that we didn't tell Lee. That was a job too. You didn't say anything about that."

"That's different. You know that's different."

"He's scared out of his mind, North. He's shaking. I'm not taking him back."

"It's not up to you."

"I think it is. I think we have a responsibility to do what's best for him."

"We are doing what's best for him!" North tried to tamp down the shout; part of him was vaguely aware that he might be overheard, but most of him was too busy struggling with his anger to care. "He's a child. You can't just put him out on the streets with no identity and no resources and expect him to be able to take care of himself. He'll be turning tricks and hooked on street shit in less than a week, Shaw. That's it. That's the end of his life. Is that what you want?"

"Obviously not. But I'm not going to force him to go back when he desperately doesn't want to. Things were so weird with his parents; we both felt it. I don't want to put him in the middle of that again."

"He's almost eighteen. We asked him if he was being abused. He said no. He doesn't like being there? Tough shit. He can stick it out for a few more months; Christ, I did it."

Shaw's face softened, but it was actually more upsetting that way. "So that's what this is about."

"Don't do that."

"This is another rich, spoiled kid running away from his problems, and you don't like that. If you could pull yourself up by your bootstraps, so can he. North McKinney versus every rich, pampered, prissy son of a bitch in the entire world."

"You're being a dick about it, but yeah, there's something to that. If I did it, so can he. I didn't want to be with my dad, but I didn't have the luxury of running away and assuming the world would bend over backwards to make sure my life still turned out all right."

"People's choices aren't always about how much money they come from. Not everything in life is about money."

"Easy for you to say."

"It's not my fault your parents didn't have money. It's certainly not Flip's. The whole time I've known you, you've had a chip on your shoulder against anybody you thought was better off, even though nobody else ever cared if you had money or didn't. You couldn't let it go. And now you're allowing it to affect your judgment about this."

"Nobody else cared?" North laughed. "Right, Shaw. Whatever. Fuck you. This is you easing your white, rich, privileged guilt by telling me money doesn't matter. I've heard it before. I'm sure I'll hear it again. But just in case you forgot, you're my boyfriend; you're not my fucking therapist."

"It sure feels like I am sometimes. Especially when you refuse to see one."

North was aware of his shredded, accelerated breaths.

"I shouldn't have said that." Shaw's voice was thick, and he looked down at Flip. "I shouldn't have said any of that. I'm sorry."

"We can take him to child services," North said. He didn't even recognize the words as his. He didn't feel like he was inside his own body anymore; someone else was driving now. "I'm not going to let you dump him on the streets, and I'm not going to let you put yourself and the business at risk, but I'm trying to meet you partway. We can take him to child services, and he can tell them why he doesn't want to go home, and we'll do whatever we can after that."

"He doesn't want to go to child services."

North dragged a hand down his face; a cold, dark wave of exhaustion crashed over him. "Then do whatever you want, Shaw. You always do. And you can be the one to tell them that their son is gone just like their daughter. You can look them in the eye and tell them that."

Flip let out a tiny cry. He shrank down, curling up inside the circle of Shaw's arm, eyes squeezed shut.

"Flip—" Shaw began.

"I'll go," he whispered. "Stop fighting. Stop. Just stop." He opened his eyes. "I'll go home."

Chapter 28

FLIP MADE THEM GO to the police.

"So there will be a record," he said.

"A record of what?" Shaw asked.

But Flip wouldn't say anything else, and North either didn't hear or didn't care, and eventually, Shaw had to call Diamond as they drove Flip to the station.

After that, the hours lengthened and took on a cross-eyed kind of doubling, blurred by exhaustion both emotional and physical. Much of the time, Shaw and North waited at Diamond's desk in the Juvenile Division's squad room. A beefy detective was the only other occupant; the collar of his dress shirt was yellow with sweat and age, and he passed the time by playing word games on his phone and rolling clove cigarettes while he pretended not to keep an eye on them. A pregnant woman staggered past them, strapped into a backpack vacuum and sweeping the hose back and forth carelessly. On top of a filing cabinet at the next workstation, a coffee maker gurgled and hissed, coffee dripping into the pot until only a single, fat drop hung suspended. It had a fairytale quality, a world locked in stasis by a magic spell, and when it finally fell with a plonk, Shaw shuddered and covered his face with his hands, his eyes so dry the lids seemed to stick.

"You can go home," Diamond said.

Shaw jerked out of the half-doze, wiped his mouth, and blinked. He'd left a wet patch the size of a softball on North's shoulder.

"We'll need to talk to you again. There are things he's saying that don't add up, and we'll have follow-up questions. But you can go."

"What doesn't add up?"

Diamond shook her head. "Raskowski and I are driving him home right now. My gut tells me that it's going to be a circus, but if you want to come, you can follow us. You might even get your fifteen minutes of fame."

Shaw glanced at North, but North was looking straight ahead, his face washed clean of any emotion.

"We'd better not," Shaw said.

"Want to do the kid a favor, then? The jackals are already showing up. You could keep their attention while Raskowski and I take him out the back."

Still nothing from North; a failing fluorescent cast a faint, fluttering shadow across one side of his face.

"Yeah," Shaw said. "Ok."

When they stepped out of the building, Shaw recognized two women from local TV stations, complete with cameras and lights and vans. A dumpy-looking guy in sweats and battered kicks must have been print journalism's delegate, probably from the *Post-Dispatch*. The camera lights flared. Voices swelled. Shielding his eyes from the glare, Shaw stuck close to North as they hurried to the GTO. He had been sure there were only three of them, but now, blinded by lights, he would have sworn that dozens were thronging them.

"—tell us anything about Philip's condition—"

"—allegations of sexual abuse by staff, can you comment—"

"—true that he was being held prisoner in a bunker on campus—"

No matter how many times Shaw and North repeated, "No comment," the journalists hounded them all the way to the car. When the doors finally thunked shut, steel and glass dropped the volume to a tolerable level, although one woman with teased-out hair and a recent round of lip fillers shouted at North through the window, holding out the microphone at intervals as though the GTO might like to make a comment. The guy in the battered kicks kept looking at an ancient Impala parked down the street, as though considering following them.

"Fucking hyenas," North growled as he started the car.

They drove home; no one followed them. North parked in the garage, and they let themselves into the house. The puppy was going wild with barking, and North let him out of the crate. Instead of his usual combination of inspecting North, prancing with joy, and offering the occasional warning bark to Shaw, the puppy shot into the kitchen. North and Shaw found him at the back door, which hung ajar. The puppy was sniffing furiously.

"God damn it," North said as he shut the door and locked it. He scooped up the puppy, who now turned his full attention to licking North's hand, face, and neck—wherever he could reach. Then he powered down Shaw's laptop, where their poor excuse for a dog sitter had probably been watching porn. "I don't know which one is less responsible: Truck or Pari."

"At least they took care of the puppy."

North grunted. After checking the dog's water and food, he opened the fridge and took out a Schlafly. He carried it to the table; when he sat, the puppy jumped out of his lap and sprinted over to yip a reminder warning at Shaw. Shaw squatted, holding out his fingers, which the puppy sniffed dubiously and then offered a tentative lick. North was hitting the Schlafly hard, pounding down the first one, Adam's apple bobbing as he drank. The light made him an outline of gold and shadow; the glass glinted in his hand.

"North, I'm really sorry."

He finished the beer and set the bottle down. He picked up the bottle cap and rolled it on its edge.

"Flip was just so scared, and then I got scared for him, and—"

"Go to bed, Shaw." He lifted his hand, and the bottle cap fell flat with a soft clack against the wood. "It's been a long day. We're both tired."

Grabbing the puppy, Shaw buried his face in the warm fur, eyes stinging. After a moment of the puppy scrambling desperately to be released, Shaw put him down and ran fingers under his eyes. "Ok." He stopped in the hall to ask, "Are you coming too?"

The answer was North's heavy steps, the sound of the refrigerator opening, the whisper of another bottle cap coming loose.

At some point in that night of restless sleeping and waking, Shaw realized North wasn't coming to bed. He padded out into the living room. North was curled up on the sofa, a too-small throw pulled over him, the puppy curled up under his arm. A half-drunk beer stood on the floor next to him, the label peeled away in large sections, flakes of paper peppering the rug. His only concession to sleep had been to ditch the Redwings; in dingy white socks and with his face softened by sleep, he reminded Shaw of the boy he had met more than eight years ago. Shaw went back to the bedroom, took one of the blankets from the bed, and tucked North in. North grumbled once, rolling onto his side, and his arm tightened protectively around the puppy. But he didn't wake.

The days after that seemed unending. Part of it was the surreal feeling of being trapped—the first two days, reporters lurked outside, waiting for North and Shaw to show their faces. Being followed by reporters wasn't exactly conducive to investigative work, so North delegated their outstanding jobs to Zion and Truck, and North and Shaw holed up in the duplex. Pari picked up two new MacBooks for them, and they tried to rebuild what they had lost in the fire, North restoring files from backups, reaching out to clients, redirecting mail and paperwork for Borealis, and Shaw spending hours on the phone with the insurance company.

But part of what made the days drag on was that after that first night, Shaw and North had both committed themselves to some kind of inescapable ballet. North set up his laptop in the living room, where he kept ESPN on at a low murmur. Shaw set up his in the kitchen, where the window over the sink looked out on the privacy fence and the alley. When North went into the kitchen for a glass of water, Shaw had to use the bathroom. When Shaw stretched his legs by walking up and down the hall, North needed something in the basement.

In what Shaw realized was a kind of karmic retribution from the universe, they came closest to each other at moments when they both seemed most vulnerable. North came out of the bathroom with nothing but a towel around his waist, smelling like wet hair and Irish Spring soap, and at the exact same moment, Shaw came around the corner and stumbled into him. They righted each other, mumbled apologies, and separated, but not before Shaw had noticed that North's eyes were red and his cheeks splotchy. Or when Shaw got tangled in yet more red tape with his insurance company, and he sat on the back stoop to have a vicious, screaming-and-crying-and-venting moment, North let himself in from the alley, tucking a rectangular package of something into his jeans' pocket.

North froze and then finished putting whatever it was in his pocket. He crossed the tiny backyard with his usual long stride. "Everything ok?"

"Peachy."

North hesitated; the opening was there.

"What were you doing in the alley?" Shaw asked.

North squeezed past him, the smell of cigarette smoke trailing him, and took the steps up into the house in one lunge. Over his shoulder, he said, "Trying not to go out of my fucking mind."

Nothing from the Chittendens, although the story was splashed all over the local news, and in what must have been a slow news cycle, even made it to national primetime for a single evening. Someone had coined the phrase "Bunker Boy," which didn't come close to the truth but which made a nice spin for a story about a young man with mental health problems who had been found by his loving family.

The story was so outrageous that Shaw said, "Turn it off."

"I want to hear if they mention us."

Shaw stood and left.

Behind him, the volume increased to a roar. Then, a minute later, the TV went silent, and North swore, and something plastic cracked when it hit the wall.

On Wednesday, the reporters evaporated, drawn by the churn of fresh chum in the waters. That afternoon, Gavin the assistant appeared on their doorstep. He was holding a manila envelope.

"They're very grateful." He held out the envelope, which North took. "This should cover the additional time you spent on the investigation after you parted ways."

"After they canned our asses, you mean," North said.

"You understand why they're not officially recognizing your part in this happy ending."

"Because they're lying." Shaw's breath hitched in his chest. "Because they're lying about all of it."

"There's also a little something in here for your discretion."

"We're professionals," North said. "We don't talk about our clients, and we don't need to be bribed."

Gavin shrugged. His face was oily in the spring sunlight, and it looked like he might be trying to grow in a wispy mustache. Maybe he'd just hit puberty.

"Then consider it an expression of thanks. The senator has also asked me to communicate that she will be recommending your services to her friends." He waited, probably hoping for the gratitude and awe that ought to have naturally followed a pronouncement of Providence turning her gentle face to them.

Instead, North spat on the stoop, barely missing Gavin's shiny oxfords. "Fuck off."

The shock on Gavin's face was the last thing Shaw saw before North shut the door.

"Sorry," North mumbled. "If you want to talk to him some more, I'll apologize."

"No." Shaw tried to figure out what to say, but all he could come up with was "That was perfect."

But that night, when Shaw walked into the living room and kissed the back of North's neck, North walked out of the house without a word and stayed in the alley for forty-five minutes, pinned under the cone of the security light. Shaw had retreated to the bedroom by the time he came back inside; he couldn't stand the thought of North rejecting him again, even if it was only in his expression.

On Thursday, Shaw had to get out of the house. He called one of those we'll-pick-you-up rental car services, and he left without saying a word to North. The last thing he saw, as he pulled the door shut behind him, was North glancing over his shoulder with a question on his face.

He spent the day shopping. New clothes. New shoes. The most important herbal supplements. Some new tea blends. Body oils and butters and creams. Bath salts. Books. A parchment roll and a quill made from a raven's feather that had been blessed by the local high priestess of Hecate, who also did real estate, and was he looking to rent or buy? In the clearance aisle of Scent-sory Impressions, he found a candle called Blue Snow Cone. He remembered the summer after freshman year, when he'd been recovering from the Slasher attack, and North bringing him snow cones day after day because Shaw wasn't eating much and sometimes he was hot with fever. He remembered North getting the Fourth of July flavor—red, white and blue—but only eating the blue because, quote, "blue is the best flavor." North had sworn for a minute solid when Shaw pointed out he could have ordered a snow cone that was only blue.

Shaw bought the candle. The knot between his shoulder blades loosened. He took what felt like the first deep breaths in the last week. He tried a new açai bowl. He ate two theater-style boxes of peanut M&Ms. He got a massage, and while Candy dug her elbow into a knot in his back, she told him she made her own CBD oil, and he bought two bottles of it.

When Shaw came home, loaded down with bags, North was still in the living room, and ESPN was aggressively loud. Two guys were yammering at each other about baseball. One of them had a face like tomato soup.

North's head came up; his eyes were chips of ice. "You look like you had a nice day."

"I did." Shaw wobbled, steadied some of the bags, and managed to shut the door with his foot. "I needed to pick up some basics—"

North started to laugh.

Heat rushed into Shaw's face. He shifted; one of the bags slid down his arm, and when he tried to bump it back up, a tub of face cream fell out.

"I'll get it," Shaw said.

But North, still laughing, had picked up the tub and was inspecting it. "Leaf your skin beautiful with the only non-prescription face cream infused with real, healing flakes of twenty-four karat gold leaf." He tossed the tub in the air and caught it. "Just the basics, right? Fuck me, Shaw. You're a trip."

Shaw couldn't even say why that was the last straw, but it was. A riptide of hurt washed the ground out from under him. He dumped the bags, shoved North away—"Come on, I was just joking!"—and headed down the hall on autopilot. He'd spent the last week retreating to the bedroom; that's where he went now, instinct and routine guiding him there. He set the thumb lock and fell onto the bed, pressing the heels of his hands against his eyes, trying to summon the mantra that Master Hermes had revealed to him or the breathing exercise Dr. Farr had taught him or just a memory of a time when everything hadn't been quite so horrible. He kept himself on the edge of breaking down completely, and after a few moments, his eyes were hot and puffy, and his breathing was wet, but he wasn't crying.

North knocked softly.

"Go away," Shaw said. "Please."

"I want to apologize."

"Ok. Fine. Thank you. I'd like to be alone right now."

"Shaw, please?"

"Just give me a few minutes."

After a moment, North's steps moved away, but he was back—according to the clock—in less than five minutes, knocking again.

"North," Shaw groaned, throwing a pillow at the door. "Go away!"

"No, I feel bad, and I don't like what I did, and I want to apologize. And I hate when you're sad because you get my pillows all snotty and then I have to change the sheets."

"Well," Shaw scrambled for a slightly softer version of *fuck you* and settled on "Too bad. I don't want you to come in. And if I want to get the pillows snotty, I will. And I'm not changing the sheets because there aren't any clean ones. And I'm not doing your laundry because you've got boot socks in there."

"What the fuck are boot socks? Don't answer that."

"Boot socks are the socks you wear when—"

A massive crack made Shaw stop, and he sat up as the door shot open, the latch tearing away from the frame. North stood there, framed by the light from the hallway, holding something in each hand.

"You can't do that!"

"Sure I can." North stepped inside the bedroom, catching the door with his shoulder when it bounced back. "It's my house."

"It's not your house. You rent."

"Guess I won't get my deposit back."

North was still coming toward the bed, so Shaw scrambled back, sliding on the mattress until his shoulders hit the wall. When North reached the foot of the bed, though, he dropped onto the corner, the mattress shifting under his weight. He set whatever he was carrying on the floor. After a sidelong glance at Shaw, he lay back and stared up at the ceiling.

"You made your point," Shaw said. "You're this big, macho guy, and you can kick down doors, and wow, I'm so impressed and very turned on. Can you go now?"

Without looking over, North patted the bed next to him.

"I'm going to make myself something to eat," Shaw said. "I haven't eaten all day, and I don't want to do this with you right now."

"I'll come with. I want some cheese. And I'm not going to slice it, either. I'm going to take bites out of the wedge, the way cheese is meant to be eaten."

"That is so gross!" Shaw rubbed his mouth. "Fine. I'll go play with the puppy in the backyard. You and I need some space."

"I've been meaning to work on my tan. It's a nice day, plenty of sun."

"No, God, you're so white I'll go blind if I look at you."

From Mr. Winns's unit above them came the theme song for *The Young and the Restless.*

North patted the bed beside him again.

"You're so annoying."

"I haven't even gotten started."

"You don't know how to respect boundaries. How am I supposed to believe you respect me as a person when you won't respect my boundaries?"

"Come over here," North said in that low smolder of a voice, "and I'll whisper the answer in your ear."

With the most dramatic sigh Shaw could muster, he flopped his way down the length of the bed, bouncing as much as possible until he lay next to North.

"So," North said, still looking up at the ceiling, "I've been doing some thinking recently, and I might have some issues with money."

"How recently?"

"The last seven minutes. But I think they might have been there for a while."

Mr. Winns was puttering around upstairs, joists creaking under his steps, and then a mysterious clunk. What had fallen? The Pepsi off his TV tray? A stack of vintage *Penthouse*? One of the crystal angels he kept in a china cabinet in the front room?

"It makes me feel like you hate me," Shaw said. "No, that's not right. But like you resent me. And I don't know what to do. Do you want me to give it all away to charity? Because I'll—"

North started laughing so hard that he curled up on the bed, rolling onto his side as the laughter rocked his body. Shaw rolled his eyes and started to scoot away, but North looped an arm around his waist and pulled him closer.

"God," North whispered, a hint of laughter still in the background, "you rich boys say some really dumb things."

Shaw pried at his fingers. "Ok, you said what you wanted to say, and now you're laughing at me, so—"

North rolled on top of him. They were close to the same height, although North was built more solidly, and his weight pinned Shaw to the mattress.

"Get off!"

"I'm sorry I talked to you like that. And I'm sorry for what I said. You're generous, and you're kind, you use what you've got to make people happy. I'm happy you grew up with people who could take care of you. It's certainly not your fault that I feel so…out of place. I've felt that way since my first day at Chouteau, and that's part of why Tucker—" He cut off and closed his eyes. When he opened them again, they were wet, and he leaned forward and brushed his lips against Shaw's. It was a schoolboy kiss, shy, almost fearful.

Shaw raised his head and kissed him again, and this time, North's mouth parted, and Shaw slipped his tongue inside. Shaw was instantly hard; he'd been sporting a semi since North kicked in the door, and now the erection was painful. He rocked up into North's substantial body, their bodies meeting at the right spot, and North groaned.

"Slow down," he whispered, stroking Shaw's hair with trembling fingers. His fingers smelled like candlewax and blue snow cone. "I want to talk about this some more."

"No talking," Shaw said. He worked his hands between them, fumbling with North's waistband.

"You like talking." North kissed him. "You always want to talk. I want to figure out some healthy ways to talk about money situations—" The button of his waistband came undone, and he said, "Shaw, I'm serious. We can have make-up sex after—" He cut off with a throaty noise as Shaw wrapped a hand around him. He thrust into Shaw's grip, and then again, his hips giving abortive little jerks like he was trying to hold back. They went like that for a few minutes, Shaw teasing him when North's self-control threatened to reassert itself, his grip increasingly slick and North's hips stuttering faster and faster. "Shit, baby, it's been too long. Let me go or I'm gonna—"

"You kicked down that door," Shaw said, his voice husky as he tightened his grip, "you big fucking brute, and now look at you."

North made a noise Shaw hadn't heard before, arousal and desperation. "Yeah. Fuck yeah. Yell at me. Tell me what a piece of shit I am." He made the noise again, rutting into Shaw. "Tell me how I don't deserve you."

And what Shaw wanted to say was that he didn't think that at all. He thought North was the best man he'd ever met. He thought he didn't deserve North, not the other way around. But he couldn't seem to think straight, and instead, he grabbed a handful of North's hair and pulled, and what came out of his mouth was "You come in here, just a big swinging dick, thinking you can do whatever the fuck you want and I'll let you get away with it?"

"Yes, shit, own me—own my ass—" North's face screwed up like a man with an unbearable secret, and then terror and release comingled in his expression. A strained, "Oh fuck," ripped out of him, and warm, wet heat sprayed Shaw's belly.

North buried his face in the crook of Shaw's neck. His tears were hot against Shaw's skin. Shaw undid his own fly and jerked himself off in a few quick strokes, adding to the mess between them, shuddering through the orgasm. When he came down, North was kissing his neck softly, whispering to him: "I love you, you're so beautiful, you're the best thing in my entire life." A string of sweet things tying them together.

Shaw stroked his hair and the back of his head with one messy hand. He was surprised to feel tears again, North's body shaking under his touch.

"North, I didn't mean—"

"I know," North said, finally managing to wipe his face on Shaw's shirt. "I know. Sorry. That was just a lot. All of it. After the fight, and then…what you said at the end. It all kind of got in my head." He was quiet for a moment, taking big breaths, his exhalations warm against Shaw's chest. "Are we ok?"

"We will be."

Chapter 29

SATURDAY NIGHT FOUND NORTH McKinney in khakis and a blue blazer that was too tight across the shoulders. He stood under an amethyst sky, killing a Boston Lager, the first handful of glitter-dust stars competing with the strings of party lights hung across the Aldrich's back patio. Jazz was playing softly in the background, which sounded like somebody had let five-year-olds run amok, plucking a bass string here, slapping a cymbal there, a woman's voice like honey going down a garbage disposal.

The woman across from him was talking stocks. "And James insists that it's all a bubble, of course, but I really don't think I should be taking advice from a man who sends his kids to public school, do you?"

Whether North did or not was irrelevant, because the woman, in her linen smock and her diamond tennis bracelet and strappy heels, was already talking again. He made himself focus: easy smile, deep breaths, if you're going to make this relationship work, Shaw's got to feel like he can bring you to things like this. Preferably without you telling the other guests that you couldn't give two shits about the Dow.

Shaw had gone to get them fresh drinks, but that had been fifteen minutes ago. North didn't wear a watch, and he was pretty sure that even though this woman didn't seem to require much from him in the way of a conversational partner, she wouldn't look kindly on North pulling out his phone to check the time and, hell, see how the Cardinals were doing.

"—told me she saw Albion in a Target, and not even the one in Brentwood, and I said that I knew they'd been having money trouble ever since Edie started driving a Volvo." She seemed to surprise herself—she certainly surprised the hell out of North—with a tinkling, cut-glass laugh. "I mean, honestly, a Volvo!"

The murmur of voices ebbed and flowed with the jazz. A haze of cigar smoke floated with the party lights, and the chocolatey tobacco smell tempered the overpowering perfume—something citrusy and migraine-inducing—that the woman was wearing. People stood in small knots. A man in a too-small polo and pleated chinos. A woman in a pink wrap. A man talking golf; three other men waiting for their turn to talk golf. A woman explaining that you only had to say fibromyalgia, and Effie, whoever the fuck that was, would set you right up. A woman explaining that the Savage Clinic was the only place she'd go to get her 'tune-ups' from now on. A man, with watchful looks over his shoulder, bitching that the Savage Clinic was putting him in the poorhouse.

Words came on a gust of citrusy perfume. "—remember how you know Wilson and Phoebe?"

North's gaze cut to the happy couple, who were circulating now, spending a little time with each group, and then back to the woman. "I'm a friend of Shaw's."

"Oh." She made the word sound dirty. "How fabulous. He really did a wonderful job on his speech, didn't he?"

North made a noise.

"He's always had a way with words," the woman continued. "He knows just how to put his finger on whatever everyone wants to say."

Sure, North thought. Like how he told the electrician last week that he'd be doing the world a public service if he spent more time inventing electric dildos and less time rewiring old houses. And something in there about knob-and-tube wiring, of course. Out loud, though, all he said was "He really does."

The problem wasn't that the woman was wrong; the speech had been perfect. The problem was that Shaw seemed perfect too. Perfectly not Shaw.

Shaw emerged from the house. He was carrying another Boston Lager and a lowball glass with what North hoped was Coke and only Coke. He was wearing a navy suit that managed to look modern and stylish with its cut, emphasizing Shaw's slender musculature, while still being conservative. A floral-print button-down offered a subdued reminder that he was, after all, gay. Oxblood wingtips completed the ensemble. His hair wasn't pulled back, and he'd done something to it with a series of products that turned the wild poof into a perfectly tousled mess of curls. He'd even found a tasteful oil painting for his parents' gift, without any of the usual spins he put on things like bull semen or hoodoo dust or astral infusions. When Shaw had come out of the bathroom earlier that day, when North had seen the clothes and the hair and the complete absence of anything unicorn related, he had made the mistake of asking, "What the fuck is going on?"

Another gust of perfume. "—horrible business, of course, but you know all about that, I'm sure. Shaw, darling, I was just talking to your…friend." A salacious curve of the lips. It would have been less awkward if she'd just licked her chops and made a porking noise.

"Hi, Bitsy." Shaw bussed her cheek as he passed North the beer. "Are you keeping out of trouble?"

"I have to, darling, I absolutely have to. The police said that next time they'll throw me in the slammer!" Another of those cut-glass laughs with the suddenness of a falling chandelier. "They really said that!"

"Shoplifting is against the law, you know."

She made a dismissive noise. "Those earrings were sterling silver. The real crime was that someone was selling them in the first place."

"Wild, come here." Wilson Aldrich waved to his son. "I want you to say hi to Tyler." He gestured to the young man next to him, who looked like he'd barely hit his twenties. He was poured into jeans and a blazer, and his jawline looked sharp enough to cut titanium.

"Sorry," Shaw whispered to North.

North plastered a smile on his face. "Go on."

"I'm really sorry."

"It's fine."

When Shaw reached his father and Tyler, Tyler said something, and Shaw laughed, his whole face lighting up. North set the bottle to his lips and pounded half of it.

Bitsy was staring at him.

"Uh oh," she sing-songed.

The plaster smile was feeling scraped thin. "Excuse me."

Her eyes followed him as he plunged into the house. The party was denser here, the music louder, the smell of expensive colognes and expensive perfumes and raw silk and cigar smoke spinning like a drill bit against the side of North's head. He slipped between bodies, making his way to the bar set up on the far side of the room. The bartender was a middle-aged woman with a stylish undercut and the hints of tattoo sleeves poking out from under the cuffs of her shirts.

"Sam Adams," North said.

The jazz sounded like somebody was hitting a cat with a bagful of violins.

The bartender handed him the beer, and North dropped a couple of bucks in the tip jar. Then he spotted the fives and tens and twenties. He glanced up in time to see the look of annoyance on the woman's face before the professional mask dropped back into place.

"A Negroni, please." The voice was familiar, and North tried to take off in the opposite direction. He was too slow. A manicured hand dropped a twenty into the tip jar, and then that same hand squeezed North's shoulder. He sighed and turned to face Wilson.

"Nice of you to be here, North. Thanks for coming. We really appreciate it."

"Of course. I mean, I'm happy to be here. I mean, thanks for having me."

Wilson's face didn't change, but North knew another Aldrich pretty damn well, and he could sense the mixture of annoyance and bemusement behind the smile. "What do you think of Tyler?"

"Who?" North asked, which was a kind of lie.

"He's on the fast track, an absolute whiz with numbers. His dad runs a couple of major hedge funds—apple didn't fall far from the tree."

"Sounds like you want Shaw to trade up."

Wilson's eyes cut down to North's hands, where North carried a fresh beer in one and, in the other, the beer he had just finished. The smile took on a patronizing indulgence. "That's one way to a handle a boring party, I guess."

"No, I was just—"

"Be careful, North. That's a slippery road."

He laughed too loud. "Don't worry about me. I've seen what that looks like up close; I'm not going to make that mistake."

Wilson's answer was a faint arch of his eyebrows.

"I just meant—" North's face was on fire. "It's just a little social lubricant, you know? Grease the wheels."

"I'm sorry you feel like we're so hard to get along with," Wilson said.

"That's not—"

But the bartender had returned with the Negroni, and Wilson headed off into the crowd.

North ran through his options: buy a one-way plane ticket to Colombia and learn Spanish; join the French Foreign Legion; scream, "Fire," at the top of his lungs and hope to get trampled to death.

Instead, he pounded back the rest of the beer.

When he lowered the bottle, Phoebe Archibald, Shaw's mother, was staring at him. "I'm glad to see you're enjoying the party, North."

"Mrs. Aldrich, hi."

She was a pretty woman, trim, in her late fifties. Shaw had gotten his build from his father, but his face, with those refined features and their sharp symmetry, had come from his mother. Her sheath dress was a blue so pale that it was almost white, and the lace ruffles gave it bridal echoes, probably intentional considering it was her anniversary. Chunky ebony bangles, with sharp lines and rough edges, slipped and clattered along one arm, and the contrast with the dress and the refined features was shocking, an effect that North guessed was, again, intentional.

"Pace yourself," she said, and her clipped tone reminded North that this woman was a professor at a prestigious university as well as an accomplished painter. "Wilson had an uncle who always said a beer in each hand kept him grounded."

"No, one of them is—"

"Had, North. Past tense. The poor man didn't go easily either. Maybe a soft drink next time." Her hazel eyes—Shaw's hazel eyes—narrowed. "They do have meetings for this kind of thing."

"I was just holding it," North said, and when he heard his own words, the old teenage defense, the flush spread into his chest. He felt dizzy. He tried for the plaster smile, but it flaked away. Over the speakers, someone was bopping and scatting, nonsense syllables that made North feel like he'd gotten trapped in a nightmare.

Phoebe offered a tiny smile and patted his arm. She turned.

North envisioned the rest of his life like this, year after year, the parties where he didn't know what to do or what to say or where to be, while this Shaw who was a stranger fluttered and flitted and smiled at guys who were a ten out of ten on the boner scale. He tried to figure out what he could do, how he could make this work for Shaw's sake.

"You look beautiful," North said. "Congratulations. Thirty years is very impressive."

Phoebe redirected her attention at him, and this time, the smile was fractionally warmer. "Thank you, North. That's kind of you." She paused, and voices from the rest of the room rushed to fill the vacuum between them. "You could have brought Tucker, of course."

The words didn't make any sense, so North laughed because he didn't know what else to do. Confusion slipped across Phoebe's narrow features. North's laughter dried up. He swallowed and said, "That's nice, but why would I—I mean, I don't think he'd—" He laughed again, and this time, it hurt. "I'm sorry. Maybe I did have too much to drink."

In a confidential voice, Phoebe said, "That's why it's a good idea to bring your husband. Next time, then. I know Wilson enjoys talking shop with him. And Shaw needs to see examples of men in committed relationships. I worry about him; he's getting too good at being single."

The music was suddenly way too loud. North stared at her. His face felt stiff, the flesh plasticized. Bodies jostled him. Bebop-ba-bop. Scatting cool cats all the way. The heat in the room suffocated him, and he had to fight the urge to drop the beers, let them shatter on the fancy floor, and rip his tie and collar loose so he could get one motherfucking breath.

"North, dear, are you all right? You're white as a sheet."

He plunged toward the front door.

"Wilson?" Phoebe's voice was a tin-can call at the other end of the universe. "Shaw? Has anyone seen Shaw?"

Chapter 30

SCHNUCKS HAD THE TWELVE-packs of Schlafly on an endcap, which was good, because North's eyes weren't focusing right, and he wasn't sure he could have found them otherwise. He loaded four into the cart, ran blearily through the self-checkout, and was back in the GTO in seven minutes. He was home ten minutes later, lugging the beer inside in two trips, the pain in his chest making him wonder, dimly, if he was having a heart attack. North didn't bother stocking the beer in the fridge; tonight wasn't that kind of night.

He let the puppy out and killed two beers standing in the doorway, the May air warm and humid. Like a breath, North thought, sweat popping out across his forehead. Like someone's breathing on my face, garbage breath, but that's just the dumpsters in the alley. Shaw had taken the trash out that morning, wearing another pair of those godawful Dutch clogs that he managed to find somewhere. North had to squeeze his eyes shut then, and he clutched the jamb so hard that one of his knuckles popped. He coughed, wiped his eyes, and did two little jump shots, the bottles tinkling as they shattered in the recycling bin. Then he got another beer, unwrapped a fresh pack of American Spirit, and really went to work.

When he heard an unfamiliar car out front, he stubbed out the cigarette, returned it to the pack, and stuffed the American Spirits into his pocket. In the middle of investigating a blackberry bramble, the puppy paused and cast a worried look at North. For a moment, North managed to sit perfectly still, and then he put his head back, opened his throat, and chugged the rest of the beer. He was getting another—his fourth? his fifth?—when the knock came at the door. North closed the fridge, staring at the painted steel, where a magnet held a picture Truck had drawn. It might have been a child's work, done in crayon, the stick figures disproportionate. They were holding hands. One had yellow hair and one had brown. NORTH AND SHAW, in Truck's scrawl, ran along the bottom, BUTT BUDDIES. North unclipped it from the magnet and folded it into a square, and then a smaller square, and then a smaller.

The knocking was getting louder.

The beer and tiny square of paper in one hand. One hand on the wall. His eyes had never really cleared up, so he had to blink as he opened the door and wedged his body in the gap.

"You fucking piece of shit."

Shaw had obviously been crying. Still was crying, maybe, although North's blurred vision made it hard to tell. "North, I am so—"

"You didn't tell your parents we're dating?"

Shaw opened his mouth.

"If you lie to me, we're done."

"It's not that I didn't tell them. It just never came up."

For a moment, North had nothing. Then he started to shut the door. "You are unbelievable."

"North, no, please—"

"It didn't come up? It didn't come up when they were trying to talk you into leaving Borealis? It didn't come up when they were trying to talk you into moving to Chicago or Boston or wherever the fuck they want you to be? It didn't come up when they were playing matchmaker with Tyler? Oh my God, it wasn't just him, was it? How many other guys have they set you up with?"

"Oh no, Tyler wasn't—"

"God damn it, Shaw!" He hurled the bottle. Brown glass shattered on the stoop, speckling Shaw's suit with beer suds. "You know what the worst part is? The worst part is I thought they hated me because they didn't think I was good enough for you. But that's not it, is it? They hate me just because I'm me. They hate me, and I'm not even your boyfriend. Jesus Christ. Can you imagine how they'd react if they knew? No wonder you never told them."

"North, please let me explain." Shaw dashed his sleeve across his eyes. "Please."

"No, I'm talking now. You wanted me to talk, remember? So I'm talking now. It's my turn to talk. This is about the lowest fucking way to treat someone, do you understand that? Like I'm not even a person. That's bad, Shaw. But what's even worse is that you lied to me. You let me believe they knew. You let me walk into that party, in their home, with all their friends, and you let me think they knew. For fuck's sake, what if I'd tried to kiss you? Were you going to run away? Were you going to pretend to faint? Is that why you spent as much time as possible away from me, left me alone with people I don't know, with fucking Bitsy?"

"I—"

"Shut up!" Aggravated breathing threatened to choke North. "Here's the funny thing, Shaw. We've always been able to joke around; maybe you'll get a laugh out of this. When I left Tucker, I told myself I'd never let someone treat me like that again. He hit me, and he cheated on me, and he fucked with my head about every way imaginable. And then I turn around, and I'm immediately in the same kind of relationship again, only even worse. And do you know why it's worse? Because Tucker treated me like a worthless fucking nobody. But at least he wasn't ashamed of me."

The color bled from Shaw's face. North had seen Shaw after some pretty serious injuries; he recognized the waxy cast, the blue-gray tinge to his lips, the lusterless quality of his eyes.

"North." Shaw stopped. He gripped the porch's handrail, swaying. "Please?"

Chest heaving, North fought with the image of shoving Shaw down the steps, of following him out onto the lawn, of landing a slap and then maybe another one, harder, something that would put him on his ass. His throat tightened. His eyes stung. He didn't trust himself to speak, so he nodded.

"I am so sorry—"

"Stop saying that." North cleared his throat. "If that's all you have to say, then you should go."

"I didn't tell them. You're right. But it's not because I'm ashamed of you. I love you. You're the best, most wonderful man in the entire world, and I don't deserve you. Especially after this. But I'll never stop loving you because you're amazing." Shaw made a noise that sounded like an animal in pain, and he scrubbed one-handed at his face. "There's something inside me that doesn't want to do what people want me to do. It's messed up. I know it is. But sometimes everything seems so ordinary, so basic, and this part of me just refuses to go along with it. Sometimes it's a good thing. If I were normal, I wouldn't have started Borealis with you; I would have gone to a PhD program or law school. If I were normal, I might not have met you—my parents wanted me to go to Wash U, not Chouteau. But a lot of the times, it's a bad thing. I know I annoy you with my weird clothes and my weird food and my weird ideas. I know I'm not an easy person to get along with, and the fact that you put up with me makes me love you even more."

"So I'm ordinary or basic or whatever, and what, if I'd shown up tonight with a unicorn-tail butt plug, you'd have marched me right up to your parents and told them we were together?"

"No, no, no." Shaw was staring at the stoop. "My parents have this way of getting inside my head. They push and push and push, and they think they're doing it for the best. They have these huge hopes and dreams for me. But they're not my hopes and dreams. And they're so good at all these games that sometimes the only way I can win is if I don't play by their rules. They want me to get together with someone like Tyler. They want me to get a surrogate in the next three years and have two kids. They want me to go back to school while Tyler brings home the big bucks. They want me to buy a house in the Central West End or Lafayette Square. I thought if I changed my clothes and pretended to think about grad school, they'd stop pressuring me about guys. That was stupid; I know that. But it's more than that. I...I just hated the thought of bringing you into that. I hated the thought of having to listen to their disapproval of you, even though they would have made everything sound like they were just pointing out facts and worrying about what was best for me. I hated having to play that basic hetero game of bringing a partner home for my parents' approval. I just wanted it to be us because we're so good together."

The sun was finally setting. The last light seemed intensely bright at the horizon, a final surge of brilliance that caught on the hi-vis reflective tape that marked off a section of pavement, glittered on the windshields of parked cars, danced on tin flashing. Two kids burst out of the house down the street, laughing, roller blades and hockey sticks in hand.

"Watch for cars," their mom shouted from the doorway as the boys set up their game in the street.

"You know what, Shaw? Maybe that's what you think you were doing. Maybe that's what you tell yourself. But you know what the problem is? It's not just you anymore. I matter too. What I want matters."

"I know—"

"Really? Because it sure as fuck seems like you don't. You do what you want, Shaw. Always. It's how you dress. It's how you spend your money. It's what you do with my fucking food. And it's one of the things I love about you, but fuck, Shaw, we're in this together now. You won't even talk about moving in together; that's not what you want, so it's not even an option. You show up high to jobs. We take the cases you want to take, even when we're already booked. You forgave Johanna Griffin's debt without asking me. You went to talk to Ronnie behind my back, for fuck's sake."

A spark of something angry and defensive ignited in Shaw's eyes, and he opened his mouth.

North talked over him. "It's everything. You did it with Flip; you fought and fought and fought until I backed down. You do it with sex. It doesn't matter what I want—you push and you push until you get what you want. You can't do whatever you want and then say, 'I love you,' and expect things to be ok again. You're part of something bigger now. We're together; we do things together, we decide things together.'"

"That's not what I do!"

"Oh yeah? When I was too tired last week, did that stop you? When I said I wanted you to fuck me, is that what we did? What about a couple weeks before that, when I said I didn't want to play with those new toys, and ten minutes later you're shoving an alien-tentacle dildo inside me? God, Shaw, I'm not a sex doll, all right? And I'm not a wet dream. I'm a person, even if I am an asshole most of the time. And this thing, with your parents, it's the same fucking thing. Did you ask me how I felt about you not telling them? Did you even let me know that's what you had decided? Did you ever consider that it's a relationship, that we're a couple, and that we need to decide things together? We've spent the last week dealing with kids whose batshit parents try to run their lives, but it's not just parents who want to run people's lives and live out their fantasies through them, Shaw. You're doing it too. To me. And I'm so fucking sick of it I'm going out of my mind!" Between the adrenaline and the Schlaflys, North's legs were starting to shake, and he had to lean harder against the jamb. His rage cycled up and up; the last tenuous thread of control snapped. He felt like he was shouting up from the bottom of a well, shouting as hard as he could, and his voice still barely audible. "For fuck's sake, Tucker, I'm a person!"

If anything, Shaw's color had gotten worse. He white-knuckled the handrail, and the other hand was pressed low over his belly. Where the Slasher had stabbed him, North thought.

The slap of a stick against a ball echoed up the street. One of the boys cheered, while the other shouted, "That's not fair! That's not fair!" The boy who had scored skated victory laps, whooping and pumping his arm.

"I don't know where that came from," North managed to say. "I'm sorry. I don't think of you two—"

"Please stop."

The breeze riffled North's hair. He focused on the shards of glass sparkling on the stoop. "I think we should take some time off."

Shaw nodded jerkily.

"From each other, I mean."

"I knew what you meant."

"Do you want to come inside," North dragged his gaze up, "and get a few things?"

Shaw closed his eyes slowly. When he opened them again, North couldn't make out the variegated green and brown, and he realized how dark it had gotten. Shaw shook his head.

"I know you're tired of me saying this," Shaw said, voice low but firm. "But I really am sorry, North. I love you so much, and I never, ever wanted to make you feel this way."

His waiting was a question, and North didn't have the answer.

"Night, Shaw," he said and closed the door.

Chapter 31

HALFWAY THROUGH THE BEER, North decided a drive was a good idea.

He found himself going west on I-44, exiting at Elm, heading north. Webster Groves was one of the inner-most suburbs, with old, expensive homes on tree-lined lots. The Schaflys were navigating, so North was half surprised and half not when he found himself parked in front of a Japanese maple, looking down a long drive to a two-story house with a detached garage. Night hung over everything in thick, velvet folds, but the house was bright and shining. North jingled the keys in the ignition. He could walk up to the door. His key would still work; he knew it would. He could walk inside, into the smell of boutique cologne and furniture polish and the Bath and Body Works air fresheners, and he could sprawl on the sofa, and he could flip channels with a beer on the floor next to him, the condensation making a ring on the rug that Tucker would bitch about. He could go home.

He leaned back, closed his eyes, and came unmoored for a while.

Tapping woke him, and he looked over at the passenger window. The texture of the night had coarsened to felt; he could almost feel it between his fingers. Everything had a dreamlike quality. Everything was unreal and hyperreal at the same time. Tucker's face was the moon, his hair spilling out of its neat part, his expression unreadable. He tapped the glass again, and North leaned over to roll the window down.

"Hi," Tucker said.

North stared at him; he felt his head wobbling on his neck.

"You don't look so good."

North's mouth was fuzzy. He tried to work moisture into it.

With a small smile, Tucker cocked his head. "I saw you sitting out here, and I got myself all worked up for a fight, and now I'm thinking maybe that's not why you came over."

"It is." North's voice was rough. He swallowed. "I want a fight. I came over here for a fight."

Neither of them moved. The crickets were making their usual racket, and a whiff of Tucker's cologne floated through the car.

"Maybe you should come inside for a little while," Tucker said softly. "Before we fight, I mean."

North gave a jerky shake of his head. It took him two tries to start the GTO, and Tucker stepped back with a sigh.

"You really don't look good. Are you sure you should drive?"

Another five seconds, and it might have worked. Instead, North turned too sharply as he pulled away from the curb, overcorrected, and barely avoided hitting a utility pole. When he got home, he called himself every bad name he could think of as he sat in the garage, head in his hands, and tried not to cry.

He drank himself unconscious that night, spent the next day on the sofa, and got black-out drunk again. Monday, he woke to a hangover and his phone buzzing. Groaning, he rolled to reach for it. The puppy let out a startled squawk and squeezed out from under him, turning to offer a barking reprimand when he was clear.

"Sorry," North mumbled as he answered the phone.

"You should be," Haw said. "Why does it take me three tries to get you on the phone?"

North sat up; the headache banged twice as hard, and he put a hand over his mouth to keep from being sick. After a moment, he said, "Shit went down. What do you want?"

"I want my private investigator to get his ass over to the lab. That guy who impersonated a delivery driver? I think he's going to try again. Today."

"What?" North scraped crusties from his eyes. "Why?"

"Because Borer Logistics, that's the delivery company he infiltrated last time, is making another delivery today."

Somehow, North managed to get to his feet, although his headache went nuclear, and he had to brace himself on the back of the sofa. He wondered, vaguely, what Haw would think of her private investigator puking down the front of his tank and boxers. When he wasn't going to puke anymore, he asked, "You think he's stupid enough to try the same scam again?"

"I don't know. But I know I'm not stupid enough to risk it. I need you here all day; put whatever you want on the invoice."

"Half an hour."

It was more like an hour: he drank water until his stomach sloshed every time he took a step, and he put down four ibuprofen; by the time he'd showered and picked up coffee, he felt quasi human again. He must not have looked it, though, because the guard at the security booth gave him a commiserating nod, and Haw snorted when she met him in the lobby.

"Did you get hit by a truck?"

"Rough night."

"I'll say. Where's Shaw?"

"He's working on something else."

"You're kidding me, right? This is the family business; what could be more important than that?"

"Call him," North bit off, "and ask him yourself."

Footsteps echoed from somewhere down the hall, and then the sound of a door opening and closing. The kid at reception was typing frantically—probably hoping he could type himself into invisibility.

All Haw said, though, was "What do you need to get started?"

"When does the truck usually get here?"

"Afternoon."

"Ok. I'll start by looking around, checking for weak spots. If you're right, they'll probably change up the timing; the truck will get here early or late because they'll be trying to throw off your routine, catch you while you're busy with something else. Call me as soon as it gets here. Oh, shit. I'll need another access card. Shaw took—Shaw has the one you gave him."

"We can do that," Haw said. She didn't look like a woman capable of much pity, but her gaze did suggest that she considered North pathetic. "You're sure you should be here?"

"I'll be fine." Then a wave of nausea broke over him, and North gritted out: "Just point me to the restroom."

After some enthusiastic puking, he wiped his face with wet paper towels, which were cool against his flushed skin and smelled like public school bathrooms. Haw was waiting for him with another access card, which he took, and then he began to make his rounds. Any real security operation had multiple levels, and some of those were beyond North's paygrade, figuratively and literally. Electronic, operational, and information security weren't in this job description, and even if he'd wanted to inspect them, he wasn't equipped to do so. But the physical security, well, that was something he could handle.

After some help gearing up with PPE, he started at Lab 14, which he had begun to think of as a kind of vault—a vault that Ronnie wanted to crack. His access card granted him entrance. As far as North was concerned, the inside of any self-respecting vault should resemble Scrooge McDuck's swimming pool full of gold coins. The lab, though, wasn't a vault. It wasn't even a single room, the way North had been imagining it, but rather a complex, with windows and sightlines that made it easy for North to move around the perimeter, once he was inside the controlled area, and examine the space without entering each individual room. Some of the lab was what he'd expected, with its fluorescent lighting, shelves of reagents, intimidatingly featureless machines, gaping fume hoods, and cream-colored linoleum. But there was also a separate office space, a cryostorage room (which had something in it that looked like a little R2D2), safety showers, eye-wash stations, decontamination kits mounted in high-visibility locations—on and on like that. Even though it didn't look like a vault, North thought, if Wilson Aldrich was right, the information in this building was worth billions. North still would have taken the swimming pool and the gold coins.

After a thorough search, he decided the only access point was the secured door through which he had entered. The lab had a self-contained HVAC system, according to Haw, and there was no way that Ronnie would be able to pull a John McClane-style crawl-through-the-ducts entrance, for the simple reason that the ducts were much too small. The door itself looked secure too; North couldn't spot any signs of tampering with the electronic lock, the card reader, or the frame. If Ronnie was going to get in, he'd need something seriously destructive—or he'd need inside help.

He worked his way through the building in a spiral pattern, checking doors and windows and locks, testing cameras, even elbowing aside acoustic tiles to hammer on the roof access hatch. It was solid and secure, just like everything else North had checked. Spitting foam particles, he lowered himself from the drop ceiling and headed outside.

Aside from the main entrance, the Nonavie building had three points of access: fire doors on each side, and the docks at the back. He gave the fire doors a careful inspection, but like everything else at the facility, they seemed to be in good condition, with no obvious signs of tampering. They didn't even have exterior locks fitted for keys; the only way in through the fire doors was with an access card. One area did give North pause; a few cigarette butts and webbed lawn chairs, folded now and leaning against the side of the building, told him this was the smoke-break zone. He'd worked on enough job sites to know how frequently those smoke breaks could come, and how quickly people became tired of keying in and out of secure locations. He eyed the base of the door, looking for chipped paint or scratches that would suggest a rock or paver had been used to prop it open, but he didn't see anything of the sort. As far as he could tell, the Nonavie employees weren't taking any shortcuts when it came to security. Well, aside from the security asshat who had sold out to Ronnie in the first place.

He was working his way along the fence when his dad called. North ignored him the first two times and answered the third.

"I'm working."

"That'd be a change. What's this I hear about you bailing on a job for Ronnie?"

"I don't have time for this. I'll talk to you later."

"Ronnie's been coming around. He says you're slacking. He says he gave you a cake job, one that's right on the beam for the airy-fairy detective agency. He says you're not doing shit, and somebody might be in trouble because of it."

North stopped and leaned against the cyclone fencing; it sagged under his weight, rattling and chiming, and he breathed in hints of rust. The day was bright, and the concertina wire held a glare along its razor edges. "What do you mean he's been coming around? Did he hurt you? Did he try something?"

Silence. And then, in a tone of pure shock, "Ronnie?"

"Answer the question."

"He comes around to bitch about your lazy ass and about how ungrateful you are. Like usual. Just what a father likes to hear. You didn't tell me the airy-fairy agency burned down."

The light on the wire sharpened, and North squeezed his eyes shut. The smell of wet earth. The smell of wild sage he'd trampled. "I'm not sure it matters. Shaw's—he's doing his own thing now. I think. I don't know, it's all messed up."

More of that silence. North forced himself to stand up straight, and the cyclone fence chittered in relief.

"Well," his father said, "it's about fucking time."

"What?"

"He's a dead weight. He's always been a dead weight. It's about fucking time you cut him loose. Look, you've gotten your name out there. People know you. People know you do good work. What do you need him for, now? You get your butt to a bank today, fill out the small business loan papers, and get your own thing going. Drop the queer stuff."

"Yeah, well, if that was an option, we wouldn't be here, would we?"

"You know what I mean. You are who you are. I'm talking about the business. Drop the homo angle, and just run a damn good agency. But first, you do what Ronnie asked you to do."

North kicked the fence; the impact rippled along the chain links with more of those rattling chimes. "Do you know what Ronnie wants me to do?"

David McKinney huffed.

"Fuck, Dad. And you're still on his side?"

"He's asking you for a favor. The same way he did us a favor—he's done you plenty, you know. We owe him. We gave our word. David McKinney's word means something."

"And mine doesn't?"

"Not if you're going to leave Ronnie hanging."

"He's asking me to help him steal something. He wanted me to help him blackmail a guy."

"He's asking you to help him take a tiny bit from somebody who already has too much. He's asking you to give that money to somebody who could use it."

"Holy shit." North laughed, and his stomach gave a queasy lurch. "He's giving you a cut?"

"Listen to me, North—"

"What about all that 'earn your own way' bullshit? What about putting me on a job when I was sixteen and making me pay for my own car and my own gas and my own insurance? What about all the shit I had to eat so I could pay for college and a place to stay?"

"You could have stayed here. You know you always—"

"You know what? Dr. Farr would have a fucking field day with this. No wonder I can't have a healthy relationship."

"Who's Dr. Farr? What are you talking about?"

"Doesn't matter. I've got to go."

"You think you're better than me, but I've got news for you: you're cut from the same cloth, kiddo. Take a look in the mirror sometime. You can ride your high horse now, but when you're not even sixty but you feel eighty, when the cancer's eating you from the inside out, come back and talk to me again about earning your own way. Life's short; you've got to get yours while you can. I wish I had."

An incoming call buzzed. Haw's name showed on the screen.

In a slightly gentler voice, North said, "I've got to go."

"Sure you do," his father said and disconnected.

"The truck's at the gate," Haw said. "Early, like you said."

The fire dancing along the concertina wire made his head throb and his eyes water. He wiped his face. "On my way."

When he got to the dock, the Borer truck was backing up, a steady beep-beep-beep warning off anyone standing behind it. North eyed the driver in the cab. It wasn't Ronnie; this guy was lanky, with a narrow face, and he had thin, stringy hair that North guessed was an attempt to hide baldness.

"That doesn't look like the guy in the photographs." Haw stood at his elbow; judging by the bulge under her jacket, North figured she was carrying.

"It's not him," North said. "He might have abandoned this approach. Hell, he might have called off the whole thing; I was sure he was going to try when I went out of town, but nothing happened."

"Wishful thinking. I put extra guys in the warehouse; we're going to watch every move this guy makes until he's back on the truck and getting the hell out of here."

North nodded. The truck rocked up against the dock bumpers, and then the brakes engaged, and the driver killed the engine. He got down from the cab slowly, an aluminum storage clipboard under one arm, and gave North a glance. Then he took a second look, obviously sensing North's interest. He made a tough guy face and strutted to meet the dock manager. Haw moved to follow.

"Check everything they unload," North said.

Haw frowned and then nodded. "You're thinking a Trojan-horse kind of situation."

The urge to make a crack about that, the certainty that Shaw wouldn't miss the opportunity, was so engrained that it hurt when North remembered Shaw wasn't with him. He just nodded and followed Haw into the warehouse.

Everyone tried to pretend the delivery was normal, but nobody bought it. The guys who worked the dock threw uncertain glances at each other and at the stern-faced security guards who drifted among them. The driver was babbling, telling joke after joke, as though he could laugh his way out of there. The dock manager was a woman with buzzed hair and carpenter jeans, and after the fourteenth or fifteenth joke, she snapped at the driver to shut up while she checked the paperwork. Haw spoke quietly with several of the guards, and they moved to follow the men who were unloading the truck. North went with them to inspect each box and crate, in case Ronnie had managed to buy someone else off.

He was digging through a box of toilet paper when he heard Haw say, "No, I said that area was closed off. I know what you're saying. What I'm saying is, why the fuck is it happening?"

And then North knew. It was happening right now. Right under their noses.

"He's not even supposed to be in the building." Her head whipped toward North. "Why is your partner inside Lab 14?"

North pulled out his phone, grabbed his temporary access card, and placed the call as he ran.

"Pick up, pick up, pick up," he whispered. "Shaw put down the blunt or the yoga mat or the rayon lederhosen and pick up the goddamn phone."

"North?" Shaw's voice was tentative and achingly full of hope. "God, you have no idea how happy—"

"Do you have your access card?"

"What?"

"The access card your dad had them make for you. Do you have it?"

"I don't—"

"Shaw, for fuck's sake, do you have it?"

"No, it's not in my wallet. I left it at your house. Why? Are you at the lab?"

And then North remembered coming home from the trip to Sikeston, the hours they'd spent getting Danny on a bus, and then coming home to find the back door ajar and Shaw's computer powered on. He'd thought Truck or Pari had watched some porn and forgotten to pull the door shut all the way when they'd left. The door had to be slammed; it swung open if you didn't slam it. But now it all made sense: Danny had been a distraction, just like North had suspected. Only Ronnie hadn't been planning on breaking into the lab by himself. That's why he hadn't had a cryoflask on that initial try. The whole thing, from Ronnie's first, seemingly botched attempt, had been a setup. He'd wanted to fail, wanted to be seen. He'd known they'd be pulled in to help with security. He'd known they'd be given access. And then he'd sent them chasing their own tails while he lifted the card from the duplex.

He'd been able to walk right into the Nonavie lab.

When North got to Lab 14, it took him two tries with the access card to get the door open. He stepped inside and knew he was too late: the cryostorage door propped open; the smell of gunpowder; the bullet hole in the fume hood on the other side of the room; the blood trickling around a lab bench. North went to find the first body, squatted to check for vitals. Her nametag said Dr. Lishi; she looked tiny in death, bird bones bundled in a lab coat now stained crimson.

Behind him, Haw was shouting into a walkie.

North shook his head, so tired that for a moment, he didn't think he could stand up. "He's already gone."

Chapter 32

THE CALL FROM NORTH sent Shaw into a spiral. He lay in his childhood bed in his childhood bedroom, the walls still decorated with his teenage preoccupations: a planar map of the Forgotten Realms spiderwebbed across one wall, with Cthulhu fanfiction stapled between the lengths of yarn that knit the whole thing together; on another wall, he'd used a projector to trace Whitman's Catullus poems, and he'd used paint pens and lots of glitter to create his own kind of blackout poems from the text; on another, larger-than-life posters of Paul Wesley and Ian Somerhalder stared down at him from where a teenage Shaw had tried to make them kiss. The curtains were drawn. His joint had burned itself out in the saucer that served as an improvised ashtray. Outside, someone was running a rototiller.

North had hung up on him.

North hadn't wanted to talk to him.

North had needed information, that was all. That was the only reason he had called.

Shaw thought about dragging himself across the bed and lighting the joint, but in the end, it seemed like too much effort.

The knock at the door sent a treacherous spike of hope through Shaw: North. He raised himself on one elbow, opened his mouth, and hesitated.

What if it wasn't North?

The answer came a moment later when the door opened and Shaw's mom called, "Sweetheart? Are you masturbating?"

Shaw flopped back onto the bed and closed his eyes. "No."

"If you are, it's all right."

"I know it's all right. We had this conversation when I was eleven. You made it perfectly clear that it was all right."

"We just want you to feel comfortable here," his father said. "We've heard you watching some pretty violent-sounding pornography—"

"Not that we're judging," his mom put in hastily.

"Not that we're judging, but we are a little worried. If you're interested in the BDSM scene, it's important to explore it safely. Your mother knows a man who's a very competent dom, and—"

"Oh my God, it's research for a case."

The pause was just long enough to hold the old, familiar, parental subtext: *bullshit.* But all his mom said was, "Well, that's nice, then."

"I appreciate you checking on me," Shaw said, "and I want you to know that I recognize and validate your worry. I'm really grateful that you can vocalize your concern, but I really want you to hear me when I say that I'd like to be alone."

He'd peppered in all the magic words, but this time, the spell didn't work. Their footsteps were muffled by the thick carpet, but he could still hear them moving across the room. The mattress dipped on one side of him, and then on the other. Cool, soft fingers—his mother's fingers—brushed hair away from his forehead.

"Sweetheart, your father and I think you might be experiencing some mild depression."

"I'm not."

"Buddy," his dad began.

"It's not mild. It's extreme. It's clinical. It's Nessus, the ninth and deepest level of hell, under the cruel lash of the Overlord Asmodeus." Shaw thought about this and added, "While Cthulhu watches."

"Well, that's—" His mother began her refrain and managed, somehow, to cut herself off.

The rototiller was still chugging along outside. The bed springs creaked under shifting weight.

"It's just," Shaw's mother said, "you're not taking care of yourself. Don't you think you'll feel better if you get up and have a shower and eat something? And then we can see about getting you an appointment with Dr. Farr, and a prescription—"

"All right."

Shaw's mother let out a soft breath that sounded relieved.

"In a few days, maybe," Shaw said. "I just need to process this a little more before I talk about it with anyone."

Her fingers, still stroking his forehead, stilled. "Don't you think you'll feel better if you focus on the future? Laura's on the admissions committee at Chicago this year, and she'd love to talk to you. Just a phone call, sweetie. She really thinks their poetics program would be a great fit for you."

"Mom, I hear what you're saying, and I know that you're trying to help. But when you talk to me about grad school, it makes me feel like nothing I've done in my life until now is meaningful. Thanks for making this a safe space and letting me share that with you."

The mattress rocked slightly as his mother stood, her breath hitching as she moved out of the room. The click of her shoes faded down the hall.

Shaw's father let out a heavy breath. "She blames herself, you know. For what happened with North. Even though I'm the one who wanted you to meet Tyler."

"It's not her fault." Shaw's eyes burned, and he turned into the pillow. "It's my fault. I ruined everything, and he hates me, and he's never going to forgive me."

"Maybe," his father said with startling frankness. "And maybe you could keep that in mind, Wild, instead of punishing your mother when she's trying to help."

"I wasn't—"

"You're better at these games. You always were. But you might have the consideration to recognize that what you're doing is hurting her, and all she wants is to make things better."

Shaw sat up, dashing tears from his cheeks. "She can't make things better. Neither of you can. Grad school and law school and money and jobs. Those aren't going to make anything better. Both of you have always thought you knew how to fix me, how to make me into whatever you wanted me to be, and I'm so fucking sick of it!"

The last word cracked like a whip, and Wilson Aldrich flinched. He hesitated, and suddenly Shaw was aware of how old his father looked, with his stooped shoulders and thin chest. Before his father could say anything, though, a jazzy ringtone filled the space between them. His dad answered.

"What are you talking about? How is that—" His gaze cut to Shaw. "Where is the access card I gave you?"

"I left it at North's. Is this about the lab? North called me; what's going on?"

"You left it at North's? I told you to keep it safe! Good Lord, Shaw, what did you not understand about that?"

"I made sure—"

"I trusted you."

"Dad, I didn't—"

"Yes, I'm listening," his father barked into the phone. "I'll be there as soon as I can."

"Do you want me to go with you?"

"No," his dad said sharply. Then, into the phone, "Get Campbell. I want to know—" He was still talking as he slammed the door behind him.

For a luxurious moment, Shaw considered calling North. This was the perfect excuse. Instead, he sparked the joint, pulled up Netflix on his tablet, and for a while, all he had to think about was the Salvatore brothers.

He must have slept because knocking woke him. He sat up, the tablet sliding off him and bumping the roach, which had burned a hole in the quilt.

"Go away! I don't want—"

"Too bad," Pari announced as she walked into the room. Today, the bindi was saffron colored, and her long, dark hair left trailers of smoke in Shaw's vision—although that might have been the last of the grass. She made a face and fanned the air. "God, Shaw, did you stop using soap again?"

Shaw stared at her.

"Because you have to use soap."

"I—"

"And you have to wash under your arms."

"I use soap."

"And your, you know, boy parts."

"I wash my—I know—"

"And your feet."

"Pari, I know how to take a shower."

"Well, you stink, so I don't think you do."

Face hot, Shaw managed to say, "What do you want? Why are you here?" And then, more cogently, "Go away!"

"No." She looked around, raised her eyebrows at the mandatory kissing imposed on Paul and Ian, and dragged a chair next to the bed. From her purse, she produced a packet of documents, which she tossed on the bed. "The insurance company keeps sending things to North, and then he gets sad and stomps around, or he gets sad and cuddles the puppy, or he gets sad and goes out to the alley to—" She stopped, pursed her lips, and added tactfully, "—bird watch. And it's exhausting. I can't keep up with boys and all their emotions. Why can't you just have a good hate fuck, get it all out of your system, and go back to normal?"

"Because North hates me now. Because I ruined everything."

"That doesn't matter. I hate Truck three or four times a day. Ze ruins everything all the time. And look at us—we've never been stronger."

"Pari, please, please, please go away."

"Your parents said you're watching scary porn, and Truck wants to know what it is."

"Oh my God. I'm not watching scary porn. I'm doing research—you know what? It doesn't matter. Tell Truck whatever you want. Tell hir that it's all electrostim and tickling. But get out of my room, now!"

Instead, Pari checked her phone. "Well, that's everything."

"Great."

"I should probably get back to work."

"Goodbye."

"We're busy now that you quit. So busy that I don't have time to listen to your relationship dramas and hear about how you ruined your one shot with a man who actually seems like he might be able to stand you."

"Wow, Pari. Wow. Thanks so much."

She settled back in the chair and adjusted the pillows.

There wasn't a mechanical clock in the room—or in the house, for that matter; Shaw disassembled all of them when he was twelve to make an owl orrery, which he had had to explain to North years later "was exactly what it sounds like"—but Shaw thought he could hear the seconds ticking away. Or maybe it was the timer on a bomb. He pried his fingers from the quilt and tried to smooth out the wrinkles.

"If you're so busy, maybe you should go."

Pari waved a hand absently in his direction. Still looking around her, projecting an extremely forced air of nonchalance, she said, "North's been talking to me a lot. Probably because he has no one else to talk to. He's been telling me things he'd never tell anyone else in the whole world."

"I doubt that."

"The other day, he was looking at me across the desk, and he basically told me I'm the best and only friend he has."

"Really? North Squidworth McKinney told you that? In those exact words?"

Pari gave him a disgusted look. "It was his tone, Shaw. Grow up."

"Pari, I don't have any cash. I don't have anything particularly valuable. But what is it going to take to get you to leave me alone so I can die in peace?"

Releasing a sharp breath, Pari flopped back in the chair. She gathered her hair, pulling it over her shoulder and running her fingers through it. She stared at Paul and Ian while she talked. "When Chuck and Nels broke up with me, I thought I was going to die. Of course, unlike you, that's not because I love drama and I'm basically the embodiment of a Victorian waif inside a teenage goth inside a man who desperately needs to start using deodorant again. It's because I'd gotten stabbed, Shaw, and I really might have died."

"Yes, Pari. I remember. Thank you for putting it so clearly."

"Unlike you and your New Age, hippie-loving, hemp toilet paper, I-want-to-slit-my-wrists-while-listening-to-Good-Charlotte-in-my-parents'-basement—"

"I got it!"

Pari smoothed her skirt. "Nothing hurts more than realizing someone doesn't love you the way you love them. North has had a lot of that in his life. Maybe you should think about that."

"But I do love him. I love him more than anyone in the entire world. He's the best man I've ever—" He cut off when Pari held up a hand, a wry smile crossing her lips. After a moment, Shaw added, "And I explained why I didn't tell my parents. It's not about him or how I feel about him. It's about me."

With a quiet laugh, Pari stood. She fluffed the cushions and returned the chair to its spot along the wall. Then, facing Shaw again, she studied him for a long moment. "Shaw, when you're in a relationship, nothing is only about you. If you love North, North needs to know it in North terms, not in Shaw's I-write-emo-song-lyrics-on-my-Chucks-and-still-talk-about-MySpace-even-though-I-was-too-young—"

"Jesus Christ, Pari! First of all, I have never talked about MySpace. Second of all, North and I are grown men. We talk about our feelings. I've told him I love him."

The look of disappointment on Pari's face was infinite. She stood there, silent, hands on hips.

"What?" Shaw finally muttered.

"A couple of weeks ago, I had the therapist-inducing experience of walking in on the two of you."

"You saw us—"

"Not that! God, I'd be in a coma. Or in a morgue. No, you two were jackassing around like usual while I was doing all the work. North was pinning you to the wall with a chair, and you were screaming 'Rape, rape, rape!' And then you stopped screaming to tell him that rape jokes weren't funny even though you were the one screaming it."

Shaw tugged on the collar of his shirt, suddenly unable to meet Pari's eyes. "He wanted me to say that *Bring It On* was better than *Mean Girls*."

Pari snorted. "That's how North tells you he loves you, Shaw. And since he didn't break up with you when you tried to 'trim,'" she drew quotes around the word, "his hair with nail scissors while he was asleep, I'd say he's probably the only human being in existence you have a shot with. So you'd better fix this mess before I have to hear another of his fifteen-minute disquisitions on why the bridge in a Fall Out Boy song is the single deepest philosophical statement any human being has ever uttered. I do not get paid enough for that kind of thing."

Shaw pressed his hands to his cheeks; the skin was hot and slightly sticky. After a few deep breaths, he managed to say, "Disquisitions is a big word for someone in community college."

"Goodbye, Shaw," Pari said as she scowled and strode toward the door. "I'm going to tell North to go into witness protection so you can't find him."

The door crashed shut behind her.

Shaw lay there for a while. From the wall, Paul stared down at him with some seriously judgy eyes. Shaw considered the dresser, where several more joints were already rolled inside a plastic baggie; door number one. Instead, he sat up and headed for the bathroom; door number two. He showered, decided—judiciously, in light of Pari's comments—to scrub extra hard with the loofa, and let the warm water sluice him clean. Back in his room, he dressed in clean clothes. He was thinking about North, which meant he ended up in a blue chambray shirt with rhinestones along the cuffs and collar, midnight-black jeans, and the closest thing he had to boots: his vellies.

He didn't have anywhere to go, but the act of showering and dressing had helped, and he left the bedroom. He found a quiet spot in the formal living room, curled up on the chesterfield, and pulled out his phone. He opened the messaging app. He told himself to let it go. Flip was home, safe, and whatever trouble he'd been running from, he was beyond Shaw's reach. Then he thought of Hiwet, and whoever had burned down his home and tried to kill him. For a few minutes, he traced the phone's screen with his thumb. What would North tell him to do? Then he sighed, called himself a coward, and closed the blank message. Instead, he opened up the MyFans videos and watched them again.

The slap of flesh against flesh filled the room, interspersed with grunted commands to "Take it, faggot," and demands like "You deserve this, don't you, bitch?" His parents and Pari had both asked about the content of the videos, but it was another term Pari had used that was now percolating through Shaw's subconscious. A hate fuck. What he was watching looked remarkably like a hate fuck. And not something that had been staged. Not your typical stilted dialogue and passionless delivery. The man in the mask—in this video, a red Power Ranger—meant what he was saying. And Flip, drifting in a haze of weed and whatever else he was on, seemed to want it. Seemed to need it.

Again, Shaw tried to match the masked figure in the videos to someone he'd met on campus. Louis had denied knowing that Flip was gay and denied any involvement in the videos. He'd told them about his distinctive freckles, and after some very graphic rim-job shots, Shaw was convinced that the man in the mask was not Louis. Kishor was the next logical choice. Flip's teacher had light brown skin and dark hair, and he had the right build and body type to match the man in the mask. But Shaw wasn't convinced. It seemed too obvious. And while that wasn't exactly a rational explanation for why he didn't believe that Kishor was the man in the videos, Shaw still believed it. Kishor liked attention. He liked feeling looked up to. He liked being admired. In a porno, Kishor would want to lie back while his partner paid lavish attention to his body. Kishor, Shaw was pretty sure, would want kisses. None of which matched the figure on screen.

Shaw had watched the MyFans videos more times than he wanted to count by this point. The content had lost any erotic charge it might have once had. Now it was just mechanics: pump, thrust, pivot, part A into part B. He knew that in the next minute or two, Flip would make a noise that was half despairing and half exultant as he shot a load across his own stomach, and the masked man would keep pounding him until the drugged-out Flip tried to squirm away and the masked man dragged him back and pinned him under with his weight and the force of his thrusts. When he finally nutted, he'd release Flip and grab a towel to wipe away the—

Shaw dragged his finger across the screen, scrubbing forward in the video.

He watched the final minutes play out exactly the way he had remembered—with one detail he hadn't noticed before. The sweat. Dark beads of sweat. He tried another video. And another. And it was there in all of them.

For a moment, Shaw tried to think through the chain of events. Then he tapped out a quick message to North: *I know you don't want to talk to me, and I don't expect a response, but I just needed someone to know: I'm going to talk to Jos.*

Chapter 33

EARLY EVENING, THE campus of The Gouverneur Morris School glowed: a jewel-box city against the dusky sunset. A girl in a long skirt, hoop earrings, and a headscarf was dancing under a sycamore to some sort of knockoff Celtic music—lots of fiddles and flutes and pennywhistles. The smell of the moldering cherry blossoms that North remembered from his last visit was gone; that slightly sweet rankness had been swept away along with the petals pasted to the sidewalks, and once again, The Gouverneur Morris school was impeccable. Aside, that was, from the shouting.

Ahead, at the front door to Washington, Shaw's slender frame was outlined by the light from inside the residence. His words became clearer with every step North took. "—ahead and call them. They'll want to hear this too!"

He tried to take a step forward, and whoever was inside shoved him hard enough that Shaw stumbled and fell flat on his ass. North broke into a jog.

He reached Shaw in time to grab his arm and steady him as he stood. Shaw glanced up, his face fixed like he was ready for a fight, and then it cleared. For an instant, the old trust and hope and happiness were there. And then his face closed into wariness again.

"I didn't think you would—" he began.

"Fuck that," North said. "Where else would I be?"

"At the lab. I should have been there with you—"

"We'll talk about that later." He squeezed Shaw's arm and gave him a cautious smile. "You ok?"

Shaw gave a microscopic smile back, shrugged, and then let his gaze slide to the door. "Mr. Virani refuses to let me into the residence. The police took the access card, so I couldn't—"

"So you couldn't do exactly what you were trying to do." Kishor's voice was hard. He was in gray mesh shorts and a white tank, the total amount of fabric approximately enough to cover a dinner plate, exposing good shoulders and great arms. "So you couldn't enter a student residence without authorization and a trusted adult accompanying you."

"Yeah." North gave him a hard grin. "Wouldn't want anyone poaching on your grounds, would we?"

A blush worked across Kishor's face. "Get the hell off campus. I'm calling security right now."

"Hold on," North said. "I need to show you something."

Kishor's response was automatic and understandable: he waited as North approached. When North got within range of the door, though, he must have realized something else was happening. He tried to shut the door. He was too late. North kicked, catching the door just below the handle, and the force of the blow threw the door back. It caught Kishor in the gut, and he stumbled. North kicked again, and this time, the door flew all the way open.

North pushed into the residence, catching the rebounding door on his shoulder, and glanced at the boot print he'd left on the polished wood. Then he looked back at Shaw.

"Just like Gladys the Groovy Mule," Shaw whispered.

"Mules kick backward, dumbshit."

"North, it was very impressive. And mules are powerful animals. I was giving you a compliment."

"Next time, I'll stand back and watch him hand you your ass."

Shaw raised his chin. "It was a trap. I was luring him into a trap."

Wheezing, Kishor had managed to get himself up on one elbow. He was staring at them with a dazed expression as North headed toward the stairs, Shaw trailing after him.

"Stay down," North said.

Kishor made a wet, coughing noise and flopped onto his stomach. As North reached the first landing, a boy with floppy brown hair stepped out of the hallway, his eyes going from them to the stairs.

"Where's Jos?"

The boy must have seen Kishor, who was still gasping for breath, because his eyes got huge.

"Jos!" North snapped.

"205," the boy said, pointing to the hall on the other side of the landing. "What's—"

"Everything's fine," Kishor managed in a rough voice. "Go back to your room, Chance."

Taking Shaw's arm, North hustled him in the direction the boy had indicated. A glance back told him that the teacher had regained his feet and was coming after them.

"A little faster," North said to Shaw, "if you can manage it in your dancing boots."

"These aren't dancing boots, they're vellies, and they're really comfortable." A frown creased Shaw's lips. "I could probably do a jig in them if you—"

"Just walk faster, for God's sake."

The door to 205 was open a few inches; from inside came the steady thump of a bassline and a whiff of noxious, strawberry incense that was covering up something else—body odor and cigarettes, North guessed. He elbowed the door open, nudged Shaw inside, and then stepped in after him. He pulled the door shut and set the lock.

"What the shit?" Jos sat up on the bed, knocking aside a calculus textbook and a graphing calculator. His blond hair was mussed. He wore a black v-neck tee and black joggers, and although the clothes softened the lines of his body somewhat, they didn't hide the fact that he had a man's build—not a boy's.

"This is your show," North said to Shaw. "I don't think you have a lot of time."

"My show would be called Gladys the Groovy Mule and Friends. No, wait. It would be called Gladys the Groovy Mule's Fun-in-the-Sun Party Hour. No—"

"Hey, faggot brigade," Jos said. "What the hell are you doing in my room?"

"North," Shaw said, "did you know that extreme homophobia is often an externalized manifestation of an internal struggle with one's own homosexual desires?"

"No shit," North said. "Everyone knows that."

Jos's face had gone strangely still. Almost dead. Only his eyes were alive, and bright with what North thought was hate.

"How long have you been in love with Flip?" Shaw asked.

"I'm not—" Jos checked himself with a visible struggle. After a moment, a sickle smile cut across his face. "Get lost, faggots."

"We saw the videos."

"What videos?"

"Jos, we know it's you."

"What videos?" But sweat beaded at his forehead, and his smile had dulled.

"I didn't understand at first. In the videos, it sounds like you hate him. Like you want to punish him. But it wasn't that, was it? You hated yourself. You wanted to punish yourself. And then I saw the sweat and it all fell into place. You used a spray tan and dye to make yourself look different; you couldn't stand the risk of anyone figuring out it was you. But you used cheap dye; it came off with your sweat sometimes. We'd been looking for a brunet, but we should have been looking for a blond."

"You don't know what you're talking about." He looked like he was trying to stop himself, but the words slipped out: "You don't understand."

"I understand," Shaw said gently. "Your parents are Bosnian, but you're American. Your friends are rich, but you're a scholarship student. Your parents are Muslim, but you're gay, and you can't let that happen."

"I'm not!" Jos slipped off the bed, chest puffing up, shoulders back. "I'm not—that, what you said. I'm not!"

"Everyone likes Flip. He's nice. He's sweet. He's attractive. He's a white-bread, high-achieving rich boy. Basically every closeted kid's heroin. You both found each other, realized you had more in common than either of you suspected. And then what?"

Jos stared at them. He was breathing too fast, a slight whistling noise accompanying each inhalation.

"Why did you make the movies? Were you going to run away together? Was that the plan? No matter how much you love someone—"

The laughter was so abrupt and so harsh that it took North a moment to recognize it as such. Jos threw his head back, brittle laughs rolling out of him.

"I didn't love him. Jesus." Jos touched feverish cheeks. "I needed money. He needed money. A hole is a hole. Simple."

"Then help us understand," North said. "What was the plan here? It makes sense that Flip would have someone helping him from inside the house, but why do it at all?"

"I didn't help him. I didn't even know he was here. We fucked a few times. I let him record it. That was over winter break." A smile like a live wire crackled on his face. "The spray tan had worn off by the time we were back in classes. The first few months, he gave me my cut just like we agreed. Then, a couple of weeks ago, when he was supposed to give me my cut for April, he blew me off. I thought—I don't know what I thought. I went up to his room. The door was locked. I kicked it open because it was my money, and I needed it."

"Wait," Shaw said. "When we got to his room, when we found the door kicked in—that was you?"

Jos looked down at the bed and played with a loose thread. "I was going to tell someone that I did that, just so people would stop saying he'd been kidnapped, but then the cops got involved, and Flip really was missing. I didn't think it mattered."

"It mattered a whole hell of a lot." North shook his head. "No wonder we were chasing our tails."

"And then what happened?" Shaw asked.

"Nothing. I didn't know where he was; I figured he'd run off with the money, and he'd be back after he'd blown it all. You know how Flip is; he winds himself up until he pops his top, and then he goes back to being a good boy."

"You weren't sneaking him food, checking on him, talking to him to keep him from going crazy?"

"Are you even listening to me? I told you: I didn't know he was down there. Like he'd even tell me, right? I was a good fuck, and then when I wasn't useful to him anymore, boom, sayonara. I guess it's not like he ever pretended we were anything else. He acted like we barely knew each other in public, which, fuck, whatever. I don't care."

A key turned in the door, and North braced his shoulder against it as the knob turned.

"Open up," Kishor shouted, pounding on the door. "Open up right now, or I'm calling the cops."

Jos flinched.

"Jos," Shaw said. "It's ok to feel hurt by how Flip treated you. That wasn't right. You didn't deserve that."

"I told you, I don't care."

"I think you might care. I think maybe you care a lot. There's a lot of emotion in those videos you made."

"We were fucking," Jos snapped. "Was I supposed to be reading the *New Yorker* while I boned him?"

"You just highlighted Shaw's niche porn." North grunted as Kishor threw his weight into the door, forcing it open a few inches. "If you add garden gnomes and Elvira and Groucho Marx twiddling his cigar. Shaw, this door is some seriously weak shit. Hurry it up."

Kishor hit the door again, and North slid a few more inches.

"I know some of that emotion was what you feel about yourself," Shaw said. "And I'm sorry about that. Growing up Muslim, feeling what you feel, not being able to reconcile those two—"

"You're not my therapist. You know fuck-all about me."

"—but I think some of that emotion was what you felt for Flip. You cared about him. You had some really big feelings for him. And those feelings were all tangled up because you wanted more than he gave you, and you hated yourself for wanting more, but you kept wanting it."

Jos's jaw trembled. His eyes were wet, but no tears fell.

Kishor crashed into the door, and North stumbled back, allowing the door to fly open. Kishor stumbled to a stop, breathing hard, tank askew.

"I didn't give two shits about Flip," Jos said, his expression suddenly hard and smooth. "He kept my secret. I kept his. We had a nice thing going. And if he opened his mouth, he knew I'd nuke him. Mutually assured destruction, that's what I told that bitch. We learned about it in Kish's class."

"What was Flip's secret?" North asked, rubbing his shoulder, careful to keep himself between Kishor and Shaw.

Jos held Kishor with an unwavering gaze.

"Don't do this," Kishor said, his voice broken. He glanced away, straightening the tank, and whispered, "Jos, you don't have to do this."

Voice tinged with cruel satisfaction, Jos said, "It didn't matter if I felt anything for Flip. Wouldn't have changed anything. He only had eyes for one person."

Kishor put a hand over his face.

"I walked in on them fucking in the classroom, a hot little scene." Jos shrugged, as though he might have agreed. "You want to know who was helping Flip? The inside man? You're looking at him."

A shudder tore through Kishor. Then he drew several deep breaths, squared his shoulders, and dropped his hands. His eyes were red but dry when he met North's gaze.

"You fucking son of a bitch," North said. "You're going to prison for this."

Kishor shook his head.

"Let's start with murder. Tack on statutory rape. Then we'll throw in kidnapping. Arson and attempted murder. We might as well add harboring a runaway, just for fucking funsies—"

"Oh my God," Shaw whispered, "please say that every time we catch a killer."

Shock obliterated the weary resignation in Kishor's face. "Murder? Arson? What are you talking about?"

"You killed Hiwet Zerai. She found out about you and Flip, and she tried to blackmail you. That's why you told Flip he had to run away. That's why you had to get rid of Hiwet. You tried to burn down my partner's house while he was sleeping—"

"Are you kidding?" As shock faded, a strange kind of relief flooded Kishor's features. "Oh my God, I was at a soccer game. In St. Charles. The police already talked to me; they talked to all the staff."

North risked a glance at Shaw. Shaw was frowning.

"You'd better tell us everything," North finally said.

Shifting his weight, Kishor shot a furtive look at Jos. "Can he—"

"No, he's staying in case you try to bullshit us."

Kishor sighed and nodded. "Flip and I were...involved."

"You were fucking him."

"We were in love. We are in love."

"I've seen the movie; I know how this ends. In a few years, he's not your twinkie treat—"

"Oh my God," Shaw breathed with excitement.

"—anymore, and you break up until you find the next teenager you can cornhole."

"You don't know the first thing about me. About us." Kishor pushed his dark, wavy hair back with both hands. "Flip comes from this terrible home, and he's under unbelievable pressure to be perfect. He's had this horrible life, and somehow he turned out to be good and sweet and wonderful. He's amazing."

North snorted at the same time as Jos, and when he turned, he was surprised by the smile breaking the teen's sullen façade.

"Fine. He has it rough at home. He didn't get those two-thousand-dollar Nikes, and Daddy doesn't come to his soccer games. Really rough. All of which justifies statutory rape, I guess."

"It's not statutory—it's not that," Kishor snapped. "He's seventeen. That's the age of consent."

"But you'd be fired if the school found out," Shaw said slowly. "Possibly sued."

After a moment, Kishor gave a grudging nod.

"Is that why you helped him try to run?"

Down the hall, a door opened, and a Post Malone song thundered through the residence. Boys laughed, and then a chorus of them picked up the lyrics, belting out the song in varying degrees of pitchiness.

"I don't understand." North studied the teacher, trying to get past the pretty surface to glimpse the monster underneath. "You took advantage of a position of authority, you took advantage of a vulnerable kid, you fucked up his head so you could have fun with him, and as far as I can tell, you're in shit up to your nose. You need to start digging yourself out. If you talk now, maybe things will go easier on you when the police get involved."

"I did what you said." A boy ran past them, feet slapping the floor, and Kishor flinched. Then a door slammed, and the music cut off, and the house was quiet. "I helped Flip. He was determined to run. I begged him to finish the school year. We had a plan. He would go to school at Wash U, and we'd be together in secret for a couple of years, until we could make things public without people thinking it had started while he was a student here. But he was…he was out of control. It was scary. He was insane about it, wouldn't listen to me, wouldn't tell me why. He just kept saying he had to go. He just kept saying he had to do it or he'd never be free. I begged him to tell me why. He was shoving clothes into a bag, and I grabbed his arm." Kishor touched his cheek, a note of amazement infusing his words. "He hit me. I'd never seen him like that. I was scared. Of him. For him. So I agreed to help him. I made sure he got food. I talked to him. I gave him the all clear when he just wanted to stretch his legs and get out of that room. It was only supposed to be for a few days, but then you were here, and the police thought it was a kidnapping, and instead of a few days, it turned into a week. And then you found him, and—and I haven't talked to him since. He won't return my messages."

"Boo hoo," North said. "I smell some serious horseshit. He wanted to run away, but you didn't know why? And you still helped him? Whatever else, that's harboring a fugitive, and at his age, they might slap you with kidnapping too."

"It's the truth! He wouldn't tell me!"

"You're a fucking liar. You wanted the kid all to yourself, and you convinced him that running away together was the only way, and it didn't matter to you that this kid had a family, that they'd be worried sick—"

"They don't care about him. This was all a publicity stunt! That's all they wanted out of it!"

"—people who had already lost a daughter and now were going to lose a son—"

"See? See? You don't know what you're talking about! They didn't lose a daughter."

"What are you talking about?" Shaw said, his voice taut with an energy North didn't understand.

"Sara Beth," Kishor said, faltering under the intensity of Shaw's gaze. "Flip's sister. She's not dead; she's alive. She's in one of those treatment centers for troubled teens."

Chapter 34

THEY DROVE TO THE Chittenden home in silence. The evening had a crystalline quality, a fragility and clarity accentuated by the purple light decanted into the hollow of the sky. It was the last time, Shaw knew, that he would make this drive. The farmhouse was lit up against the dusk, the white clapboard glowing. The last homely house, Shaw thought, and he thought of Tolkien, and how power made monsters of everyone. North parked, and when Shaw opened the door, the smell of corruption met them. Roadkill. Or something that had died behind the tree line and been left to rot. Shaw adjusted the satchel on his shoulder and got out of the car. They climbed the stairs to the porch, and one of the barn doors swung in the wind, clapping against the siding, hinges squeaking.

When North knocked, only silence answered them, and the clapping of the barn door, and the protesting hinges. He knocked again, harder.

"So help me God," North muttered, "if I have to deal with Gavin because she's giving an interview or doing a photo shoot or—"

The door opened. Celia stood there in nothing but rumpled flannel pajamas. Her short blond curls were mussed, and one side of her face had a red line, as though she been sleeping somewhere uncomfortable. She had also, Shaw decided after an experimental sniff, been bathing in whiskey.

"Yes?" She loaded an experienced drunk's caution into the word. "What do you want?"

"Mrs. Chittenden, we need to talk to your son."

She shook her head, wobbled, and clutched the door. "Flip's not—Flip's not—" She drew herself up and with exaggerated poise managed, "Flip is indisposed."

"It's very important, Mrs. Chittenden," Shaw said. "It's about a murder, and we think Flip is the only one who can give us the answers we need."

"Is it that girl?" Celia swayed again. "She was his friend. He's been crying all week."

"Yes, it's about Hiwet."

"We're not supposed to—we're not supposed to—Flip was just confused. He had a breakdown. My son is receiving the best mental health care our great country can provide."

North's eyebrows shot up. "That's very fucking reassuring."

"Mrs. Chittenden, please. We only need a few minutes."

After another wobble, Celia stepped back. She didn't motion them in, but she left the door open as she tottered toward the stairs. She made a vague motion toward the office just off the entry hall, and then she was pulling herself up the banister two-handed, calling out, "Flip, Flip, sweetheart."

North stepped inside. Shaw followed, and he shut the front door to block out the squeal of hinges and the clap-clap-clap of the barn door.

"I guess—" North nodded at the office.

Shaw led the way this time, and they turned on the lights. The only additions since their last visit were an empty bottle of Kentucky Deluxe, a rocks glass with Celia's lipstick going all the way around the rim, and a dark spot of drool on the blotter. North studied the pictures again and made a disgusted noise.

"It's not our fault," Shaw said. "There's no sign a girl lives here, and there's only the one picture of her, and she keeps it facing away from visitors so no one will see it and ask, and nobody seemed to know what had really happened to her."

"We should have run it down."

"It's not our fault," Shaw repeated. "People were working pretty hard to make sure we were looking in another direction."

Footsteps silenced them. Celia entered first, clutching the placket of her pajama top as she stumbled to her seat behind the desk. Francis came second, blowing gin fumes the way a dragon breathes fire, still dressed in a polo, khakis, and loafers. Flip came last, tousled brown hair hanging over his forehead, his eyes red, holding himself as though his entire body were one raw nerve. Francis took the window seat; Flip hovered in the doorway, hugging himself.

North nodded to him.

"Hi, Flip," Shaw said quietly.

Flip stared past them.

"We need to talk to you about Hiwet, Flip. Someone killed her. And someone tried to kill me. And we think that's because someone wanted you to disappear. Someone wanted you to be gone for good."

Shaw was looking for it, so he spotted the flash of fear, total and all-consuming, before Flip managed to tamp down the emotion.

"Flip," North said, "we can make sure no one hurts you again."

Nothing. The boy's expression remained fixed and chalky blank.

"And no one will ever hurt Sara Beth again either," Shaw said.

This time, Flip flinched.

"What are you talking about?" Francis said. He rose from the window seat, gesticulating wildly. "What the hell is this? You said you needed to talk to him about a murder, but now you're bringing up Sara Beth. Can't you see that he's not well? Can't you see that he's not up to this? He's leaving tomorrow for a treatment center—" He cut off, seeming to realize he had said too much, but managed to say, "Get out. I want you out of my house right now."

"Be quiet, Francis," Celia said.

"I want them—"

"Be quiet!" Celia slid the Kentucky Deluxe away from her, and the sound of the bottle chittering against the wood made the hair on the back of Shaw's neck stand up. "What are you talking about?"

"We're talking about your daughter." North nodded to Shaw, and Shaw produced a pile of documents from the satchel.

Francis made a quivering movement toward the desk before halting again.

"What are these?" Celia asked, stirring the papers with one finger.

"Medical records from Disciplemakers Ranch. Years of them. Enough, I'd say, to raise some pretty serious questions about abuse."

"Those records are confidential!" Francis took another step before checking himself again. "You're breaking the law just by—"

"You know the interesting thing about people who will take your money to be quiet?" North said. "They'll be happy to take even more money to tell you anything you want to know."

Squinting at one of the pages, Celia plucked it from the pile and examined it. The alcohol ruddle in her cheeks turned to ash.

"What is this?" she asked, a quaver rocking her voice. "Where did you get this?"

"It didn't make sense at first," North said. "Flip's behavior. Most kids who run away are trying to escape trouble at home, but Flip didn't fit the pattern of the abused kid. He got into trouble in spurts, instead of a regular pattern. His friends all noticed it—they described it in different ways, but they all talked about Flip winding himself up and then exploding. That sounds like a kid who's coping with some really bad shit, but who's also trying as hard as he can to be good. That sounds like a kid who's being held hostage."

"This is ridiculous," Francis shouted. He rocked forward, but when North turned a look in his direction, he settled back on his heels. "This isn't making any sense."

"Flip," Shaw said, "you knew your father was hurting your sister. Did he threaten to hurt you if you told anyone?"

Flip was a statue. The tendons in his neck stood out. His face was a greasepaint white.

"This is your chance," Shaw said. "You can tell us now and we'll help you, but tomorrow, he's sending you away, and you'll never have a chance after that. He'll make sure of it.

"What is this?" Celia asked again, still paging through the pile, the drunken slur to the words failing to mask her shrill horror. "What is this?

"I won't let you talk to my son—" Francis bellowed as he rushed forward.

North shoved him back toward the window seat. Francis stumbled, hit the ledge at the knees, and half fell, half sat back. He stared at North, stupefied.

"Stay there." North jabbed a finger in his direction.

"Flip," Shaw said, "your dad killed Hiwet. She knew about the MyFans videos. She knew they'd be damaging to your mom's career. She contacted him and tried to blackmail him; she had a survivor's instincts, up to a point, and she thought she could get something out of him. He killed her, though, and he planted those travel papers on her. Then he tried to kill Shaw—and me, since he assumed I was in the building. He didn't know your mother was going to fire us the next day; he wanted us to stop investigating. People were getting too close to the secrets he kept buried, and Francis was desperate for everyone to think you'd disappeared, Flip. He was going to kill you once he tracked you down."

"I got bored." Flip's first words had a weightless quality: paper caught in the updraft of a bonfire. "I messaged Hiwet while I was waiting for everyone to go away. I thought she'd get a kick out of the apartment; she always liked learning people's secrets. I didn't tell her about the videos, but—" He had to stop to swallow, the sound painfully dry in the silent room. "But she always knew Jos's secrets. I didn't know she'd go there. I didn't know she'd—she'd get hurt."

"That's not on you," North said, directing his words to the blank-faced Celia. "Hiwet got killed for the same reason Francis needed Flip dead. See, that's what we couldn't figure out. Francis didn't have a motive to want Flip dead. The opposite, in fact. If Flip were alive, and if he managed to begin divorce proceedings while Flip was in his custody, then he stood to gain control of a good chunk of money. But we knew someone was trying to cover something up; that's why Hiwet had to die, and that's why Shaw was almost killed. It didn't make sense until we realized Francis wanted something even more than he wanted financial independence. He wanted to keep his secrets buried. That's why, after you faked your suicide, we found your dad drunk. He wasn't grieving; he was celebrating. The last loose thread had just tied itself off. Isn't that right, Flip?"

Two tears slipped free, tracing sinuous tracks down Flip's face. "He said he'd hurt her more if I told anyone. He said no one would believe me, and he'd hurt her to punish me. That's how it was with everything: if I didn't get good grades, if I didn't get into an Ivy, if I didn't score over a 1520 on the SAT, if I caused any trouble at school. I tried as long as I could and then—and then I'd lose it. I threw out everything in my room and broke up with Abby; I tried to be a monk. That didn't work. I tried to get high. That just made things worse.

I just wanted to leave. I didn't want him to hurt her, but I couldn't live like that anymore. I told them I was leaving. I told them I'd never bother them again."

The slight unevenness in Shaw's next breath matched North's.

"You knew?" North asked.

"He called and said he was running away," Celia mumbled. She tried to push herself upright, planting both hands on the desk, but one hand slipped and shot out. She sent the rocks glass flying, and it shattered against the honey-colored floorboards. Celia paused. She considered the broken glass. Her movements were jerky and uncoordinated, a marionette with all its strings tangled. "We talked about it. We decided it would be good press. We thought we'd find him in a day or two. That's why I hired you. Celebrities. All those famous cases. You'd bring him home. Nice bump in the polls. But then someone had broken into his room, and Philip really was gone, and the girl died—" She staggered around the desk. "Philip, angel, what—what—what—what—"

Her scratchy voice skipped like a record.

When she moved to embrace Flip, he exploded, a flurry of blows striking her in the face and chest. She staggered back, falling with a sharp cry, and landed in the broken glass. In the dim light of the office, the first drops of blood patterned the wood like a Rorschach test. A moth. The thin man. Abyss.

"You let him do it!" Flip screamed down at his mother, spittle flecking his lips. "You knew, and you let him do it, and then you let him send her away!"

Moaning, Celia shook her head, cradling her cut hand against her chest. "No, no, no. You never told me—"

"You didn't want to know! You didn't want to know about me. You didn't want to know about her. You didn't want to know about anything that messed up your perfect family and your perfect home and your perfect life, and there was no one else I could tell!" The last words came out in a strangled shriek: "I needed you!"

Shaw pulled Flip into his arms, and for a moment, Flip fought him, flailing to free himself. Then something extinguished the fight in him, and he sagged. Shaw tightened his grip and held the shaking boy. He gazed over Flip's shoulder to where Francis perched on the window seat, still massaging his chest where North had shoved him. A horrible serenity had dropped over Francis, smothering whatever humanity had lingered in his mask. He smiled a Jimmy Stewart smile that had a little bit of aww, shucks in it.

"This is nonsense, Celia. Philip is obviously having some sort of reaction to the trauma from the last few weeks. He's sick, just like Sara Beth. He spent days by himself, alone, cooking up these fantasies. And these two are helping him, although I won't pretend I know why."

"The records—" Shaw began.

"I'm sure someone from Disciplemakers will explain in the morning that those records were falsified by a disgruntled employee, possibly one who has an axe to grind because of my wife's politics. The story about this girl trying to blackmail me is tragic, but there's no evidence. It's another fantasy. And I have no idea who tried to burn down your home, Mr. Aldrich, but the police haven't talked to us, so I'm sure that they have another person of interest. Men in your line of work make all sorts of enemies."

Celia pushed herself up; she left a bloody handprint on the pale boards. Her glassy eyes swung from Francis to Flip and back to Francis.

"Except," North said, "I bet you tried to be clever. I bet you tried to tie up all your loose strings at once. You weren't going to let Hiwet's death go to waste; you'd already started setting up Celia by telling us that she would rather have had a dead son than a gay one. It's not much of a leap from there. You wanted everyone to believe a crazy conservative politician might have killed the girl who tried to blackmail her. Very neat: you got rid of Flip, got rid of Hiwet, got rid of Celia. But to do it, you had to use her gun. Lucky for you, she leaves it out to impress visitors." North's gaze settled on the red-felt display case. "I'm sure the police can match that gun to the bullet that killed Hiwet."

Francis stood. He shook his head and smiled. "Nice story, Mr. McKinney, but you won't find my fingerprints anywhere on that gun. Of course, you might find Celia's on the cartridge casing. She might not have been thinking about fingerprints when she loaded the gun. She might have been in a blind fury, determined to get rid of a threat to her tiddlywinks career in politics."

Celia stared at her husband. One blood-streaked hand ran across the display case, leaving behind a red smear.

"It's time for you to go," Francis said. "I'll be calling the police to report your visit, and—"

It didn't happen fast. Any of them could have stopped her. But the unreality of the moment held all of them, even Shaw. Only at the last moment did he pull Flip's head into his shoulder so that the boy wouldn't have to see.

Celia flipped open the case, took the gun in her lacerated hand, and shot her husband in the head.

Blood, bone, and brain spattered the window behind him; the sound was like a squall of spring rain hitting a tin roof. Flip jerked in Shaw's arms and began to cry.

"Get him out of here," North barked, and Shaw pulled Flip toward the double doors.

Celia raised the gun to her head, and North lunged, catching her wrist on his second step and twisting the gun away. A second shot tore open the ceiling, and plaster rained down, the house belching out a cloud of dust.

"Get him out of here!" North shouted as Celia began to scream, twisting and thrashing as she fought North. Flip fought too, a wildcat now, tooth and nail as he tried to get free. Shaw managed to keep the boy from seeing what had happened to his father; that was the only victory in that long, awful night.

Chapter 35

NORTH SAT IN THE borrowed Ford Focus; every time he shifted, the upholstery off-gassed the smell of fried food, ancient cigarette smoke, and farts. He cracked the window, which helped, but for the hundredth time he promised himself that when Borealis had some breathing room, he was going to buy a cheap car at auction just for stakeouts.

For now, he just watched the two-story house at the end of the block, one eye on the clock, and rested a hand on the Mossberg that lay across his lap. The shotgun's black plastic was smooth and cool under his fingers.

Six am. Nice, quiet little street in Maplewood. Two-story houses, some brick, most frame with clapboard siding. The lawns were more crabgrass than anything else, and the sidewalks had cracked and buckled in places, but the houses were well maintained. The morning light, the dew, the humidity in the air—they all combined to soften the scene. An opening shot, maybe, in a John Hughes film. A nice place to raise a family.

When North heard the garbage truck, he got out of the car. He hopped two fences and came out behind the house that he'd been watching. He pressed himself up against the side of the house. He held the Mossberg across his chest. A few minutes later, the garage door rumbled up, and plastic wheels scraped on cement.

He counted to three and moved, clearing the corner of the house at almost a full sprint. Ronnie had one moment of shock before the butt of the Mossberg connected with the side of his head, and then he dropped. He was wearing a robe, a dumpy Hugh Heffner knockoff, and it had flapped open when he had fallen. North slung the shotgun over one shoulder, grabbed Ronnie's ankle, and hauled him into the house. He zip-tied him to the table, ran the trash down to the curb, and went back inside. On the way in, he slapped the garage door control, and it rattled back down.

Ronnie was coming around, so North sped things up by shoving the Mossberg's muzzle between Ronnie's teeth.

"Morning," North said. "Hope I didn't chip a veneer."

Ronnie's answer was a squawking string of swears that were mostly unintelligible around the blued steel.

North glanced around the kitchen. A floral border at the top of the walls. Blue check wallpaper that had to have come from the 90s. Laminate countertop and oak cabinets. He took a breath of fried eggs. The toaster popped, and Ronnie flinched.

Grinning, North said, "Damn. Spooked me too."

Ronnie tried talking again.

"No," North said. "You listen. I'm going to talk. You fucked us pretty good, Ronnie. We did right what you wanted. We went after Danny. We tried to figure out how you were going to use him or Lee to get access to the Nonavie lab. We went chasing after him when he called for help. And you waltzed right into my place and stole the access card Shaw's dad had given him. You couldn't have known he'd leave it, though. So what was your plan if he'd taken it with him?"

North withdrew the Mossberg. Ronnie grimaced and ran his tongue across his teeth. "North, my lad," he snarled, "you are seriously fucked."

"You didn't have a backup plan. Is that it?"

"You have no idea what a mistake you just made. No goddamn clue."

"Keep it up, and I'll give you your binky again. Lots of guys find it comforting to suck on something. You seem to be one of them. Now, answer my question."

Ronnie blinked, and color rose in his fleshy face. "There are devices. Scanners. I was going to place one in the nightstand; I've seen where he leaves his wallet. It doesn't even have to touch the card."

"Jesus. And poor Shaw made it so much easier for you. What about his login information? You left his computer powered on—you're getting sloppy in your old age."

"Your boyfriend needs a better password; the Aldrich Acquisitions admin account had strong security, but his personal account leaves something to be desired. He made the mistake of saving the admin login information in his email."

"I guess we're as stupid as you thought we'd be; Shaw was the perfect patsy, and I just stood there in the loading dock, dick in my hand, while you walked right into the lab. Pretending to be servicing some equipment was smart; it got you in close, and then you could use the access card. Smart, smart, smart. And we were so stupid. That's how most industrial espionage happens, though, right? People who are greedy or stupid, or usually both."

Ronnie's answer was to peel back his lips—a smile, maybe, but mostly a threat.

"I'll admit," North said, "we didn't know how you were manipulating us. But we're not totally incompetent. We made some contingency plans, just in case we couldn't figure out how to catch you with your hand in the cookie jar, so to speak. Have you gotten any offers yet?"

"Entrapment is almost as ugly as betrayal, North."

North's grin got bigger. "No, I'm not recording you. I'm not interested in a recording. I came here to deliver a message. And that message is, no matter how pissed you are about what happens in the next twenty minutes, stay the fuck away from me and the people I care about. Anything happens to Shaw or my dad or my employees, I will come after you, and they don't have a hole deep enough where I won't be able to find you." He stood and rested the Mossberg on his shoulder again. "Now, let's see. You were hired to steal a sample of Nonavie's prize project. That's all. In fact, I bet you were told not to bother with the computers because the buyer only needed a genetic sample. But I know you, Ronnie. You got greedy. You went for the computers anyway. Was that going to be a separate deal with someone else? Or did you think your buyer would pay extra? Either way, you fucked up. You opened the stolen data last night at 7:17pm, and because you're an ancient, stupid, human-sized scrotal sack, you didn't even bother to check it for any little extras. That means the Trojan horse that a couple of the tech gals at Aldrich Acquisitions cooked up went straight to work. And that means that last night, the police got a warrant to search your home and computer for stolen intellectual property, and of course, I just happened to get your address from some of the pings that the spyware sent back. And now here we are, all caught up."

Shock was giving way to horror. "You can't—" Then Ronnie managed to shut himself up.

"You're a thug, Ronnie, and a bully, and a blackmailer, and for a long time you've managed to run a pretty good game. But you're small shit, and you messed with the wrong people. And you shouldn't have gone to my dad's house; you were threatening me, and I don't like threats. Anyway, that's over now. Remember what I said: they can lock you up and throw away the key, but you send anyone after me or mine, and I will end you, no matter where you are. I'm going to let myself out the back." Through the opening to the dining room, a sliver of the front windows was visible. An unmarked car was pulling into the driveway. A police cruiser idled at the curb. "Hang tight, Uncle Ronnie. Help is on the way."

Chapter 36

SHAW STAYED NEAR THE outer walls of his burned-out Benton Park home. The floorboards were burned through completely in places, and he didn't trust the remaining ones to hold his weight—he had no way of telling how serious the damage had been. The spring day was hot, the sun scorching the back of his neck. The smell of stale char and smoke filled his nose; occasionally an eddy of air would kick up, breaking the day's slumber, and he'd get a lungful of hot asphalt, and the police caution tape would snap and flutter. But mostly he breathed in the smell of ashes as he picked through the rubble.

He'd started a pile near the front of the house: four teaspoons, a Farberware pot, the faceplate and handle from the drawer of a filing cabinet, a rock that he'd found when North had taken him to Lone Elk Park. He gripped an exposed stud to steady himself; the burned wood was greasy under his touch, and when he pulled his hand away, his fingers and palm were black. He scrubbed them on the pink chinos.

"You're ruining a perfectly good pair of pants," North said.

Shaw glanced over his shoulder and dug up a smile. "When I bought these, the first thing I thought was that you were going to tell me they looked like Pepto Bismol."

"They do look like Pepto Bismol."

Shaw's smile felt a little more real. He gave another look at the devastation and shook his head. "What am I doing? Everything is gone; this is a waste of time."

"Not everything. You found your rock."

This time when Shaw looked over, North was bouncing the rock on his palm.

"You remember that?" Shaw asked.

"You told me a ley line used to run through there, and the rock was probably magic, and I said it was doing a pretty good magic trick of looking like an ordinary rock."

"And then you said if I wanted to see a real ley line, you had some serious warlock magic in your pants, which I think is offensive to ley lines in general and to warlocks in particular."

North burst into laughter, and it sounded so purely happy that Shaw grinned in response. The May sun made North's hair shine, picking out the golden fuzz along the shell of his ear, erasing lines from his face. For a moment, he could have been seventeen again, the boy Shaw fell in love with over dining hall food and episodes of *Supernatural* and late-night study sessions when they tried to see how many cupcakes they could cram in their mouths at one time.

Turning away, North started to cry. It only lasted a moment, a single shake of his shoulders, and then he was still again. He wiped his face.

Shaw dragged himself through the sagging window frame. He crashed into North, wrapping him in a hug, and to his surprise, North hugged him back. Another of those huge shakes tore through North.

"North, it's ok. It's ok."

"No," he said, the word mangled by pain. "No, things are not ok. Oh my God, how can this hurt so much?"

Shaw turned his face into North's chest, the auto parts t-shirt smelling like Tide, and under that, the smell of Irish Spring soap and North's body. His face was hot for a moment, and for one final moment, he took refuge in the man who had been his hideout from the world for almost nine years. Then he stepped back, blinked his eyes clear, and met North's gaze.

"Can I say anything that will make you change your mind? I'm sorry I didn't tell my parents. I'm sorry I didn't show you how much I love you. I'm sorry I've been selfish in so many ways, when you deserve so much better. Can I do anything? I will do anything. Anything."

"Shaw," North tried again, but his voice broke.

Rucking up his shirt, Shaw wiped his eyes and clamped down on the sob that was working its way through him. He could do this much for North. He could at least make it easy.

"North Dingleberry McKinney—"

"Not my middle name," North whispered.

"—get on with it and break up with me."

North wiped his face again. "I don't want to break up with you. I want to be with you. I love you. I've loved you since freshman year. But I don't like where I am in my life. I don't like how that's affecting us. I know I threw a lot of blame on you when I found out that you—when I realized your parents didn't know. I said some pretty awful things, things I didn't even realize I thought about you, things I didn't even realize I was collecting like…like weapons to use against you. And I think I was doing that because it was easier to focus on you, and what you were doing, than to think about what was going on inside me. I feel like everything has been that way lately. I'm so focused on one thing that I miss what's really important. I don't want it to be that way with us. You're what's important. You're the only thing that's important."

Shaw swallowed against the hard, dry wedge in his throat. "Your breakup speeches need some work."

North wiped his face on his shoulder.

"Do you even know what a breakup speech is supposed to sound like?"

"I don't want to break up. But I think I've got some stuff I haven't resolved yet. From Tucker. From my parents, too, if I'm being honest. And even though I don't want to lose you, I think—I think the last few days have helped me see that I might have jumped into this. I wanted to be with you for so long, and I never had time to get past...things."

"That was a little better. Now, this is where you say, 'I think we should break up.'"

"Please don't make me," North whispered. His jaw trembled.

"Here, I'll help. I'm tired of you. You're boring. You track mud all over the house, and your boots smell funny. You don't get any of my jokes, and I found that garnet cock ring I gave you in the trash, and you always make me be the little spoon."

"You like being the little spoon."

"Maybe it's not a breakup. Maybe it's like you said earlier. We need some time off, that's all."

"But what if I lose you?" The words were thin and pitchy and struggling.

Shaw didn't say anything; he didn't know what he could say.

"Right," North said, and then he cleared his throat and hocked a wad of spit onto the grass and wiped his face. "Sorry. That was a shitty thing to ask."

Shading his eyes from the sun, Shaw considered the man in front of him. A minute might have passed, the only sound a breeze picking up, the creak of burned timbers, the traffic on Gravois.

"What do we do now?" Shaw asked.

"Maybe we start with what we're good at." He shoved his hands into his pockets, shoulders hunching slightly. "Would you—could you—oh for fuck's sake. Will you still be my friend?"

The breeze picked up, and ash spun into the air, a river of it washing around Shaw's ankles, fat flakes drifting between the two men. It might have been the slow dissolve of the universe. Entropy. Disintegration.

Shaw reached through it, tugged North's hand from its pocket, and threaded their fingers together.

"Always."

REDIRECTION

Keep reading for a sneak preview of *Redirection*, book three of Borealis: Without a Compass.

Chapter 1

"DO YOU THINK one of my balls is bigger than the other?" Shaw glanced down at his American-flag hot pants. Cowboy boots and a spangled cropped tank completed the outfit. He inspected himself for several long seconds. He wished he'd brought a ruler.

Around them, Teddi's Fourth of July party was in full swing. According to the ubiquitous rainbow banners, the theme was LAND OF THE FREE, HOME OF THE GAY. Rainbow bunting and fairy lights ran riot. The guests were almost exclusively guys, a fresh set of pretty boys that Teddi had just taken out of the plastic. Most of them were shirtless, and some of them wore nothing but patriotic jocks or briefs. Some hardcore groping and making out was happening in dark corners. Miley Cyrus and Lady Gaga played endlessly over the speakers.

North had worn his Redwings, jeans, and a t-shirt that said First Community Credit Union. He picked at the label on the brown-glass bottle he held and leveled a look at Shaw. "We agreed we were going to do stuff like this."

"What?"

"As friends, Shaw."

"Oh my God, what?"

"If we can't go to parties as friends, that's fine, but let's be honest about it."

"North, I asked you one simple question about my balls."

"It's a party. There are hot guys here. We're just friends now."

"And?"

"And that means, ideally, we're each other's wingman, and we help each other get laid tonight. And if we can't do that, then at the very least we don't cockblock each other."

"Yeah, and?"

"And the first thing you do is ask me to stare at your junk like you're trying to pick me up."

"Ok, well, first of all, I didn't want you to stare, I wanted you to measure—wait, North, are you getting a ruler?"

Before North could make it more than a few steps, though, he must have spotted something because he drew to a stop and muttered. "I need more beer for this shit."

"Shaw, darling, it's so good to see you." Teddi, their host, swooped in to peck Shaw on the cheek. He wore his usual jacket and slacks and loafers, and his head was gleaming. His only concession to the party was an American flag bow tie. Next to him, his boyfriend, Jack, wore fireworks suspenders and low-rise navy briefs that looked like they provided tremendous lift and support. The suspenders showed off his pecs and abs. The briefs showed off—

"If you ask nicely," North said, "maybe he'll pull down his panties and wave it in your face. You know, so you can get a better look."

Shaw's eyes jerked up. Jack was smiling shyly, and he leaned against Teddi and laced their fingers together.

"Hello, North," Teddi said. "Shaw didn't drive by a convenient dumpster where he could abandon you, I suppose."

"Actually, we did drive by three dumpsters," Shaw said. "I was counting because North said he'd rather dig through garbage with possums all night than have to pretend to—ow!"

"Whoops," North said, slapping the spot where he'd pinched Shaw's hip and then lifting the bottle to his lips.

"Always a pleasure, North," Teddi said. He seized Shaw's arm. "Sweetheart, give me five minutes and then find me in the kitchen. I have so many people I want you to meet. Ciao, ciao, North. Stay as long as you like."

With a flutter of his fingers, Teddi disappeared into the grind of sweating, muscled bodies. Jack's eyes drifted between North and Shaw, and for some reason his shy smile got a little bigger.

"So," North said. "Looks like things are working out."

"Oh yeah," Jack said in his soft drawl. "Teddi's perfect." His gaze ping-ponged from Shaw to North. "I heard you guys are, um—"

"Friends," North said.

"Good friends," Shaw put in quickly. "Best friends."

North rolled his eyes at that and took another drink.

"Well," a blush blossomed across Jack's bare chest, spreading up his neck and into his cheeks as he shot a glance at North, "Teddi and I, we've got an open thing."

Shaw looked at North.

North took another drink.

"I didn't know if you knew that," Jack said, barely audible over the pounding music. The poor kid's face was on fire.

North's eyes raked him up and down.

"North's taking some time off from dating," Shaw shouted. He must have been too loud because Jack flinched and North put a hand over his ear. "He's figuring some stuff out. You know. Doing a deep dive into his subconscious. Projecting himself into past lives. Working out his issues. Processing things." North's gaze still hadn't shifted away from Jack. "Isn't that right, North? Aren't you doing a lot of processing?"

"So much processing," North said in a distant voice. He raised the brown glass to his lips again. His eyes were the color of a fresh snowfield, like light breaking on a sheet of ice. When he drank, he lifted his chin enough that his Adam's apple bobbed, but his eyes never left Jack. Goosebumps chased the blush across Jack's chest.

"So, you should probably go try to seduce someone else tonight, Jack," Shaw said, "I mean, if that's what you were doing, because it was kind of hard to tell and you weren't doing a very good job, and maybe next time you should squeeze your nipples and run your tongue around your mouth, you know, so he gets the picture."

Jack blinked, and the splotches of color in his face didn't look like they had anything to do with embarrassment now.

"Shaw," North passed the empty to him, pressing it into Shaw's hand so that Shaw either had to accept it or let it fall, "aren't you supposed to go find Teddi?"

"I think that was more of a suggestion or an invitation—"

"It wasn't. Go find Teddi."

"But—"

North leaned in, his voice quieter now, barely audible over the droning music. "Go have fun. Pick up a cute guy. Remember: friends, wingman, get laid. That hot bartender has checked you out three times already—go read his future in his scrotal sack or something."

"Actually, you really can read the future with—"

North stepped back. "And just so you know, one of your balls is swinging low, sweet chariot." North squeezed Jack's shoulder, steering the younger man into the crowd. Over his shoulder, North glanced back, directing a pointed look. "It might be the big one."

Swearing, Shaw ditched the empty on an accent table. He stuffed himself back into the shorts, wincing when the spandex compressed a little too effectively, and waddled off to find Teddi. He told himself not to look. Then he looked. Totally by accident. North had both hands on the younger man's shoulders and was whispering in his ear as they made their way to the iced beers.

The crowds and the July heat made the rooms sweltering. By the time Shaw had squeezed between a hundred different bodies and neared the kitchen, he could smell a hundred different colognes that had wiped off on him. Sweat plastered the cropped tank to his back. He caught a brief glimpse of Peter and

Paul, college friends who had married each other. They wore matching polos and were lurking in a corner, faces drawn with unhappiness. A guy in a Union Jack thong stumbled into Shaw, the thin material stretched over some prodigious goods and leaving the rest of his smooth brown skin and well-muscled body on excellent display. He smiled at Shaw, turned, mouthing an apology that the music swallowed. Then the crowd closed between them, and the press of bodies bore Shaw into the kitchen.

"Shaw!" Teddi was standing with a cluster of three men and one woman. The three men were white. The woman was black. Shaw knew two of the men. Percy Herbert, Shaw's freshman crush, was the genetic mix of a WASP recruiting poster and an Esquire cover model, all cheekbones and tumbling blond curls and a natural athlete's build. Tucker Laguerre, the second man, was North's abusive ex-husband, and he had the same WASPy features that somehow managed to be more toned and tanned and coiffed than Percy's. The third man, Shaw recognized but couldn't name. He was older than the other two, blond and bearded, and he'd kept himself in seriously good shape for a guy who had to be pushing fifty. The daddy vibes coming off him were so strong that half of the Ken dolls were circling like sharks in the water, but he had his arm around the woman. She was tall, and an ungenerous description would have been rawboned, although the way she held herself and the intelligence in her eyes suggested a confidence that had its own allure. Tucker and Percy were in shorts and tanks, and the third man in t-shirt and jeans. The woman wore a simple dress, pale linen with a geometric pattern banding the hem.

Percy smiled at Shaw and rolled his eyes.

Tucker met him with a flat, empty stare.

The third man cocked his head as though trying to place Shaw.

The woman offered a small nod.

Shaw tried to retreat.

"Come here," Teddi said, drawing Shaw into their circle. "You know Percy, but he says you haven't seen each other in ages. He didn't even know that you're a hero and that you almost died!"

"No," Shaw shook his head, "I didn't—"

"And obviously you know Tucker. I know there was bad blood, but he told me you've smoothed everything out."

Tucker's thousand-yard stare didn't seem to have gotten the same message.

"And Rik says you look familiar, but he can't place you. Rik, this is Shaw Aldrich," and in a campy falsetto, "of Aldrich Acquisitions." Rik's eyebrows went up, and he smiled and extended a hand. "Shaw, this is Rik Slooves. He was a professor at Chouteau College before he went to the dark side and started making millions of dollars in Chicago."

Rik's smile was indulgent.

Then Shaw remembered him. Rik had been a big deal during Shaw's junior and senior years—the business professor who had separated from his wife and screwed his way through the gay boys at Chouteau College like a thresher, leaving a trail of ruined relationships and broken hearts. Including, if Shaw's memory wasn't failing him, both Percy and Tucker.

"Nice to meet you, Shaw." Rik had a deep, self-assured voice that went with the rest of the daddy vibe. He gripped Shaw's hand just this side of too hard and held on just that side of too long. His gaze roved over Shaw, and his smile got bigger. "It sounds like we ran in some of the same circles back then. I'm sorry we didn't cross paths."

The woman's face crumpled into anger before she managed to smooth it back into pleasant neutrality.

"My wife, Jean." Rik gave her a squeeze. "We recently moved back. St. Louis is home, and we're not getting any younger."

"No matter how hard we try," Jean said, the words lightly accented. She gave a dry laugh.

Percy and Tucker laughed too, but Rik shot her sidelong look and managed nothing more than a chuckle.

"I know this is a party," Rik said, "but I'd love to get you alone for a few minutes and talk to you about what I do. It's never too early to start thinking about the future, and I've got some investment opportunities that you'd be interested in."

"You work in investments?"

"That's right. Percy brought me on board at Herbert and Galleli. Small world, right? He used to be my student, now he's my boss."

"I'm hardly your boss," Percy said in his quiet, smooth, slightly-boarding-school tones.

"Well, that's settled then," Teddi said. "Shaw, you and Rik have to sit down tonight and get to know each other. I've already handed him the keys to the vault—this man is a wizard with money, and I'm not going to let him slip away. Before you two boys wander off, though," Teddi took Jean's hand and squeezed, "I'm going to put Rik and Jean through the most barbaric torture imaginable: meeting my neighbor. She does her house in all pastels, darling. It's like being buried in a Rococo tissue box. You're going to hate her—it'll be so much fun."

Before Rik or Jean could agree—or protest—Teddi had whisked them away, leaving Shaw standing with Percy and Tucker.

"I think I'm going to get a drink," Shaw said. "Good seeing you guys."

Tucker's upper lip pulled back in what might have been a grin. Or a snarl.

The bar, though, wasn't much better. The guy serving drinks was barefoot, wearing nothing but cutoffs, and he had huge, dark nipples and a droolable patch of chest hair. His eyes widened when he saw Shaw, and his smile was slow and steady as he leaned across the bar to say, "Hey, gorgeous. What can I get you?"

"Do you have any Coke?"

"For you, absolutely." He opened a can, poured some into a tumbler with ice, and slid it across the bar. "Anything else I can do for you? Seriously, anything?" He bit his lower lip; his teeth left white pressure marks.

Shaw cast about the room, the question barely registering. It didn't take long to spot North, who had cornered Jack near a window, with barely three inches of empty air between them. North was laughing, and Jack was smiling and saying something, probably in that adorably soft drawl.

"That your boyfriend?" the bartender asked.

"Oh. No. Just a friend."

"Want to make him jealous? I could kiss you."

Shaw frowned. "Well, he's not looking right now, so I'm not sure how that would make him jealous."

"It couldn't hurt." He hooked one strap of Shaw's tank and tugged him closer.

Shaw stumbled, and a firm hand on his waist steadied him. He looked up to find Percy's green eyes wrinkled in amusement.

"A mojito, please. And—" He eyed Shaw. "A hurricane."

The bartender was silent for a moment. When Percy glanced over, he released Shaw's tank, made a face, and said, "Yeah, sure."

"Um, thanks, I guess," Shaw said. His gaze slid past Percy and back to North, and at the same time North looked over his shoulder. When their eyes met, North winked. Shaw yanked his attention back to Percy. The bartender returned, and Shaw accepted the drink without even looking at it. In his mind, he kept seeing that wink. He thought about finding a table to put down the hurricane, which would have been the responsible thing to do. Then he saw that asinine wink again, and before he could reconsider, he took a gulp of his drink and began to cough.

"Maybe you should sit down," the bartender said. "Let me get Rico to cover the bar, and I'll take you—"

"We're fine, thanks," Percy said coolly.

He caught Shaw's elbow and guided Shaw away from the bar. With a wary glance at Percy, Shaw took a few more gulps of the hurricane. It tasted surprisingly good, although his stomach was already doing an unsteady rumble. For a few minutes, neither of them spoke. Percy swayed in time with the music; fairy light gleamed along the bronze ridge of his shoulder. The song changed. And then that song ended, and it changed again. Percy might have been humming, or maybe Shaw was finally tuning in to the astral vibrations of the universe. The alcohol was hitting Shaw now, making him sweat, a full-body flush running through him. He barely realized that Percy had maneuvered him to the far side of the room. When he glanced around again, he met North's eyes, and this time there was no mistaking the hard edge to the look. Shaw threw him a big smile and gulped more of the hurricane.

"Slow down," Percy said, laughing as he caught the base of the glass.

"'tsogood."

More of that gentle laughter. "I forgot you're a lightweight."

"I'm not a—" The next rush of alcohol was like the surf washing sand out from underfoot. "Not a—" Shaw blinked. "Hi, Percy."

"Hello. It's been a while, Shaw."

"The bartender was being nice to me. I think I knew him from when I got reincarnated as an otter."

Percy burst out laughing. "Same old Shaw." He shifted his weight. He'd put on muscle in the years since college, and he carried it well, most of it exposed by the thin white cotton of his tank. His hand settled on Shaw's hip, and one finger played with the waistband of the hot pants. "It's good to see you again."

"It's good to see you again too." Blinking, Shaw tried to make out what was happening over Percy's shoulder. Even though it seemed impossible, it looked like another of their college friends was here. Rufus, in biker leathers, was pointing a finger at Rik's face, saying something that was lost in the ambient noise. Whatever it was, though, the body language communicated the tone: Rufus kept advancing, getting bigger in his leather vest, and Rik kept retreating. It didn't make any sense; Rufus wasn't one of Teddi's friends, and Shaw was sure he hadn't been here a few minutes ago. Before Shaw could consider it further, though, his stomach gave a queasy lurch. "Percy, I think I've got food poisoning."

"You had such a crush on me freshman year," Percy said. His breath was warm against Shaw's face, sweet with rum and lime. "And I was a total idiot. I've thought about that a lot lately. When I heard you and North were together, I was crazy, crazy jealous."

The suffocating heat of the room seemed pleasant in comparison with the blaze inside Shaw. His stomach flip-flopped again.

"I did some stupid stuff in college," Percy said, his fingers growing more adventurous, sliding past the waistband to press against bare skin. "But the stupidest thing was not telling you how much I like you."

"You liked Tucker," Shaw said, and then he had to swallow, hard, against a wave of nausea. "And North. Or maybe both of them."

"No, I played with Tucker and North. I liked you. I was just too much of a coward to go for you." Percy leaned closer. His lips brushed Shaw's ear. "And then I saw you tonight, looking so very fuckable, and I didn't want to be stupid again."

Shaw closed his eyes, battling the sudden need to vomit.

North's voice broke through party's clamor. "Hey Percy."

"North—"

"Let's get you a drink."

Shaw opened his eyes. North was gripping Percy's arm. Livid spots marked Percy's golden skin where North's fingers dug in.

"I've got a drink," Percy displayed the mojito, "and since you were so busy with that kid with the great shoulders, Shaw and I decided to catch up—"

"Great, Percy. That's fucking great. Here we go." North hauled on Percy so hard that his heels came up off the floor. Percy shot a look at Shaw, and then North was towing him into the crush of bodies, and then they were gone.

Blearily, Shaw tried to find a place to put down the rest of his hurricane.

A hand took it from him, and then another hand caught his shoulder, bracing him. "Oh boy. Who let you into the booze?" Tucker whistled. "North is going to be pissed."

Tucker's perfectly coiffed looks doubled and recombined and doubled again. Shaw's gut twisted, but he tried to keep his face smooth as he looked at North's ex. "North and Percy—"

"Yeah, I saw. It's kind of fun, being on this side of his whole insane jealousy thing."

Shaw had an answer for that, but he lost it in the struggle to keep from puking. In spite of the heat, he felt clammy now, and he was pretty sure Tucker was the only thing keeping him on his feet.

Tucker was staring across the room, and Shaw followed his line of sight to where North and Percy were getting in each other's faces, their shouts swallowed up by the party's roar. With a sigh, Tucker shook his head. His attention settled on Shaw again, and he brushed a sweaty curl away from Shaw's forehead. "Jesus," he said, so quietly that Shaw almost couldn't hear him. "I never had a chance, did I?"

"Tucker, I think I'm going to puke."

For a white-bread prep-school boy, Tucker sure knew how to haul ass, which Shaw was distantly able to appreciate as he upchucked in Teddi's hall bathroom.

Later, leaning against a wall painted a color that Shaw decided to call sea foam, he said, "I'm dying."

"You're not dying," Tucker said, laughing as he passed over a cool washcloth.

Shaw wiped his face and neck. He closed his eyes again. "North is going to be so mad. He wanted to hook up tonight, and then I made it weird, and then he made it even weirder, and then I got mad and drank one-hundred-percent pure poison, and now I'm dying, and he's going to be really, really mad."

"Yeah, well," the note in Tucker's voice was strange, and Shaw opened his eyes to see a shadow on his face, "somehow I doubt he'll stay mad at you for long."

"He's going to make me rip up carpet or fix a toilet float valve or cut my nails."

"Right."

"He will."

Tucker rolled his eyes.

"What's that supposed to mean?" Shaw said. "And why are you being nice to me?"

"Oh, you mean, 'after I beat the shit out of you with a nine iron, why are you being nice to me?' Is that what you're asking?"

"I didn't know it was a nine iron."

"Look, Shaw, I fucked up a lot of things in my life. You were…kind of a wake-up call. Not one I enjoyed, by the way, and not one that needs to be repeated. I spent a lot of my life hating you because I was so afraid of how much North loved you." Tucker ran a hand through the perfectly barbered blond locks. "And, according to Dr. Farr, that might be why I sabotaged my own marriage by being the worst piece of shit imaginable." He fell silent, his gaze on the tile, his eyes dark.

The thud of music pulsed through the house. Bodies crashed up against the closed door, and someone giggled, and then footsteps staggered away.

Shaw twisted the washcloth. "North and I broke up. Well, he broke up with me. Well, kind of. He was doing a terrible job, so I had to do most of it for him. Like when he was trying to shave the back of his neck and he kept dropping the mirror and—"

Tucker rolled his eyes again.

"He did! He thinks he's athletic, but sometimes he's not coordinated at all, like when he was standing on the chair, trying to change a light bulb, and I jumped out and shouted, 'Boo,' and he fell right off and then wouldn't talk to me for the rest of the day, even though it was Samhain."

"Oh my God. I honestly can't with you two."

"North—"

"North is still in love with you, Shaw. Honestly, it's a little…intense how much he loves you. You guys might be going through a rough patch, but nothing's going to keep you apart permanently." His voice took on a dry note. "Trust me; I tried."

"No, we're just friends, which he made abundantly clear when he couldn't keep his hands off Jack and—"

"And I guess when North crawled up Percy's ass, it had nothing to do with Percy trying to give you the Harvard handshake through your booty shorts?"

Shaw smoothed the washcloth over his knee. The cotton was rough and damp. He folded the tag back and forth.

"Still wondering why I'm being nice to you?" Tucker asked.

"Is it rude if I say kind of?"

"I...hurt North. Bad. And I know we're finished, and I know I can't make it up to him. But I'd like to see him be happy. And, honestly, I'd like to see him be happy with you. I mean, what's the point of living in terror that he'd leave me for you, spending my entire marriage scared that I'd wake up and he'd realize what he had with you was so much better, if the two of you don't end up together?"

All Shaw could manage in answer to that was "Oh."

"Come on." Tucker held out a hand. "Up." When Shaw was on his feet, Tucker straightened Shaw's tank top, and he shot Shaw a crooked smile. "Feeling better?"

"A little."

"You want to speed things up between you and North? Hurry things along so you can get back together?"

"Um."

"You saw how North lost his shit when Percy got handsy with you?"

"I think he was getting Percy a drink."

"Yeah, sure, that's why Percy's going to have bruises on his arm for a week. Look, North lives for that macho possessive crap. He likes feeling like the alpha, or whatever you want to call it. So, you go out there, you find the hottest guy you can, and you're all over him. Channel your sluttiest inner Shaw."

"Actually, we don't use the word slut anymore because—"

"And I'll bet you a hundred bucks that North goes out of his mind. He'll be over there so fast your head will spin."

"I don't know if using jealousy is a healthy way to patch up a relationship."

Tucker shrugged. "I'm not saying it's healthy; I'm saying it'll work. But if I'm wrong, what's the worst that happens? You and North are friends. You agreed you were going to find someone to hook up with. I mean, if North doesn't come charging in, you cruise a hot guy and have fantastic sex."

After a moment, Shaw shrugged.

"Just a tip," Tucker said as he slipped out of the bathroom. "Mouthwash. And play it cool."

Shaw swished mouthwash. He checked himself in the mirror. He let down his hair, long enough now that it tumbled to his jaw, and he shook his head a few times to loosen it up. Working his way through the press of bodies, the sweat and heat making his head pound, he tried to decide what he wanted to do. He decided to get a bottled water, and he worked his way over to the coolers to give himself time to think.

A guy with a nice ass, on display in skimpy Union Jack briefs, was digging through the ice. He stood, glanced over his shoulder, and did a double take. Then he smiled. His teeth were white against his dark brown skin.

"I was hoping I'd see you again," he shouted over the roar of the party. He had a swimmer's build, every muscle cut clean.

Play it cool, Tucker had said.

Shaw leaned against the wall, doing his best impersonation of nonchalance, and offered a reserved smile.

Then he slipped.

He caught himself, but by then, he'd gotten tangled in the bunting, which disoriented him. He took a few more steps, lost his balance again, and went down hard. He pulled the bunting with him. The bunting pulled the fairy lights. Like some terrible, Fourth-of-July domino set, the decorations came tumbling down, first on one wall, then the next, then the next. People screamed. Then they stopped screaming.

The music continued to pound, but the party had fallen strangely silent.

Union Jack was frowning, obviously torn between helping Shaw and getting the hell out of there.

Shaw felt a draft.

"You know what?" North said, standing over him and pausing to take a pull from his beer. "One of them is definitely bigger."

Shaw groaned and willed the earth to swallow him.

"Like," North said with a frown, "see-a-doctor bigger."

Chapter 2

"SLUT!"

Shaw ducked his head and walked faster through the reception area.

Not fast enough, though, because Pari, their office manager (a promotion she had given herself), caught the strap of his tank and spun him around.

After a killer had burned down Shaw's home a few months before, Borealis Investigations had needed a new base of operations. A number of factors had led to their new digs, located in an aging Benton Park strip mall well off the beaten path. The main factor had been North McKinney's cheapness, which explained the cinderblock walls; the peeling paint that was the color, as North had once remarked, of old man dandruff; the mustard-colored shag carpeting; the warped wood-grain paneling peeling away from the studs; the threatening ceiling fan (which Pari insisted was possessed); the weird stain in the hallway (which Shaw insisted was Our Lady of the Pestalozzi Street Shopping Plaza (ALDI COMING SOON!!!)); and the french-fry smell (which North insisted Shaw was imagining, and which Shaw now believed might be psychic evidence of a crime).

Currently, Shaw was sending a prayer up to Our Lady of the Pestalozzi Street Shopping Plaza (ALDI COMING SOON!!!), asking that the murdered french fries manifest, or that the ceiling fan make a few ominous swipes, or that the building collapse on top of them.

"You. Are. A. Slut." Pari wrinkled her nose. "And you stink. Like sex. Go take a whore's bath in the sink."

"First of all, both slut and whore—"

"Oh my God!" The words were one unbroken squeal. "Are those hickeys?"

Shaw tugged on the tank. "No."

"They are!"

"No, I was doing something with a vacuum." Shaw scrambled. "Something auto-erotic."

"Those are totally hickeys." Pari perched on the desk, knocking over several stacks of papers in her excitement, and adjusted her long, dark hair. Today, the bindi was gunmetal gray. "Ok, what's his name?"

"Well, it's rude that you assume that it was a guy because, as I told you, I'm pretty sure I'm bisexual now because I was watching that cologne commercial, and there was a lady in it, and I had a physical reaction."

"Your thing," Pari said, wrinkling up her nose, "did its thing because North came in from a run and was wiping his gross, sweaty, hairy chest with his shirt."

"That cologne lady had a bikini on! Like a…like a temptress!"

"No," North muttered from the front door, only halfway across the threshold. He was wearing dark sunglasses and rubbing a spot between his eyes. "No fucking way. I am too hungover for this shit."

"Shaw is a slut."

"As I was saying," Shaw tried, "slut isn't a word we use anymore because—"

"Of course, you're a man-whore," Pari said to North. "Or a fuck-boy. I'm not sure which yet." She shrugged. "I'm not sure which is better, actually."

"Fuck-boy," North said.

"Man-whore," Shaw said.

"I'm going home," North said, shouldering open the door again. "We're closed. We're closed forever."

"That's good, right? So I can shred all those papers on your desk—"

"Don't go anywhere near my fucking desk." North leveled a finger at Shaw. After a moment, when it seemed like he'd made his point, he growled out some grumbling subvocalizations, pushed his way past the two of them, and disappeared into the back office.

"Did you see who North went home with?" Pari whispered.

Shaw shook his head.

"Come on, you had to have seen." She leaned closer. "I mean, I know he's still in love with you, but if this new guy has good equipment, you might need to move a little faster with your plan."

"What plan?"

"Your plan to win back North and prove that for some reason—you have to fill in the blanks here because I honestly have no idea what you'd say—he should get back together with you, even though you've got those bushy pits and sometimes you don't brush your teeth and still think pig Latin is cute and—"

"Ok, ok, ok," Shaw whispered furiously. "I'm working on it."

"You're serious? You didn't see his new guy?"

"No!"

"What about your new guy?" Pari's expression grew concerned. "Is it serious?"

"What? No. Of course not. He's just—it was just fun."

Pari made a face. "You really do smell like sex. Whore's bath. Now."

After scrubbing the most important parts in the tiny bathroom—a lady-of-the-night's bath, Shaw decided was the best name for it—he checked on North. The blond man had his head on his desk, a bottle of ibuprofen next to him, letting out a whistling snore. Shaw shut the door gently, went back to the reception area, and began sorting promotional materials.

While North's cheapness extended to picking a new office in an ancient strip mall with half its storefronts empty, it apparently did not include promotional materials. New business cards. Window decals. Banner stands. Flyers. So many flyers. The original design—North's—had featured a picture of North and Shaw standing back-to-back with their arms folded, like they were posing for a '90s hip-hop album's cover art, or doing a bus ad for a law firm. After Pari had laughed so hard that she had fallen over, North had redesigned the flyers to feature text only. They'd arrived on Wednesday, the day before yesterday, and Shaw guessed that his afternoon assignment was going to be wandering in the brutal Midwestern heat, stapling these to every utility pole he could find.

"Shaw." North's voice was a growl from their office door. "I need your help with this new parabolic mic."

Shaw hid a smile by digging deeper in the boxes. "Why do you need my help?"

"With the instructions."

"You can read them yourself."

"Shaw."

"I don't understand why you need my help."

"Because I do. Right now."

"I better work on these flyers. You told me on Wednesday that they were top priority. You went on and on about it for like an hour."

"Like two hours," Pari said, eyes still locked on her monitor.

North grunted something and shut the door.

Five minutes later, though: "Shaw, get your ass back here."

"I told you: I'll help you with the mic—"

"Not that. The numbers on the Pasco invoice are fucked to shit."

"You can fix it."

"It's your invoice. You typed it up. Get your ass back here and fix it."

Shaw extracted himself from the boxes long enough to direct a soft smile in North's direction. "You know I'm not any good with numbers. You go ahead and fix it. It'll be faster anyway."

"No, I want you to—"

"Oh my God," Pari said. "Fix it yourself, North, so I don't have to hear about Shaw's alternative mathematics where one plus one equals three."

This time, there was some definite snarling.

Seven and a half minutes later: "I need to show you something."

Shaw glanced up. North's messy thatch of blond hair was even more mussed than usual, and red circles marked his cheeks. His eyes were narrow and promising some serious payback for this bullshit.

"What?" Shaw asked, head down again to hide his grin.

"That's what I'm going to show you."

"Can't you tell me?"

"Motherfucking son of a bitch—" North cut off. "No, I can't tell you. That's the whole reason I want to show you."

"It's not about that parabolic mic, is it?"

"No."

"It's not a bug, is it? Because if you want me to kill a bug, I'm not going to do it. We've got enough ghosts in here already."

"I can kill a bug by my own goddamn self, thank you very much. Get your ass up. Walk your ass back here. Right now, Shaw."

"Ok," Shaw said, letting doubt creep into his voice as he set aside the stacks of promotional materials. As he gathered himself up, he shook his head. "No, wait. I just remembered. I've got to call the power company because we keep getting that electric bill from the ethereal plane, and—"

North's voice had come unraveled, and it rose into a shout. "For the last fucking time, it's not the ethereal plane, it's for the goddamn last tenant!" Then the door crashed shut.

Pari flicked a look at Shaw. "He's grumpy for a guy who got some last night."

"He's North," Shaw said with a shrug. "He's always grumpy."

Half an hour later, Pari stood, stretched, and grabbed her purse. "I'm taking my break. Do you want anything from Shameless Grounds?"

"Actually, yes, they have this vegan pita—"

"I didn't think so," she said as she flounced out the door.

No sooner had it shut behind her than the inner office door flew open, and North stood there, chest rising and falling with huge, labored breaths.

"You son of a bitch," he growled as he launched himself across the room.

Trying not to laugh, Shaw let North manhandle him into their office. North shut the door and pressed the thumb lock. Shaw, grinning, backed away.

"Why," North cast his sunglasses on the desk and tugged off his shirt, "do you have to be so fucking difficult sometimes?"

"I don't like feeling objectified."

"Get those stupid shorts off right now," North snapped as he shucked his jeans.

Shaw wriggled out of the hot pants but said, "I don't like feeling like a cheap trick."

Hopping out of his boxers, North made an aggravated noise. Then, naked and hard, he advanced. Shaw gave up and started to laugh.

"What the fuck is so funny?" North asked as he caught Shaw by the arms and settled him in a chair. For a moment, his dick bobbed inches from Shaw's face, and then he lowered himself to straddle Shaw's lap. Shaw whimpered when their erections slid against each other. North had a wicked grin as he grabbed the cropped tank and gave Shaw a light shake. "I asked you a question."

Shaw opened his mouth to answer, but North rutted against him, and all that came out was garbled noises.

North bent, kissing Shaw's mouth, his jaw, his neck and collarbone and shoulder. He sucked and bit at the marks he'd left the night before.

"Fuck yeah," he whispered. "Walking around half-naked, my marks all over you."

Taking both of them together in one hand, Shaw began to pump.

"Fuck," North groaned. "I never should have let you out of bed this morning."

The thin paneling, the distant noise of traffic, the unfamiliar setting, even the knowledge that Pari could walk in on them at any moment—they all combined to set Shaw on fire. But it was more than that. It was this change in North, the sudden lack of inhibitions, his seemingly insatiable need.

"Yeah, yeah, you got me there, oh shit." North rutted into Shaw's hand and came, the strain of controlling his volume outlined in his face. When he finished, he slumped forward, forehead on Shaw's shoulder.

Shaw let his head fall back and finished. As he was coming down from the orgasm's crest, he felt North's mouth moving gently across his throat, kisses and murmured words that he couldn't assemble into anything meaningful.

"Well," Shaw finally croaked. That was all he could come up with.

"Yeah," North said with a chuckle. "God, sometimes I feel like I could get off just looking at you. Especially when you play so fucking hard to get."

They were both quiet for a few minutes, North's face against Shaw's shoulder again, the bigger man's body still. Come was cooling and drying on Shaw's belly. He ran his hand down the bumps of North's spine, pressed his palm against the small of North's back, a position that was almost an embrace. North settled against Shaw's hand with a contented noise.

"This is fun," Shaw whispered. He had to stop because his mouth was so dry. He tried again. "Sneaking around like this, it's hot."

North made a pleased noise.

"But don't you—I mean, maybe if we told a few people, so they didn't keep trying to set us up—"

North's head came up. His ice-rim eyes were unreadable. "Tell them what?"

In the storefront next to them, the Jonas Brothers were wailing about being suckers for you.

North leaned back, tapped Shaw's arm, and tugged the tank up and off. He used it to clean up Shaw's belly and then held it, crumpled, in one hand.

Shaw focused on an ominous-looking bulge in the acoustic tiles. It suggested water damage. Maybe a serious structural problem.

"Come on," North said, and the friendly tone couldn't hide the irritation in his voice. "We talked about this. We're friends."

"Friends with benefits," Shaw said. "Will you get off me, please?"

"I don't get why we have to have this fight over and over again. We're so good at this, Shaw. We're good at being friends. We're good at giving each other shit. We're good at working together. We're good at fucking together."

"You weigh a ton." He pressed on North's chest. "And I want to clean up before Pari comes back."

"Look, every relationship has its natural level. This is ours. Best friends and fantastic sex. When we tried it without sex, we had problems. When we tried to make it more than friends and sex—"

Shaw moved, rising fast enough to dump North on his ass.

"Jesus Christ!"

Moving around the desk, Shaw shrugged. "I asked you twice."

"Damn it, Shaw. I'm going to have bruises on my ass."

In the bottom drawer of his desk, Shaw found a change of clothes. "That'll give you a good story for all your other hookups."

"For fuck's sake." North gathered himself, but Shaw was already moving toward the door. "We broke up. We agreed that if we were going to do this, add sex to our friendship, we weren't going to get weird about it."

Shaw threw open the door. He huffed, trying to get close to laughter while being a hundred miles away from it.

"Hey, I'm talking to you."

But Shaw was already out in the hall. He shut himself in the bathroom.

North hammered on it once. "Open the fucking door."

Shaw stared at the yellow tiles, the yellow sink, the yellow toilet. Chartreuse, he thought. Maybe someone had called this color chartreuse instead of old tennis ball or moldy orange.

With a muttered "Fuck this," North moved away from the door.

Warm water. Soap. Paper towels. Then Shaw pulled on the clothes: a sailor-collar shirt of peach-colored linen, and cutoffs. Cold water for puffy eyes. In the reception area, the bell jangled, which meant Pari was back from break and it was now safe to exit. North wouldn't press the issue while Pari was around. At least, Shaw hoped he wouldn't.

When Shaw opened the bathroom door, though, North popped out of their office like an angry Norse jack-in-the-box. He was dressed again, and the t-shirt was tight around his biceps.

"You know what? When we're having a fucking conversation—"

"North?"

The voice was older, cultured, self-assured. Shaw turned.

He recognized the man: Mr. Laguerre. Tucker's father. Which, in some nightmare logic, made sense right now. Why wouldn't he be here, Shaw thought, when everything else is so awful?

"Dick," North said. "I'm sorry, I didn't know—" He shook his head. "Are you—is Cathy—" He laughed and rubbed his mouth. "I'm sorry, I don't know what's going on."

"I need to hire you," Dick Laguerre said. "Tucker's been arrested for murder."

Chapter 3

THE WORDS ECHOED IN North's ears, and for a moment, they were gibberish. Tucker's father stood in front of him, here, in the Borealis office. Dick Laguerre, talking about murder. The summer sunlight coming in through the front windows was too bright; North wiped his eyes.

"Why don't you come back to our office?" Shaw said. "North, do you want me to—"

"No." North's head bobbed as though on a loose string. "I mean, yes. Come on, Dick. Let's sit down. This has got to be some kind of misunderstanding."

Impossible, back in their office, to miss the smell of sex. Impossible to miss the faux-walnut paneling peeling back from the studs. Impossible to miss the water-damaged acoustic tiles and the rusty bleed-out from the drop ceiling's grid. Impossible to miss Shaw's desk, it's usual insanity: the Five Below wall clock he had disassembled, turning the second hand into a "phallic gnomon to represent the sexual dimension of time"; the charcoal-stained toothbrush being used to clean a coach-pitch trophy that had once belonged, according to the plaque, to a girl named Seema Naidu; an uncapped Speed Stick; a rubber band ball that Shaw had once spent an entire afternoon trying to saw through with an eight-and-a-half by eleven printout of Adrienne Rich poems; and a boxed set reprint of *The Little House on the Prairie* books. Impossible to miss, in other words, the fuckery of North's life.

They sat. Dick looked around. His face didn't show anything, and he was too polite to say anything. He was an older version of Tucker, with a more patrician cast to his features but the same classically good looks, the same boarding-school coloring. Today, he wore a salmon-colored polo and preppy khaki shorts. He was tan from hours on the back nine. Once, in a moment of drunken bitterness, Tucker had claimed that his father's proudest moment had been when he birdied on Tea Olive at Augusta. Maybe that explained why, in those first shocked seconds of seeing his soon-to-be-ex father-in-law, North had thought Dick Laguerre had driven all the way down to Benton Park to talk golf.

"Mr. Laguerre," Shaw said, "why don't you tell us what happened?"

"Please, Shaw. Call me Dick. We're all adults here, and whatever—" His gaze slid from Shaw to North and back to Shaw. "—unpleasantness might have occurred, I think we can all behave appropriately."

The Laguerres, North thought with a sudden smile. The house could be burning down, and Dick and Cathy wouldn't drop that amiable detachment. What had North expected? For Dick to lose his shit because here North was, with the man he had left Tucker for, and the office smelled like a horny teenager's laundry hamper? Then the smile died. He leaned forward, elbows on the desk. "Dick, what are you talking about? There's no way Tucker killed someone." North ignored the shadow on Shaw's face. "If the police took him in for an interview—"

Dick held up a hand. "Not an interview. He was arrested, North. He called our lawyer, and our lawyer called us. Biff is convinced he can get Tucker out on bail, but the earliest he could get a hearing was Monday." For a moment, Dick looked older, and his hand trembled as he smoothed the hem of his shorts. "Biff says—well, it doesn't matter. Tucker will be out of that awful place on Monday; that's what matters. What we have to do now is begin preparing for his defense."

"Who do the police think he killed?" Shaw asked.

"A man named Rik Slooves."

Shaw shot a look at North.

"You know him?" Dick asked. "I understand he used to be a professor at Chouteau, but now he's some kind of banker or investor or something."

"We know him," North said. He didn't add that Rik Slooves had fucked every boy he could convince to hold still for five seconds. He didn't add that Tucker and Percy and most of their other friends had, at one point or another, fallen victim to Rik's charms. "Why do they think Tucker killed him?"

"Biff said Tucker was upset. He said Tucker was doing his best to explain, but certain facts remain unclear." Dick's smile was worn thin. "I believe that means my son had been drinking and doesn't remember clearly what happened, but from what Biff was able to gather and pass along, they found Tucker with this man. After he had been—well, you understand."

"Mr. Laguerre," Shaw said, "if Tucker was drinking, and if they found him with the victim, it sounds like—I guess I'm saying, I'm not sure what you're asking us to do."

"I know how it sounds, Shaw. I'm well aware of how it sounds. But my son is not a murderer. I refuse to believe that he had anything to do with this man's death, no matter what the circumstances suggest. And I'm disappointed—very disappointed—that you'd think anything to the contrary, although I suppose, considering the nature of your relationship, it's not unbelievable that you'd wish the absolute worst for Tucker."

Shaw's cheeks reddened, and he leaned back slightly.

"That's not fair to Shaw," North said. "And it's not fair to me either."

In reception, the bell jangled again, and Pari called, "I'm back."

Dick crossed his legs. His foot beat an empty measure in the air. "I'm sorry," he finally said. "Biff called sometime after three, and as you can imagine, I couldn't fall back asleep. I've spent most of the morning reaching out to friends. They all want to help, but of course, they all have their excuses. 'You have to let it play out' is what I've heard most often. The most I could get was a promise from an old fraternity brother to do his best to make sure Tucker made bail, although I'm not even sure when he'll be arraigned. It's all been…frustrating. But that's no excuse, and I'm sorry for saying what I did."

"You've been through a lot," Shaw said. "I'm sorry you have to deal with this."

With a stiff nod, Dick said, "Thank you."

"Do you have some reason," North tried to find the right words, "to believe Tucker was framed? Or that he was simply in the wrong place at the wrong time?"

"It seems…unlikely that he was simply in the wrong place at the wrong time. From what Biff conveyed, that does not seem possible." Dick held up a hand to forestall North. "I'll let Tucker explain that to you. I'm not sure what I want you to do, if I'm being honest. I suppose I want you to find the truth. If we know what happened that night, what really happened, it will exonerate my son."

"We'll—" North began.

"We'll need a moment to discuss things," Shaw broke in.

North flipped the bail pull on the center drawer a few times. He straightened in his chair. He looked over at Shaw.

"Just a few minutes," Shaw said, smoothly but firmly. "If you'd wait in the hall, Mr. Laguerre."

"Of course," he said, standing. "And please, it's Dick, Shaw. We can drop the formalities."

When the door had closed behind him, North said, "We're taking this case."

"I don't—"

"We're taking it, Shaw. That's final."

Some of Shaw's hair had slipped free from its tie, and he blew it out of his eyes. "North—"

"Unless the next words out of your mouth are 'I agree completely,' stop."

"Can you hear yourself right now?"

"Ok, let me get this straight." North pushed back from the desk. The chair glided across the mat and then bogged down in the shag carpeting. He lurched out of the seat, didn't know what to do with his hands, and made fists at his sides. "You get to say what cases we take, no matter what I think."

Shaw drew his knees up to his chest.

"When Matty came to us, I didn't want to take the case, but we did. Because you decided we would."

"I—"

"And when Chuck's boss went missing, remember that? We took that case because you wanted to, even though I thought it was a bad idea."

Fingers laced together, Shaw pulled his knees up tighter.

"And the Slasher, Shaw. Everything we went through with the Slasher. That was you. And that stupid romance convention. And for fuck's sake, we spent six hours in May turning over rocks looking for a leprechaun Peeping Tom because your witch friend claimed he was watching her when she celebrated her black Sabbath naked. So fuck what you want. We're taking this case."

Ruddy streaks marked the hollows of Shaw's cheeks. He lowered his feet slowly. Then he stood. For some reason, North was surprised by how tall he was, as though he'd forgotten or misremembered, or as though Shaw were a stranger to him.

"Do I get to say something now?"

"What do you want to say?"

"If you want to do this, fine. I know I—I know how I've done things in the past, insisting I get my way, I recognize that's been a problem. For us. For how you and I—for the way things ended, I guess. So I'll support you in this, and I'll do whatever I can. But can I at least ask why?"

"Why?"

"Why do you want to do this? After everything Tucker did to you—"

"This isn't about him."

"Oh North." Shaw sounded so infinitely sad about it that for a moment, rage scrambled North's vision.

Struggling to keep his voice even, North managed: "It's not. Tucker's a piece of shit; I don't want anything to do with him. But his family was always good to me. They're decent people, and they're kind, and hell, Dick treated me more like a son than my own dad ever did." That slip, and the look on Shaw's face, made North hurry on. "So I'm going to do it because he's asking me to do it. And you know what? Even if Tucker is a piece of shit, he deserves justice."

"You know what he's capable of."

"Yeah. I do. Better than you, Shaw, actually."

"So you know he could have killed Rik. If he'd been angry enough, he could have. The night I saw him—"

"Stop talking."

North didn't recognize his own voice, the dead quality of it. He did, however, recognize the adrenaline that went through him like a chill, pimpling his skin.

"You won't be able to be impartial about this," Shaw said quietly.

"Fuck that. And fuck you for saying that."

"It's not just me. No defense attorney worth the name would put you on the stand; a prosecutor would shred your testimony in two questions."

"You know what?" North shook his head and headed for the door. "I don't ask for a lot from you."

"North, come on, I'm trying—"

"So it'd be really fucking nice if everyone once in a while, if it wasn't too fucking inconvenient, you could show me a little support." He threw open the door and met Dick Laguerre's tired gaze. "We'll take the case."

Acknowledgments

My deepest thanks go out to the following people (in reverse alphabetical order):

Wendy Wickett, who did a *very* thorough (see what I did there?) job of helping me with my excesses, who consulted the Sacred Text (Urban Dictionary) and let me know when it had nothing to offer, and who made me smile by pointing out the unexpected educational benefits of this book.

Jo Wegstein, who helped me gut and rebuild (correctly, this time), the Nonavie lab, who explained the best way to steal a highly valuable biotech intellectual property, and who helped me make sure Ronnie got his comeuppance at the end.

Tray Stephenson, who offered word choice suggestions, who caught my many typos, and who provided some helpful advice about real-life problems when I sorely needed it.

Cheryl Oakley, who was the first to write back (always the first!) to tell me that she was angry at Shaw, who helped me tease out the promise of relationship trouble to come in the next book, and who helped me hammer down what exactly was happening in the confrontation with Celia and Francis.

Steve Leonard, who reminded me of the distinction between extra skin and extra crispy, who kept track of timelines—as he always does!—and who told me not to change a thing, which is what I needed to hear, even though it hurt.

Austin Gwin, who offered his usual (and always exceptional) insight into the characters, who helped me think about the soft threat buried in the ending, and who gave me more to think about in terms of clarity (and lack thereof) in the resolution (or, again, lack thereof).

About the Author

Learn more about Gregory Ashe and forthcoming works at
www.gregoryashe.com.

For advanced access, exclusive content, limited-time promotions, and insider
information, please sign up for my mailing list at
http://bit.ly/ashemailinglist.

www.ingramcontent.com/pod-product-compliance
Lightning Source LLC
Chambersburg PA
CBHW052032240626
47153CB00006B/2050